The Border Wolves

Damion Hunter is a pseudonym of Amanda Cockrell. Along with the Centurions Trilogy, she is also the author of *Pomegranate Seed*, *What We Keep Is Not Always What Will Stay*, the historical trilogies *The Deer Dancers* and *The Horse Catchers*, and *The Legions of the Mist*, a Roman historical adventure novel. She lives in Roanoke, Virginia.

Also by Damion Hunter

The Legions of the Mist
The Wall at the Edge of the World

The Centurions Trilogy

The Centurions
Barbarian Princess
The Emperor's Games
The Border Wolves

THE BORDER WOLVES

AMANDA COCKRELL *writing as*

DAMION HUNTER

1☰CANELO

First published in the United Kingdom in 2021 by

Canelo
31 Helen Road
Oxford OX2 0DF
United Kingdom

A CIP catalogue record for this book is available from the British Library.

Print ISBN 978 1 80032 289 9
Ebook ISBN 978 1 80032 288 2

This book is a work of fiction. Names, characters, businesses, organizations, places and events are either the product of the author's imagination or are used fictitiously. Any resemblance to actual persons, living or dead, events or locales is entirely coincidental.

Look for more great books at www.canelo.co

Printed and bound in Great Britain by Clays Ltd, Elcograf S.p.A.

1

For Felix

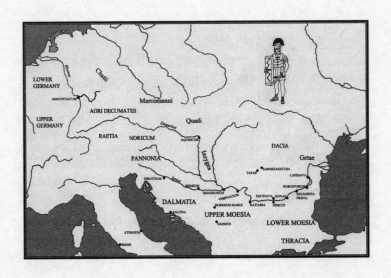

Cast of Characters

The House of Appius

Appius

Flavius Appius Julianus The Elder

Antonia (deceased): wife of Appius, mother of Flavius and Julia

Decima: Helva's maid

Diulius: horsemaster of the chariot ponies

Forst: German freedman, Appius's horsemaster

Helva: slave mistress of Appius, mother of Correus

Niarchos: head of the household servants

Philippos: household steward

Correus

Correus Appius Julianus: adopted slave-born son of Appius

Cottia: Ygerna's maid

Eilenn: Appia Eilena, daughter of Correus and Ygerna

Eumenes: slave belonging to Correus

Felix: Frontinus Appius Julianus, Correus's son by Freita, a German freedwoman

Marcus: Correus Marcus, son of Correus and Ygerna

Julius: slave of Correus Marcus

Nurse: Marcus's nurse

Septima: nursery maid

Ygerna (Flavia Agricolina): British wife of Correus, she was a princess of the Silures

Flavius

Flavius Appius Julianus The Younger: half-brother to Correus, legitimate son of Appius

Aemelia: wife of Flavius

Appia: daughter of Flavius and Aemelia

Bericus: Flavius's slave

Rusonia: Aemelia's maid

Julia

Appia Julia: sister of Flavius, half-sister of Correus

Lucius Paulinus: husband of Julia

Lucian: son of Julia and Paulinus

Paulilla: daughter of Julia and Paulinus

Tullius: free servant of Paulinus

Rome

Didia Longina: distant cousin of Prosper Rufius

Domitian: Titus Flavius Domitianus, emperor of Rome

Gentilius Paulinus: uncle of Lucius Paulinus

Livilla Drusa Major: Livilla Minor's aunt

Livilla Drusa Minor: Prosper Rufius's wife

Prosper Rufius: a senator

Blaesus: Correus's second-in-command at Singidunum

Cominius: Messala Cominius, legate of the Seventh Legion Claudia

Decius: Aurelius Decius, legate of the Fourth Legion Flavia

Dotos: frontier scout

Favonius: Favonius Marcellinus, tribune of the Fifth Legion Macedonica

Frontinus: Julius Frontinus, general and military engineer

Fuscus: Cornelius Fuscus, commander of the Praetorian Guard

Hirtius: junior surgeon at Viminacium

Licinus: Marcus Licinius, legate of the First Legion Italica

Maximus: Lappius Maximus, governor of Lower Germany

Nicomedes: military surgeon to Correus's command at Singidunum

Nigrinus: Cornelius Nigrinus, governor of Lower Moesia

Rufus: Velius Rufus, Roman general

Saturninus: Antonius Saturninus, governor of Upper Germany

Sosius Alpinus: primus pilus of the Fifth Legion Macedonica

Tettius Julianus: new commander of Roman army in Moesia

Tsiru: frontier scout

Vindex: Silvius Vindex, primus pilus of the Fourth Legion Flavia

Dacia

Decebalus: elder son of Duras

Diegis: younger son of Duras

Duras: king of Dacia

Gudila: king of the Getae

Natoporus: Diegis's translator

Rescuturme: younger sister of Decebalus and Diegis

Ziais: sister of Decebalus and Diegis

Germany

Arni: Semnone lord

Armin: Semnone landholder

Barden: priest of the Semnones

Commius: a river pirate

Fiorgyn: widow of Nyall Sigmundson, wife of Ingvar

Haddon: chieftain of the Chatti, nephew of Marbod

Hauk: Semnone lord

Horst: Semnone lord

Ingvar: Semnone lord

Nyall Sigmundson (deceased): former chieftain of the Semnones

Ranvig: chieftain of the Semnones

Signy: wife of Ranvig

Steinvar: Semnone lord

Thrain: Semnone lord

Parthia

Artapan: minister of the court of Pacorus

Pacorus: king of Parthia

Sallustius Lucullus: governor of Britain

Zosines: chieftain of the Iazyges

Prologue

Sarmizegetusa

The king's palace at Sarmizegetusa occupied the top three levels of the complex that rose up over multiple terraces, atop the holy mountain Cogaeonum. Decebalus, warlord of the uneasily allied cities of Dacia, sat in its lamplit Council Hall and prepared to bargain with the German.

"This is not as many men as we agreed." Decebalus was a young prince with an aging father and the look of a man who intends to sort the world to suit himself. He had a heavy, straight brow and a square jaw, with curling hair, a brown beard, and a mouth half-hidden under a mustache. He wore a richly embroidered tunic, loose breeches, fawnskin boots and a cap made of a red fox's fur against the cold of the mountain winter. A gold bracelet of many loops ending in horned beasts' heads covered most of his left arm. His brother Diegis sat to his left, watching silently but with a certain catlike interest.

The German regarded them unmoved. "It is all that we can spare. We are not many, after the last war, and I have no intention of tempting another one in my own hunting runs. The last one served its purpose and the Romans have stayed out of the Free Lands. I brought you these to show you how the Romans fight, not to be spear fodder. As we agreed."

Ranvig, chieftain of the Semnones, lords of the German Free Lands, was not as finely dressed as the Dacian prince, but his shirt, breeches, and wolfskin cloak were of suitable quality for a chieftain, and he wore a heavy gold torque around his neck. His pale hair spilled over his shoulders in two thick plaits, rather than twisted into a knot at the side of his head in the fashion of his inherited tribe. Ranvig had been of the Nicretes before they had gone down before Rome and their remnants scattered to the Semnone lands. Afterward, Nyall Sigmundson of the Semnones had been taken by Rome. The Council and the remaining Kindred, two of whom sat beside him now, had spoken for Ranvig to lead them, and if they wanted him, they had been told to take him as he was. He had an odd, crooked face, his blue eyes set slightly askew and his front teeth also crooked, which gave him a wolflike aspect. When he smiled, which he was not doing at the moment, his mouth slanted up farther on one side than the other.

Decebalus wondered how much further he could push him. The Semnone lands were a substantial distance to the west, north of the Rhenus. It was not somewhere he could express his displeasure at the end of a spear. A slave appeared with a pitcher and five silver cups, and Decebalus nodded at her to fill them. It was Roman wine, very good, and not cut with water as the effete populace in Rome drank it. He took a sip and waited as Ranvig inspected his cup, possibly to see if there was anything else in it. There wasn't. That would have served no purpose. "We also agreed that you would see that your kinsmen the Quadi and the Marcomanni give us their support," Decebalus said.

Ranvig contemplated him for a long moment. "The warlord misremembers. I said that we would urge them not to help Rome against you."

"They are one and the same thing."

"They are not!" Arni snapped. He half rose from his chair beside Ranvig and glowered at Decebalus.

Ranvig gave Arni a look and he subsided. "Nor will I trade more men for the Dacian bride that Duras the king offered me last night," Ranvig said. "I have a wife."

"Duras is old and he drinks." Decebalus grinned. "I am keeping my sister to persuade the Getae to finalize our confederation. Although there is a younger one. She is only ten, but such

2

an alliance would not be a bad thing. We will be a great empire. Greater than Rome."

"No." Ranvig considered that a permanent alliance with Decebalus would be an appallingly bad thing. He was glad that he was not the king of the Getae, who were related to the Dacians and were going to be "persuaded" one way or the other.

"If the Free Lands wished to be part of an empire, we would not have fought Rome," Arni said and Ranvig didn't quiet him this time.

Decebalus considered. He had got what he thought he would, which was the neutrality of the Semnones' eastward relatives, and a tactical lesson in Roman armor, weapons, and maneuvers to supplement what he had gleaned from Roman deserters who had crossed the river into Dacia fleeing punishment or boredom. "I could keep your men here," he suggested. It would be easy enough; they were greatly outnumbered.

Arni started to stand again and Ranvig laid a hand on his arm. "Do not threaten me, warlord. None of us will be of use to you dead, and none will fight for you willingly. Are you ready to sacrifice your agreement with the Quadi and the Marcomanni for that? When the snow clears enough to travel," Ranvig informed him, "we will make our way home. Good fortune in your endeavors, prince." He nodded at the other two and they all rose.

When the Germans had left, Diegis said, "Gudila is wavering. It would give him things to think about if you kill the Germans."

Decebalus poured the rest of the wine into his cup. "Ranvig is more useful alive. Also, he is right about the Quadi and Marcomanni. The German chieftains all have tempers like wolverines. It is why they will never be great, and I will. They'll bite the Romans eventually. It just has to be arranged."

"In that case," Diegis said, "you had best go and sweeten Gudila with rapturous descriptions of our sister's tits. And you might wish to sweeten Ziais too. She's angry."

"When you have something to offer that I have not thought of, be certain to tell me," Decebalus said. He turned his own wine cup in his hand, studying the embossed horseman who rode around its midsection, spear leveled at a fleeing enemy. He would drive the Romans from the Ister, which they called the Danuvius, all the way south into Macedonia. And maybe when that was done, he would conquer Macedonia too, and then the Parthian lands where Alexander had died. He would be Alexander reborn, and unlike Alexander, he would live to rule. The priests had seen it in the stars, if only because he had told them to.

I

Mourning

Correus Appius Julianus stood with his parade helmet tucked under one arm and let himself cry. Against the marble doors on the end of a small casket, carved in hope of the soul's journey, leaned a marble spindle and basket of wool. Above them a marble dove fluttered, caught between the spindle and the mourning wreaths that flanked those immoveable doors.

The howls of the mourners beat against the air unendingly, but the grief was real. There had been no need of hired mourners to lament Lady Antonia. Family, slaves, freedmen, and half the great families of Rome had stretched the funeral procession from the house on the hill in an unbroken line to the green lawn and masonry monuments beside the road that were the graves of the house of Appius Julianus. There had been other deaths this winter from the epidemic that had taken its toll mainly on the very young and very old, but Lady Antonia's had been the unexpected one, the loss without warning that is always the most devastating. She had nursed her slaves and household through the worst of it all autumn before she caught the fever herself. Her body had been burned weeks ago, but the funeral had been postponed to give the family time to come home.

The bier passed by him to the sad, sweet processional of flutes, and Correus, watching his half-brother's face, thought that of them all, Flavius was the most torn. Antonia had loved both her children, and her unasked-for stepson Correus, but it was Flavius who had had the deepest place in her heart. His dark face was etched now with grief renewed, and Correus wished that they had not waited for his own arrival, but had buried her when she died, rather than put Flavius through this again. Correus was still road-weary with the long ride from the Danuvius in Moesia, and then a sea journey to Italy, but Flavius was on the emperor's staff and had been in Rome all along, and while his mother's ashes were unburied, there had been no place for him to lay his grief to rest. They should not have waited for him. And being away from an unstable frontier was making Correus's neck itch.

A priest was pouring oil and wine on the steps of the burial vault as the keening of the slaves rose in an anguished howl. It was like fingernails scraping on slate. Correus wanted to shout at them to be still, but they must not be denied their right to mourn her. Correus was aware of his wife's silent presence at his elbow, standing very still with the baby, looking back over her shoulder at the mourners. Ygerna was British but this would not be her first Roman funeral. There had been too many deaths this fall and winter already and, as a daughter of the house, Ygerna would have attended them all. He followed her gaze and saw that she was watching his father.

Appius Julianus stood rigidly, formal in the dark gray toga of mourning, leaning on a staff that Correus could not remember seeing him use before. His aquiline face, so like his sons', was stretched taut and his dark eyes were tired. He had been married to his wife for thirty-three years; never a love match, but she had been a part of his life, and now there was an empty place. He seemed to Correus to be a little lost, a little uncertain, in a way that was not like Appius at all. *He is old*, Correus thought suddenly, and felt his chest tighten. *One day we will lose him too.*

The bearers who carried the painted bier upon which the casket rested halted before the open doors of the burial vault. The other mourners stood back to let the family come, each in turn, to lay a hand upon the marble: Appius brushed the carved spindle and wool with a light, familiar touch – how many times had Correus seen his father thus lay a hand on his wife's hand? Then Flavius, who put both hands on the lid for a moment as if he would lift it. His wife, Aemelia, took his arm and turned him away. There would be nothing in the glass vase of ashes that lay inside to soothe his heart. Their daughter Appia touched the marble gingerly, one hand clutching her mother's veil. Above the bier, on the steps of the vault, a statue of Antonia stood as she had been in life, a spoon in one hand and a basket of roses in the other, beside the funerary inscription.

DIS MANIBUS
ANTONIA MARCELLINA, BELOVED WIFE
OF FLAVIUS APPIUS JULIANUS,
MOTHER OF TWO AND MOTHER IN HER
HEART TO MANY.
WITH KINDNESS SHE BLESSED US AND
WITH SORROW WE LET HER GO.
SHE LIVED 51 YEARS.

Antonia's daughter Julia, Correus's half-sister, laid a sheaf of freshly cut roses across the marble ones, and her husband, Lucius Paulinus, lifted their children in turn to let them say farewell to a familiar face and not a coffin.

Correus shepherded his own brood forward behind Lucius and Julia: the baby Marcus, five-year-old Eilenn who was officially Appia Eilena, and Felix, his eldest son, his green eyes wet and rebellious and looking so like his own dead mother that Correus nearly stopped right there.

"You must," Ygerna said gently in his ear, and he put his arm around his wife's slim shoulders gratefully. He would not forget Freita, but it had been ten years since he buried her. His mourning was long since done, and Correus had the gods who had sent him Ygerna to thank for that.

Correus laid a hand on the stone, cool and unfamiliar. There was none of Antonia's presence left in it. A little spray of petals dropped from the statue's marble arms onto the bier. Never once in all his life, even when Appius had adopted him against Antonia's wishes, had Antonia ever let Correus think that she resented his presence because his mother was a slave and her husband's mistress. He glanced at Helva, standing slightly apart from the others of the household, and wondered uneasily if he would be able to mourn her with the genuine sorrow he gave now to Antonia. He shook the thought from his head as ill luck.

Felix was crying silently, and Correus put a hand on his shoulder and shooed him gently down the steps with Ygerna and the small ones. The household slaves must have their turn now. Correus eyed his mother jumpily. Helva's beautiful face was solemn and her gold hair was decently veiled, but at forty-seven she was still a woman who could stop traffic in the streets, and she had never had an inconspicuous day in her life. The expression on her face was thoughtful and stubborn, and Correus found himself earnestly wishing himself elsewhere. All these funeral guests would have to be fed tonight, which meant that Julia and Helva would butt heads again over the orchestration of the meal, the cook would have a temperament from being given two conflicting sets of orders, and everything would go to Hades on a horse. He frowned at his mother, angry with her because she was patently incapable of filling Antonia's shoes, and she looked hurt. He put his arm around her, repentant. He supposed Antonia's death had not been easy on Helva either. It had upset the orderly pattern of her world.

"Father should have freed you years ago," he said.

Helva's lovely face was horrified. She was terribly afraid that Appius might be planning to do that now. "But where would I go?"

"Father would be generous—" He stopped, exasperated. They had been over this before. Helva didn't *want* to be free, and Correus, who had wanted it so badly that it had amounted to an obsession, found it hard to forgive her for that. "Never mind. Come away before we make a scandal. People are looking at us."

"I will pay my respects with the others," Helva said with monumental dignity. Correus watched her warily as she drifted toward the bier in a cloud of somber draperies and put a white hand on the stone. Antonia undoubtedly would have liked to fly up out of the casket and snatch her, but nothing untoward occurred. Helva tripped sedately down the steps again and gave her arm to Correus.

The important guests began to move back up the cypress-lined road to the house with its rose-tiled roof which capped the hill above them. Overhead, a skein of starlings folded and unfolded itself in the evening sky, and below, the brood mares' pasture spread away toward the edge of the hayfields. Appius Julianus bred remounts for the army and chariot ponies for the circus. The tall blond figure of the horsemaster, Forst, could be seen striding away across the pasture to make sure that the excitement hadn't provoked any of his mares into foaling early. The air was unseasonably warm, touched with the first balminess of the coming spring, which was an excellent thing. There were too many here to be fed in the dining room.

Ygerna put Eilenn's hand in Felix's and took Appius's arm.

"When I die," Ygerna said seriously, "I hope that so many people will be sorry for it. I never knew anyone so greatly loved."

"Nor I," Appius said.

"There will be a war tonight over this dinner, though," Ygerna observed.

Appius's mouth twitched in spite of himself. His daughter-in-law's candor amused him. And he found himself grateful for a conversation with no further condolences. He never knew how to answer them, and they changed nothing. Since Antonia's death, Appius had found Ygerna to be the one unfailingly practical person in his household. "I shall strive to keep the peace," he commented, "but I shan't blame you if you flee."

Ygerna watched her mother-in-law stroll away on Correus's arm, head bent to his. If Helva was fit for nothing but to be some man's toy, Ygerna thought, striving with difficulty to be fair, then that was only what Appius had made of her.

The main doors of the house stood open, spilling a gold haze of lamplight into the first insubstantial shadows of dusk. Like all Roman houses, the estate presented a mostly blank face to the outside world, with its balconies, windows, and colonnades all turned in toward the central court around which it was built. Philippos the steward stood gravely at the door under the portico, ushering in the guests. Inside, the atrium and gardens were full of people indulging in the usual gossip and speculation in the midst of their mourning.

Ygerna stood on tiptoe to kiss her father-in-law's cheek and left him to greet his guests in the atrium. Helva was his business after all, and he would have her on his hands, turning the peace of his home upside down and shaking it, no doubt for the rest of his life, which was a large price to be paid for a man's single indiscretion.

She took the baby to the green and gold room that had been allotted as her private chamber and handed him over to his nurse. Eilenn had disappeared with Felix, probably being fed cakes in the kitchen. Ygerna set the schoolroom maid on their trail, and sat down to straighten her hair in the silver mirror propped on her dressing table. She peered at her reflection thoughtfully and a pale, triangular face with winging dark brows peered back at her. Her black hair was pinned into an arrangement of curls dressed with studied carelessness, and her face painted in the current fashion. A gown of dark gray silk was ornamented with a necklace of coral and pearls, and coral ear drops. Her woolen mantle, the only wrap permitted to the fashionable, was striped in funereal gray and dark blue and fringed with gray silk. Ygerna had long ago decided that if she was going to be a Roman, then she would be a Roman down to her sandal laces, not an oddity to be pointed out like the provincial princes who were half hostage and half visiting dignitary, who sat in their own box at the circus like a cageful of tame lions.

A high thin chant, an insubstantial keening just on the edge of hearing, drew her to the balcony. It came and went, fluttering in her ears above the noise from the gardens below. The rose garden and the courtyard of Athena were thronged with the white togas of the guests, with flashes of purple and military scarlet, and the delicate flowerlike silks of their wives. Appius and Antonia had commanded the respect of the elite of Rome; senators, magistrates, and provincial governors had all come with their wives to give them their due. The house servants moved among them with trays of sweets, skewers of meat, and silver wine cups, and the gathering was turning, as funeral feasts so often did when the burying was done and no one had to think of death anymore, into a party. The keening came not from the guests in the garden, but from the slaves in their quarters, or gathered in small knots, like to like, in the terraced vineyard on the rear slope of the hill. There were Britons among them, and Gauls, Greeks, Egyptians, and Germans. And all had had their own dead to mourn.

Old Thais, who had been nurse to children now grown, and Alan, who had been horsemaster before Forst, lay buried with the family along the tree-lined road that led from the house on the hill to the main trunk road to Rome. It was the honor due long service. But there were other graves, row on row of them, in the slave cemetery. The fever had spread like wildfire through the slaves of the house before it had reached out a hand for the mistress. Ygerna had watched Antonia work beyond her strength, in an old gown with a sacking apron tied over it. They had boiled or burned everything that the fever had touched, according to orders from Appius, who said that was what the army surgeons did, but still it spread. Ygerna tried to close the sounds of mourning out of her ears. So many of the graves were small ones, and if the children of the family had been spared, that was small comfort to a slave with empty arms. Even now, Ygerna, Aemelia, and Julia watched their children like hawks, breath held every time they sneezed.

Ygerna decided that she had skulked on the balcony long enough, despite Appius's permission. She descended to the garden, threading her way past a bulky senator named Prosper Rufius, who was holding forth on the decline of respect for tradition among the young, while his wife Livilla Drusa Minor chattered with Aemelia. Aemelia didn't look happy but Livilla Minor was a malicious gossip and her predatory appraisal of Ygerna made Ygerna disinclined toward rescue. Livilla's terrifying old aunt, Livilla Drusa Major, was discussing her digestion with a trapped senator's wife, and Ygerna skirted around her as well before she could advise her to make sure Correus ate egg yolks every day and ask her about her sex life. She found Correus still in his mother's company, ruthlessly abandoned him too with a fleeting smile, and went to pay her respects to Julius Frontinus, currently proconsul of the province of Asia. Frontinus had been governor of Britain when Correus had served there, and chief of engineers in the last Rhenus campaign.

"My dear child!" Frontinus beamed at her with transparent approval. He was a tall, angular man with heavy, callused hands that moved restlessly when there was no task to put them to. He had a passion for waterworks and bridges, and an avuncular interest in Ygerna, who had been a rebellious thirteen-year-old hostage when he had first known her. "You look delightful, even in mourning dress."

Ygerna gave him a grin and motioned to a slave who was sidling through the milling throng with a tray. "Have you seen Correus yet? He only came home last night and is already looking like he wants to leave. Here, have some of these, they're very good."

"Very good indeed." Frontinus made a long arm for a cup of wine as another tray went by, and leaned comfortably against the weathered brick wall between the bare arms of espaliered apricot trees. He cocked an eye at Ygerna. "You've been here since you left the Rhenus?"

Ygerna made a face. "Having another baby, which is a thing that everybody seems to feel they know a great deal more about than I do. Correus's mother kept telling me I was too thin to carry it properly, and about all the women she knows of who have died in childbirth – I expect that's wishful thinking. And Aemelia said I should never look at fire or cows. And Forst – *Forst!* The Mother save me from men! – said that horses never have any trouble. His wife had a baby while he was in Germany, so he knows *all* about it, and the last time I saw Forst he was facedown in the mud with his arm halfway up a horse that was having trouble. I expect I am being indiscreet," she added.

Julius Frontinus burst out laughing. "Not at all. I take it that you want to go out to Moesia?"

"If I don't," Ygerna said flatly, "I shall go mad. Marcus is old enough to travel now, but Felix needs to stay here, which he won't like. His grandfather is insistent about proper tutoring, although he's had three tutors and they all developed tics after a week. Whenever he's driven one off, he trails about after old Diulius and Julius, and learns to swear like the race drivers."

"I saw young Julius drive in the Lupercalia races," Frontinus commented. "I bet on him on your husband's word and he made me a great deal of money."

"He's getting a swelled head," Ygerna said. "Women throw flowers at him."

"A most unsuitable example for the master's grandson. I may know of a tutor who is made of stronger stuff."

"If *you* told him to mind his lessons, I think he would," Ygerna said. "Appius is right that he's getting too old to run tame in an army camp and talk like the soldiers."

"I'll do what I can. He's my namesake, after all." Felix was a pet name; his full name was Frontinus Appius Julianus. "I owe him that. I've always felt I cost that child his mother."

Felix's mother had been eight months pregnant and ill, in a rainy, half-built fort. The governor had put her in his bed out of kindness and she had died because a man with a knife had come there looking for Frontinus. An army surgeon had cut the baby out of her dead body. The man with the knife had been an ally of Ygerna's uncle Bendigeid, then king of the Silures and at war with the governor's army. It was all very long ago and complicated, Ygerna thought.

"You did a kindness. No one can do more than that. And you've been more than kind to Felix. He thinks you are finer than the emperor and Jupiter Capitolinus rolled into one."

Frontinus chuckled. "A discerning child, and plainly destined for great things. He was born in a camp of the Eagles and swaddled in a military governor's cloak. I don't see how he can miss."

"The opinion in the household," Ygerna said, "is that if he didn't look so much like Correus, it would be a general assumption that a demon had fathered him."

"According to the old general," Frontinus said – Appius Julianus had been a famous man in his day and his name was still a byword in the army – "he is *greatly* like Correus."

"No doubt," Ygerna said dryly.

"It strikes me," said Julius Frontinus, "that there is more to this matter of your joining Correus in camp than finding a tutor for young Felix."

"Correus thinks the Danuvius frontier is going to make trouble," Ygerna said. "I expect he's right – he usually is. But I am going anyway as soon as I can talk him around. I doubt this Decebalus is worse than my uncle."

Julius Frontinus pricked up his ears. Her uncle had nearly won. Dusk was falling and the garden was splashed with light from lamps hung along the colonnades. Under one of them he could see Correus Julianus with his father and his brother and Lucius Paulinus. Correus's hands moved in an angry pattern in the air. "Ah, well, I daresay he'll come around." Julius Frontinus patted Ygerna in a fatherly, abstracted fashion and moved away toward them like a hound on the scent.

Some of the guests had begun to depart already, and others were talking suitable trivialities or careful politics under the broad trellises that ran from the dining chamber to the fountain. Frontinus wriggled his way through them, declining to be detained, skirted the stone-flagged courtyard of Athena where the goddess of wisdom kept watch over Appius's gardens, and fetched up in the south colonnade with an interested expression on his square, heavy-boned face.

Appius shifted a little to make room for him, leaning on his staff. "Join us. I'm afraid I'm disinclined to make small talk this evening."

"Understandable." Frontinus surveyed the four of them. This had all the earmarks of a quiet family quarrel. Flavius lounged against the plaster wall, soaking up the heat that came from the baths on the other side. His oddly elongated hands curved around an empty wine cup, his dark curls hung in a carefully brushed fringe across his forehead, and he wore a dark toga like his father's. The missing fingers that marred his hands had been hacked off by an enemy who had wanted, and not gotten, a military secret. There was more to Flavius Julianus than there seemed. Beside him, his brother Correus might have been his reflection in an unreliable mirror. He was left-handed and slightly taller, and his brown hair grew in erratic waves that refused to lie down unless he stuck a helmet on them, but his sharp-angled brows and aquiline features marked him for his father's son and were enough like Flavius's that they could have been twins and not half-blood kin. The gilded mail and scarlet field cloak of a cavalry prefect gave him a look of restless energy. Beside Appius Julianus and his brood, the sandy hair and homely freckled face of Appius's son-in-law Lucius Paulinus had an air of vague and guileless innocence, but Frontinus knew better. Lucius Paulinus was a student of modern history, or so he said. Privately, Frontinus had always thought he was a spy. Certainly he had been the late Emperor Vespasian's eyes and ears, and Titus's. His relationship with Domitian was cloudier. His somber mourning toga gave the impression of a man attempting to be invisible.

"We might talk shop," Frontinus suggested. "Moesia, for instance."

Correus gave his old commander a half-smile. "Am I that transparent? Moesia gives me the fidgets. There are too many rumors flying, and my men have caught too many tribal Dacians from the wrong side of the Danuvius in the towns in our sector, with no satisfactory accounting of themselves."

"We thought something was brewing two years ago," Frontinus said, brows raised. "That's why you were posted out there."

"I wasn't the only one," Correus said with disgust. "We're top-heavy with commanders just now." A fair amount of new blood had been shifted from the Rhenus to Danuvius commands, and there they now sat while the governor of Moesia decided whether he really ought to be worried or not. For most of them, the promised reinforcements in the ranks had not materialized. "Oppius Sabinus has 'come to the conclusion that the threat from Dacia was unduly magnified,'" Correus said.

Frontinus grunted. "I know Oppius Sabinus." He shot a glance at Appius. "I served with him when I was a junior. Under you, in fact. He had a way even then of telling himself whatever would cost him the least exertion."

"Well, this time he's told it to the emperor," Flavius said quietly. "And Sabinus was co-consul with him two years ago, so the emperor is inclined to listen. For that and other reasons." Unsaid was that too great a concentration of troops in any one province was always considered unwise. An army had put Domitian's father on the throne and one could very well put Domitian off it. Flavius knew the moods of his emperor better than any of them. Domitian did not care to be disagreed with. He was disposed to see disagreement as synonymous with treason.

Lucius Paulinus cast a watchful eye up and down the colonnade. "Tricky times," he murmured quietly. "They tend to breed adventure on the frontiers. So now the Dacians have a new warlord."

"Decebalus," Correus said. "He's about as harmless as a strung catapult. The frontier scouts have said it. I've said it. A few of the other commanders have said it. Oppius Sabinus thinks he's a tribal chief with a little cattle raiding on his mind."

"That's been their pattern in the past," Flavius admitted.

"Yes and no," Correus said. "These people are not barbarians. There's a loose confederacy of kingdoms made up of the Dacians and the Getae, who are some sort of kin to them, and the Roxolani and some others. But they're literate, they mint their own coinage, they build cities." He ticked off his points irritably on his fingers. "And every so often someone comes along and pulls them all together, and then they're dangerous. Burebista did it and started to meddle in Julius Caesar's war with Pompeius. Before he died, Caesar had every intention of marching on Burebista, and he had excellent reasons. After that Burebista played off Augustus and Marcus Antonius against each other until his own lords saw some kind of opportunity and murdered him. That's when Dacia split into a handful of petty kingdoms again and confined themselves to raiding the frontier because there was too much internal squabbling to do anything else. Now they have Decebalus. And Oppius Sabinus, may Ahriman snatch him by the hair, doesn't see the change in matters."

"Stop grinding your teeth," Appius said mildly.

"I'm sorry, Father." Correus had the look of a man who finds it trying to be a prefect on the Danuvius and the son of the household at home. "I've just been attempting to explain this to Mother, who either can't or won't see it, and wants me to stay in Rome for a few months, may Mithras help me."

"That would be pleasant."

Correus glowered at his father. "You want me to stay and make Mother behave. *You* do it."

"I'm far too old," Appius said. "And you're being rude." Lucius Paulinus and Julius Frontinus studied their toes.

"Well, I can't stay. Assuming that I had enough leave coming, which I don't, I can't leave an undermanned fort without a senior commander while the Danuvius is this touchy." He lifted an eyebrow at Flavius. "My scouts say there are Germans hanging around Decebalus's court. Tell *that* to the emperor. Semnones," Correus added. "In Sarmizegetusa. Ranvig, by the man's description. That means a high-level treaty."

"We made a treaty with them two years ago," Frontinus said thoughtfully. "But the chieftain of the Semnones is not a man I would trust greatly farther than I could throw the Capitoline."

"Nor he us," Correus said. "I thought at the time that a war with Dacia might be Ranvig's suggestion for keeping the emperor busy and his eyes off Semnone lands."

"Borders have a way of breeding wars," Frontinus said. "If we win them and don't annex, the next generation just has to fight the war again."

Paulinus opened his mouth, closed it again, and reassembled his words in a more tactful order. "It has occurred, just now and again, that Rome started the war. To keep our hand in, so to speak."

Frontinus contemplated him. "You're as vague as a thin mist. Wise of you, maybe. But if you mean the German war, *I'm* not Domitian's spy."

"It is important that the emperor be respected as a military man," Appius intervened. "It fosters stability. Domitian needed that triumph and he earned it in Germany. Let us leave it at that."

"I'd feel happier if Rome did start a war in Dacia," Correus said, "and got a jump on it. There's going to be one, whether Oppius Sabinus puts his head under his pillow or not."

"If so, you'll see troops shifted out there fast enough," Frontinus said.

Correus leaned against a pillar and crossed his arms on his gilded fishscale. "I don't like last stands," he said succinctly.

Julius Frontinus nodded, not without sympathy. "An avenging army does very little for the men already buried. Alas, sometimes that's what it takes." He straightened the folds of his toga and the long, purple-striped senatorial tunic under it. He nodded at Appius. "My condolences. She was a very great lady. Worthy of an old house." Antonia had been of the family of Marcus Antonius himself, a point in which she had taken pride. Frontinus clapped a hand for a moment on Appius's shoulder, somber in its dark toga, and turned to Correus. "I think I know of a tutor for that young hellion of yours. That's about all I can offer. The Senate's very nervy these days."

"The Senate is shaking in its senatorial boots!" Correus exploded as soon as Frontinus was out of earshot.

"The Senate has good reason to," Flavius said. "You've been on the Danuvius all year. The emperor collects informers for a hobby. The palace is thick with them, underfoot like rats."

"That's unusually frank for you, Flavius," Correus said.

"That's too frank," Appius said. "For any of us. Julius Frontinus is no coward, and if he isn't willing to tell a home truth to the emperor, then he has a reason, and you know what it is, Flavius."

Flavius stared into his wine cup. There was nothing to see in it but a distorted reflection of his own face. He had served Domitian loyally, for Rome, which was very different from the reasons he had served and loved Domitian's brother Titus. But Domitian had reasons to cultivate informers, which unfortunately also bred more need for them. "I may be able to speak to him," Flavius said. "Oddly enough, he still trusts me. At least he won't order me to open my veins for it, but I doubt he'll listen either." He looked at Paulinus. "You, maybe."

Lucius Paulinus shifted uncomfortably. "Domitian uses me because his father and brother did, and he's afraid I know things. I work for him because I can't afford not to. That's not the most amiable arrangement. Still... I've a fancy to see the Danuvius again. I'll go and find Julia, Correus, before she puts nightshade in your mother's wine." He drifted off, and Appius turned a shrewd gaze on both his sons.

"Rome has survived capricious emperors before now. Rome will survive this one. But I intend for my family to be here to see it. This is a time for discretion. Do I make myself clear?"

"Uncomfortably so," Correus said. "We shall behave with the circumspection of Vestal Virgins. Don't expect us to like it."

"I don't. But I have buried all the bodies I am willing to."

II

Family Matters

It was not a restful night.

Six-year-old Appia thrashed wildly at the woolen bedcovers and shrieked, "*Grandmother!*", her night shift rumpled and sweat-stained. The unfamiliar room was lit by a little silver night lamp shaped like a pomegranate, but all the dark corners seemed to gape the way the opened tomb had. Her grandmother's death had never seemed quite real to her so long as the casket had lain in state, unburied. Now it closed around her, terrifying and inevitable.

"Shall I send for Nurse?" Aemelia put her arms around her daughter helplessly.

"Noooo! *Grandmother!*" Appia's voice rose in an anguished howl and Flavius appeared in the doorway, rubbing his eyes.

"Now you've woken Papa. You'll wake the whole house," Aemelia said. "Hush now, like a good girl."

Appia uttered another inarticulate shriek and hurled herself to the far end of the bed, tangled in the coverlets.

Flavius strode into the room. "How did she get in this state? And the Hades with the rest of the house!" He shook his daughter out of the bedclothes and held her while she beat at his back with her fists. "Who left her alone like this?"

"I told Nurse to go to bed," Aemelia said. "And you know she doesn't hear well. Appia was all right when she went to sleep." Aemelia's delicate face was smudged with gray under the eyes and she gave him a furious look as she put a tentative hand on Appia's dark hair. "Please, precious, try to be quiet."

Appia's flailing fist connected with Flavius's ear and he swore. He grabbed both the child's wrists in one hand and wrapped the other arm around her more tightly. "Go back to bed," he said over his shoulder. "I'll deal with this."

"Flavius—"

"Go back to bed. You're not being any help."

Aemelia glared at him and left, and Flavius rocked his daughter, cursing himself under his breath. It wasn't Aemelia's fault that the child had nightmares. And certainly not that Livilla had chosen his mother's funeral as the occasion to tell Aemelia gossip about her husband that must be all over Rome by now. They had had a furious argument before the guests had even left, Aemelia hissing at him under the trellised grapevines at the end of the garden.

In her father's firm grip, Appia had subsided into broken sobs, and Flavius crooned to her gently, an old lullaby half-remembered from his childhood. His wife had not been so easy to deal with. He had tried to deny it like a fool, and then to pacify her, and only succeeded in making her burst into tears and run into the house. That too would be all over Rome tomorrow, he thought ruefully. Correus had warned him not to fall into a love affair on the frontier, especially with a woman who could be no part of his life. And it was a German chieftain's widow of all the ill-advised choices, who had her own people to look to, as he had his.

He stroked Appia's hair and kissed her on the ear, and she burrowed her face into his night tunic. "We all miss Grandmother," he whispered, "but she wouldn't want you to be this unhappy."

"But she's *gone*," Appia wailed into his shoulder. It was the stark terror of it that had woken her screaming.

There was no denial to be made to that, Flavius thought. He had waked in a sweat more nights than one to find himself staring into the darkness, reaching for the irretrievable. Fiorgyn, gone from him, and now his mother too. And his son, stillborn, *gone*. Flavius tightened his arms around Appia, willing himself not to blame her because she wasn't a boy. He had been so delighted with her when she was born. There had been plenty of time for boys, for a child who would carry his name. Then the boy had come, born dead, and the physicians had said he must father no more children on Aemelia or risk losing her too. And had that been in some way his fault, he had asked himself in the middle of the night, because he had very likely been in Fiorgyn's bed when it had happened?

Appia's breathing was slow and regular now. When Flavius laid her down on the bed, she burrowed into the pillow, and he drew the covers back over her. He started for the door, then changed his mind and settled into the cushioned wicker chair by the window. A spare blanket lay on the bench at the foot of the bed and he pulled it over his knees. *This is beneath my dignity*, he thought wryly. *I should send for Nurse*. But Appia didn't want Nurse; Nurse didn't share her mourning. He would sit with her for tonight, he decided. He'd be gone again for days at a time soon enough on the emperor's business. At least he was in a position to tamp down most of the rumors and dangerous machinations of palace intrigue. At the moment, Domitian was embarked on a campaign to improve public morals, and to root out fraud in the various government offices, where he had let it prosper in his first years. The unwisdom of that had now been seen and a new broom was being employed, which made the Senate nervous. Domitian was still capricious, but he was determinedly growing into the job of emperor as he adjusted to possessing the power that his father and brother had never let him have. He had given Flavius grudging leave to spend two nights at his father's house for his mother's funeral, with the promise of no urgent summons back to Rome. Domitian had almost balked at that, but Flavius knew that without it, some inconsequential upheaval would have had the emperor shouting for his presence before he was halfway home. He expected he would have to pay for it when he went back.

–

In the adjoining chamber, Aemelia propped herself up on the pillow and stared at the faint glow that came from her daughter's room, trying to unravel what had happened to Flavius. He wasn't the same man he had been when she married him, and it couldn't all be because he had found a tart in Germany. When Titus had been alive, there had been such a heady air of excitement to their life in the inner circle of the palace. Aemelia had gleefully hoarded scraps of knowledge on the interior workings of the government with which to impress less favored friends. Great men had come to dine and found her charming. Now Flavius wouldn't talk to her about government matters at all, and when there was company, the conversation was so casual that she grew bored and restless and it seemed simpler just to dine alone. But Flavius had changed in other ways too. Of course the physicians had told her that she mustn't have any more children, but he didn't seem to mind. That would have been almost a relief if Aemelia hadn't suspected that this response wasn't normal. There were things that Flavius could wear – horrid, flaccid things that looked like worms. The physician had given her one, but she couldn't bear to touch it. Then he had given her a little silver cap and a horrid greasy ointment and something that smelled vile to wash with afterward, and told her interminably how to smear the ointment on a piece of wool and put it and the silver cap inside her when her husband wished to exercise his marital rights. Aemelia had been mortified and had listened to him with her eyes on the frescoes on the far wall. They had used the silver cap once, but after that, Flavius hadn't mentioned his marital rights, so the cap stayed in its ivory box on her dressing table, lost among the perfume bottles.

Aemelia had been almost unendurably grateful. She had lived in mortal terror that the silver cap wouldn't work and she would be pregnant and have another dead baby, or die of it herself. She had asked Flavius if he wanted to divorce her, and he had said certainly not, she was his wife and he loved her, what did she think he was? Then he had gone out riding, bareback, on a horse that everyone said was dangerous.

And then last night, Livilla had told her, whispering confidentially over a dish of oysters, that there was something she thought Aemelia ought to know, and of course it was only gossip and probably not true at all, but the person who had told Livilla had a husband whose sister's cousin was stationed on the Rhenus, and well, husbands did this sort of thing all the time, but she did think Aemelia should *know*.

–

Helva, brushing out her gold hair by lamplight, could hear a pacing on the flagstones under the statue of Athena. She knew by the familiar footfall it was Appius. She had sent her maid away in case he should want to come to her, but he wasn't going to, she thought dismally. Lady Antonia's death had made everything difficult and uncomfortable. There was no possibility that Appius might marry Helva now; that would be an insult to Antonia's children and Antonia's memory, and Helva was not so foolish that she couldn't see it. She wanted only for things to go on as they had been – to be someone's pampered darling, to have pretty clothes and jewelry, and her apartments done over whenever she liked; to be part of a great house.

Helva laid the coral-backed brush down on the table and pulled the twin lamps closer to stare at her face in the mirror. The lamps were silver, Charon in his boat, and triple-headed Cerberus with the oil flame glowing behind all three mouths, the guardians of the underworld. She had liked them immensely when Appius had given them to her, but now they had begun to give her the horrors. Even her bedchamber, newly painted in sky blue with poppies abloom on the walls, seemed malign and disturbing in their light. Helva studied her face again. She was still beautiful, but not so beautiful as she had been when Appius had bought her out of a slave market in Gallia Belgica after her tribe had unwisely tried to fight with Rome, and had taken her with him from camp to camp until she was pregnant with Correus. Then he had installed her among his young wife's waiting women without consulting the wife. Antonia had otherwise been given the respect that was due to Appius's wife, but Helva had discovered that she had a power of her own in the year that she had followed the army with Appius. She had been willful, cajoling, greedy, and beautiful, and she made him laugh. When she had given him a son, on the same day that Antonia had borne Flavius, her position in the household was assured. As Appius had grown older, her hold on him rested more in Correus than in her beauty, but she could still charm him and he still came to her bed when he was in the mood. Until Antonia died.

Helva listened, lonesome, to the restless pacing in the courtyard. Would Appius, bereft of his wife, feel that he owed it to her memory to part with his mistress as well? He would never sell her, but Helva was terrified that he might free her. It was not in Helva to love Appius, and he had never required that she should, but after so many years, she did not think that she could bear to be alone.

"If you took me back to the Danuvius with you now, we could do this every night," Ygerna told Correus, wrapping her arms around his shoulders. Both Appia's shrieks and her grandfather's restless footsteps could be heard through the bedchamber windows, and they were resolutely ignoring both.

"As soon as it settles down, I promise." He bent his head and kissed the tips of her breasts and then the faded gray-blue five-petaled flower between them: the mark of a priestess of the Mother and a royal woman of the Silures. It was permanent, pricked indelibly into the skin with blue woad, and she would carry it to the grave. The moon flowed through a tree beyond the open window, leaving her skin tiger-striped with shadow. The first time he had lain with her had been by moonlight. Correus put his hands on the insides of her thighs, the memory achingly clear. It had been on a hidden trail in the Silure hills, while all around them her uncle's hunt had been prowling for them. She had been fifteen. What night madness had prompted him then, he never knew, but it had not let go of him since.

Afterward they lay cuddled together spoon fashion, soaking each other up. There were only a few more days before he would have to go back.

—

In the morning, the family gathered for a communal breakfast of bread and honey, eggs and olives, no one looking as if they had had much sleep. Helva ate in her apartment since despite her place in the household, dining with the family was unsuitable.

"Julius Frontinus thinks he knows of a tutor," Correus said, as the children bobbed in and out of the dining room, nurses in pursuit. "His current master's children are out of the schoolroom this year and they are looking for a place for him. He is said to have nerves of iron."

Appius smiled. "He will need them. If Frontinus recommends him, I will buy him as a present for you."

"That is generous of you." Correus looked mildly suspicious. The larger a household he acquired, the more reasonable it would seem to have his mother in it. But the offer was generous. A tutor was an expensive purchase. Correus, as a second son, had his army pay and an allowance from his father. Ygerna had a small dowry, conferred upon her by the Senate along with her citizenship. It did not make them rich.

Appius held out his cup and a slave poured the exact proportions of water and wine that he knew the master liked at breakfast. A shriek from the corridor announced that someone was doing something that should not be done, probably Felix. "Money well spent, I think."

"It is kind of you," Ygerna said. "Felix will be happier if he has something to interest him before I leave, besides chasing his father to the frontier with me and learning curse words." Her voice held the tone of a woman whose trunks were packed.

26

"I'm afraid you may have plenty of time," Correus said. As Ygerna opened her mouth, he said, "You know I can't take you out there the way things are."

"I can't think why you would want to go," Aemelia told her. She shuddered delicately, nibbling bread and honey. "One trip to the frontier was enough for me. I am glad that Flavius doesn't have to go there anymore." She gave Flavius a thoughtful look that was not lost on either Correus or Lucius Paulinus.

"If you get reinforcements, the border will settle down," Paulinus said. "I spoke with Tettius Julianus last night after we talked and he thinks that if they come from anywhere, they will come from the Rhenus, and that's overdue. He has three legions out there quartered at Moguntiacum. Two of them have old bad blood with the other one so that may have been wishful thinking. But on the other hand, that makes five legions just in Upper Germany, and that's a lot. The emperor would do well to thin that out."

"It was kind of him to come all that way for Mother's memory," Flavius said.

"Who is Tettius Julianus?" Ygerna asked. "Is he a relative?" The intricacies of Roman family connections were as tangled as the royal house of the Silures had been.

"Not exactly," Flavius said. "Maybe one of those fourth cousins by marriage and adoption twice removed sort of thing."

"That's close," Appius said. "Julianus as a cognomen doesn't necessarily make him related," he told Ygerna. "The important name is the middle one. The Appii are our gens, our clan. The first name is at the discretion of the parents. Ours, Flavius's and mine, is unusual in that the Flavians are a gens. It usually isn't given as a praenomen, but it was given my grandfather to flatter some Flavian who had done him a favor."

"He was probably a connection of the current emperor," Flavius said, cracking an egg. "So it's been useful."

"My people have one name generally," Ygerna said, "and the Druids, who of course do not exist anymore, keep track of who is related to whom."

Appius chuckled at that, and Lucius Paulinus said, "They are very efficient for nonexistent people." The Druids were the old priesthood of Britain and Gaul and one of the few religious entities that Rome had banned in its conquered provinces, for the reason that rebellion sprang up like weeds everywhere they went.

"What about the Julianus part?" Ygerna asked. "Why doesn't that mean he's related?"

"The cognomen is sometimes inherited, and sometimes acquired," Appius said. "Julianus indicates some connection with the Julian gens. A maternal line maybe, or an adoption. An adopted son takes his adoptive father's name but may keep that form of his original gens as a cognomen. We've kept Julianus without changing it for so long that I'm not really sure how it came about."

"It seems odd for an Appian to have adopted a Julian," Flavius said. "One would expect the other way around." The Julian gens was the family of the first Caesar, wealthy and with a long, distinguished history. The Appii were an obscure clan, risen to prominence only on the military career of Appius Julianus.

"Could have been the need for an heir," Paulinus said. There was a small silence and he looked like a man who has had a sudden uncomfortable thought. He gave his attention to peeling an egg.

Ygerna watched the unspoken thought go around the room. Flavius had no heir and unless he divorced Aemelia was unlikely to have one. Correus had two sons, both of whom would benefit by the adoption of either of them. The adopted son – Felix, for instance – would inherit Appius's estate eventually. Then Marcus would not be a second son and would inherit whatever Correus could amass rather than starting with nothing. Or vice versa. She knew without asking that everyone in the family had thought about this and no one was ready to mention it. Which was probably wise.

The necessity for a change of subject was removed by the steward Philippos, an imposing figure in a blue woolen tunic and the silver armband of Appius's house. "This came by courier, Prefect," he said, addressing Correus with the dignity of his rank – as if he had not, when Correus was five, put him over his knee for pouring ink in the fountain. He handed Correus a sealed tablet.

Correus broke the seal with his thumb and swore. He looked ruefully at his wife. "I am sorry. This must have started chasing me days after I left."

"What is it?"

"It's from my second. And of course it's weeks late. Our scouts have found signs of mass movement of men and horses across the river, more than before. When I left, it was still frozen, which is practically a highway saying 'Invade Here' along the whole length of it. I can't stay any longer."

"Of course," Appius said. "We are grateful that you came." He eyed Ygerna, whose face was grim. "Send word, please, as often as you can."

"It will take a day to send a courier to Aternum, to make sure we have transport. I'll leave in the morning." He held out his hand to Ygerna and they disappeared.

–

Julia floated on her back in the warm pool of the household baths. She was sorry to see Correus leave again, but that was the army. Splashes and shrieks from the next room proclaimed that her children, Paulilla and Lucian, were being persuaded by their nurse to take a cold plunge for their health. Her husband came in, in tunic and sandals, and squatted on the edge of the bath. Julia made shooing motions at him. "Go away. It's the women's hours. You'll have them all squawking like hens."

"Aemelia is fighting with Flavius," Paulinus said. "Ygerna has gone back to bed with Correus. And Helva wouldn't care."

Julia displayed an expression indicative of her opinion of Helva's character, then cocked an eye up at him. "Why is Aemelia fighting with Flavius?"

Paulinus looked embarrassed. "That harpy Livilla Minor told her the gossip last night. It was bound to get around. And my remark about adoption didn't help."

"It didn't." Julia flipped over in the water, dove down, and came up at the edge of the pool with a splash. She shook wet brown hair out of a pair of suspicious eyes. "But that isn't why you're invading the bath just now."

Paulinus sat down on the damp stone and put his arms around his knees. "Stop splashing. I'm getting my backside wet. I'm going out to Moesia with Correus."

Julia narrowed her eyes. "Do I bore you, Lucius?"

"Don't be an ass," Paulinus said irritably. "Correus thinks something's brewing out there. Since the governor doesn't seem inclined to listen to him, I think I had better. And I can't tell Domitian much without going out there."

"No one ever likes you nosing around," Julia pointed out. "Even when you're on their side. And for Domitian?"

"More like for your brother and every other commander out there. But I made my peace with the emperor. I thought that was what you and Flavius wanted."

Julia lowered her voice. Her maid was lurking somewhere in the corridor with towels and rubbing oil. "You were courting a treason trial," she hissed. "You had to."

"No. I promised Flavius, after he and Correus saved my skin."

"They saved all our skins," Julia said somberly. "I'm not sure I've forgiven you for that."

Paulinus's homely, freckled countenance had begun to show all of its thirty-six years lately. His brush with treason had left its mark on both of them. It had been a fine idea, he thought bitterly – for "the good of the empire" – to replace an unstable emperor with a man capable of keeping control. But then the chosen successor had died, and the plot had proved almost impossible to stop. It had come within an inch of bringing half the honest men in Rome down with it.

Paulinus put a hand over Julia's wet one and she pulled it away to untangle a strand of hair from one of the gold drops in her ears. "Correus told me that the emperor doesn't want to hear any warnings out of Moesia," Julia said. "What makes you think he wants you to go?"

"I don't think he does," Paulinus said. "But if Correus is right and the whole frontier boils over, he will certainly hold me to blame for *not* having warned him."

"You pick a very fine time. You may not even be here when the baby comes," Julia said. Standing on the lowest step, the bath came just below her breasts. Through the rippling water, Paulinus could see that her belly was already taking on a familiar curve, and said a fervent mental prayer of thanks to Juno and Mother Cybele for his wife's pregnancy. Ordinarily they traveled together, babies and all, and saw the sights. Lucius Paulinus was not a soldier and could command a lodging far more agreeable than the frontier housing in which Correus's wife frequently found herself. But this was not an expedition on which he wanted his wife. A frontier about to go up in flames beneath an oblivious commander would be dangerous even in the Roman zone.

"I think in this case, Ju, it's probably just as well. The Danuvius is tricky country just now. But after the baby comes, we'll go somewhere. Would you like to see the pyramids? Or Greece again? There's a sunken city off the coast of Achaea – you can rent a boat and go out and see the ruins through the water."

Julia pinned her hair into a knot on her head with the gold-tipped pins that lay scattered on the stone and waded from the pool. "I am not a child, Lucius. Don't offer me treats."

–

"And the worst of it is that she has every right to be angry still," Paulinus told Correus on the road.

"That she does," Correus said, in no mood to mince words. He had been part of the perilous effort that had pulled Paulinus out of the fire. And he had only had three days with his own wife.

The sanded bridleway ran beside the stone-paved Via Tiburtina out from the City to Aternum on the Adriatic coast. Correus

31

carried his kit rolled up behind his saddle on Briseis, a sleek chestnut mare who had replaced the now elderly troop horse that had been his father's commissioning gift. Correus's slave Eumenes and Tullius, Paulinus's servant, rode behind them with two mules loaded with Paulinus's gear.

It was starting to rain. Paulinus sighed and pulled a battered straw hat and a cloak from behind his saddle, while Correus tipped his helmet forward a little to keep the rain out of his eyes.

"I shall take an ague," Paulinus said dolefully, "and die of it in Aternum." He did not particularly care for being wet.

Correus chuckled. "If you didn't take an ague on the Rhenus, you won't get one in Italy. But please die before Aternum if you're going to do it. If you expire while we're crossing the mountains, I'll leave your body there."

"Be sure and tell Julia," Paulinus said, "so that she's properly sorry. I don't know whether she was angrier at my going or at my not letting her come with me. I expect she's having an indignation meeting with your wife at the moment."

"Ygerna wasn't best pleased," Correus admitted.

"That is the disadvantage in marrying for love," Paulinus said thoughtfully as the rain dripped from his hat. "One cares so violently what the other one does."

III

Viminacium

I used to have a plow,
Two oxen and a cow—

Tullius was whistling one of the old marching songs of the Legions, and Correus and Eumenes, who knew them all, joined in with feeling.

And it didn't seem too grand to leave behind
When I signed on with the Legions
For a tour of other regions—
But now I rather think I've changed my mind!

It was at least half a month's journey from Rome to Singidunum on the Danuvius, and that was traveling fast, with a military transport across the Adriatic to Salona, on which they had all been miserably seasick. The late winter had brought with it the *boreas*, the cold, gusty wind that churned the Adriatic into froth and deformed what few trees grew in its path. It was still blowing, catching the notes of Tullius's song and hurling them into the ravine that dropped steeply away from the mountain road beyond Salona. They kept the horses hugging the shelter of the cliffs on the other side. The *boreas* had been known to blow a traveler right off the road. The dry limestone hills were clothed in juniper, thyme, and twisted, stunted trees clinging precariously to the

33

mountainside in the teeth of the wind, and the coastal villages of Dalmatia all put rocks on their roofs to hold them down.

It was still early in the year for anyone to be traveling who had not been forced to it by necessity. The mountain inns that clung to their promontories like windblown birds were generally bare of any company save an occasional farmer with a crock of honey to sell, or a flock of goats being driven down to market. They came to another of these way stations at nightfall and turned into the inn yard gratefully. The landlord's boy led the horses away to be rubbed down, and they walked stiff-legged into the one long room that was the dining hall, wine shop, and sleeping chamber combined. A fire roared in the hearth. Paulinus sat down in front of it and stuck his hands nearly in the flames.

Correus pulled his helmet off, dropped down onto the bench beside Paulinus, and sent Eumenes to find someone to bring them dinner.

"Goat meat," Eumenes said with conviction. It had been goat meat every night so far. But he was glad just to be on the road again and on dry land. Kicking his heels in the prefect's father's house in Rome was too pointed a reminder of how Eumenes had come into the prefect's service. Eumenes had served in the auxiliaries once, and gone swiftly from there onto a slave ship after he had tried to kill his decurion, who made a habit of tormenting the men under him for amusement. From the slave ship he had gone into the arena for trying to kill an overseer. It was there that Correus had fished him out of the water, half-drowned but unaccountably still alive at the end of a mock sea battle, and had found himself unable to send a man through the arena twice. Thus Eumenes had come into Correus's service, and he was grateful, but he had taken a dislike to Rome as well as to water. The Adriatic crossing had terrified him.

Eumenes nosed about the kitchen that opened off the main chamber, sniffed at the stewpot that hung on a hook over the kitchen fire – goat meat – and prodded a stocky woman with a mustache and an unpleasant-looking apron toward the door.

"Food," he said, assuming correctly that she would know that much Latin. "And wine. Good wine," he added hopefully. "*Festina!*" Hurry.

She nodded, wiping her hands on the dubious apron, and took a stack of earthenware bowls off a shelf. Romans were always in a hurry. She had never seen one that wasn't.

In the main room, the company had been expanded by a farmer in a sheepskin jacket that grew more noticeable the closer it came to the fire, and a burly man of indeterminate profession with three knives in his belt. Correus, Paulinus, Tullius, and Eumenes took one look at him and decided simultaneously to sleep on top of their saddlebags.

The stew proved to be passable, flavored with parsley, onions, and wild thyme, and the wine was unexpectedly good – and therefore almost undoubtedly smuggled. Since they were drinking it, Correus felt disinclined to take any official notice of that. He was not, after all, a customs agent. He settled in contentedly on the far side of the fire from the sheepskin jacket, while outside the *boreas* howled and battered at the shutters.

–

The air grew colder as they climbed higher inland, although the wind ceased to blow with such force. The Dalmatian uplands resembled nothing so much as a petrified sponge. The limestone was fissured and honeycombed with underground caverns in which dwelt unpleasant, sightless creatures, and with subterranean watercourses which drew most of the rainfall into their depths. Even the few surface rivers vanished abruptly underground to emerge again miles later. Farther from the coast, oak, pine, and beech forests clothed the lower slopes, and in the sheltered valleys olives, almonds, figs, and wild cherries grew. There were only beginning to be signs of spring – wind-tossed mountain roses leafing out among the rocks, tortoises come out to sun themselves in a brief warmth, and, in the dry hillsides, waking scorpions, lizards, and a sudden hatch of sandflies. They rode through clouds of them, shooing them away with hats and riding crops as the weather warmed. Briseis, bitten on the rump by a horsefly, nearly dumped Correus into a ravine a hundred feet below the road. At Servitium on the Savus, they found the river ice-free enough for traffic, as Correus had hoped, and they loaded the horses onto a merchant ship bound for the Danuvius, under the captain's protest and Correus's determined pulling of rank. Finishing the trip by river would shave days off their journey. The Savus flowed into the Danuvius at Singidunum, where the corners of Moesia, Pannonia, and Dalmatia touched.

Singidunum Fortress sat on the chalk cliffs above the confluence of the rivers, with its vicus, the usual motley civil settlement of soldiers' women, wine sellers, native peddlers, and frontier entrepreneurs spread out to the south and east. It was a massive timber-built fortress, considerably enlarged of late, in the so far unfulfilled hope that it would be called upon to house greater numbers than the thousand-strong cavalry ala currently occupying it. Downriver lay the provincial capital Viminacium, home fort of the Seventh Legion Claudia, one of only three stationed on the six-hundred-mile length of the Moesian frontier.

They rode in late afternoon up the slope from the river to Singidunum's western gate and the hastily snapped salute of a sentry who touched his pilum to his breast and nearly knocked his helmet off. Correus returned the salute gravely and smiled a little under the shadow of his helmet at the rapid clatter of hastily disappearing military sandals. Someone had gone to report that the prefect was back. Correus drew rein for a moment just inside the gate to give the senior decurion a chance to get his men in order. The Ala Dardanorum was a good unit, and Correus disliked pouncing on his men from around corners. It spoiled their dignity.

"Good to see you back, sir." His second, Decurion Blaesus, gave him a salute and a look that said plainly that he was telling the truth. "Sorry to chase you down at your mother's funeral, though."

"I got three days out of the saddle," Correus said. "My backside aches." He swung down from Briseis and smacked her on the rump as Eumenes led her off to the stable block. Behind Blaesus, Correus's headquarters optio had appeared, wearing a face of morose welcome. Correus decided that he didn't like the look of either of them.

"The scouts came in not an hour ago," Blaesus said. "Tsiru and Dotos. They're one man short, and they say there's a war band the size of two legions out there somewhere, across the river."

"We came down the Savus and there wasn't enough ice left on the river to hold up a cat," Paulinus said. There weren't any bridges over the Danuvius.

Blaesus didn't bother asking who Paulinus was. "They'll swim it or use boats. You don't know the Dacians." His voice was brisk and slightly accented. Like the ala itself, he was a man of the Dardani of Moesia. "I sent a courier to Viminacium, sir," he told Correus.

Correus headed for the Principia, talking as he went with Blaesus and the optio trailing him. "Is there any chance they're just picking a quarrel with the Getae?"

Paulinus handed his horse to Tullius and followed along behind. In the courtyard of the Principia, the troop standards and the blue and gold silk banner of the ala were displayed. The prefect saluted them as he passed and turned into the headquarters building.

"I doubt it, sir," Blaesus was saying. "That's too many men just to go horse-stealing. There are also rumors about a marriage between one of the Dacian princesses and the king of the Getae, so that argues against a raiding party too. I told the governor my assessment," he added. "I wish you had been here to put your name to it. Do you want to see the scouts, and send another message on, concurring?"

"Yes, fetch them in." Correus pulled his helmet off and set it on the desk in his office, rubbing at the callus that the helmet strap had left under his chin. Nearly fourteen years under a helmet, he thought. It was a wonder that his head didn't fly off without it. "Oh, and Optio—" Correus halted him as he went in search of the scouts "—This is Lucius Paulinus. My sister's husband. He'll be staying a while with us – that is, if there aren't Dacians coming in the windows tomorrow morning. He's a mind to see the frontier."

"I'll have someone find a room in the Praetorium for him," the optio said. He glanced at Paulinus. "You've picked a lively time, sir." If the prefect wanted to let his civilian relatives loose in a war zone, it was no business of his.

Correus was sifting through the stacks of papyrus and wax and wooden tablets that littered his desk – quartermaster's lists, hospital lists, duty rosters, requests for leave. "Is any of this important?"

"Nothing that won't keep," Blaesus said.

"Good." Correus looked at Blaesus. "Get your wife out of here. Send her east to Servitium. I doubt they'll head that way."

"You think they're going to cross the river, sir." It wasn't exactly a question.

"I've been thinking they were going to for a year." Correus put his head in his hands as Blaesus left. And telling the governor for nearly as long. Well, ten thousand men should wake Oppius Sabinus up, if they didn't burn Moesia to the ground first. And if that's all there were. He looked up at Paulinus. "It's a bit late in the day, I'm afraid, to take a report to Domitian."

Paulinus drew up a chair and flicked a finger through the scarlet horsetail crest on Correus's helmet. "So it would seem. What do you do now?"

"We wait for orders," Correus said grimly. The Ala Dardanorum was one of the new milliary alae, a thousand strong instead of the usual five hundred, but he couldn't take on ten thousand with it, even if the ala were up to strength. There were a thousand men on paper. There were eight hundred and four fit to ride in Singidunum. "Where are those scouts?" Correus shouted. The optio returned, and Correus glared at him.

"They were in the baths, sir," the optio said.

"Merciful Diana and my departed ancestors, I don't care if they're *clean*! Get them in here!"

The scouts appeared, damp hair hanging in their eyes, and sandal laces trailing. "Why this sudden passion for the proprieties?" Correus snapped. The border wolves, a different breed from the regular scouts who moved ahead of any march, could live off the land and blend in with the natives. Their hair was long and shaggy, they shaved once a week when they thought about it, and no one should throw dice with them.

"Governor's orders," the senior of them, Tsiru, said briefly. "He was through here last week. No one to report to his superior until properly attired."

Correus ground his teeth. "Very well, you may take that as rescinded unless the governor is in Singidunum. What in Mithras's name is going on out there? And what happened to you?" Both were somewhat battered and Tsiru had a newly stitched gash down his arm.

"We got caught. Seen, anyway," Dotos said. "They killed Beto; at least I hope so. Otherwise, they just take them back to cut pieces out of."

Correus's expression became less wrathful. The border wolves were a close-knit brotherhood. "We'll say the Prayer for the Slain tonight," he said gently. "If the Dacians give us time. Sit down before you fall over, and report."

Tsiru and Dotos remained adamant in their count of the Dacian numbers. Mostly infantry, with some archers and scale-armored cavalry, they said. And not a raiding party – not with those numbers pouring out of the Dacian mountain strongholds. And there were more behind them, they thought. Just to put an army of that size on the march without eating their own country bare meant superior organization and an established supply line. The scouts could say where the Dacian army had been massing when they had spotted them two days since, but not where they were now. There were several places where the Danuvius could be swum or crossed on a temporary boat bridge.

By the time the scouts had finished, the prefect was in a rising fury. The war that Oppius Sabinus had declined to believe in was about to start. Two-thirds of the fort commanders on the Danuvius had predicted it, and it gave Correus very little satisfaction to be proven right.

He thought of the other fort commanders, and of how little Governor Oppius Sabinus would like it if Prefect Julianus of Singidunum took it on his own head to send them a warning without waiting for the governor's reply. He decided that he didn't want any burned-out towns on his conscience and shouted for the optio again.

"Send a rider to the governor at Viminacium with my concurrence of Blaesus's report, and make sure the legate of the Claudia there sees it too. Send someone with a reasonable amount of discretion. Tell him to stop in Tricornium on the way and give the same report, very unofficially, to the commander there. And when he leaves Viminacium, unless the governor has a return message, he's not to come back here but go on to Pincum, with a strong personal suggestion from me that the commander at Pincum pass the message down the road."

The optio departed with a scribbled message on a wax tablet, and Correus sent the scouts after him, to sleep while they could. There was little point in sending them out again. Decebalus and his army – Correus had little doubt that it was Decebalus at the head of it – had seen them now. And, Correus thought, cursing Governor Sabinus, he was going to need them to fight at Singidunum.

–

Correus reviewed the ala by torchlight on the camp parade ground outside the fortress walls, while the civil settlement to the southeast swarmed like an overturned anthill. To stay and trust the protection of Singidunum Fortress, or flee south and maybe get caught on the road? They sent delegation after delegation to the prefect, and all the prefect could tell them was that he didn't know. The Ala Dardanorum made the Prayer for the Slain and the proper sacrifices for battle before the ala standards and banner, and Correus gave a speech which he didn't remember afterward. The troop horses spent the night tethered and saddled in their stalls, while their riders dozed restlessly, one ear open to the night.

Tullius and Eumenes had shaken out a disused room in the Praetorium, the fort commander's house, and Paulinus settled in, wondering how big a mistake it would be to go to bed. The room was plain but inviting, with a sanded plank floor overlain with bright native rugs. The writing table was also local work, ornamented with roughly carved dragons writhing down its legs. A bronze lamp on a base of coiled snakes illuminated the tabletop. The snakes looked benign and scholarly.

Paulinus rummaged in the locked bronze box where he kept his private journal and sat down with it at the table. In the next chamber Tullius, who had long ago acquired the soldier's habit of sleeping now because the chance might not come later, snored rhythmically. There was a ewer of water by the bed, and Paulinus mixed some of his store of dry ink with it, and pared the nib of a reed pen to suit him.

Notes at the start of war, he wrote, and drew a sketch of Singidunum Fortress beneath it while he considered.

> *An interesting country, Moesia – absorbed into the empire with almost no protest, content to become Roman and reap the benefits of civilization thereby. Correus's ala, officially the Vespasiana Dardanorum, are mostly local boys, recruited by the emperor's father from the Dardani and serving in their homeland – a sure sign of a loyal province. What foreign culture has been acquired before our coming is mostly Greek, and they have a taste for luxury and the settled life. It is fine grain-growing country here, and we could ill afford to lose it.*
>
> *The Dacians are another matter entirely. They make alliance with the wild tribes to the west of them when it suits them – with barbarian Germany, according to*

Correus's spies — but Dacia itself is not barbarian by any definition of the word. Their people are literate, having adopted both Greek and Latin letters to their use. They mint their own coinage, based on the wealth of their gold mines. Trade and production are well organized, and their mountain fastnesses such as Sarmizegetusa have become cities in their own right, sites of centralized government, power and commerce, defended by a network of minor forts and outposts. In short, all the hallmarks of an empire. Small wonder that we are about to come head-to-head with them.

I have never been into Dacian lands myself, which all lie across the Danuvius, the river that the Dacians call the Ister, but I am told that the heart of their country is not in the plains but in the high mountains, guarded by only a few known passes. It is there that all their cities lie, virtually impregnable to any attack except with elaborate siege weapons. There they have developed a high craftsmanship in gold and silver, factories for ironworking, and a great many other talents that make them dangerous.

What gods they worship is uncertain — amorphous figures which they decline to depict in statuary — but they are advanced astronomers, and so far their formless gods have smiled upon them. They are on the verge of being a great people, I think, and I cannot wish their destruction, even now with them breathing down our necks at midnight. A twitchy feeling, that. It is a pity that Oppius Sabinus should be a blind fool, but that is plain speaking and plain truth. I wonder if all this could have been forestalled if we had better defenses out here, but the fear in Rome of too much troop concentration in any one place is great, and perhaps justified. That is our dilemma — a great empire takes a great army to hold it, and a great army gets ideas of its own in its head occasionally. We had too many sword-made emperors when Nero died, and no one wants to risk another civil war, even at the price of letting Domitian wear

the purple, while we ignore that the instability of the frontier
is mirrored in the capriciousness of the emperor.

Paulinus looked at the last sentence and inked it carefully into obliteration. Some thoughts were best left unwritten. He locked his journal away again before he found himself tempted to further treason, stood up, and stretched. Voices and the click of hobnailed sandals could still be heard in the corridors of the prefect's private quarters. He blew out the lamp, feeling foolishly late and unnecessary here, and stretched out on the bed. The mattress smelled invitingly of clean straw and rosemary. Outside the Praetorium, Singidunum slept with one eye open. Paulinus put a knife under his pillow, drew the heavy blankets over him, and attempted to do the same.

He awoke, two hours before dawn, to the sound of troop horses going by. The smell of rosemary was obliterated by the faint scent of fire in the wind.

The glow of a pottery lamp illuminated the doorway with Tullius behind it. "The prefect's compliments, sir, and we're to sit tight. That's Viminacium burning."

"Vimi— dear gods." Paulinus sat up in bed and felt on the rug for his sandals. "Where is he?"

"Gone, I expect." Tullius propped the shutters of the window open and the smell of smoke came strongly on the breeze. "The second courier never made it past Tricornium – there was a rider from Viminacium coming the other way like he had the Furies on his heels. There's no saying if the governor paid any mind to the first rider from here, but it doesn't sound like it. The Viminacium man had a bad story to tell."

Paulinus knotted his sandal laces and stuck his knife through his belt. "And where are the Dacians now?"

"Loose on the countryside," Tullius said, "if they're finished with Viminacium. The prefect's taking a relief column out tonight. He's left orders we're to stay well back."

"Indeed?" Paulinus said. "I knew the prefect when he was a junior centurion with a two-month-old commission."

"You'll stay here, Lucius, or I'll send you back to Rome in a mule cart," Correus's voice said unequivocally. The lamplight flickered on the gilded, overlapping fishscale of a cavalry hauberk. Beneath it he wore a white leather harness tunic, and the blue undertunic and knee-length breeches of the Ala Dardanorum. His face was shadowed by the close-fitting cavalry helmet. A spatha, the long cutting sword of Rome's mounted troops, hung from his belt and the buckle was decorated with the ala's mountain rose insignia. He pointed a finger at Lucius Paulinus. "If you think I'm going to tell Julia I let you ride in a cavalry fight and the Dacians took your head home on a pole, you've gone mad."

"If I want a nursemaid, I've brought Tullius," Paulinus said, pulling his cloak around his shoulders. "You've never thrown me out of a camp before."

"I was never the commander before," Correus said frankly. "And I'm not throwing you out, I'm locking you in. If I catch you in catapult range of the front lines, I'll shoot you back to Singidunum with one." He disappeared again, shouting for the optio, and Paulinus looked after him reflectively, with his cloak pin in his hands.

"I used to amuse myself seeing if I could slip past the commander's eye," Paulinus said finally. "Not this time, I think."

–

The Ala Dardanorum rode out under the first graying of false dawn to the strident sound of cavalry trumpets. They made a swift-moving column on the road, riding light behind the winged silver troop standards and the ala banner. Anything that couldn't be tied behind a horse was left behind in Singidunum, while to the east rose a sullen glow that no one was foolish enough to mistake for dawn.

Below the chalk cliffs the road traveled directly along the riverbank, just above the towpath. In some places to the east the Danuvius gorge narrowed to such a chasm that road and towpath were only a single narrow track suspended on wooden trestles above the water, but between Singidunum and Viminacium the going was fairly clear. Tricornium was nearly empty when they passed through, and the senior officer remaining said that the commander had pulled out for Viminacium an hour ago. They changed horses there and kept going. Correus pushed the ala into a gallop but not even the fact that he knew what he would find prepared him for Viminacium.

The Dacians had come over the river like hunting wolves and the Seventh Legion Claudia, half their strength, had gone out to meet them lest Decebalus turn his attentions on the undefended countryside instead. Governor Oppius Sabinus, to give him credit, had ridden at their head, and the Claudia had broken the force of the Dacian onslaught at a cost that Correus could count in the piled dead and the half-burned timbers of Viminacium. Decebalus's war band had scattered southward, leaving Viminacium smoldering behind it, and the governor of Moesia dead in the field.

His body lay in state in the Principia now, while the legate of the Seventh Claudia, with smoke-blackened hands, composed a letter to the emperor and orders to the garrison commanders of the Danuvius. He wasn't sure which of the three legionary legates of Moesia was technically in command now, but the other two were far to the east and he was here in Viminacium. Until someone should send orders to the contrary, that made him accountable.

Correus halted before the legate's desk and saluted, fist to chest, weaving on his feet – no one had slept. He had known Messala Cominius a long time, which made some things unnecessary to say. The legate's face and dark hair were streaked gray with soot and the crest of eagle feathers on his helmet was nearly burned away.

"You made good time, Julianus. My thanks for it." He grimaced. "And for your scouts' intelligence, which comes somewhat late."

"My decurion sent a rider as soon as the scouts came in," Correus said steadily.

45

"Not precisely what I meant," Cominius said. "Still, that's water down the stream." The rider from Singidunum had come too late to make ready for a war in which Governor Oppius Sabinus had refused to believe until the Singidunum scouts had shoved it in his face. "I've ordered the Tricornium troops east to pick up what men they can from Pincum and Taliata, if the Dacians haven't got there first. Take yours south to Horreum and then swing down through Naissus. Even stragglers from Decebalus's troops can burn those civilian towns to the ground and our warehouses are in Horreum."

"What sort of state is the Dacian war band in now?"

"I think we cost them nearly a third of their strength," Cominius said wearily. "And Mithras knows we paid dearly to do it. I don't think they can regroup in under three days, but if we don't have an army on their tail by then…"

Correus nodded. Six or seven thousand Dacians loose on the civilian countryside didn't bear thinking about. And there was his scouts' further report. "My men thought that wasn't all," he told Cominius. "There may be more."

"There are," Cominius said grimly. "There are beacons burning all along the river. Details are sketchy but another band hit Oescus and the Macedonica has taken serious losses – worse than ours."

Correus closed his eyes for a moment.

"We'll hold our western posts. It's all we can do," Cominius said somberly. "The surgeons tell me my men will be mostly fit to march in three days. They will have to do it in two, but I can't cut it finer than that. In the meantime, I will burn the governor's body and earn myself a reprimand from Rome."

Correus Julianus had served under Messala Cominius as a very junior centurion, with Cominius his cohort commander. It made them inclined to be frank with each other. Undoubtedly the family of Oppius Sabinus would not take kindly to a frontier funeral.

"I can't spare the men to escort a body home," Correus said bluntly. "Can you?"

Cominius smiled. "You always did see the point of things, Julianus. No, they can have a pot of ashes when I have leisure to send it."

"We can ride after six hours' sleep, not before," Correus said, "and I need to send for the baggage wagons to follow us. We traveled light getting here."

Cominius waved a hand through the doorway into an adjoining office. "Use the governor's. There's nobody needing it at the moment. I think your decurion's rider is still in one piece. At least he wasn't on the Dead List."

Correus settled himself at the governor's desk, pushing aside stacks of papyrus inscribed in Oppius Sabinus's finicky hand. He didn't look at them. It would give him no pleasure to read the complacent reports of a dead fool. He pawed through them until he found a stack of wax-faced wooden tablets and a stylus. He scratched out orders for the baggage train to catch up to him at Horreum Margi, and for the optio at Singidunum to see that the prefect's brother-in-law stayed put, even if he had to tie him up.

Correus found Blaesus's courier, with a burned hand but otherwise undamaged, indignantly telling his tale to his troop mates outside the gates. "I thought the governor was going to bust his gut. Epona and the Horseman help me, you never saw anything like his face when the sentries came barreling in, shouting that the road's full of Dacians – and that just after he'd been looking down his Roman nose at me, asking if the scouts couldn't have seen a herd of pigs instead!"

Correus shoved the tablet in the courier's hand from behind and the courier jumped.

"*Ride*," Correus said grimly. "Get your tail back to Singidunum, give that message to the headquarters optio, get that burn looked at, and *keep your mouth shut!*"

"Sir!" The courier saluted and vanished.

Correus swung his head around to the rest of the ala. "Any further gossip on the actions of your superiors and the man doing the talking won't be able to ride for a week. Mount up!"

IV

Decebalus

That they still talked among themselves, Correus was aware, but they didn't do it in his hearing, which was all he could reasonably ask for. The ala had a right to be aggrieved; if Governor Sabinus, newly come to Moesia, had listened to any of the experienced frontier commanders, the Ala Dardanorum would not now be chasing a still-dangerous Dacian army through civilian country, and trying to patch up the horrors that the fleeing Dacians had left behind them. Most of the ala were Moesian-born. This was their country. To give the Dacians credit, they had not slaughtered the civilian population wholesale, but they had burned and looted with a savage ferocity. To a Moesian peasant with his field in flames, there was little difference between death by the sword and death by starvation.

Correus set up a temporary relief station at Horreum Margi, where the grain warehouses were, and tried to shepherd as many of the homeless that way as he could. Someone in Rome would likely be angry over that too – much of the grain in the warehouses was destined for shipment to Rome – but neither Correus nor Messala Cominius had a wish to fight the Dacians with a hostile local population at their backs as well. Where the Dacians weren't, the roads were clogged with fleeing civilians, while the Dacians roamed in small bands through the hills, fighting when they outnumbered the Romans, and running when they didn't.

The Ala Dardanorum encountered Decebalus's warriors more than once and managed to pin a small band of them down in

48

the rocky hills above Naissus. Despite their suspicions, among Decebalus's fighters they saw no Germans, who would have been distinguishable even at a distance. A Dacian warrior was marked by the peaked cap, point pulled low over the forehead, which was the privilege of the freeborn man. A few, the lords probably, wore helmets peaked in similar style, while most wore mail or scale hauberks, and all had iron weapons, mostly the falx, a scythe-shaped sword or pole arm that was as deadly as anything Correus had ever fought.

Correus kicked Briseis up the hill, with Decurion Blaesus and the ala banner at his side, and the Dardanorum behind him. The Dacians hadn't run soon enough this time, and there was the ruined countryside around Naissus to avenge. The cavalry ponies of the Dardanorum were used to Moesian mountains and they scrambled like goats, their riders throwing up their shields against the flight of arrows that sang down at them. Three or four horses went down with their hooves scrabbling at the loose stones on the hillside, and then the ala was too close for arrow fire. They ran the Dacians down ruthlessly, spearing the archers out of the low-growing oaks on the summit, fighting savagely with the foot soldiers. Correus drove his spear past an oval shield of cowhide, scarlet-painted and incongruously patterned with a wreath of flowers, and it slipped from his hand, lodged in a scale hauberk. The shield wavered and he swung his sword at the stumbling warrior behind it, dodging the wicked falx blade. He swung again at the throat. The man went down in a spray of blood, and Briseis gathered her haunches and leaped over him. Cavalry ponies were taught to jump high; a man on the ground could still have a knife.

The ala had had a long ride and bad provisions for too many weeks in a country stripped bare by Decebalus's marauders. There were no prisoners taken. Correus patted Briseis's sweat-soaked shoulder and surveyed the carnage.

"Leave them," he said, and turned Briseis down the hill, with the ala carrying their own dead and wounded across their mounts. Already the carrion birds were circling over the Dacian corpses and the wolves would be out with the dusk. Just now Correus didn't care what the wolves ate so long as it wasn't the few remaining lambs of the Moesian villagers.

They made camp in the valley below, in a trampled patch of yarrow and scrub grass, digging a double row of ditch and wall by moon and torchlight. No Roman army ever slept in an unfortified camp, or left it standing afterward for the enemy to make use of. Correus wondered how many miles of ditch he had dug in his time. Now he was a prefect the work was below him, but there were times when he wouldn't have minded changing back. It was hard to brood over a grievance when a man was putting his energies into a spade handle. He leaned against Briseis's wet flank, rubbing the foam away from under the girth and bridle straps, until Eumenes came up to take her.

"That's a fine mare," Eumenes said. "Seems a pity to drive her up and down the mountains like a wagon mule."

"That's what she's bred for," Correus said, but it seemed a pity to him too. Eumenes led her away and was replaced by Decurion Blaesus with a neat bandage pinned around one thigh and a troop roster in his hand.

"All accounted for, sir. Four dead, but the surgeon says all the rest of them are fit to ride, thank the Horseman. Light losses for a good day's work, I'm thinking."

Correus grimaced. "Light losses, if I thought those four would ever be replaced, Decurion." Slowly, as they pushed Decebalus's raiders back from the province, their own numbers were being whittled down. In the meantime, the Dacian raiders had grown to an estimated thirty thousand, if not more, and were running loose from one end of the Moesian frontier to the other, with only three undermanned legions and their auxiliaries to counter them. Every commander in Moesia had been screaming for months for replacements, and so far, even now, not a single man had been sent. The emperor was gathering an army, it was said.

"I'd like to know why we're not getting them," Blaesus said. "If I may ask."

"You may ask, Decurion. I've been asking, and no satisfactory answer has been forthcoming. It is my private opinion that the emperor wishes to avenge so great an insult as the death of a provincial governor personally, but I shouldn't care to be quoted."

"No, sir. And what do we do in the meantime, sir?"

"We hold them with what we've got," Correus said. "What else?"

He nodded dismissal to Blaesus and strode down the passage between the barracks tents and the horse lines that constituted the Via Principalis in a marching camp. In the red Principia tent, which served as both Correus's private quarters and his office, he found the quartermaster and the vet awaiting him, urgent and mutually aggrieved. When he had sifted the matter over, it appeared that liniment and poultices for the troop horses' legs had been brought in insufficient stores. The vet announced that all the horses would undoubtedly go lame tomorrow and suggested sending the quartermaster back to Singidunum on foot to see how he liked it. The quartermaster replied that everything had been brought as ordered, and if the vet's thieving orderlies were wasteful, he had only himself to blame.

Correus glowered at the quartermaster and told the vet, "Go and buy what you need in Naissus. Give them a chit for it."

"They don't take chits," the quartermaster said.

"They'll have to. I haven't got anything else."

When they had gone, Correus put his helmet on the desk, the long scarlet horsetails showing dark as bloodstains in the lamplight. He pulled the tent flaps closed. In the hills a jackal yelped and was answered by the nervous yips of the town dogs.

Eumenes stuck a cup of wine under the prefect's nose. "You'll be wanting this."

Correus wondered if he could stay awake long enough to drink it. They had been chasing Decebalus's scattered war bands for over two months now. Contrary to expectation, the Dacians had not joined forces to make a single army, and no one knew for certain how many they were fighting. Was the unit that had besieged

Ratiaria the same that had attacked Timacum Minus or another? The invaders had crossed and recrossed the Danuvius several times, tempting the Romans to follow. The Romans, undermanned and stretched thin, stayed in their own zone, hoping only to push the Dacians over the river one last time and keep them there. Correus suspected that Decebalus was testing the Roman defenses with this game and was finding them encouragingly slim.

He took a drink of the watered wine, the last of his private stock, discovered that he had swallowed a bug, and spat the rest out. "Jupiter Thunderer blast this country! I'm going to bed."

"Does the prefect wish to bathe?" Eumenes inquired.

"The prefect wishes that the gods would strike Decebalus, the emperor and the ghost of Oppius Sabinus with lightning," Correus said. "Yes, I wish to bathe, Eumenes, thank you." Eumenes dragged water in a bucket every night from whatever stream was handy and heated it in a cauldron. One of the privileges of rank. Correus stripped his armor and harness tunic off and stood shivering while Eumenes rubbed him with oil and scraped his skin clean with a strigil. He stood in the shallow tub and let Eumenes pour warm water over him.

Eumenes wrapped him in a wool blanket to dry off, and Correus sat down by the three-legged iron brazier that heated the Principia tent. He sneezed.

The optio came for the evening password. Correus told him "Ague," then, "No, wait, I didn't mean that. Make it 'Tartarus.' That's where I want Decebalus." He ran his hands through his wet hair and shook it. "Did that courier go out this morning?"

"Yes, sir. At first light, with an escort."

The legates of the Fifth Macedonica at Oescus and the First Italica at Novae were attempting to coordinate with Messala Cominius and the Claudia to build a line with no holes in it that could sweep the invading Dacians toward the river. With no central place of command, communication was complicated and was made more so by the necessity to ride through what might on any given day be hostile territory. Even the military road along the Danuvius was chancy. There was only so much that could be communicated with a beacon fire and smoke.

Lucius Paulinus had been firmly sent back upriver and on the road to Rome not long after Viminacium burned and he had been uncharacteristically willing to go. He had carried the governor's ashes, a request from Messala Cominius to bend the emperor's ear to put on speed, and one from Correus to please tell Ygerna that he was personally in no danger, which she wouldn't believe, and simultaneously that it was too dangerous to send for her.

Correus lay down on the camp bed and Eumenes settled on the pallet at its foot. "Boreas blow Decebalus into the Adriatic," Correus said. Maybe then he could see his wife again.

–

Decebalus viewed the Roman head stuck like a battle standard on a pole outside his tent with interest. "Was he carrying anything interesting or were you hunting for sport?" he inquired, amused. His brown, thick-lidded eyes considered the head and the three warriors who had brought it.

His brother Diegis, a youthful, less forceful version of himself, hooked his thumbs in his belt and grinned at Decebalus. "He had an escort, all riding very fast. Also, he had a good horse, which I myself wished to own. There were letters in his pouch, which we brought you, concerning their troop movements. Also the head, for a present. One seemed enough."

"You honor me. But he smells somewhat and it is going to be hot. Put him in a sack and we will take him to my father the king. A head might be a useful thing to make my point with."

Diegis looked interested. "We're going home? To Sarmize-getusa?"

"I am. Not you. You are going to stay and be a trouble to the Romans until I have cemented our alliance with the Getae."

"Ziais will fight you."

"That does not trouble me."

"She will go to our father."

"Our father already offered her to the chieftain of the Germans when he was drunk. Ziais will do as she's told. And so will he. When we have the Getae, we can make a proper war, and I wish to be king when we do it."

Diegis leaned on his spear and forbore to remark that his brother had wished to be king for a great time now. Their father Duras was too old to ride in battle anymore, but the subject of abdication was touchy. No man liked to be succeeded by his pup in his lifetime. Still, with a summer's loot from Moesia to bring home behind Decebalus's banner, the Dacian lords might force Duras to it.

A light breeze picked up the tail of the warlord's dragon banner and lifted it above the tents. It had a wolf's head of finely worked gold, open-mouthed, sewn at the neck to a column of green silk that formed the body when the wind filled it.

"And when you are king, then what?" Diegis said.

Decebalus looked at the banner and then at his brother's gift head. "Then I will push the Romans off the Ister entirely. There is not enough room here for two empires to grow great."

Diegis shrugged. In the meantime, there were the chieftains of the Roxolani and the Bastarnae to bring into the fold. Despite what Decebalus had told the Germans, and despite the fact that they had been fighting under Decebalus's banner all winter, no formal alliance had been made. There wouldn't be either, Diegis thought, until Gudila of the Getae made his pledge.

–

"And why should the Roxolani fight to make the warlord of the Dacians great?" the Roxolani chieftain inquired.

"For the reason that we are all kin and a great empire will make even lesser kings great," Decebalus said.

The Roxolani chief snorted. "If your empire does not shatter into pieces like a green pot in the kiln. When was the last time any king held the cities together since Burebista?"

"None," Decebalus said. "Until me." He looked from each of the three chieftains to the next, forcing their eyes to his. It had begun to rain, the drops spattering on the tent roof, and the Dacian lords stretched their legs toward the fire burning in a brazier between them.

Gudila spat into the flames. "Burebista reigned over a hundred years ago. And you are not Burebista." He was a stocky man with an ugly snouted face and heavy mouth above his red beard. His arms and shoulders were heavily muscled, and the hands he stretched to the fire were short-fingered and thick with gold rings.

"And was killed by his own lords," the Bastarnae chief murmured and Decebalus shot him a dark look.

"As Gudila said, I am not Burebista," he said quietly. "I do, however, command an army as great as his, which may turn its attention to rebellious allies when I have finished with the Romans."

The Roxolani and Bastarnae chiefs shifted uncomfortably in their chairs. They had not the strength to stand up to Decebalus if he wished to press the matter, although doing so would weaken Decebalus's forces. The question, always, was whether Decebalus could beat the Romans. If he could, then to cast their lots with his was not even a question. If he could not, then...

"You are not king yet, either," Gudila said. He disliked Decebalus for his arrogance.

"I shall be king shortly," Decebalus said. "And you will be brother to the king when you have taken my sister home to Capidava."

Gudila was more than aware of the power that rank would hand him, and the larger share of loot from the campaign. He had seen the girl in Sarmizegetusa. She was as arrogant as her brother but also one that anyone would be pleased to have in his bed, and wide-hipped enough for easy childbearing. The matter of an heir was important lest the Dacian king look toward Capidava to add to his holdings when Gudila grew old.

"*When* you are king," Gudila said, "and we have assurance that your father will not countermand you."

Decebalus smiled. "He will not. But I will be king within the season and prove it to you. And I will remember who doubted me."

–

"It is always a disappointment, Caesar, when a trusted friend proves foolish." Lucius Paulinus looked at the floor, attempting tact. The floor was composed of intricate patterns in exotic marble with lions chasing gazelles around the borders, and Paulinus felt rather like the gazelles at the moment. The delivery of Oppius Sabinus's ashes had been a touchy moment despite, or possibly because of, the invitation to dine with the emperor, who had a habit of feeding his foes before they were executed.

The Emperor Titus Flavius Caesar Domitianus Augustus adjusted the purple and gold folds of his toga. Two slaves in the white tunics of the imperial household hovered with flagons of water and wine, and the ebony table was laid with silver dishes of delicacies, some identifiable to Paulinus only by wild guess. Domitian prided himself on a cook who provided the unusual, and hence the expensive. His taster, now dismissed, had already consumed a bite of each.

Flavius was stretched out on a couch between Paulinus's and Domitian's, his dark hair brushed in neat curls that mimicked the emperor's, his odd hands resting on the pale silk cushions.

Domitian gestured to the slaves and they padded out of the room, bare feet silent on the marble floor.

"Indeed," he said to Paulinus. "We are all grateful to you for bringing the remains home for a suitable interment." He paused and selected a bite of meat from one of the silver dishes. "I am too trusting," he said sadly.

They were silent while they waited to see which way the wind would blow.

"I must send a new governor out there as soon as may be, and then bring considerable reinforcements."

"You intend to ride with them, sir?" Flavius asked.

"Certainly," Domitian said. "A situation that has got so out of hand must be attended to." He looked at Flavius. "I am aware that the lower ranking commanders on the Danuvius have been warning of this, and that I was badly advised. There will be no more of that. I shall go personally and see to things."

"A most wise decision," Paulinus said with a sinking feeling. To organize an army with the emperor at its head would take weeks, far longer than a less top-heavy relief column. "They will take heart from the emperor's presence," he added.

"Just so." Domitian's solid, square-jawed face and beaked nose gave him the look of a man whose convictions should not be argued with. He sat up, signaling the end of the meal. "Julianus, I intend for you to come with me. I shall be sorry to take you from your father so soon after your loss."

"I am sure that my father will understand the need," Flavius said. "He is your loyal supporter, as you know."

Appius had been Vespasian's loyal supporter and a diplomatic sleight of hand could extend it to his son; a nicety which Paulinus complimented when they had left.

"You're almost as devious as I am."

"I am not. And don't think you're going back out to the Danuvius for your own purposes, because you're not."

"Oddly, that was what your brother said. I would have once, Flavius, but I have Julia now, and the children and another one imminent. I grow cautious."

"That is excellent," Flavius said. "Because if you get killed my sister will move back to our father's house to argue with Helva more conveniently, and he will probably fall on his sword."

–

"So this is where you've gone to earth, Appius." Gentilius Paulinus, uncle of Lucius, eased his girth into the steam room of the Baths of Titus and settled onto a bench. "My physician says this cleanses the skin," he grunted, "but I wonder. I knew a man once who fell asleep in the steam room and died. No one noticed until the next morning. Gave the bath a bad name, I can tell you."

Appius looked up from the bench where he was ensconced with a scroll that was rapidly going limp. "You should bring something to read, Gentilius. It will keep you awake. And out of my business."

Gentilius Paulinus inspected him pensively. "I think you evade me out of habit." They were old comrades and onetime rivals, going back a long way. Neither had ever been so shortsighted as to completely trust the other. "No one's seen so much as the back of your cloak since Antonia died. I thought you were rusticating in that country house of yours. Why come to the City and not show your face in the Forum?"

"The Forum's full of lawyers," Appius said, "and civic reformers, and innumerable people whose failing memory prompts them to believe I owe them favors. When I leave, someone drops a slop pot on my head." The towering tenements of Rome leaned inward over the narrow streets. It could be risky to pass beneath them at night.

Gentilius snorted. "That doesn't tell me why you're lurking in this cauldron. You have an excellent bath at home."

Appius stretched his bare legs out on his bench, rearranged the towel that provided minimal modesty, and propped his back against a column. "I came here for solitude," he remarked, laying the scroll down regretfully. "Something which, I might add, I do not get at home either."

"You're becoming a recluse, like those whatchamacallums – those African birds that stick their silly heads in the sand. It isn't good for you."

Appius looked at him with surprise. "Dear me, I believe you're worried about me."

"Of course I'm worried about you," Gentilius said testily. "There aren't that many of our generation left, especially in these times. And that's another point. If you don't stick your head up and look around, you'll never see what hit you."

Appius sighed. He pushed the band of linen that had kept the sweat out of his eyes a little up on his forehead. "I'm not so blind as all that," he said, looking Gentilius in the eye. "I know what nearly hit me."

Gentilius shifted his bulk on the bench. "Amazing the way you've kept your figure. I used to be thin once," he added regretfully.

Appius grinned, with a look that was reminiscent of his sons. "You should have stayed in the army. It's very difficult to keep a good cook in the army."

"Maybe you should have stayed in," Gentilius said. "Give you something to turn your hand to."

"I put in thirty-five years with the Eagles," Appius said. "That's enough for any man."

"Well, I don't like the look of you," Gentilius said frankly. "Go and do something, man, before you rot!"

–

Despite his protestations to Gentilius, Appius strolled from the baths to the Forum and read the *Acta Diurna* before leaving the City. Ordinarily he waited for his secretary to bring him a copy, but it was another way to dawdle on the homeward path. The Forum was the usual madhouse of politicians, lawyers, astrologers, and everyone else with a cause to proclaim haranguing the crowd. Outside the Basilica Julia, a reader was loudly relaying the contents of the *Acta* for the illiterate, hand outstretched for tips. Appius put a coin in his hand and muttered, "A quarter hour's silence, blast you."

He bent his eye to the lead tablets incised with the usual collection of legal judgments, marriages and divorces, military news, and imperial edicts, interspersed with advertisements (*Thrassalus the glassblower is having a sale*) and human interest stories (*dog follows condemned master's corpse to river, attempts rescue*). The *Acta* was posted daily on the wall of the Basilica Julia with copies disseminated widely through Italy and as far as the provinces.

Today's edition featured the announcement of the upcoming races sponsored by the emperor himself and a list of prizes.

Maybe there was something in Gentilius's advice, Appius thought moodily as he progressed homeward out of the City, with a wary eye open for slop pots. No wheeled traffic was allowed in the City of Rome by day, and Appius was not yet so old that he could be carried in a litter without feeling like a fool. *I shall accept Prosper Rufius's invitation to dine*, he thought. Rufius owned a team bred by Appius that was entered for the Blue faction in the races. That young demon Julius was driving them and they were the popular favorite. Prosper Rufius was planning his victory celebration in advance.

He would make the day a household holiday, Appius decided. It would give them somewhere to go besides for each other's throats. The peace and order that Antonia had brought to Appius's household had shattered with her death, and Helva was no more capable of restoring it than she was likely to sprout feathers and fly. The other slaves did not take kindly to her trying, and Julia, with her husband absent and time on her hands, had felt impelled to step into the breach. Paulinus's return did not appear to have distracted her. Appius found his carriage, left to wait for him outside the City, and settled into it with some trepidation. War had been imminent at his departure.

Upon his return, the smell of burning fowl proclaimed that hostilities had escalated in his absence. Cook never burned the dinner except in righteous indignation. Having achieved this protest against constantly conflicting orders, Cook had retired to his apartment to sulk, as Helva informed Appius at the door.

"Such a nice dinner, too," she wailed. "Quail in little pies, and fresh berries, and—"

"Eat the berries," Appius said.

"They aren't the way you like them," Julia informed him. She gave Helva a look of disdain. "You'd think after all these years you'd know that. You must have done *something* besides—"

"That will do," Appius said. He eyed his daughter. "When do you find the time to manage your own house, Julia? Especially now that Lucius is home? Doesn't your husband require your attention?"

"I am only trying," Julia said with dignity, "to see that yours doesn't go to ruin. *None* of the strawberry beds have been strawed up yet. And there are *crows* in the kitchen garden."

"One could hardly expect me to chase crows away," Helva said. "With all the other things that have to be seen to."

"I hardly expect you to do anything but give yourself airs and not work!" Julia snapped. "*Mother* was up at sunrise. And the crows wouldn't be there if you'd thought to set a slave to chase them away. I don't suppose you thought to set anyone to pick the bugs off the lettuces at night either."

"There were no bugs on them in the daytime," Helva said with hauteur. "Why would I go look at them at night?"

"That is *enough*!"

They both stared at him reproachfully.

Appius unwound his toga and handed it to a slave who had been maintaining a discreet silence. "Julia, go home. Helva, find Philippos and tell him I want to see him. I think this house needs a holiday from itself."

"Where are you going?" Julia demanded.

"For the moment, to the kitchen," Appius said. "To mollify the cook. If possible."

In the kitchen he found not the cook but Ygerna and a teary kitchen maid, plucking a duck.

He sneezed as a puff of down drifted past his nose. "What are you doing plucking fowl?"

"I wished to eat," Ygerna said. "It did not seem likely other-wise."

Appius chuckled. "A practical woman. I'll help you."

The kitchen maid regarded the master with horror. "It's all bloody, sir."

"So it is, but you don't seem to be very good at it."

The kitchen maid sniffled. "It isn't my place."

"She was handy," Ygerna said.

"Lady Helva said I was to make pies," the kitchen maid muttered.

"They're very jealous of their position," Appius said. "I believe this one – Tirza, isn't it? – is a pastry cook."

"Then go and make pastry," Ygerna said, wrestling with the duck.

Tirza departed, outraged.

"There," Ygerna said. She wiped her hands on the apron she had tied over her gown. "Now it is only to cook it."

Appius considered the duck. "No, we want Cook for that, I think. I shall go and make amends. He will demand to buy his freedom – he has quite enough saved – and I will appease him, and we will be back on an even keel again for the moment, as long as Helva stays out of the kitchen."

He sounded quite cheerful about it, Ygerna thought, but she suspected that it was simply because Appius had excellent manners. The upheaval of his household had only intensified his mourning for his wife. Most men would have gotten drunk and thrown things at the slaves.

Ygerna hung up the apron and scooped up the cat who had come in to keep an eye on the duck. Paulinus had brought her a message from Correus saying she was to stay put in his father's house until sent for. Paulinus's description of the burning of Viminacium was gruesome. She couldn't risk the children or distract Correus from his business with worrying about all of them. All the same, much longer under the same roof with Helva would stretch her temper thin enough to do something irreparable.

–

"Livilla will be at Prosper Rufius's dinner," Aemelia said. "If his wife is there, I don't see why I can't go." She eyed Flavius in her mirror as her maid pinned up her hair.

"It's not the kind of dinner I want you at," Flavius said. "I don't like Livilla or her friends."

Aemelia's mouth tightened. "However, you are going."

"Prosper Rufius bought that team from my father. He is also a friend of the emperor. I am being diplomatic."

Aemelia selected a topaz necklace and ear drops from her jewelry case and handed them to her maid. "Or perhaps you just don't want me there while you are being 'diplomatic' with Livilla's friends that you dislike so much." She sat stiffly while the maid worked the wires through her ears.

"You might be a little more diplomatic yourself," Flavius commented. "Rusonia, leave us, please."

The maid fastened Aemelia's necklace and fled.

"It is not your business to order Rusonia about," Aemelia said. "She belongs to me. And since everyone in Rome seems to know about your 'diplomacy' in Germany, I don't see why you care."

Flavius sat down in one of the small gilded chairs that furnished his wife's dressing room. "Aemelia, I am sorry. I have said I am sorry. I don't know what else to say." He should have known there would be gossip and that eventually someone like Livilla would tell her. Rome lived on gossip. What had startled him was the change in her personality that the information had wrought. Until Antonia's funeral, Aemelia had been weepy and apologetic, constantly looking for reassurance that he was not going to divorce her, first over her father's financial troubles, and then over the lack of a son. Now she was still weepy but apparently felt that he could divorce her and be damned.

"Do *you* want a divorce?" he asked her bluntly.

Aemelia sniffled. "Not really." She turned to look at him. "I just want things back. Back the way they were. When Emperor Titus was alive and you took me to dinners, and I still thought you loved me, and there were parties."

Flavius smiled. "I see." He wasn't sure which she missed most, but it might have been the parties. Considering his behavior, he couldn't really blame her. "I do love you," he said, which was mostly true. "I can't change things at court, but we might have a party, if you like. As soon as I get back," he added, rethinking that.

"I'm sorry about this too, but the emperor is going out to Moesia himself and taking me with him, and I'm afraid you'll have to go stay with my father while I'm gone. I don't want you alone in the City. It isn't safe."

"When?"

"I don't know yet, but it needs to be as soon as we can shift him if he insists on leading the army himself." He paused. "And please don't repeat that."

"Since I'm not going anywhere, I shan't have a chance to," Aemelia said. She turned back to her dressing table. The ivory box with the silver cap and horrible ointments caught her eye among the perfume bottles and her hand closed around it.

"Throw it at me if you want to," Flavius said.

She set it down and started to cry.

"Oh, Typhon." Flavius pulled his chair next to her bench and put his arms around her. "I've made a mess of everything and it isn't your fault. I'll find some way to start us fresh, I promise." He felt like one of the jugglers they had seen throwing glass balls in the air at the seaside. One more ball and then another.

She sat stiffly in his arms until he gave up. As he left, he heard her burst into tears again.

V

Prosper Rufius's Horses and His Wife

An air of constrained civility prevailed as the house of Appius set out for the City and the races. Marcus, who was too young to care, was at home with his nurse, but Ygerna had taken Eilenn with her, and Felix rode beside their carriage on his pony, looking so grown-up that Ygerna wondered why childhood, that seemed so long to the child, fled so quickly in the parents' eyes. Julia had brought Paulilla and Lucian, who sat twitching with excitement in the carriage with their mother and Ygerna. Helva rode in lonely splendor in her own carriage with enough maids and pages accompanying her to have filled a tier of seats on their own, as Julia said acidly. Appius and Lucius Paulinus, a reluctant participant, rode beside the carriages, and behind them rumbled a ragtag traffic of wagons, mules, and donkeys. Appius had given a day's holiday to every slave on the estate, with Philippos to see that they stayed out of tavern brawls and all came home again.

At the outskirts of the City the ladies exchanged their carriages for hired litters, with the household slaves beside them to help shove a path through the holiday crowd that jammed the streets all the way from the Gardens of Sallust past the Flavian Amphitheater and around the Palatine Hill to the Circus. Master and slave, rich and poor, Rome took its chariot racing seriously, and the Circus Maximus, which could hold two hundred thousand racegoers, would be full to overflowing. Lesser folk might have to fight for the free entrance tokens, but the family of Appius could view the spectacle in comfort from the marble boxes reserved for the senatorial and equestrian houses of Rome.

Appius offered a seat in his box in the equestrian tier to Diulius, the estate's chariot master, but the old man just shook his head and grinned.

"Better view down below."

Appius put a hand on Felix's shoulder to prevent him from accompanying Diulius. Felix looked wistfully at the arched doorways under the consuls' balcony. All the interesting things would be happening in the stables, but his grandfather did not see eye to eye with him on the propriety of Felix's spending the day there.

Appius saw his brood settled in their box with cushions, shawls, and sunshades, sent a page to buy a box of sweets and pears on ice from the vendors who hawked their wares up and down the aisles, and went to pay his respects to Prosper Rufius.

"I'm told your team is the favorite today," he said, resting his arms on the edge of the senator's box.

"They had better be," Rufius said jovially, "considering what I paid you for them." He was a short, stocky man with a broad nose and straight brows that met above it. Beside him, his wife Livilla was eating sweets and sending her page scurrying back and forth with messages to her friends. She had a pointed, fox's face and bright gold hair that was very fashionable just now.

"It's charming of you to dine with us," she chirped. "It should be an amusing dinner. Julius is going to join us."

"I don't see that that was necessary," Prosper Rufius said, but there was no real argument in his voice. He generally let his wife do as she pleased with these parties.

"My dear, Julius is the most famous man in Rome," Livilla said. "All the women will be green with envy."

"He's a fine driver," Rufius said. "I don't see the need to have him to dine. Still, if you wish it…"

"I do." Livilla ignored him and beamed at Appius. "Do bring your ladies with you tonight if you like."

"Thank you, but they will wish to take their children home, I think," Appius said gravely. This was not going to be the sort of dinner party that he wished Ygerna or Julia to attend, and he was reasonably sure that Lucius Paulinus would agree with him. He also knew that while Livilla might amuse herself dining with race drivers, she would never dream of inviting Appius to bring Helva. A man could take his mistress only to an all-male party. Unless, of course, she was a married woman of rank. The social niceties were complex.

Livilla had become distracted, watching the opening procession. She didn't really want Julia or Appius's British daughter-in-law there anyway, at least not without their husbands, and Lucius Paulinus had already made his regrets. It would unbalance the party. Livilla preferred an overabundance of men. The trumpet and horn players blared their way through the triumphal arch that formed the east entrance, followed by the suffect consuls, riding in chariots behind their twelve lictors. Livilla craned her head. She wasn't interested in the consuls. The real power was to be found on the emperor's balcony – the private, garlanded viewing stand built to be entered directly from his palace on the Palatine Hill that towered over the Circus. It was empty at the moment, but one never knew when the emperor would choose to show himself. The populace had best notice it if he did.

Behind the consuls, who were resplendent in scarlet, purple, and gold, and almost dwarfed by the monstrous golden garlands held over their heads by their attendants, came the chariots entered for the day's races, churning up the yellow sand of the track. There were over twenty of them, brilliant in the colors of the six racing factions of Rome – Red, White, Green, Blue, Purple, and Gold. A rain of flowers, perfume, and coins showered down, and the drivers – young, lean, and a little dangerous – waved with cocky grins at the cheering crowd. Livilla hung forward over the railing in excitement. When Julius's team went by, she flipped a gold coin expertly into the chariot, and blew him a kiss when he looked up.

At the end of the circuit, the chariots disappeared into the starting stalls at the west end of the track, and the consuls took up their posts on the balcony above.

The four teams for the first race lined up behind the ropes stretched between marble posts outside each of the stall doors, while the other drivers got theirs back out of the way; the chariot ponies had a tendency to start the race whether they were entered in it or not. Julius found Diulius awaiting him, heavy with advice and last-minute instruction. Julius brushed the flower petals out of his hair, listening with one ear to Diulius and with the other to the catcalls of his friends and rivals.

"Hai, Julius! Looks like the owner's lady's got a liking for your ugly face!" The race drivers never missed much.

Julius made a rude sign with the back of his hand and ducked under the near horse's neck to inspect the harness of the middle two where it was hitched to the shaft. They were sorrels, their sleek hides brushed to the color of a new minted gold aureus, tails bundled into a tight knot, and their braided manes starred with pearls. The Blue faction was wealthy and spared no expense on its turnout. Blue ribbons fluttered from the harness and the feather-light chariot itself was blue, ornamented with painted sunbursts. The drivers were nearly as gaudy as their horses in tunics to match their faction colors under the tight strapping that was designed to protect ribcage and thighs. Sometimes it did and sometimes it didn't. Most had broken a limb or two and the driver with all his teeth was assumed to be an amateur. Julius, short, wiry and agile as a monkey, was rapidly gaining a reputation as the best of them, and he had the missing teeth to prove it. His face, under a cap of mousy hair, would have been more attractive if it had not been scarred by a broken chariot pole a year before, but Julius didn't really care. The races had made him somebody.

He slapped the near shaft horse on the rump to make her move over and called over the ponies' backs to the Gold faction's driver: "You'd best stay clear today, Gaius, or we'll wipe up the sand with those spindly blacks of yours!"

The Gold driver called back, grinning, "What's the favorite got to be worried about?" But Diulius, watching his eyes, thought the boy looked uncomfortable.

The Gold faction hadn't a prayer of winning the main race, Diulius thought, and he inspected the other teams suspiciously. The strongest competition would come from the Greens, a team of showy white ponies with green and silver trappings. They stamped nervously in their stall. Overtrained, Diulius thought. He said as much.

"I don't doubt it," Julius said, serious now. "The owner's been pushing them hard enough to break them, to get another bit of speed out. Ought to be ashamed of himself," he added. "*I* won't drive for him."

"Made you an offer, did he?" Diulius said.

Julius nodded, tightening a strap and rubbing the off horse under the chin. "Wouldn't take it. Bastard doesn't treat his horses right."

"Well, watch them," Diulius said. "And watch that Gold driver too."

"What for? Gold's going to get left in the gate."

"Because I've spent more time on a track in my day than you've racked up yet," Diulius said. He spat through the gap between his own teeth. "That's why."

A roar from the crowd and the thunder of hooves proclaimed that the consuls had dropped the handkerchief for the first race. Diulius pushed his way through the crowd of grooms, stable guards, water carriers, and cheering section that accompanied each team, and took a spot in the arch of one of the starting stalls to watch. Beside him, the drivers' surgeon and the veterinary surgeon kept a wary eye on the race. The sole object of a Circus race was to finish first and no tactics short of outright murder were considered unfair. The chariots were paper-thin boxes kept upright only by the balance of their drivers. Only the center ponies, generally mares, were harnessed to the chariot itself; the stallions in the outer positions were attached to their teammates by thin traces and took the brunt of the sharp turns at either end of a lap. To control them, each driver lashed his reins around his waist, and carried a knife to cut himself free if he overturned. The cemeteries were full of drivers who hadn't been quick enough. The man who survived and won was Rome's darling.

Diulius sighed. He'd had all the ladies throwing him flowers once, but he hadn't really expected to live to old age, so he'd spent the money as it came in. Still, it had been a fine, wild life while it lasted, and young Julius was a protégé to be proud of. When he was in the mood to listen.

The laps were marked by seven bronze dolphins at one end of the spina, and seven marble eggs at the other. As the last dolphin flipped over, the first race ended as the chariots thundered across the finish, with the Purple team in the lead by half a length.

The drivers' surgeon picked up his kit and strolled off to the rear of the stalls where the Reds' driver had dismounted with a pulled tendon. He whistled between his teeth as he taped it. If he got nothing worse than a lame leg today, he'd thank Aesculapius. In the next stall the veterinary surgeon was checking over the ponies as they came in, before they were led off to walk dry. The racehorses were as famous as their drivers and were frequently in better health since the horses didn't go carousing after a race.

Two more minor chariot races, a bareback race, and a team of jugglers were on the bill before the day's main event, sponsored by the emperor, for which all six factions had entered their best teams. The jugglers juggled with a tame tiger, who caught the balls in his mouth, and all the ponies had hysterics as the wind shifted in their direction. A groom went running furiously onto the track to tell the jugglers to take their accursed cat to the other end of the spina. The crowd, bored with these amusements, began to shriek for their favorites, and fist fights broke out between rival factions in the upper stands. Around Prosper Rufius's box, the patrician supporters of the Blue faction gathered, betting records in hand, to toast the hope of fortune and the Blues' honor in Chian wine.

Julius put his helmet on, balanced himself carefully in the Blue chariot, and lashed the reins around his waist. The grooms gave the ponies a last brush and they cocked their copper-colored ears to the sound of the crowd shouting their names: "Victor! Lotos! Luna! Acceptor!"

"Mind what I said." Diulius jabbed a forefinger at Julius.

The sorrel ponies lined up in their stall, with the Gold team to their right and the White to the left. The ponies frisked restlessly, ears swiveling, while the drivers cursed under their breath because the Emperor Domitian had chosen that moment to appear in his viewing box and the resultant halt while he acknowledged the adulation of his subjects was taking the edge off the ponies' mettle.

"I think, sir," Flavius murmured in the emperor's ear, observing the restive horses, "that we had best begin."

"Of course," Domitian said benignly.

Flavius made sure that Aemelia had a good view, a parasol, and a cup of the emperor's excellent wine, well watered. That she had agreed to come with him to the races, as a sop for missing the dinner that night, might be a good sign, or might just be a sign that she liked the races and sitting in the emperor's box more than she was mad at him.

Domitian raised a ringed hand to the consuls in their balcony and the handkerchief fluttered down. The ponies shot forward in a cloud of sand.

"There's Julius!" Felix swung a leg over the front of his grand-father's box for a better view of the track below, and Ygerna and Julia both shot out a hand for his tunic hem.

"Get down!" Ygerna hissed. "You aren't an ape!"

A marble egg slid down its pole as the chariots careened around the first turn, with Julius and the Blue faction's sorrels in the lead. The position nearest the spina was the fastest, but also the most dangerous. If a driver took the turn too closely, he could crack his chariot into pieces on the end pillar; too wide, and another driver might cut him off. Julius pulled on the left rein and leaned into the second turn as the first bronze dolphin flipped over. Beside and behind him, the Green, Gold, and Red chariots thundered, whips cracking. Unlike most charioteers, Julius never used a whip on his horses, but he carried one anyway, to use on the other drivers. All was fair in a circus race – he had once seen one driver bite another when the chariots collided.

The sorrels still had the inside slot when Julius gathered his reins for the fourth turn. From the stands, they were only a cloud of yellow sand with bright flashes of color and the flying heads of the horses visible from moment to moment. Very little more was to be seen on the track, but Julius was aware of the Gold team hard on his right, with the Greens beside them. The black ponies of the Gold faction's team were pushing hard into Julius's off stallion, Acceptor. Acceptor swung his head and bit at them and the near black pony screamed and shot its head out to bite back. On the chariot pole, Lotos and Luna lost their stride a little.

"Jupiter blast you, Gaius, get over!" Julius shouted at the Gold faction's driver.

Gaius shook his head grimly and edged his horses closer. On Julius's left, Victor was running dangerously close to the end pillar, his sleek red hide wet with foam. Beyond the Gold faction's blacks, the white horses of the Greens loomed through the sandstorm. Old Diulius wasn't such a fool after all, Julius thought, gathering his reins. It wasn't uncommon for a rival to bribe a lesser team to run the favorite into the spina and take them out of the race. But it could be dangerous. It was going to be *very* dangerous for Gaius, Julius decided furiously. He swung his whip hard into Gaius's face and dragged on his right rein. The sorrels swerved hard with a crash of bumping chariots. Julius pulled to the left again immediately, and Gaius's chariot continued to careen right. It caromed off the Green chariot this time, and Gaius's black ponies reared up in panic. The Greens' driver swerved his team past his ally, cursing, as the Gold chariot splintered around a broken axle box and Gaius grabbed desperately at his knife.

Prosper Rufius's sorrels swept into the lead with Julius leaning low over the rail crooning to them and praying that nothing in the chariot had been snapped in the scuffle. There was no time to look back at Gaius, but he knew from the howl of mingled sympathy and excitement from the crowd that the Gold chariot was down.

Livilla watched with satisfaction from the stands as the black team plunged wildly across the track, dragging a bloody form in a broken chariot behind it in the sand. She followed this spectacle until the driver finally managed to saw his reins in half. The blacks shot free and the race attendants and the surgeon came running to pull the motionless driver from the track. As they lifted him, he turned his head; not dead after all then. Livilla turned her attention back to Julius a little regretfully. It would have been more exciting if the driver had died.

The Green team had lost ground in the altercation, and they were nervy, overtrained horses to begin with. Their form vanished completely and the crowd booed and jeered as the white ponies limped in third behind the Reds, while the Blues' sorrels sailed to victory.

The emperor beamed as he prepared to award the victory palm. "An excellent race." He patted Aemelia's hand. "I'm glad you could join us. I understand the driver belongs to your household?"

"To my brother," Flavius said. Most of the drivers were slaves, but if they could survive a few years, they'd quickly grow rich enough to buy their freedom. Julius was well on the way.

"Highly unsuitable name," Domitian said reprovingly.

"Alas, it's the one he came with," Flavius said, embarrassed. "It was more trouble than it was worth to get the brat to answer to anything else." In truth, Correus hadn't tried.

In the stables, Julius laid down the palm and went stalking the driver of the Greens. "Try that again and I'll wrap your head up in a sack. Where's Gaius?"

"I wouldn't know," the Green driver sniffed. "*You* wrecked him."

"Wish it had been you." Julius stuck his fist under the Green driver's nose. "Tell your boss to leave Gaius alone. He needs the money too bad to stand up to you, but I don't."

The Green driver, bitterly aware that his team's owner would have hired Julius instead of himself if he could have got him, growled and turned away. He was still smarting from the jeering crowd, but he knew better than to provoke Julius in this mood.

Julius spat on the stable floor with great emphasis and went off to find Gaius. The Gold driver was stretched on a cot, his face ashen, while the surgeon worked on him.

"Cracked ribs," the surgeon said briefly. "Lucky it wasn't worse."

"Fool," Julius growled. "You should have known you couldn't bring that off. Not against me." He wasted no sympathy on the cracked ribs; Gaius had been trying to give him the same. He squatted down by the cot. "Look here – stick to the country races and get out of the Circus. You aren't up to it. You're just all the Golds can afford. That's why they took Green's money."

Gaius gave him the ghost of a grin through split lips. He was sixteen. "I will be – you wait."

"Maybe," Julius said. "Probably. If you live long enough." He put a coin on the edge of the cot. "You'll need something to eat off till those ribs heal, if I know the Golds." His owner was probably a Gold and wouldn't be openhanded just now.

Gaius closed his hand around the coin and Julius edged his way through the crowd again to his own stable, to be pounded on the back by a throng of jubilant Blues. In the next stall, the owner of the Green team interrupted the dressing-down he was giving his seething driver to shoot him a venomous look. Julius could practically feel it on the back of his neck, and he turned around and bowed rudely.

–

Prosper Rufius's steward welcomed Julius into his master's house, firmly shutting the door in the faces of the plebeian mob that trailed after him, shouting his name. Deprived of their hero, the crowd in the street shouted "*Julius! Julius!*" a few times at the blank wall of the house, and then drifted off in search of other amusement. The steward clicked his tongue with displeasure. Most of them had consumed a skinful of wine already, and the emperor was footing the bill for a free dinner for the whole City mob on the track of the Circus tonight. At least one fire would break out, and there would be racing slogans and drivers' pictures chalked up on the walls all over the City by morning. He regarded Julius disapprovingly; the guest of honor wore a bright blue tunic sewn all over with gold sunbursts, and a wreath of vine leaves trailed through his mousy hair to hang rakishly over one ear. Like Prosper Rufius, the steward had won a good deal of money on Julius, and like his master, he saw no reason to have him to dine. He stumped down the corridor and through a corridor lined with statuary to the dining chamber, beckoning for Julius to follow.

It was a large party – Prosper Rufius, Livilla, Appius Julianus and his son Flavius Julianus, a woman in her forties named Didia Longina who was kin in some way to Prosper Rufius, and several couples of Livilla's choosing – young, fashionable, wealthy, and growing very drunk. Appius, reclining on a couch beside his host, blinked in amusement at Julius's entrance and the reception accorded him by Livilla and her friends. No doubt Julius would have a fine time. Appius supposed that the women's husbands were either too drunk to notice or didn't care if their wives made fools of themselves over a chariot driver. It was definitely not a party to bring Ygerna or Julia to. Appius was prepared to enjoy himself and take his pleasure where he found it, but this tolerance did not apply to his daughter. Flavius, he noted, had not brought Aemelia.

On the other hand, Prosper Rufius set an excellent table: fowl and suckling pig, a joint, an excellent mullet, blue-veined cheese from Gaul, goose liver, and fruit cooked with honey, much of it constructed by Prosper Rufius's cook to resemble something else entirely. The goose liver, for instance, had been molded into a ship with wooden oars that were used to serve it. A silver bowl of grapes and peaches made the centerpiece, with crouching silver figures that looked like weasels holding it aloft. It was still daylight and a golden glow flowed in through the open end of the room, from which green marble steps led down to a pleasant garden of topiary and rose bushes.

Livilla bore Julius triumphantly to her own couch and waved a graceful hand at her page to bring him wine.

"You honor me, lady," Julius said. "You should be having Victor and Acceptor to dinner, not me. They won your husband's race for him."

Livilla giggled, her blond fox's face flushed with wine. A wreath of hothouse roses in her hair gave off a heady scent. "How would I ever get a horse on my couch?"

"Nonsense, Livilla." The pretty young matron on Julius's other side laughed. "You've always had a liking for stallions."

Livilla laughed too but she shot the other woman a glance that was not entirely pleasant. She wriggled a little closer to Julius and he grinned into his wine cup as he felt her hand slip unobtrusively under the hem of his tunic. Rome was a gossipy city and Livilla had a reputation for liking gladiators and race drivers. It was the excitement of never knowing if her lovers were going to be killed in their next appearance, Julius expected, but he didn't mind. He liked the excitement himself. Julius was City-born, one of Rome's thousands of street urchins until his father sold him when there was nothing else left to sell, to buy himself another month's worth of wine. Julius expected the old man was dead of it by now, but he had never bothered to find out. He would shortly be free again. He was as famous as the emperor, and the City mob put up plaster busts of him in their houses.

Prosper Rufius's banquet was growing raucous. The couches, arranged like wheel spokes about a round table, were rumpled and the guests no less so. A pair of nearly nude dancing girls with pan pipes and Egyptian braiding in their hair pranced across the wave-and-clouds mosaic on the floor, dodging nimbly as the men reached for them; most of the men were too drunk to stand up and pursue them if they tried. Flavius, who Appius thought was not drunk, was watching them appreciatively but that was all.

Only the woman on the couch next to Appius's seemed to maintain a kind of amused serenity, and Appius wondered what she was doing there. They had been introduced: her name was

Didia, she was a widow and a distant cousin of Prosper Rufius. Beneath a dinner party wreath of leaves and flowers, she had a coiffure of curling brown hair with strands of gray in it, a pleasant face, and wide dark eyes. Appius thought she might be forty-five. He studied her out of the corner of his eye and caught her looking back at him. Her lips twitched.

"You are thinking that this isn't my sort of party at all," she whispered, "and that I am far too old to be chasing race drivers."

"You are a great deal younger than I am," Appius whispered back, "so I wouldn't be so rude. You don't appear to me to be chasing race drivers."

"I'm not," Didia said primly. "I don't approve of my cousin doing it either, but no one has ever been able to stop Livilla from doing things that they didn't approve of, so I don't see why *I* should try," she added practically.

Appius laughed. "Then why *are* you here? I thought you might be her chaperone."

"Juno forfend," Didia said. "I should sooner try to chaperone a rabbit."

She watched Julius, across the table from them, peeling an apple so that the peel fell into a neat coil on his napkin. Livilla, giggling, dropped a little scrap of papyrus into the coil when she thought no one else was looking. Julius stuck it down his tunic front, putting his elbow nearly in his wine cup.

"He belongs to your house, doesn't he?" Didia murmured to Appius. "I hope he's careful. Prosper has his limits and Livilla's reckless. I had to be in the City on business today," she added, returning to his question, "so I decided that I might as well dine at Prosper's expense as my own." She lifted her cup to her lips.

"Business?" Appius raised an eyebrow. For a woman to handle her own affairs was unusual, although a widow had considerably more independence than a wife or an unmarried girl.

"When my husband died" – Didia did not sound as if she regretted his departure very much – "I spent a great deal of time and trouble convincing the court to let me choose my own guardian. There is an elderly uncle, for form's sake, but I actually take care of his accounts as well as my own, so I can't afford to let anything get in a tangle."

"And you never remarried?" A young girl often did not have much say in her marriage, but a widow could have her choice. And surely Didia was much in demand. Her gown and jewelry spoke of a comfortable fortune.

"I have never seen any reason to," Didia said. "I find that as matters stand, I have just enough money to support me in the sort of comfortable, fashionable life I like, and I am my own mistress. I wasn't so greatly fond of being married the first time."

"Then you had the wrong husband," Appius found himself saying and wondered if he was drunker than he had thought.

Didia regarded his saturnine countenance curiously. An attractive man, Appius Julianus, even at sixty-eight. One needn't look at his son to know what he had been like in his youth. And a famous man – she had known who he was before they had been introduced. She had never heard that he had a reputation as a gallant. Didia stared into her cup suspiciously. Maybe it was the wine, she thought, conscious of Appius's eyes on her face. "Prosper's slaves should put more water in this," she said. "It's wasteful."

"I wondered if I might be drunk," Appius said. "I don't think I am."

"No." Didia considered. "No, I don't suppose I am either."

Appius leaned on one elbow, resting his head in his hand. The wreath of ivy in his iron-gray hair tipped a little over one ear. He took it off. At least he had kept his hair and his figure. Maybe he didn't look as foolish as he felt. Had he ever in his life gone courting before? He couldn't remember it. "I should like," he said carefully, "to call on you, when you are at home again."

VI

The Dead List

There were too many holes in the net. The Roman commanders were slowly drawing a ring around the bulk of Decebalus's army, but the Dacians were still slipping through the gaps to raid the civilian towns, from Naissus in the west as far east as the coastal settlements of the Pontus Euxinus. A column of smoke rising might be a military beacon or the beacon of a burning town.

The border was six hundred miles long and it was like hunting ghosts. The fastest travel east was by river, but cavalry horses were notoriously reluctant to get on ships. In addition, travel through the stone-toothed rapids and whirlpools of the gorges downriver from Viminacium was dangerous under any conditions. Infantry were moved down the Danuvius on the fleet out of Sexaginta Prista until they were all seasick and terrified, but there was never enough wind to go back upriver without oars or a tow, so when they turned around to chase the Dacians in the other direction, they went by foot. The unfinished and often precipitous road along the river's edge needed to be patrolled to keep more Dacians from slipping across at night. Roads on the south side of the river forts, downriver of the gorges, ran through the wetland plain and were easier going than the mountains but thick with clouds of mosquitoes that drove horses and riders mad. Couriers rode from commander to commander, most of them getting through, and slowly they patched each hole in the net and pushed the Dacians closer to the river's lower reaches, waiting for the reinforcements that didn't come. The emperor was gathering an army, they were told in dispatches from Rome.

"Then where in Hades is it?" Correus demanded, glaring at Messala Cominius as if he were somehow in charge of the nonexistent relief column.

Cominius laid his stylus down and picked up his seal, very carefully, and Correus was aware that he had gone nearly too far. Old acquaintance had its limits.

"It is where it is, Prefect." The legate pressed the seal down on a wax tablet and slid the ring back on his finger. "In the meantime, the enemy are where they are, and we are very likely going to find them tomorrow and tackle them with what we have."

Correus counted up numbers in his head for perhaps the thousandth time. Three legions, one badly undermanned, about twelve thousand if they were lucky, and an equal number of auxiliaries and cavalry. Twenty-four thousand against probably thirty thousand Dacians, maybe forty. Rome had beaten armies often before with those odds. It was the discipline of Roman troops protected by plate and scale and armed with swords and iron pilums that made the difference, against a spear-wielding enemy whose commanders were often the only ones with any armor, and who once unleashed on the enemy were uncontrollable. The Dacians, however, were iron-rich. The smelting works at Sarmizegetusa meant that every solider carried the deadly falx, a single-edged scythe-like blade that could cut through Roman armor, particularly the segmented plates of an infantry lorica. They had also demonstrated a discipline and knowledge of legionary tactics that the Roman commanders were beginning to suspect had been taught to them by other Romans. There had been rumors for several years now that Decebalus was courting deserters.

Cominius picked up a map and began to annotate it. "Please tell my optio that I would like to speak with him on your way out, Prefect."

Correus saluted and went to see to his own command.

–

An influx of scouts and couriers in the morning confirmed Cominius's prediction. Briseis danced under Correus's weight as he sat at the head of his troops while the column formed behind them. The auxiliary infantry and the Ala Dardanorum were in the vanguard, followed by the three legates, distinguishable by the eagle feathers of their helmet crests. The legionary cavalry came next, and then the catapult mule teams, and the baggage and hospital wagons with auxiliary guards on either side. Behind them marched the bulk of the three Danuvius legions, the Claudia, the First Italica, and the scarred remnants of the Fifth Macedonica. The rest of the auxiliary cavalry brought up the rear. By common consent, and mostly because no one else much wanted it, Messala Cominius had overall command.

The land here bordered on marshes alive with wading birds, pelicans, and thousands of squawking geese that flew up in outraged clouds as the column approached. At Durostorum, the river began to flow north and they left its banks to push eastward. The few villages scattered among the low, windy hills were deserted, with signs of marauding reivers everywhere in the burned barns and trampled vineyards. A smell of ash hung in the air.

A scout on a lathered horse rode in and drew rein beside the three legates, and in a moment the Order to Engage sounded along the column. Correus tightened the strap on his helmet as the breeze caught its red horsetail crest. The wind fluttered the blue and gold banner of the ala, its bearer lifted it high, and each troop raised its winged silver standard in response. Correus looked them over, nodded at them, mouthed "Make me proud," and put his heels to Briseis's flanks.

The Dacian army blackened the plain beyond the last ruined farm. Messala Cominius, from his vantage on a low hill, gave his orders, and the cavalry moved up to spread to either flank while the auxiliary infantry prepared to take the first brunt. Here was where Roman discipline halted the headlong charges of barbarian warriors. The front ranks flung their pilums into the advancing enemy, tangling their column. A pilum's iron head went halfway down its length, but only the tip was tempered, so that it bent as it pierced its target and could not be pulled out of a shield. The Dacians who had lost shields to the weight of an embedded pilum abandoned them and closed their line. The Roman front rank knelt while the second rank sent another rain of pilums over their heads. Then up and lock shields. Stab from behind the shield wall with the efficient Roman short sword and take a step. Stab again and take another step.

But the Dacians didn't break before the shield wall as the Germans and Britons did. They kept formation and pushed back, the horrible falx blades on the ends of two-handed pole arms cutting through the shield walls, the short-handled blades slicing steel plate. The dragon standards snapping in the wind above their heads made an eldritch shriek as the wind passed through the bronze mouths. The Dacian cavalry swept down on the Roman flanks as Correus fought to keep his wing together and push them back. The intent was to drive the Dacians to the river and hold them there until they had to cross or die. There were no bridges, and unless they could bring their boats up fast enough, they would have to swim.

The catapult crews had set up on a hill behind the front lines and Correus heard one of the wicked little scorpion bolts whine overhead. In the field they were most effective against cavalry, where one bolt could tangle a troop around a downed horse. He snapped his head around as another bolt went by in the other direction and he heard a scream as it landed behind him. Someone among Decebalus's Roman deserters had been a catapult man. Correus gritted his teeth and envisioned crucifying him.

A Dacian cavalryman swung his falx at what would have been Correus's sword arm if he hadn't been left-handed. Correus brought his shield up and took a slice out of the Dacian's own arm, just below the scale of his hauberk sleeve, before he could realign his attack. It shot blood across Correus's vision, but he had the satisfaction of realizing that he had hit an artery. The Dacian swayed in his saddle as another came up to take his place, never losing formation. The wind screamed through the mouths of the dragon standards as Correus's own cavalry pressed around him, and another catapult bolt landed in their midst. The ala parted around a fallen horse, coalesced again, pushed on.

On a slight rise above the plain, Messala Cominius watched with an uneasy eye. The other two legates were at the heads of their legions, where they belonged. His was under the command of its primus pilus, and Cominius itched to be there and not where he was, making decisions that were not going to be the right ones, no matter what they were. The auxiliary front ranks, badly mauled, had fallen back to let the bulk of the legions take their place. Estimating the swarm of men darkening the low ground before him, he thought that forty thousand was closer than thirty. From there, as the river flowed north, the land rose on the east into the coastal hills. If they could put enough pressure on the Dacian army, they could push it to the river, with the hills hindering their eastward movement. If. The front ranks of the legions were falling back now; slowly, but they were falling back.

The Dacian horsemen were gradually fighting their way around the Roman flanks while the Roman cavalry fought to stop them. Correus could see the cavalry commander of the Dacians' left wing, his gilded helmet catching the light on its peak. He held a short-handled falx in his right hand, and a spear in his shield hand, behind the red and gold oval with a rose on its boss. His scale armor was much like Correus's own. Correus kicked Briseis forward through a gap in the melee. It was always useful to take the commander out. Blaesus and the ala followed him, aware that the Dacians would have the same idea.

"Leave him to us!" Blaesus shouted.

Correus braced his spear against his saddle horns and steadied it. The Dacian commander, eyes shadowed under his gilded helmet, lifted his falx, and Correus kicked Briseis forward again. The Dacian raised his shield arm, and Correus put Briseis's weight behind the spear, aiming at the last second not at the commander's head or belly but at the armpit where the falx was held high. It only tore the scale of his hauberk, but the commander's arm twisted and the falx fell as the two horses nearly tangled. Correus spun Briseis around, his long cavalry sword in hand, and caught the cavalry commander with a blow that sliced his scale above the hip. Beside him, Blaesus drove his own spear into the commander's shield and tore it away before the man could pull his arm free. The Dacian fell from his horse under the hooves of his advancing men.

"Now!" Correus shouted, and they pushed hard against the Dacian cavalry before another commander could rally them. The ala kept formation, but they were making no headway, and around him his men were dropping.

The Dacian commander's second was at the head of his wing now, his own men keeping formation and pushing back hard. He made for Correus with his riders behind him. The front lines had become a tangle of men and horses, who leaped now over the bodies of both. Correus brought his shield up as the Dacian officer thrust a spear at him. It stuck in his shield, and Correus swerved Briseis so that her weight pulled the haft out of the Dacian's grip. Correus struggled to get the point out while it dragged his shield down. He managed it finally, with Blaesus and his men encircling him, and sheathed his sword, bracing the Dacian spear against his saddle horns with the now ragged shield on his other arm. He rode hard at the Dacian line and had the satisfaction of catching one in the helmet with the spear point. The blow knocked the Dacian's head sideways but the rider kept coming, as did the rest of them. The ala braced itself stubbornly against them. Correus spotted the Dacian second officer in the melee again and they locked shields, each struggling to pull the other's from his hand. Correus let go of the spear as the Dacian swung his long falx at him. He blocked the blow with his cavalry sword and pulled his shield free. They eyed each other as the battled swirled around them. Briseis's flanks were red with blood, neither hers nor Correus's, and she stumbled over the body of a Dardanorum standard bearer. The Dacian officer's horse went down when another staggered into it, the empty saddle blood-streaked, but it righted itself and kept coming.

In the end it was no use. All the advantages that the Roman forces generally enjoyed were turned against them. The Dacians held formation with iron discipline, responding to their signal flags and wolf-headed trumpets with practiced precision. The scorpion catapults they had been taught to make rained their bolts down on the Roman troops and on the Romans' own catapult positions. And the Romans were badly outnumbered.

Cominius made his decision. He signaled the trumpeter beside him and the Fall Back sounded, and then sounded again over the noise of the battle.

Correus heard the Fall Back through a red mist of fury as he struggled with the Dacian officer, his anger at the ghosts of Oppius Sabinus and the deserter who had taught them to make catapults driving him forward, his ala behind him, damaged but still in ragged formation. The Fall Back came again and he saw his banner-bearer raise his standard higher, signaling. He swung again furiously at the Dacian officer and his sword bit through scale below the Dacian's ribs. Then reluctantly he reined Briseis back, shield up, pulling the ala with him.

The discipline that made Roman armies victorious was also the thing that saved them in defeat. Slowly they pulled back in formation, closed around the vulnerable baggage train and the wounded in the hospital wagons, drew inward into a half-circle, shields overhead, with a ring of pilums facing outward and the cavalry another ring around that one. Gradually the whole column moved backward, and the Dacians let it go, unwilling to rush the Romans' fanged defenses just to reach an enemy already in retreat.

It had been a devastating loss, mitigated only by Cominius's anguished decision to pull back before they were overwhelmed. The tipping point for that had been very close.

They slept that night in a heavily fortified camp near one of the ruined villages, tended the wounded, burned the ones who died anyway, and prayed for the shades of the ones they had had to leave on the battlefield. They would go out in the morning under a green branch if the Dacians would honor that and burn them in the field.

Correus, collecting the Dead List from the ala's surgeon, barely kept himself from weeping over it.

The surgeon, named Nicomedes, was on his first posting as a senior medical officer, and to Correus's war-weary eyes looked to be about fifteen. His expression was dismal too. "There's a score more we may lose. I need to go back to the hospital, sir. I can't leave them to my juniors for long."

"Get some sleep yourself," Correus advised him as he departed, but he supposed he wouldn't. The surgeons never did.

Decurion Blaesus took his place, rubbing at the healing scar on his thigh but otherwise unmarked. He looked at the Dead List and touched the amulet around his neck, an iron horse and rider that was common among the ala's men. The Horseman was an old god, faded mostly into folklore but perhaps more powerful for that. Like the Dacians, to whom they were kin, the Moesi worshiped a supreme god who had no image, an amorphous personification of the universe itself. The Horseman was more readily called upon in times of need.

"General Cominius sent the password," Blaesus said. "It's 'holdfast.'" He paused, looking uneasy. "May I ask a question, sir?"

Correus laid the Dead List down. "If it's about reinforce-ments—"

"No, sir. It's about where the Dacians got those catapults."

"They got them exactly where you think they got them, Decurion," Correus said.

"And don't be thinking the clever lads who taught them were with that lot today," Eumenes said from the corner of the tent where he was polishing Correus's helmet. "If it was me, I'd stay in a locked room in Sarmizegetusa." Desertion was a capital offense. Aid to the enemy was worse and the execution method would be ghastly.

"Until we take Sarmizegetusa," Blaesus said grimly.

In the morning they began the slow retreat to the territory that Cominius thought they could hold, west of Ratiaria, collecting a flood of displaced civilians as they went. Dispatches had gone out to Rome by multiple couriers, stating that they would hold there until the emperor's relief column arrived.

The civilians came clutching babies, sacks of pots, and rugs, leading donkeys or goats, hungry and exhausted and waiting for Rome to take care of them, as Rome had promised. Cominius and the other legates assigned a large garrison to Horreum Margi and herded the refugees into shelter in the empty warehouses there, doling out what grain was left, and settling squabbles over donkey ownership and petty theft. There the inevitable enterprises appeared almost overnight in cobbled-together shacks: wine shops selling drinks of no one knew exactly what and whorehouses willing to barter for onions and a chicken.

Correus retired to Singidunum with his badly damaged ala. He ordered continual patrols along the roads east to Viminacium and south to Horreum Margi. Riding at the head of one of these, he took note of the unplowed fields going to weeds, and the burned farmsteads north of Naissus. There was a garrison at Naissus where the Via Militaris from Viminacium crossed the Ratiaria road and made its way southeast into Thrace. With luck, they could hold the western half of the province until the emperor made up his mind, but it would be two years at least until the land recovered and the burned towns were rebuilt. They would have to send the army to help once peace was restored if they didn't want famine on top of war. Because he couldn't help it, he ticked all these things over in his head, plans impossible to implement while they hung onto the province by their fingernails.

–

That spring everything hung dangerously in the balance, waiting – for the emperor, for a recalcitrant king, for whatever would tip it one way or the other.

"Decebalus will be here soon," Rescuturme said. She stretched out on the rug and moved a stone on the game board. "I hate him," she added.

Ziais didn't bother to tell her sister not to be disrespectful. Ziais wasn't her nurse and Ziais hated him too, first for being treated as a game counter in the endless bargaining of treaties and alliances, and now for his demand that she marry the king of the Getae.

"What are you going to do?" Rescuturme asked.

"I've told Decebalus I won't do it," Ziais said. She moved a stone on the board. "I'll have to marry someone, but it won't be him."

"He smells," Rescuturme said. "You'll go away if you marry and leave me here. I wish Diegis was going to be king."

"Diegis isn't any better," Ziais said. "He's nicer to you is all."

"Decebalus stuck his hand down my front to see if I had breasts yet," Rescuturme said. "He'll find someone hateful for me to marry too."

"So would Diegis." That was the only use the royal family had for their women – to cement alliances.

"What if Decebalus makes you?" Rescuturme asked. Could he, if he didn't mind the scandal that an unwilling bride would make? Decebalus always did what he wanted. Ziais put her hand to her throat and the small gold figure that hung there. "I asked the Mother to keep me from him," she said.

"Vezinas High Priest told me the Mother is one of the Old Ones and doesn't listen anymore," Rescuturme said.

"Vezinas is a man. No doubt she doesn't listen to him," Ziais said.

–

Decebalus inspected his neatly oiled beard in a silver mirror. He snipped a stray curl and ignored his sister. His tunic and trousers nearly lit up the chamber with gold embroidery and his shoes were bright blue leather with gold laces. It was going to be important to outshine the allied lords.

Ziais snatched the mirror out of his hand and flung it onto the marble floor where its thin edge crumpled. He swung his palm at her and she dodged.

"I won't do it!" She spat at him now across the marble basin where he had begun to wash his hands. When he looked up, she turned to the window. "I'll jump first!"

"Don't be childish." He directed his attention back to the basin. "You'll do as you're told. And that would hurt. You wouldn't like it."

Decebalus's private chamber lay within the palace complex occupying the top three of Sarmizegetusa's thirteen terraces. The windows gave a view some three thousand feet down a rock-fanged, tree-studded cliff to the river below.

Ziais faced him furiously. "You can't make me do this, Decebalus. I'll call on the Mother." The Goddess, like the Horseman, was a remnant of the old ways, but among the women she had some power, and it was generally directed at men. He took note of the small gold figure strung from a gold and lapis lazuli collar around Ziais's neck, over the bright blue and yellow silks of her gown and overtunic. Lapis lazuli drops hung in her ears and she wore her dark hair in the flowing waterfall of an unmarried woman, bound with a gold fillet.

"The Mother should be happy to see you married. Lots of babies. That's what she likes." He dried his hands on a linen towel.

"He's a pig. He smells."

"Gudila is king of the Getae. I need him. Hold your nose."

"Do you really think you can hold all these princes under your command? You can't even convince Father to abdicate."

"That is a matter open to discussion," Decebalus said. "And not your business."

Ziais's mouth tightened. "You get too big for your boots. You aren't Burebista."

"And you aren't important, except that Gudila wants you. Go tell your women to get you ready for the wedding." He grinned at her. "You can be married tied up in a sack as well as on your feet."

Ziais clenched her fist around the little gold figure. "You will pay for this, Decebalus."

The look in her eye made him twitch but he ignored it. When she had gone – to choose her bridal clothes or not, it didn't matter – he found his father in his Council Hall, attended by various scribes and servants who scattered when Decebalus pointed at the door.

Duras had much the look of his sons, with a heavy oblong head and angular jaw covered by a curling beard. A gold fillet sat in his gray hair, which was thinning at the crown. His shoulders were wrapped in a fringed woolen shawl and a hot brick had been set beneath his chair to warm his feet.

"Diegis has sent another caravan with loot from the south," Decebalus said. "Have you seen it?"

"The contents were brought before me first," Duras said. "Since, as it happens, I am still king."

Decebalus touched his forehead. "The allied lords will be here tomorrow for the wedding. We'll have to give them some, but there is plenty. No heads this time, since you didn't like the last one."

"I prefer live Romans," Duras said. "The head may know things, but it is not in a position to tell them."

"I've had the skull cleaned," Decebalus said. "It will make an excellent standard and can tell the Romans what it knows."

Duras stretched his arms out from under the shawl, wincing, and shifted his weight in his chair.

"May I send someone for a cushion?" Decebalus asked. "You shouldn't have been on a horse yesterday. It's made your hips worse."

"Thank you for your solicitude." Duras gave him a black look.

"The allied lords share my concern. A king should lead his army."

"I suppose I am lucky you haven't had me poisoned," Duras said.

"That would be most unlucky. You should listen to the allied lords."

90

From the window of her silk-hung chamber, Ziais watched each cavalcade as it made its way up the terraces of her father's capital. The heights of Cogaeonum, the Holy Mountain, were still snow-covered in mid-spring. The lords and their retinues clattered through the gates in the outer curtain wall, banners flying, sending up showers of snow, past the villages and cultivated fields in the lower terraces, where children came out to gawk at their finery. They rode in procession to the temple complex with its columned sanctuaries and great sundial, past the ironworks above the temples, then the counting rooms and granaries, and came finally to the marble walls of the palace.

She saw Gudila at the head of his men, his gilded helmet pulled down over his heavy brow. His saddle trappings were red and heavy with gold fittings to show his rank. The allied lords would stay three days, eating and drinking everything in sight and bothering the serving women, and then ride south again to their armies, to further hound the Romans along the Ister. Ziais would have to bed the pig king of the Getae and then he too would ride out, following her brother. The Mother send an evil fate on them both. She would give the Mother a gift so she could hear her through the wall that Vezinas High Priest put around the old gods.

Ziais turned to the little altar in the corner of her sitting room and thought for a moment of what to offer. Finally she took the scissors from her needlework basket and began to hack off her hair below her ears.

When it was a dark pile on the floor at her feet, Ziais dragged the little iron brazier from the opposite corner, spilling ash, and set it before the altar. She heaped the hair in it, stirring up the banked coals. The hair refused to burn. It only smoldered and shriveled where the dark waves touched the coals. She snatched the silver lamp from beside her bed and poured the oil out onto the hair. It went up then with a vicious flame and she watched it as it turned to sticky ash and filled the room with smoke.

VII

"We Were Lucky"

Livilla paused to inspect a set of sapphire-studded bangles, while her slave waited outside the jeweler's shop in the City with her mistress's parcels under one arm and her mistress's parasol in the other hand. Prosper Rufius was dining with the emperor tonight, a gathering of senators whom Domitian no doubt wished to keep an eye on, and had parted from his wife that morning to bathe and be shaved with the admonition that she stay at home and away from the race drivers. The emperor's campaign to improve public morals required impeccable behavior from senators' wives.

In Livilla's opinion, the emperor's campaign to improve public morals should have started with the emperor himself, and since it hadn't, she felt no great compunction to worry about it, particularly since her husband wouldn't be home. She bought the bangles, as well as one in a somewhat more masculine design that Julius was sure to like, and rejoined her slave.

"I want the peach-colored gown tonight and some peonies for my hair. Tell Cook we'll have dinner at sunset, just myself and one guest."

Lobsters, she thought, and some new asparagus. And that Gallic wine that Prosper was hoarding.

—

Julius made his way, whistling, past the walled villas of the Quirinal Hill and the greenery of the public pleasure gardens to the door of Prosper Rufius's house. He was mildly surprised to be met not by the steward of the household but by Livilla's personal maid, but he followed her cheerfully through the atrium into the rose and topiary garden and then to a small private dining chamber nearly hidden behind trellised vines. Livilla, with white flowers knotted in her hair and a practically transparent gown, reclined on a couch that was clearly meant for two. There were no other couches and no other guests. To Julius's mind, the prospects for the evening rose considerably. Livilla was getting a little long in the tooth, but she was still pretty, and she knew a number of interesting things to do.

She patted the cushions beside her and waved a hand at the tray of honeyed dates on the adjacent table. "These are very good," she told him, popping one in her mouth and holding out another to his.

Julius shook his head. He didn't like sweets much.

She frowned at him and then laughed. "We'll find something else you'll enjoy, then." She turned to her maid. "We'll have the dinner tray now, Lepida, and the wine and cake too, and then you may leave us to chat undisturbed."

Lepida bowed her head and padded silently away. Unless it was extremely cold, most household slaves wore no shoes, so as not to annoy their betters with their footsteps. Julius considered that unwise. He liked to know where people were.

Livilla touched Julius under the chin. "I have a present for you, if you're good. And the most enchanting day planned for us tomorrow. You can't stay the night, of course, but I'll meet you in the gardens at midday and we'll go boating."

"Can't do that," Julius said, shaking his head. "Need to run the team or they'll go flat."

Livilla pouted, as prettily as she could manage. "I might go flat too," she suggested, "if I don't get a little attention."

Julius grinned at her. "You can have all my attention tonight, until your husband comes home anyway. But the horses come first."

She smacked his face then, not very hard, but with feeling. "No, Julius, *I* come first. Keep that in mind."

Julius rubbed his cheek and blinked at her. "I hadn't thought I was so important."

"You are. I'm sorry I did that. I'm just lonesome." She looked plaintive and stroked his face where she had hit it.

And bored, he thought. Livilla didn't enjoy anything that wasn't dangerous. He couldn't blame her, he supposed. He was much the same, but his pleasure came mainly from the races. Livilla was a fill-in, a scratch to a common itch. He'd better not let her know that, though.

Lepida brought a tray burdened with silver dishes of lobster and asparagus accompanied by various other delicacies, a large pitcher of wine and a two-handled silver cup, and departed, closing the door behind her.

"Pour us some wine. It's Prosper's best."

Julius obeyed and they drank together from the cup. Livilla fed Julius bites of lobster with buttery fingers, and slid her hand under his tunic, teasing him until they spilled the wine and forgot about the asparagus.

When he left, she was asleep among the rumpled cushions in the ruins of her peony wreath, with her gown tangled around her waist. He was very drunk, but he knew better than to go to sleep there. Prosper Rufius was at the emperor's dinner party in the imperial residence on the Palatine Hill but he would come home eventually, and Julius valued his contract to drive Rufius's horses rather more than he valued Livilla. He pulled her gown down and made his way to his apartment near the Circus stables, where he left the baker on the ground floor a copper coin and a note to wake him at midday.

–

Announced by the combined alarms of a dog and a flock of geese, Appius Julianus handed the reins of his horse to the slave who emerged from the portico of Didia Longina's country house and detached a parcel from the saddle bag. "Is your mistress at home?"

The slave appeared uncertain how to answer that. An older servant, the household steward by his air of dignity and wide silver armband, bustled through the door and regarded Appius with suspicion. Appius wondered if he thought he was selling something.

He shifted the parcel under his arm. "Please tell your mistress that Appius Julianus is calling on her."

The steward looked more receptive. "Indeed, sir."

Appius inspected the parcel and waited. The steward was back in a moment. "Mistress is in the garden," he informed Appius. "Please come with me."

Didia rose from a cushioned wicker chair and held out her hand when she saw him. "How lovely to see you." She had been reading, judging by the scroll in the grass at her feet.

Appius looked embarrassed. "I thought perhaps... you mentioned your roses... that is, I have some cuttings from a bush in my garden that was trimmed back for transplanting, and I thought you might..." He trailed off and gave up. He thought she was laughing at him.

"You needn't come armed with rose cuttings to get an audience," she said. "Kallias, take the cuttings that General Julianus has kindly brought me and give them to Demippos. And bring us some wine and something to eat, please."

Appius handed over the damp parcel of cloth-wrapped cuttings with relief. The head gardener had lectured him lengthily on not allowing them to dry out.

Didia smiled at him. She wore a plain linen gown of the sort that said she wasn't expecting any other company, and her brown curls were pinned into a knot on her head with plain silver combs. A gray streak springing up just over her left temple made its own small curl, an effect that Appius found unexpectedly charming.

"Come, let me show you my gardens while we wait for Kallias," she said. "You can see that we will give them a good home."

He followed her along the stone paths between the rose bushes, coming into bloom in showers of scarlet, pink, and white. At the end, a walk lined with yew trees led to a blue-tiled fountain that sent a silver spray from a leaping fish's mouth, shimmering in the sun with rainbow scraps of color. Beyond the hedge he could see the little silver river, a tributary of the Tiber, that flowed along the edge of her estate.

"Your garden is lovely," Appius said. "I never paid much attention to mine until lately, other than to admire it. It was my wife's pride. Now my daughter and… the other women of the house argue over it, and the gardener does as he pleases, I suppose."

"Gardeners do that, I find. Demippos will be delighted with your cuttings but he won't let me advise him about them at all, I fear." Didia didn't comment on the rest of his statement. Helva was no secret, and it was beginning to be a running joke that Appius had no idea what to do with her now. Prosper Rufius had found it funny enough to add to his dinner party repertoire.

She cocked her head at him curiously, trying to decide why he had come to see her. He had told her that he would like to call on her, but she had put that down to the wine, despite his denial. Maybe just to escape his household. That was entirely possible from what she had heard. "A great shame he adopted that boy," Prosper Rufius had said, shaking his head sagely. "Now he can't shake loose of the mother and the boy brought home some foreign witch for a wife into the bargain." Didia had commented that the "boy" was now distinguishing himself in the army and the "witch" was a princess of her own people, and Livilla had sniffed. "Little dark thing. Looks like a goblin. I don't know what Correus sees in her." A certain amount of light had dawned then. Livilla would make a play for any attractive man and didn't like being turned down. Didia wondered if she had gone after father and son both, with no results.

Didia wound the garden tour back to the chairs where a pitcher of wine and two cups had appeared, along with a tray of figs and olives and good cheese. "How is your household holding up after your loss?" she asked him, experimentally.

"It's been hardest on Julia and Flavius," Appius said. "And my granddaughter, Flavius's girl. They were very close. And I still find myself thinking I must tell her something and then remembering that she is gone."

"I am so sorry."

"We were married very young," Appius said. "A match arranged by our parents, as I suppose yours must have been."

She nodded.

"She was the axle that all the wheels turned about," he said. He bit into a fig and was silent a moment. "My other son's mother is no use at all. She has never had to be. Julia insists on running home from her own house to set things straight and have a fight with her, and my daughter-in-law, who is of a practical nature, is the one who keeps things going so that we at least have breakfast, but she hasn't Antonia's authority, and in any case, she'll be off for the frontier as soon as Correus will let her."

"Have you considered running away to sea?" Didia inquired.

Appius grinned. "Multiple times. Unfortunately, I get seasick. If I weren't too old, I would join the army again."

She regarded him thoughtfully. He was dressed in riding clothes, with an old pair of what were probably army-issue breeches below his tunic, and sturdy sandals. Most men of his age and rank would have come in a carriage. His iron-gray hair was neatly oiled and barely thinning and the resemblance to his sons was startling. "You are welcome to come and hide in my garden any time you like," she told him.

"I've been hiding in the horse barns," he said, "but this is more pleasant."

"You raise cavalry remounts, don't you, as well as the chariot ponies?"

"We do. The emperor is in the process of scraping my barns bare with an order for the Moesian frontier. I am relieved that he has turned his attention that way."

"Your son is there, isn't he?"

"Yes, on the Danuvius. They are barely holding on, I think. The emperor got some very bad advice from the governor there, and the governor has paid for it by getting himself killed. I think that has shaken both Domitian and the Senate into action. Flavius is on his staff and he tells me that they are expecting to move out quickly now. It's overdue, I fear."

Didia digested this. It was the kind of information that men rarely discussed with a woman, other than perhaps a wife. There was something intimate and domestic about Appius's conversation with her, something friendly, neither careful nor courtly. She was flattered.

By the time he took his leave, she was reasonably sure that he would be back. What she intended to do about that, if anything, was another matter.

–

Appius rode home deep in thought. He had found himself thinking about Didia Longina since Rufius's dinner party. Now he was still thinking about her. That had not happened to him before, and he knew guiltily that it was far too soon after Antonia's death to let anyone else know it. It was not like the physical pull that Helva had held for him. That had diminished somehow since Antonia died, for reasons that seemed to him too complicated to untangle. It was something that was a matter of the heart perhaps, unexpected and awkward. That there was a physical attraction was undeniable. She was lovely, the more so, he thought, because she didn't henna her hair into the garish shades favored by the fashionable women of the City. But that wasn't the heart of it. If he was doomed to fall in love for the first time at sixty-eight, it seemed unfair, but perhaps sixty-eight was an age at which you could be practical about it.

These musings were driven from his head on arriving home, where a carriage and a mountainous wagonload of luggage and slaves waited at the portico steps. Flavius and Aemelia were in the atrium, quarreling furiously while Ygerna ordered Niarchos, who oversaw the indoor servants, to have a slave make up rooms, and Helva told him to use different ones. Small Appia clung to Flavius's tunic hem with both hands.

"We're marching tomorrow," Flavius said. He wore his staff officer's uniform, helmet under one arm. "I've brought Aemelia as we discussed. She shouldn't be alone in the City."

Aemelia was red-eyed and her mouth was set in a furious line.

"We are delighted to have you," Appius told her, ignoring her obvious lack of a similar sentiment.

Flavius stayed to dine and rode back to Rome at sunset, leaving Aemelia, Appia, a nursemaid, a maid, three trunks, six traveling baskets, a groom, and her personal carriage and horses. She refused to bid him farewell, and then stood in the portico and watched until his figure disappeared down the road.

–

Flavius made one detour on his way back to the emperor. He found his sister and Lucius Paulinus sitting domestically in their garden, Julia propped in a pile of cushions on a chaise. The glow of a dozen hanging lanterns illuminated the courtyard.

"Flavius! I thought you would be on the march by now." Julia inspected him. "You look awful."

"Thank you." Flavius sat down and took off his helmet. He put his head in his hands. "I just left Aemelia and Appia with Father. I told her a week ago she would need to go to him when I left, but she acted as if I had just sprung it on her and we had a thunderous quarrel. Will you please look in on them while I'm gone? And how did you know we were about to march?" He raised his head to look pointedly at Paulinus.

"Certainly," Julia said, allowing her husband to ignore that question. "Are you worried about her? They will have Ygerna and the children for company."

"She doesn't know how to talk to Ygerna. I think she's afraid of her."

"That's ridiculous." Julia had been friends with Aemelia since her betrothal to Flavius, and not overly fond of Ygerna herself, but that had shifted when she watched Ygerna during the fever, making a bonfire of soiled bedding and singing to sick babies. The family of Appius Julianus had not got to where it was burdened with an inability to alter perspective. And Aemelia was making Flavius's life a burden to him.

"She's been very sheltered," Flavius said. "And I've given her a bad time."

Julia snorted. "So you have. And done your best to make it up to her."

"That's not entirely fair, Ju," Paulinus said. "There's been open gossip about it, and she's humiliated."

"There is always open gossip about everybody," Julia pointed out. "Our father being a case in point, and I'm not having hysterics. Lucius, I'm hungry again."

Paulinus rose and poked his head in the window of the kitchen wing which overlooked the garden. "He's your father, not your husband," he pointed out when he came back, followed by a slave with a tray of bread and olives. "It's undignified but not a personal insult."

"I know. I'm sorry. I get cross when I'm hungry. It takes a lot of food to produce another human being." Julia ate an olive and dipped a piece of bread in the oil they swam in. "I'll look in on Aemelia, I promise."

"I have heard," Paulinus ventured, looking at Flavius, "that the emperor is taking the Praetorian Guard with him."

"Have you?" Flavius raised an eyebrow.

"Under Cornelius Fuscus."

"Fuscus is a good general," Flavius said, not bothering to contradict Paulinus's information.

"He's reputed to be a bit overconfident," Paulinus commented.

"He's had no reason not to be so far," Flavius said. "And he doesn't have political ambitions, which makes him a refreshing choice."

"Like Father," Julia said. "Fuscus refused senatorial rank too, as I recall."

"He prefers to risk his neck on the battlefield instead," Paulinus said. "It will be interesting to see how he handles this command.

Ju, I've been thinking that you really ought to go to your father too, until the baby comes."

Flavius snapped his head around to look at Paulinus. "Lucius, you are not going to the frontier. Correus has already thrown you out. I'll do it again if you try it."

"As it happens," Paulinus said, "I have the emperor's permission."

Flavius looked openly suspicious.

Julia sighed. "He does. It was almost a command, in fact, although I understand that it was phrased as a privilege. It's why I haven't fought him about going when the baby's nearly here."

"I am to write a firsthand account of the campaign," Paulinus said. "For posterity. His brother's early death has given the emperor to understand that surprises do happen. He's begun to think of his legacy."

"Fuscus won't like it," Flavius said flatly. "If you stick with the emperor's entourage, that's one thing. But if you go nosing about the camps, that's another. Sticking with the imperial staff is what he means for you to do."

"Of course," Paulinus said.

Flavius gave him a hunted look. "Lucius, I have nearly all I can manage. I mean it." He picked up his helmet and they walked him to the door.

Julia looked at Paulinus as her brother rode away. "He doesn't look well. Do you think it's only the trouble with Aemelia? Is he *still* thinking about that woman?"

Paulinus was silent a long moment. "We were lucky," he said, "to love someone we could have. Yes, of course he is thinking about her. She is thinking about him, I expect. It's an excellent thing he is out of Germany."

–

It was May Eve, and Fiorgyn was trying to think about cows, if Ranvig would let her. They were being rounded up to go to the high spring pasture, and she marked the stock of Ingvarshold on a tally stick as they went through the gate into the cattle pen. "Thirteen, fourteen… Ranvig, let it be!… fifteen, sixteen…"

"I need you there," Ranvig said, ignoring the cows. "Haddon of the Chatti wants a council and I don't like the sound of it. Your word carries weight as Nyall—"

Fiorgyn threw the tally stick down. "I have lost count and I am sick to death of being Nyall Sigmundson's widow! Now I am Ingvar's wife and Nyall is dead in Rome and I want no more of it! Your wars have cost me all I will pay!"

"Then come to Ranvigshold tomorrow and tell that to Haddon."

"No one ever told the Chatti anything. Haddon is like Marbod and Marbod went to Rome with his head in a bucket after the last war. May Ziu send Haddon the same!" She climbed down from her perch on the fence and picked up the tally stick. "Gert!"

A towheaded boy with a dog at his heels looked up. He waved his arm and the other boys halted the stream of cattle.

Fiorgyn handed him the stick. "Count them for me, please, as best you can. Lord Ranvig has other uses for me!" She stalked across the cattle yard, scattering a flock of chickens and holding her woolen skirts above the muck. A thrall hauling water from the well scrambled out of her way as she went up the hill, past the forge and the pony sheds and the Maytree, to the Great Hall that overlooked the home pastures and outbuildings of Ingvarshold.

Ranvig followed her in, uninvited, and found her husband Ingvar mending a saddle girth by the hearth fire. "She is in a temper," Ingvar commented. "What did you say to her?"

"That I require her presence at council."

"Just that? She would have come anyway since I am bidden there." Ingvar's voice was placid, as of someone remarking on the need for more firewood or the prospect of rain. It was a trait he was noted for and belied the fact that he was the best swordsman among the council lords. He was dressed for hunting in leather shirt and breeches, and he had taken his muddy boots off to steam before the fire. His brown hair was knotted at the side of his head in the Semnone fashion, held with a bronze pin. He shouted for a thrall and told him to bring the chieftain beer.

Ranvig sat by the hearth fire and stuck out his own boots toward the heat. Two of Ingvar's hounds shifted sleepily to make room for him. "It isn't really me she's angry at. Haddon of the Chatti is willing to stick his spear into a wasps' nest because he is tired of Roman taxes and Roman outposts on his side of the river, all of which he agreed to after the last war. I need her voice."

"A more weighty matter than broken betrothals and cattle raids," Ingvar agreed. "We will be there for council and the Mayfires. It may be that some of our own will need persuading."

Branches green with new leaf draped the roof beams of the Council Hall at Ranvigshold and the Maytree outside in the courtyard made blurred and dappled shadows on the ground. The hall doors stood open to the soft twilight where the swallows who lived in the eaves danced in the air, scooping up insects that came out with the sunset. The smell of meat turning on a spit and the voices of thralls and lesser folk making the Mayfires ready came through the open windows. Most minor council matters had been dispensed with and now Haddon, chieftain of the Chatti, rose from his chair.

The Chatti lands ran east of the Roman forts along the Rhenus between the Semnone holdings to the north and the Black Forest that was the western part of what the Romans called the Agri Decumates. Haddon, sister's son and successor to the old chieftain Marbod, was relatively young; young enough not to count the cost when he was angry, and he had been kept waiting. He was red-haired like his uncle, with a drooping mustache and braided hair. He wore a wolfskin vest and plain dark shirt and breeches, not elaborately ornamented but of fine cloth and workmanship, and an iron collar like a thrall's but elaborately worked. Chatti boys wore such an iron torque until they had killed a man in battle, and some wore it afterward to show that there were more enemies left to kill. He leaned on his war spear, not caring that to have brought it into Ranvig's hall was a rudeness in itself.

"Now is the time," he said. "Now. The Dacians have beaten the Roman army and killed their governor."

A murmur that might have been agreement came from among the council lords and Ranvig turned his head to stare at them. No one spoke further.

"The Roman army that the Dacians have beaten is stationed on the Danuvius," Fiorgyn said quietly. "Here there are five of the Romans' legions on the upper Rhenus, three of them in Moguntiacum alone. And four more downriver."

Haddon glared at the women seated on the chieftain's left and right. Fiorgyn Arngunns-daughter was the old Semnone chief's widow and the younger one was Ranvig's wife. Neither, in Haddon's mind, should be offering opinions. "Women's words," he said dismissively, and spat on the floor.

Every council lord stiffened.

"That may be the way of the Chatti," Steinvar said quietly. He was a lean, scarred man and the eldest of them except for old Hauk. "And perhaps the reason the Chatti did not fare well in the last war," he added pointedly. "Frigg who is wife of Wuotan Allfather does not look kindly on men who refuse the counsel of women."

Arni stood. "The chieftain of the Chatti should mind his manners in our Council Hall," he said. He was kin to Fiorgyn after all, and Steinvar's son-in-law. "But" – he paused to look around at them all – "he speaks of important matters."

Horst looked at Arni. "Why should we concern ourselves with Chatti matters? Did Allfather make us their nursemaid?"

Barden the priest, who would light the Mayfires later, sat unmoving in his corner. The gold sun disk around his neck reflected the flames from the hearth. He would tell Ranvig later what the gods had said, but not here in front of Haddon.

"The chieftain of the Chatti has ridden all this way to tell us something we know already," Ingvar said. "We in the Free Lands made a treaty with the Romans that involved no taxes and no outposts of the Eagle soldiers. We trade freely in their cities. We have even dined with the Roman governor in Moguntiacum. Why should we fight for Haddon to overset his own treaty?"

"For the reason that Rome may look to us next," Arni said.

Ranvig held up a hand. "This is for the council lords of the Semnones to discuss." Had there ever been a time when Arni was not persuaded by any reason to start a fight? "If the chieftain of the Chatti sees the opportunity to fight the Romans, he may do so at any time he wishes. For us, we will think on it."

Fiorgyn watched Ranvig speculatively. If there was anything she had learned of Romans in the process of tearing her own heart out, it was that Rome did not forget. If the Semnones helped Haddon start a war on the Rhenus, then Rome would come after the Semnones when it had settled Haddon, and the aftermath would be ruined fields, burned steadings and another generation of young men dead, whether Rome won or lost. The current war along the Danuvius meant nothing, other than fixing Rome's attention there unless Haddon drew their notice. That had been the whole intent of the agreement with Decebalus.

Ranvig stood, signaling the end of council, despite Haddon's objection. Haddon was not chieftain in the Free Lands. "The Mayfires are laid and ready to be lit," he said, listening to the merrymaking that had begun outside the hall. When Barden had made the offerings to Wuotan and to Freya and lit the great bonfires, his people would drive their cattle through the embers to make them fruitful, and the beer barrels would be opened. Let Haddon get drunk on Mayfire beer and go home with a sore head. The Roman emperor had got one victory in Germany to please his Senate and demonstrate his power. It was important that he not think he needed another.

VIII

Further Family Matters

The emperor's army left Rome with a flourish of trumpets, the splendidly armored Prefect Cornelius Fuscus at the head of the Praetorian Guard – almost but not quite as splendid as Domitian himself. The streets were lined with people hoping to catch a glimpse of the emperor or the generals in their gilded armor.

Julius Frontinus accompanied the emperor as chief of engineers, summoned from his proconsul's post in Ephesus, along with Cornelius Nigrinus, a lanky fair-haired man brought from Gallia Aquitania to be the new governor of Moesia. Flavius rode with them, as did his brother-in-law, on whom he kept a wary eye.

The Praetorian Guard cohorts followed smartly, ahead of the baggage train of hospital wagons, grain stores, armorers' supplies, and the officers' possessions. Behind the army trailed the draft of cavalry ponies from Appius's stables, marked with the estate brand and now with a fresh one denoting their army service and acquisition in the reign of Domitian.

The emperor's Praetorian troops would be joined on the other side of the Adriatic by two full legions supported by detachments of auxiliaries. Couriers, moving faster than the army, brought the Danuvius commanders the news, and Correus a letter from Flavius, who had wangled a spot for it in the imperial bag.

> *I hope the couriers bring welcome news. We are on the march and will join with the Fourth Flavia in Dalmatia and the Fifth Alaudae from the Rhenus, along with auxiliaries from the ends of the earth, which is to say Britain, and*

some German detachments. Cornelius Fuscus is champing at his bit to drive the Dacians into the Danuvius and brings the men to do it. We have most of the Praetorian Guard with us as well. I believe the Flavia is to be posted to Singidunum, at least to begin with.

I should warn you that Lucius Paulinus is also loose among us. The emperor has appointed him to write an account of the campaign. I do not question the wisdom of the emperor, but you know Lucius. He is one of those who always keeps a second set of books. Since you have already thrown him out of your command once, you may wish to alert the legate of the Flavia.

The family and household are generally well. Your horrible brat Julius is very popular in the City just now, particularly among women with time on their hands – Livilla Drusa Minor, for instance, who regards him as some sort of animated toy. On the other hand, he won me a great deal of money at the races.

I saw Ygerna and the children the night before I left, and they are all well. The tutor that Julius Frontinus found, whose name is Loukas, appears to be ideal. He and Felix speak Greek exclusively and build things out of rocks in the garden and then knock them down with a miniature stone-thrower they built, and thus Felix learns mathematics and geometry because the tutor makes him do all the calculations. He appears not to think that he's actually going to school.

Ygerna, on the other hand, would probably be on a horse and over the fence if she thought she could get away with it. She and your mother are not an ideal combination. I don't know what Father is planning and I hadn't the temerity to ask, but frankly your wife is holding the household together and when she joins you on the frontier, Father will have to do something. Your mother has lorded it over Philippos and Niarchos too long for them to be able to get a grip on her

now, and I can't imagine Father finding a new housekeeper
who could either, unless she is half gorgon.

Correus noted that he didn't mention the possibility of Aemelia coping with the situation in Antonia's stead. Or mention Aemelia at all. Their marriage was clearly still unhappy. Anyone else might have divorced her, for the lack of an heir and for objecting to his affairs, but Flavius was apparently not a man inclined to blame his wife for his own stupidity.

Correus tucked the letter into his desk in the Singidunum Principia, which he supposed he would shortly be sharing with the legate of the Fourth Flavia. The particularly interesting news, aside from the desperately needed reinforcements, was the appointment of Cornelius Fuscus to lead them. Prefects of the Praetorian Guard always came from the ranks of the equites, but generally legionary commands, much less the generalship of an army, went only to men of senatorial rank. That Fuscus was an eques was a sign that promotion for Correus might sidestep that requirement as well, as it had for his father. Aside from the prohibitive cost of senatorial status, freedmen were not admitted to the Senate's ranks, a fact that Correus had long known was going to be a stone in his shoe.

–

The legate of the Fourth, Aurelius Decius, proved to be a youngish career man, not unlike Correus, with the red hair of the Gaulish province of his birth. He brought with him a welcome draft of replacements for the Ala Dardanorum and a willingness to divide the Praetorium quarters and the Principia offices between them without pulling rank.

"We'll be off on the emperor's road crews soon enough anyway," he said, pulling his helmet off. "As soon as everyone stops vomiting." The weather had been rough and the river choppy. Like most infantry, the Fourth would have preferred to walk, but the river was faster and most of the Danuvius fleet had been sent upriver to aid in transport down the Savus to Singidunum and then along the Danuvius to Ratiaria, where the Alaudae would be based.

"We're to push east as far as the river road goes, and hold that while it's extended," Decius said, "at least as far as Oescus. General Fuscus wants control of the riverbank itself. The emperor is settled in Naissus, or will be, while that's done. Your brother is with him, I believe."

"He's on the emperor's staff," Correus said. "What are our chances of getting some of the civilians in Naissus and Horreum Margi back to their farms? The land is going to ruin and they're eating us out of everything edible."

"Between here and Oescus, good. We'll be starting from both ends. Downriver of that, no."

"I'm taking a patrol out tomorrow," Correus said. "We go south to Horreum and Naissus, and east as far as Viminacium on a regular route. General Fuscus may change that, but we'll stick with current orders until he does. I'll see which of the refugees there we might send home."

—

At Naissus, Correus found that Flavius had already begun to wade through sorting out the displaced. He sat at a camp desk under the cavernous roof of the basilica amid sacks of grain and stacked amphorae of oil, a sheaf of rosters spread in front of him. Everyone, from entire families to cloth merchants, drovers, uprooted civil magistrates, and a madam with three of her bedraggled charges, stood in line to tell him where they had been evacuated from, and be assigned to a group under escort or told to wait at Naissus and given a dole of grain and oil.

Flavius looked up when he saw Correus. "This is in hand now," he told the junior tribune at the desk beside him. "Just make sure everyone has a chit that says where they're being sent and that they don't lose it. I'm going to take a report on Horreum Margi and give my brother a decent lunch."

He put an arm around Correus's shoulders and edged him through the crowd. "Actually, Lucius is going to give us a decent lunch. It's fortuitous that you're here. I want you to look sternly at him. Did you get my letter?"

"I did. What is he up to?"

"Just general information gathering. You know Lucius. But the problem is that he gathers everything."

"The emperor wishes him to write a history of the campaign?"

"An official history, if you understand me."

Correus did. An official history would be flattering to Domitian, and to his generals only to such an extent as did not quite match that accorded to Domitian. And it would not contain the sort of thoroughly factual account that was Lucius Paulinus's specialty. Correus made a point of giving Flavius his update on the Horreum Margi refugees before they found Paulinus, inhabiting a tent that was nearly as palatial as Domitian's, and attended by Tullius, who was cooking an omelet on a camp stove.

"Correus!" Paulinus bounced up at the sight of him. "Tullius, get a third plate and expand that omelet, please. You're a welcome sight. Your sister sends her love and a kiss which I shan't deliver personally but you can imagine it."

"That will be quite sufficient," Correus said. He gave the tent an appreciative inspection. Besides a wooden floor and a folding camp bed of luxurious proportions, it included a desk with recesses for an inkwell and blotting sand, collapsible shelves for scrolls, lamps and braziers on folding legs, and five trunks. "How *do* you survive in these primitive conditions?" he asked.

Paulinus grinned. "It serves. We may be moving about a bit, so it doesn't pay to rent a house. In any case, the emperor and his gilded staff have commandeered all the good ones."

"You are *not* to move about a bit," Flavius informed him.

"Have a drink," Paulinus said. "They brew very good beer here."

"How is Julia?" Correus asked. He settled in a chair and took his helmet off while Tullius went round with cups and a pitcher. "She must be nearly due."

"Indeed. We packed up the current children and sent everyone off with three nurses and her maid to stay with your father. Aemelia and Appia were already in residence with their various necessities."

Correus envisioned that. "And Ygerna's there with three more children. Father must be ready to rejoin the army."

"I suspect so, yes."

"The children aren't the problem," Flavius said, digging into the omelet that Tullius presented, "as you well know. Father likes children, and when he doesn't, they have half a dozen nurses between them."

"I suppose you mean the problem is Mother," Correus said. "I can't do anything about her, particularly not at this distance. And you said yourself that you don't know what's in Father's head."

"I know what ought to be," Flavius said. "He ought to free her, settle some money on her, and turn her over to you."

Correus folded the omelet with his spoon and fingers and took a bite. "On the frontier," he commented. "With my wife."

"In Rome," Paulinus suggested. "In a nice house. Julia could manage your father's staff for him if she didn't butt heads with Helva like a pair of goats."

"She would be in debt or some other trouble in a month," Correus said flatly. "You know it, I know it, and Father knows it. That's why he hasn't done it."

"Then it's rather up to you now, isn't it?" Flavius said.

Correus glared at him.

"Father made this mess," Flavius said, "but you're the product, so it does fall into your lap. It hasn't been a bad thing for you, all in all."

"Why yes, I could have grown up in a mud hut in Gallia Belgica," Correus said. "How charming of you to point it out." He swallowed another bite of omelet, not quite annoyed enough to turn down Tullius's cooking.

"That was *not* my point," Flavius said, sounding exasperated. "But she is your mother and her status now is the direct result of our father's actions on your behalf."

"He does have a point," Paulinus said. "Tullius, bring us some more beer. We need to get the prefect drunk enough to see reason."

Tullius, who had been studiously pretending not to eavesdrop, grinned and produced the pitcher.

"Look, brother," Paulinus said, an affectionate term he employed so rarely that it caught Correus's ear. "Remember your Freita."

Correus winced.

"I'm not saying the circumstances are the same, but think of her when you think of your mother. What options did either of them have but to do what the man who bought them wanted? You wanted a wife, as it happened. Your father—"

"Wanted a lovely amusement," Correus said. "Yes. And my mother was admirably suited for that. Freita would have stuck a knife in him."

Flavius snorted with laughter and Correus grinned at him, grudgingly.

"I haven't cared for Helva," Flavius said carefully, which was an understatement, "because of the insult to *my* mother. But… Lucius is right. I've seen it when I've been there. I don't think Father goes to her bed anymore, possibly out of respect for Mother, a thought that might have occurred to him while she was alive. Still, your mother's place in the world is gone now, and she can't step into a new one in Father's house."

Correus groaned. "Do you expect me to bring her out to the frontier?"

"No," Flavius said. "Although it would enliven things. But after this campaign the chances are excellent that you will have a posting that would allow two households. That's your answer, I think. I'd hold out with Father for financing that."

Correus looked at his brother suspiciously. "I wouldn't put it past you to put in the fix with the emperor for a promotion, just to saddle me with my mother."

"Certainly not," Flavius said piously. "He wouldn't do it anyway. But you're ready to move up a rung in the natural way of things."

Correus picked up his helmet. "Tell Father, since you have access to faster post than I do, that if he is even contemplating sending Mother out here, I will resign my commission and go raise goats in Dalmatia." He jammed the helmet on his head and fastened the chin strap.

It wasn't until he was astride Briseis and riding past the city gates that he remembered that Flavius had somehow forgotten his pretext of having Correus speak sternly to Lucius Paulinus. And he was going to have a headache from Lucius's beer.

–

A great part of the newly arrived legionary cohorts had been put to work on the road crews under Julius Frontinus, and they had pushed the unfinished Danuvius road along the gorges nearly as far east as Ratiaria, wide enough for a column three abreast to skirt the cliffs above the churning water. In places where the stone dropped sheer to the river's edge, they were cutting a ledge from the living rock when possible, and when not, a wooden road was being built, supported by timbers cut from the cliff above and driven into the face. Correus's ala, among others, got orders to guard them as well as to patrol the finished sections and the older roads that ran south of the Danuvius forts. Having built far more miles of road in Germany than he had cared for, and that at least on flat ground, Correus had no regrets at the moment for a cavalry command. Eyeing the trees that clung to the cliff face like spiders above and the river frothing over the fanged rocks below him was bad enough.

He had halted the column for a rest where the unfinished road ended when he saw the unmistakable figure of Julius Frontinus, a sheaf of papyrus plans in one hand, striding along the clifftop. An engineer with a plumb line stood on the precipice consulting his calculations on a hand abacus, and another in a boat moored to the rock at the water line signaled back, running his messages up a pulley to the clifftop. The rock road ended a few feet away and was apparently to be continued with wood over a particularly tricky bit. Correus signaled to the decurions of the patrol column to turn about and eat their midday meal where they didn't have to think about what would happen if a high wind came up. He halted Briseis where the road came to a precipitous end in the lee of the cliff, and watched Julius Frontinus putting on a leather harness while his petrified engineers protested.

"General, we'll send one of the men down there!"

"Nonsense. I want to look at that rock." Frontinus buckled the harness about his spare middle and pulled on the fasteners to test them. A line of hemp rope was knotted to both shoulders and he tested that too.

"General—"

"You'll give the emperor a seizure if he sees you do that," Correus called up to him. Frontinus peered over the cliff edge.

"An excellent thing that the emperor is in Naissus then," he shouted back. "He'll have a seizure if the road gives way under his column too. Julianus, is that you? Wait there."

A crew of soldiers suspended by their own harnesses had begun work with drills and wedges on the rock face ten feet above the water where the road ended. They stopped and gaped as their general began to descend, belayed by a pair of terrified assistants on the clifftop.

Correus watched while Frontinus dropped slowly past his crew, narrowly avoiding a suspended platform full of tools, and hung against the cliff. "Set me down for a minute!" he shouted up and pointed at Correus. His assistants edged gingerly along the cliff face and set him on his feet at Briseis's head. Correus slid out of the saddle.

"I want to talk to you."

"I could have come to your headquarters," Correus said. "Sir."

"This was fortuitous," Frontinus said. "Saves time." He adjusted the harness where it had pinched him in the descent.

"You spent a winter in a pirates' camp playing Wisdom with Ranvig of the Semnones, as I recall."

"I didn't know who he was at the time, but yes," Correus said. "What's he like?"

Correus thought. "Clever. Capable of playing a very long game… I liked him," he admitted. "Why do you ask?"

"I hear things out of Germany," Frontinus said.

He would, of course. Julius Frontinus had excellent ears and heard things that were indistinguishable whispers to most people.

"I did wonder if he might have outfoxed us with that mass of troops we didn't know he had at the end of the last war," Correus said slowly. "When trouble started up out here, I started thinking that maybe he *didn't* actually have them. If they were Dacians, on loan so to speak, for the look of the thing, then he might owe Decebalus something."

"Like fomenting trouble on the Rhenus?"

"Yes. Does that seem far-fetched?"

"I don't know," Frontinus said. "The emperor thinks so. We settled the Semnones fairly thoroughly in the last war and he celebrated a triumph."

And would not like it if that war had not been as successful as proclaimed. No one needed to say that out loud.

"Something is bubbling there, I think," Frontinus said. "Probably best not to suggest the Semnones just now, if you could keep that under your helmet, but thank you for the consultation." He tugged on the line and Correus took that as a dismissal. "Give your wife my regards," he said as he rose from the road and began to maneuver his way to the work site. "She's a woman who'll be an asset as the commander's lady. Bring her out here when we've settled Decebalus."

—

Duras lifted the crown from his temples. It was old, heavy, ugly, and worn only on state occasions. Legend said that it had been Burebista's, but that was more than a hundred years ago. At any rate it hurt his head, a fact that he was philosophical enough to consider metaphorically as well as literally. No doubt it would pain Decebalus eventually.

The Great Hall of Sarmizegetusa was bright with the banners of the allied princes, gleaming in the thin sun that made its way through the high oblong windows. Outside, a warm spell melted the scattered snow.

Duras rose from his throne and the assembled lords watched as Decebalus knelt before him. Decebalus wore a coat of gilded scale over a cerulean tunic worked with gold and scarlet thread, and scarlet trousers. His arms and throat were heavy with gold jewelry. His head was bare.

"There comes a time," Duras said quietly and they strained to hear him, "when the world stands on the edge of new things. We have the army to drive the Romans from the southern lands across the Ister and take them for ourselves. The king must ride at their head."

There was a murmur of agreement from the lords. Keeping the assembled armies together required a strong hand. The king of the Getae, for one, had been bound to the pact only by the assurance that Decebalus would wear the crown.

Decebalus bent his head and felt the weight of it settle on him. It had been a near thing. He had beaten Ziais black and blue everywhere that it wouldn't show, but that would not grow her hair back. Gudila had nearly reneged. To cut a woman's hair meant that she was disgraced, unfaithful or promiscuous.

Decebalus had dragged her into Gudila's presence once he had beaten her. "My sister has been very foolish," he said. "I have disciplined her. Once you are married you may do it again."

"Whore!" Gudila glared furiously at Ziais's ragged hair hanging barely below her ears. "I will not marry a whore."

"She did it herself," Decebalus said.

"Whore," Gudila said again. "I am to marry this in front of all the lords? My own chieftains? In front of everyone who will say I am cuckold from the start?"

"She will be veiled."

Gudila spat.

"Afterward you can lock her up until it grows out."

"And you, prince? If you cannot command your sister, am I to believe you can command an army?" Gudila's face compressed in a sneer.

He did look like a pig, Decebalus thought. He pushed Ziais, who had stood stone-faced while they argued, down on her knees in front of Gudila.

"And the king your father has yet to abdicate," Gudila said. "I will take my share of the treasure and go home to find a wife."

"Don't look at her hair," Decebalus suggested. "Just at the rest of her." He yanked Ziais's gown off her shoulders, leaving her bare-breasted, and watched Gudila waver. "Stand up!" He hauled her to her feet, tore the gown the rest of the way off and held her arms behind her back to keep her from covering herself. "There. I have shamed her for you. She won't misbehave again." He let go of her and she collapsed on the floor in the shreds of her clothing, hands over her breasts.

Gudila considered her, arms folded.

"With no marriage, we have no kinship between us," Decebalus suggested. "You would be as the other lords." That would matter more than Ziais's beauty. There were other beautiful women, more easily acquired.

"When you are king then," Gudila had said. "I do not trust you."

And now he was king. Decebalus kissed his father's hand, rose, and sat down in the massive ceremonial chair, his now. Duras took the lesser seat beside him.

"We will feast tonight," Decebalus announced, "when we seal our confederation at the marriage of my sister Ziais to Gudila, king of the Getae, uniting two great kingdoms." He stared at Gudila, daring him to renege again here, publicly.

Gudila nodded back. The alliance would entitle him to a larger share of loot and command of part of the army. It was worth taking a troublesome woman for that.

Ziais's maid hovered beside her, the wedding clothes over her arm. "They will come for you soon, Lady. You must dress."

Ziais stared into her reflection in the mirror on her dressing table. The oil lamp beside it was smoking, making her face waver in the silver surface. It was Roman workmanship – there were some trade routes that wars could rarely interrupt – with a stand in the figure of Leda embracing the swan. Its beak was ugly, prodding. That tale had always frightened her.

"Very well." She rose and let the maid slip her undertunic over her head to replace it with a finer one, and then the layers of gown and undergown, pale silk and linen and fine wool, heavy with gold embroidery. She worked her hands obediently through the multiple spiraling loops of six gold bracelets with dragons' heads for finials and stood still while the maid dropped the great gold and carnelian necklace that was her bride gift from Gudila over her shorn head.

"Where is my lapis necklace?"

"In your jewelry box, Lady." The maid looked uneasy. "Your brother is going to be angry if you don't wear this one." *And he will beat me for it* didn't need to be said.

"Fetch me the box."

The maid brought it and Ziais extracted the lapis necklace and the small pair of pliers kept for repairing such bits as unfastened themselves from necklaces and ear drops. She took the gold figure of the Goddess off the lapis necklace and strung it on the one around her neck. "There. And my garnet earrings, please."

Relieved, the maid found the earrings and threaded them through Ziais's ears. She hesitated. "Your hair, Lady." An unmarried woman wore her hair down her back, often even at her wedding, but there was the difficulty of Ziais's impetuous shearing. The scandal of that and her subsequent beating by Decebalus had made its way through the palace. Her husband would be dangerously angry if he was shamed by a public showing of her cropped head.

"I am to be veiled," Ziais said stonily.

The maid pinned a coif tightly over her ragged hair and then a veil that hung below her waist. A second veil of thin silk draped her face and swept the floor. It was a shame, Ziais thought, that her features could still be seen. There were tales of men who had married demons unaware. She would have liked to make Gudila wonder.

The marriage that would unite the royal houses of Sarmizegetusa and its allies with the kingdom of the Getae would be sanctified in the Great Temple on the lower level of the terraced mountain. The bridal party made its way, preceded by trumpets and banners, down the switchback road on carpets spread to keep the thawing snow and mud from their feet. The bride rode in a litter, its curtained panels painted with flower-garlanded horses, symbols of hoped-for fertility, and Decebalus marched alongside, guardian of his sister until she should be given to the bridegroom. Her sister and maids walked on the other side. Rescuturme could see Ziais's profile through the curtain, backlit by the rising sun, chin up and rigid with fury.

At the sun disk in the Temple Court they paused, and Ziais stepped from the litter to pray to the Lord of the Universe, magically born in the old days of the Mother and the Horseman. Vezinas raised his staff and Gudila came up through the lower court, dressed in red on a great white stallion, as the Horseman had once come to claim the Mother.

Decebalus thought Gudila looked as if his temper had cooled only somewhat since the day before. This form of marriage could not be undone for anything except death and was used by the great families to seal an alliance. Even so, Gudila had not wanted to consent to it. But it was impossible to refuse without starting a brawl, and likely a war, and he had not objected with more than a black look when the bride's brother and father had led him to the horse and given him the cape of horsehide and tails that hung over his shoulders.

Decebalus took Ziais by the arm, his fingers biting into her flesh, and led her to meet Gudila as he dismounted at the steps of the Great Temple. The Getae king had bathed and his beard was clean, but the horsehide cape was ancient and smelled of death. In the darkness of the temple, the air was thick with incense and the musty scent of old hangings.

Decebalus pinched her arm again as she climbed the steps, a reminder to watch her manners. Ziais saw her father a few paces away and closed her eyes. Not one of them had ever seen her as more than a bargaining chip, just as her mother, dead these ten years, had been. Unmarried, she had wielded a good deal of power. Now, none. She opened her eyes and went up the last step.

Mother, let me be ill luck for him.

–

In the morning, Ziais watched the allied lords ride out again with their retinues, Decebalus and Gudila at their head. She stood at the window in the bedchamber to which Gudila had taken her the night before. Gudila had been staggering drunk, but had nonetheless done what he felt like to Ziais and none of her prayers and offerings had stopped him, while in the palace halls below the visiting lords had also eaten and drunk and sung and forced themselves on any serving girl who couldn't hide.

In the morning her maid had sent the bloody sheet to the priests for the proof that Gudila demanded be made public. He had made sure there would be enough blood.

Ziais fingered the gold figure of the Goddess where it lay amid the jumble of her clothes and jewelry that the maid had picked up from the floor where Ziais had sat weeping. "I gave you my hair, Mother," she whispered.

–

Decebalus watched Gudila out of the corner of his eye as they rode down the switchback road past the glow of the ironworks. He looked like a man who had enjoyed himself, although he supposed Ziais hadn't. Decebalus shrugged. That was the fate of women as the gods ordained it, just as the gods had ordained that he was going to be king, and he was.

Now they would cross the Ister on its lower reaches where the Dacian army controlled the territory and rejoin Diegis. Scouts reported that the Roman emperor had arrived in Naissus.

"Offer him a truce," Decebalus told his brother when their boats had brought the last of the lords and their escorts across, and he had inspected the camp where Diegis had consolidated their army while the Romans reinforced theirs.

"What?" Diegis stared at him.

"This is why I am king and you are not," Decebalus informed him. He lifted each foot for a slave to remove his boots. "You will see all you can of their camp. And take some measure of this emperor. Bring me a report that covers more than his answer, which I already know."

"Me? Why does not the king go, exalted as he is, to frighten the Roman emperor?" Diegis inquired.

The slave presented a clean pair of shoes and knelt again to lace them. "Because I have no intention of putting my exalted personage in their hands," Decebalus said. "They won't want you."

"And if they do?" Diegis asked.

"They won't. They know I won't ransom you."

Diegis laughed. "Their spies will have told them that already, I expect. Why not send Gudila?"

"Because you are cleverer than Gudila, I don't trust Gudila, and Gudila is not my brother. I'm not going to give him the opportunity to strike some bargain of his own. He is not expendable until our sister has given him a son."

"Very well, I will go and insult the Roman emperor for you." Diegis rose lazily from his chair and grinned at his brother. "The crown has given you a big head."

IX

The Envoy

Domitian assembled his generals and advisers at his campaign headquarters in Naissus, an elaborate villa selected by Flavius and commandeered from its owner, a wine merchant who had been happy to take the cash and go elsewhere, where there no Dacians.

"A truce," Domitian said thoughtfully, tapping the gilded silver cuirass that was his accustomed uniform when in command of the army. A military cloak in deep imperial purple hung from the back of his chair. "Do any of you believe it?"

Cornelius Fuscus snorted. "If I thought I saw the ghost of Alexander riding a goat through the marketplace, I would be more likely to believe in that."

Cornelius Nigrinus, the new governor of Moesia, nodded. "He is sounding us out, in my opinion, Caesar." He paused. "Still, it could be useful to see what terms he offers."

"Agreed," Julius Frontinus said. He had come to Naissus from the Danuvius road particularly to put his oar in, in case anyone lost their head sufficiently to trust Decebalus, or to refuse to meet. He considered that either would be a mistake. "I would advise meeting with him to see what we can pick up. They'll be trying to pick up what they can from us, of course," he added. "That's always the trade. I suggest a skilled translator."

–

"And you just happened to mention me to him," Correus said crossly to Flavius, "and that I've been here long enough to pick up the language." The Thracian dialect spoken by the civilians of Moesia and Correus's Moesian cavalry troopers was not much different from that of the Dacians except in accent.

"You've always been the one who got languages," Flavius said. "You could seduce the kitchen girls in six different ones. The emperor wants an interpreter he knows. You were invaluable in Germany. He said so. So did Julius Frontinus."

"Kind of him. Where is Lucius, incidentally?"

"Hanging about court, writing flattering passages of imperial accomplishments. Exactly what he's supposed to be doing, for a change."

"So far as we know."

Flavius looked as if Lucius gave him a headache. However, their brother-in-law appeared biddable at the moment, and Correus noted him the next day with Tullius at his side among the civilians of Naissus come to get a look at the Dacian envoy. The envoy and his retinue rode into the city on the military road that swung southeast from Ratiaria, given a safe passage by the Fifth Macedonica's garrison at Oescus. A detachment of their cavalry accompanied the Dacians on their way.

There were a hundred of them, led by a mailed and helmeted vanguard, and they came at a near gallop, green and scarlet dragon banners shrieking in the wind of their passage. They were armed, as befitted a royal delegation, and Correus eyed the long falx blades at their belts with respect. The envoy, Diegis, brother of the new king, rode just behind the vanguard in a fishscale hauberk gilded to reflect the sun in impressive fashion, and a peaked helmet that mimicked the shape of his retinue's caps. He wore a heavy gold torque around his neck and gold bracelets halfway up his arms. His cloak, thrown back about his shoulders, was of the heavy fur that winters in his home mountains bred, as were his boots, into which were tucked scarlet breeches. His white horse was as elaborately caparisoned as he, with gold embroidered saddle trappings and a bridle of scarlet leather and gold fittings.

The column slowed as they approached the first pickets outside the city gates and passed at a walk between the honor guard of

Praetorians lining the street. The Praetorians also served to keep the populace from getting too near the Dacians, and a civilian refugee of the burned lands to the east, who was armed with a rock, was stopped from throwing it just in time.

The prince and his high officers were to be housed in the best inn in the city, from which everyone else had been ruthlessly shifted. The Dacian warriors accompanying them had been assigned quarters in civilian houses within the city walls, and Flavius had been delegated to calm their terrified or furious owners with sufficient silver and the emperor's good wishes, the implication being that refusal would entail the emperor's bad wishes.

The emperor was not present, of course. Flavius was assigned to greet the prince with Correus beside him to interpret. That Domitian had sent his staff officer and not his general could be taken any way the Dacians cared to.

"The Emperor Titus Flavius Caesar Domitianus Augustus extends his greetings to the Prince of Dacia," Correus announced. "The Centurion Flavius Appius Julianus conveys them for him." He nodded at Flavius.

Diegis regarded Flavius politely. "I read Latin rather better than I speak it," he said, in Latin. "So an interpreter is welcome. Also, I have brought my own." He motioned and a slight, black-haired man in a Dacian cap and plain tunic dismounted and came to stand stiffly beside him. He eyed Correus and Flavius uneasily and his eyes fell once to Flavius's hands. "Natoporus will attend our councils with me. Just in case there are nuances of speech that I might miss."

"Very wise," Correus said. He inspected Diegis with interest. He was Decebalus's younger brother, reputed to be both brave and a hothead, and his name in Dacian meant "Shining" or "Burning." That was something to remember. Also a man who read Latin. *These are not barbarians*, he thought. *We must remember that.*

Diegis looked curiously from Correus to Flavius. "You are kin?" he asked.

"Brothers," Correus said. "I am Correus Appius Julianus." He wondered why Diegis wished to know. Perhaps just idle curiosity, as they were so alike. But another thing to note: Diegis actually looked at people and not merely their trappings.

"Allow us to show you your quarters," Flavius said. "If you will leave your men here for the moment, we will escort them once you and your officers have been housed."

Diegis nodded and signaled to his commander. The black-haired interpreter remounted and followed the prince. Correus noted his plain tunic and brown breeches again. The man must be educated if he was to interpret Latin, but he was plainly of lesser rank. Maybe a slave, but Correus wondered. There was something in his stride and his carriage that was familiar. He thought it over, wondering if Flavius had noticed, while they settled Diegis and his retinue at the inn.

Diegis inspected the furnishings with a raised eyebrow. "This is how the emperor of Rome lives?"

"The emperor of Rome lives in a palace," Flavius said. "I am sure that of your brother the king is its equal. However, this city has seen severe damage of late and this is the best we have available to offer the king's emissary."

"Ah." Diegis nodded. "If I were a soothsayer, I would have given orders to leave a few good houses standing."

–

"I don't imagine there's the slightest chance of this not coming to war," Flavius said when they had departed, leaving Diegis ordering beer and dinner for which the emperor would no doubt pay. "They killed a military governor. They must know that's not going to be overlooked."

"It might be if they offered complete surrender," Correus said. "But that's not what they're offering or I'll forfeit a year's pay. They're sizing us up."

"Of course they are," Flavius said. "Cocky bastard, too. Come and have a cup of wine with me. I've hit my tolerance for diplomacy today and you're the only person I can be rude to with impunity."

Correus laughed. "That's touching. Who has decent wine?"

"Lavinia does. And don't look like that. It's a perfectly respectable wine shop, with all other activities conducted discreetly upstairs. I expect she'll have a good deal of custom tonight from the Dacians, but if they get rough with Lavinia's girls, they'll have a knife in them. She has two monstrous bodyguards and an even more monstrous dog."

Correus noted as he followed Flavius through the streets that signs of the recent influx of refugees were beginning to recede as the ones who could go home were doing so, and the others were beginning to be absorbed into the city or the towns outside Viminacium and Ratiaria. He expected that Lavinia had been happy to see the emperor's retinue arrive. Staff officers with silver in their purses improved the local economy. Lavinia's establishment had a fresh coat of paint and a new sign above the door offering fine wines, beer, companionship, and home cooking for the homesick soldier. Even the hole under the whitewashed steps where the household snake kept his residence had a little vine-draped portico painted above it.

"Centurion Julianus!" A girl in a green tunic greeted them at the door. She had a head of improbably hennaed hair that made her look like a calendula blossom and was clearly well acquainted with Flavius.

"We'll have the rabbit stew, Merope. And a pitcher of what Lavinia passes off as Falernian."

"Will you be wanting your dinner upstairs?"

"In the dining room, please," Flavius said. "Unless...?" He glanced at Correus.

"In the dining room," Correus said firmly, but he looked around him approvingly. Lavinia's establishment reminded him of the house Rhodope had kept in Germany; a comfortable refuge in a war zone improved by a brood of friendly whores who were a pleasure to look at whether or not a man intended anything else.

He waited while Merope brought their wine and a loaf of bread with the stew. The wine was definitely not Falernian, but it wasn't bad. The bread was hot and the stew smelled appetizingly of herbs and well browned meat.

"Now then," Flavius said. "About that interpreter."

Correus looked up from his bowl. "I wondered if you'd noticed."

"He's been drilled," Flavius said. "You don't lose that once it's been knocked into you. Look at Father after all these years."

"He could have been trained by the Dacian army, I suppose. They aren't the rabble that the Germans and Britons are. They can keep formation."

"True."

"On the other hand, he doesn't have the rank I would expect of someone well-born enough to be educated in Latin, if he's a native Dacian. I'd like to hear his accent."

"And why would Diegis bring him if he's what we suspect?"

"A thumb in our eye? Or to see what he can see that Diegis might not recognize?"

"He'd better hope no one recognizes him," Flavius said.

"Are you going to mention this to the emperor?"

"I am not. It would upset the troops to commandeer the Dacian envoy's interpreter and stone him to death as a deserter. Also against the rules of treaty talks, I expect. I'd like to, though."

"So would I. Someone has built catapults for them."

"I heard that. Julius Frontinus desperately wants a firsthand look at one."

"We'll do our best. In the meantime, we'll give Diegis and his tame whatever-he-is an eyeful. The emperor wants cavalry games after the talks tomorrow. They've called my command off patrols to be the entertainment."

Flavius wiped his bowl with the last of the bread. "I'm going to report to the emperor that our royal guest is settled for the night and suggest extra troops around his quarters, and pickets at the civilian lodgings we've assigned his men."

"You think they'll make trouble?"

"No, I think our civilians will. They find it insulting to have Dacian fighters in Naissus, probably the same ones that burned their farms. Someone will see a chance at revenge. I should like to avoid that, at least until we conclude the talks. After that I doubt I'm going to care."

Correus doubted it too. Once the talks were concluded, they would be at war. The chance that they would not was approximately the size of Lavinia's wine cups.

Preliminary negotiations were conducted the following morning in the basilica of Naissus. The Emperor Domitian received the Dacian envoy from a gilded chair in the Hall of Justice, draped in imperial purple, his thick hair crowned with a gold wreath. The marble floor was strewn with roses, the walls had been freshly painted for the occasion with scarlet panels, and the column capitals newly gilded. The emperor's staff officers and interpreter stood beside him, his Praetorians behind, plumed and polished. Their commander, Cornelius Fuscus, in parade armor and a scarlet sash, occupied a seat to the right of the emperor next to Cornelius Nigrinus.

Correus eyed Fuscus with interest. Fuscus had supported Galba and then Vespasian during the civil wars of the year of Four Emperors and come out alive. He had also refused senatorial rank and done very well without its attendant complications and expenses. He was nearing forty, his hair only starting to recede, a stocky man with a muscular body beginning to go a bit soft with age and residence in Rome.

Diegis, sitting opposite the emperor in a chair not quite as ornate as Domitian's but rather more so than Fuscus's, appeared unimpressed with the show of finery. Correus noted that he was eyeing not the emperor but his general. The black-haired interpreter, Natoporus, stood stiffly beside him and cast a wary glance at Correus.

Proceedings began with an exchange of gifts, in accordance with the pretense that this was a meeting of friendly powers. Diegis presented Domitian with a falx in a scabbard of brilliant blue leather, its hilt finely worked in gold and so ornate as to be unusable. Domitian offered Diegis, in proxy for his brother, an antique bronze vase of considerable value and ancient Greek workmanship. An unusable sword and a reminder of the extent of Rome's empire: the language of diplomacy was not necessarily subtle. Correus thought both the emperor and the prince seemed amused.

The niceties observed, negotiations began with an offer from Diegis of a treaty that amounted to Rome's complete surrender and withdrawal from Moesia.

"The envoy insults Rome," Domitian said flatly, amusement vanished. Correus and the Dacian interpreter both translated, unnecessarily.

"My brother the king," Diegis observed, "at present has an army in your eastern province. This is our country, the lands along the Ister. What is Rome to come across the sea and occupy it?"

"Rome maintains the peace," Correus said, translating the emperor's response. "Where Rome dwells, there are green fields and vineyards and graze for sheep and cattle. Taxes are paid, roads are built, peace is kept. What is it like where your king's army has been?"

Diegis considered that. "No doubt the peasants do not care whose army it is. In my country they also pay their taxes."

"Then let the Dacian king go back to that country and collect his own taxes," the emperor suggested.

Diegis looked thoughtful. "It is perhaps possible that my brother the king might entertain an arrangement to coexist, as it were. I must think on that for the afternoon."

"We are encouraged if there is progress to be made," the emperor observed. "As long as it does not take too long. Rome has limited patience."

"Indeed." Diegis rose and his entourage clustered around him.

"In the meantime, the emperor invites the envoy to view an exhibition of cavalry games in the envoy's honor this afternoon," Correus said, knowing that Diegis intended no thinking whatsoever. "They are excellent entertainment."

"I shall enjoy that," Diegis said.

Correus retired to his lodging to find Decurion Blaesus already there, kitted out in sports armor, his troop horse and Briseis tethered outside and slobbering water from a pan.

"They're forming up on the parade ground," Blaesus said. "I call it a silly thing to pull them off patrol for, but I expect with the Dacian envoy here there won't be any surprise attacks. We saw you come out of the basilica. I don't suppose you've negotiated a peace?"

"Far from it." Eumenes handed Correus a bowl of stew and he wolfed it down. "We're to provide the envoy with a demonstration that should encourage him to rethink things, although I don't suppose it will."

"It will make the emperor happy," Blaesus said. "That part's important."

The cavalry games were demonstrations of skill, and rehearsing for them kept cavalry entertained as well as disciplined. Correus, a little self-consciously, had always loved them. The ala put away their regular armor and brought out the special sports armor that covered both horse and rider: silvered helmets with human faces and molded curls, crested with floating feathers, gold and silver greaves, and shields painted with scenes from famous battles. The troop horses wore red leather bridles with gilded eyeguards and polished scale that covered breast and flanks, fitted with silver trappings. Each team carried standards with long, bright snakes' tails, and wooden spears wrapped with the team colors.

Correus suited up Briseis and told her how elegant she looked when she gave her head a disgruntled shake. He settled his helmet on his own head, grateful that the sun was behind clouds at the moment. The game helmets were full-face. It was like putting an iron bowl on his head, with only the eye holes for an opening.

The Naissus arena had been fitted up with the purple and gold banners of the emperor and a special box from which Domitian and his diplomatic visitors might watch the show. The ostensible object was to score a hit on the opposing team with the brightly wrapped spears, but it was the perfect precision of the charge that really mattered, the columns interweaving at full gallop, snakes' tails flying. A visual reminder to Diegis, brother of Decebalus, of what Roman cavalry could do.

The yellow team thundered down the arena sand with Correus happily at their head, reveling in the skill required, a welcome change from the tangled negotiations of the treaty council. The yellow columns wove through the blue team's lines in precise formation, tapping each other's wooden shields with the light-weight lances, wheeling and coming around again in a different pattern. It was almost impossible to see anything through the helmet but the horse in front, but Correus hoped that Diegis was getting an eyeful. It was a simulacrum of war, a carving on a triumphal arch, but it carried the reality of Rome's might behind it: *Thus we play at war, and you will see what happens when we turn to it in earnest.*

At the end, the ala lined up before Domitian's reviewing stand to dip their lances to the emperor. Correus and Blaesus pulled off their helmets and rode forward out of the ranks to receive the emperor's laurel wreaths on the ends of their spears.

Diegis laughed as they saluted and said something over his shoulder to Natoporus, who was stationed, somewhat uneasily, Correus thought, behind him, next to Flavius. Natoporus did not translate.

–

"All the same, he was impressed," Flavius said, hiding in Correus's lodging from any further official duties. The Ala Dardanorum had returned to patrol under Blaesus, leaving its prefect to cool his heels in Naissus. "He went on digging at Domitian about our cavalry being trick riders from the circus, and Domitian just smiled. Diegis got an eyeful of what we can do. It won't change his mind, of course."

"Did you get any further impression of that interpreter?"

"I did. Diegis doesn't need him, or you, despite what he says. I think our Natoporus, and that's not his name, is here to see what he can see. Specialized knowledge about what to look for, as you suggested."

"I rather think Natoporus is a marked man if we find him in the field."

"I imagine you're unlikely to," Lucius Paulinus said, appearing in the doorway and dropping into a chair beside Flavius. "He won't risk a good spy."

"And I presume you know one when you see one," Correus murmured.

Paulinus looked insulted. "I know a diplomatic game of latrunculi when I see one. I am the oracle. Heed me." He rolled his eyes back in his head and mimed a trance. "Three days. Three days will the envoy remain, becoming ever more annoying, until the emperor has lost his patience or has heard from Julius Frontinus that the roads are now adequate for his purposes."

"The purposes being to send the envoy back across the Danuvius with a flea in his ear and General Fuscus's boot in his behind," Correus said. "I shall enjoy that."

–

In the meantime, there was diplomatic latrunculi to be played, in which the emperor pretended to think that the prince might withdraw his brother's army, and the prince pretended to think that Rome might do the same, if only an agreement could be reached.

The interpreters translated each offer and counteroffer while Paulinus took notes from his place among the emperor's scribes, and his prediction proved correct. On the third day, Diegis seemed to have learned whatever it was that he wanted and offered his final terms: Rome might remain in possession of the lands south of the Danuvius in exchange for the payment of an enormous, insulting sum. Decebalus, king of Dacia, would withdraw his army upon its receipt.

Domitian's face reddened. Correus could see him stiffen with rage. General Fuscus shifted slightly in his chair. Flavius whispered in the emperor's ear.

"The envoy of Decebalus has wasted Rome's time long enough," Domitian said finally.

The Dacian interpreter translated while Diegis looked thoughtful, as though considering this idea. "One might say that Rome has wasted my time," he commented. "And that of my brother the king."

"Rome will pay compensation to your brother the king on the Greek kalends," Domitian informed him.

Correus, translating, helpfully explained that this meant never. "The emperor says that you have an hour to remove your men from Naissus," he added.

Diegis's brows rose. "Is this how Rome addresses the envoy of a sovereign nation?"

"The envoy is fortunate that the emperor abides by protocol and does not take you hostage," Correus informed him. "One hour."

Domitian spoke again.

"There could have been peace," Correus translated. "There could have been an end to war."

Diegis stood and settled his cloak around his shoulders. "Tell your emperor, 'only the dead have seen the end of war.'"

–

The Dacian envoy left Naissus with armed riders to the front and rear despite the banner signifying that they remained under imperial protection. Correus saw the interpreter Natoporus turn in his saddle for a last look at the Roman encampment, his expression as inscrutable as the games helmets with their silver faces and blank eyes.

"That one's lucky Domitian didn't hear your opinion of him," Paulinus said as they watched the column depart. "The emperor didn't care for having a barbarian quote Plato at him, particularly not in the original Greek. He's in a temper."

"That's all the Dacians ever meant to do," Correus said. "Put Domitian in a temper. That and find out how many legions we have."

"Decebalus's spies have no doubt done that already," Paulinus said. "Let's hope it's enough to give them pause. More likely he wanted to know what shape they're in."

"So do I," Correus said. "The fighting this spring left us ragged. It's hard to integrate reinforcements into a unit that's been that badly damaged."

"The Flavia and the Alaudae came out here up to strength," Paulinus said.

"And the Italica and the Claudia got substantial reinforcements, along with the auxiliaries. It's the Macedonica I'd worry about. They took heavy losses at Oescus *and* lost their tribune. They found him later without his head. They got reinforcements but something like that hangs around a legion's neck."

"Since Domitian hasn't transferred their legate, he must think they're sound," Paulinus said. "Or Fuscus does. What does Flavius say about it? He's singularly reluctant to talk to me."

"I imagine that Flavius has been occupied in convincing Domitian that he did the right thing in not sending Decebalus's brother back to him in a sack."

"I'm not sure he did," Paulinus said. "Decebalus wouldn't have sent him if he couldn't spare him. But it would have sent a certain message."

"That kind of thing is hard to step away from and leaves a mark. Do you remember Bendigeid of the Silures?" Correus asked. "He murdered a military tribune. It didn't end well. Ask Frontinus."

"The emperor of Rome is not a British west country kinglet."

"You didn't meet Bendigeid," Correus said.

"You always talk about him as if he was something slightly other than human."

"I don't know what he was. There was some old, dark power about him. I'm not saying Domitian has it, but killing an envoy might be something that wakes that in a man. I don't know. I'm just glad he didn't."

X

Mopping Up

The army of Rome, firmly under the command of Cornelius
Fuscus, prepared to show the king of Dacia the error of his ways.
Correus's ala had been attached to the Fourth Flavia under Aurelius Decius, and multiple other cavalry units and auxiliary infantry
supported the bulk of the legionary troops. The Seventh Claudia
under Messala Cominius, the First Italica, and the damaged Fifth
Macedonica were bolstered not only by the newly arrived Fourth
but by the Fifth Alaudae and the troops of the Praetorian Guard,
both under General Fuscus. All in all, nearly fifty thousand men,
minus a handful left to garrison their base forts.

Correus, with Briseis under him and the ala's banner-bearer at
his side, watched the column move across the plain in late spring
sunlight, a great serpent of scarlet and steel, shields painted with
the legionary and auxiliary insignia. Those of the Fifth Alaudae,
the oddly named "Larks," bore a parade of five elephants in honor
of a long ago victory over a Numidian king. Their standard
rode above them, with the gilded Eagles of four other legions
interspersed along the column, and the flamboyantly uniformed
Praetorians marching under the likeness of the emperor.

Julius Frontinus rode with General Fuscus and he nodded at
Correus as the commander's entourage passed along the column.
Correus caught a glimpse of a billowing gold and purple cloak
and a gilded, purple-feathered helmet, signifying the presence of
the emperor, which meant that Flavius was there somewhere as
well.

As it marched, the column split to send a detachment down the new road to watch the riverbanks and forestall any attempt to come at them from the rear, while the rest followed the landward road. As they went, they acquired yet more troops, collecting the remaining men of the Danuvius forts as they moved east, into territory held, for the moment, by Decebalus. Decebalus had underestimated Rome, Correus thought, once Rome was sufficiently annoyed. The trick would be not to underestimate Decebalus in return.

They traveled over the same ground they had covered the last time they had met with Decebalus's army, and the battle, when it came, took much the same shape, but this time the numbers were in Rome's favor. The weather had warmed and the biting flies and mosquitoes of the marsh had come out in force, invading helmet and lorica and hauberk collar, which set every soldier's teeth on edge and put that much extra energy into his fury at the Dacians. Eumenes, stationed at the rear of the ala with Correus's spare mount, cursed them in a series of Macedonian maledictions that prompted the admiration of everyone in earshot.

Waiting for the trumpet call to move his horsemen out, Correus could see from a slight rise above the plain that the tide was flowing in their favor this time. The Dacians were pressing hard against Rome's front lines, but Rome's lines extended back and back again, past the line of scorpion catapults and the great stone-throwing onagers, to the generals on the ridge above the reserve cavalry, and back again to the emperor's camp. Each fallen man was replaced instantly by another. At a discreet signal from General Fuscus, Domitian would arrive in time to oversee the final rout of the enemy that had insulted him personally.

The cavalry trumpets sang out the Reserves Forward and Correus sent Briseis down the gentle slope at the head of the ala's wedge, their blue and gold banner waving above the bearer's head. The Dacian cavalry met their charge in disciplined ranks, fighting to push through to the Roman infantry's rear. They were spear-armed, in scale hauberks and the peaked helmets that mimicked Dacian caps, with shorter curved blades at their belts. Charge met charge on the flanks, struggling through a mass of downed men and horses, alternately falling back and surging forward. In the center the Roman infantry moved forward stubbornly in formation, sending fresh troops up through the intervals between cohorts as the front ranks tired. They pushed their way through marsh grass and bog and into higher fields where the wreckage of vineyards studded the ground with the jagged stumps of broken vines.

Correus's men forced their way through the shattered remnants of a village, tumbled stone and burned sheds still half-standing, the road through it littered with broken wagon wheels and over-turned carts and barrows, abandoned when its occupants fled. A Dacian spear ran down his left thigh and raked it open, shredding his breeches. Correus braced his own spear and thrust at the rider as the Dacian horse reared up, driven by the sword of a dismounted trooper. The Dacian cavalryman went down and Correus reached a hand down for his trooper, pulling him up behind in a shower of blood. The trooper's leg and arm were both laid open and there was a long, murderous-looking gash in his scale hauberk.

"Hold onto me!"

Correus found Eumenes trailing the rear of the ala and slid down from Briseis, who was wet and beginning to tire. He ordered the trooper into the saddle and to the surgeon's tent, and took the reins of the spare, a dark roan called Ashes, appropriated from the ala's remount pool.

"You need that seen to!" Eumenes said.

Correus inspected his thigh. The torn breeches were soaked with blood and it hurt like Hades. He wouldn't be able to keep a grip on a horse with it, but the bleeding had slowed. "Go back and collect Briseis and rub her down." He mounted Ashes, not easily, and kicked him forward into the battle, counting on balance to keep him in the saddle. Blaesus would hold the ala together but it mattered for the commander to be visible, to be at their head.

They had seen him pull the injured trooper onto Briseis, and they saw him now, his leg dripping blood and guiding Ashes by the reins, and shouted, tightening formation around him. Correus nodded to the banner-bearer and they drove forward as an unhorsed Dacian opened a gap in the lines, tumbling under the ala's hooves.

On both flanks, the Roman cavalry pushed harder against the Dacian horsemen, shields up, spears out, forming and re-forming to drive a wedge into them here, to flatten out a charge there, finding any small opening, any tiring enemy, until the momentum shifted once more, and Correus thought they had turned them. His head was swimming, but he was still astride his horse.

–

It was not an easy victory all the same, and when it came, the retreat of the Dacian army was not a rout. Flavius, at the emperor's side, watched as Dacian ships drew up to the shore from where they had been anchored in mid-current, to take the retreating ranks aboard in orderly fashion, while the cavalry and rear guard held off the pursuers until they had loaded and put out across the river. There were more ships than had been estimated by the Roman scouts. The big catapults, hastily brought forward, landed a few well-placed stones through the deck timbers, sinking a number of them and tangling the oars of more in the wreckage, but foot soldiers and cavalry both stripped off their armor and swam alongside the loaded boats, heaving the armor into the current to keep it from the Romans. They set fire to their own catapults as a parting gesture.

The emperor's army made camp well back from the boggy land near the river, laying out the grid of streets, headquarters tents, and hospital that was the same in any Roman army camp in the world, throwing up earthworks of ditch and wall in the dusk. Roman losses this time had been minimal, and while the dead were collected and listed, General Frontinus rode out to the riverbank to inspect the charred remnants of the Dacian catapults. He knelt and peered at the iron undercarriage, and felt in the ashes for scattered rivets, while his optio held his horse.

Flavius appeared at his side with a lantern. "The emperor and General Fuscus send their compliments and would like to know where in Bellona's name those catapults came from."

Frontinus stood and kicked a booted toe at the half-burned carriage. "I'm told that they may have made off with one of ours when they hit Oescus, but by the fittings and the ironwork on the wheels, I'd say these are Dacian-made." He stared thoughtfully at the remains of the trigger mechanism. "With some excellent instruction."

Flavius inspected Frontinus's handful of rivets and springs. "My brother tells me that the scouts here claim they've been recruiting our deserters," he suggested.

"No doubt they have." Frontinus put the bits of ironwork in his pouch. "It's tempting to just go over the river if you've had a bellyful of your centurion. Border posts are always trouble."

Flavius made his preliminary report to Domitian and to Cornelius Fuscus – who said briskly that Decebalus was going to be sorry about that – and was dismissed, so he went in search of Correus, and found him in his tent having his leg attended by Nicomedes. Eumenes was heating wine over a brazier.

"That looks bad. Why aren't you in the hospital?"

"Eumenes thinks I'm too important to go to the hospital and has sent for my personal physician," Correus said. He sounded as if he had had a good deal of the wine already, although he winced when Nicomedes poured vinegar into the gash.

"If the prefect will hold still, I am going to stitch this," Nicomedes said. He produced a suture needle and a fine thread of tendon.

"What I thought," Eumenes said, "was that you wouldn't get yourself seen to until every last man with a scratch on him had been seen. Sir."

"They have a light load in the hospital," Nicomedes said. He set in a stitch while Correus gritted his teeth. "We took very small losses, Aesculapius be thanked. They can spare me."

"How is Mucapor?" Correus asked between stitches. "I sent him to the rear earlier in a bad way."

"Barring an infection, he'll manage, and he'll be fit to ride again too."

Correus nodded, foggily grateful. A trooper invalided out did not have an easy life. He set his teeth again while Nicomedes put in the last stitch and smeared the length of the gash with salve. He wrapped it lightly with a clean cloth.

"You'll need to let me look at this tomorrow afternoon," the surgeon said. "If you bathe, try to keep it dry. But get in the saddle right away so it doesn't stiffen. That'll hurt," he added.

A trooper appeared with the Dead List, this time mercifully short. "You need to certify this, sir," he said to Nicomedes, and they went out together.

"That's going to make an impressive scar," Flavius said, sitting down and helping himself to the hot wine.

"Badge of the cavalryman," Correus grunted. "And kindly leave it out of any letters home. I need to write to Ygerna, but I've had too much wine to think straight."

"Put him in bed," Flavius told Eumenes, and took his leave. A Praetorian optio found him almost immediately because, of course, the emperor had thought of something else he wished him to do. Flavius sighed and turned back toward the emperor's headquarters again, a monstrous tent of imperial purple leather and gold fringe that overshadowed the Principia and the lantern-lit hospital.

Domitian had abandoned his desk and was now reclined on a couch eating dinner. Flavius thought he looked pleased, which was not necessarily a good sign. Julius Frontinus and Cornelius Nigrinus sat opposite him around an elaborate brazier and looked less pleased.

"We shall be setting out for Rome in the morning," Domitian informed Flavius. "The Praetorian Guard cohorts will accompany us. General Fuscus remains in Moesia to oversee the peace."

Frontinus looked uncomfortable, and Flavius thought there had probably been conversation about this already. Frontinus's voice carried the tone of a man giving it one more try. "Are you sure General Fuscus isn't needed in Rome, sir? Governor Nigrinus is here and our Danuvius garrisons are up to strength. There won't be any more surprises from the Dacians."

"Cornelius Fuscus feels that we need a firm hand on the military just now," Domitian said. "I should be *most* unhappy to celebrate a well-earned triumph in Rome and have the frontier unravel behind me."

"Does General Fuscus feel that is likely?" Cornelius Nigrinus asked.

"He feels vigilance is required. And possible preemptive action."

"General Fuscus has a reputation as a bold man," Frontinus said. "In all senses. Even as a bit overconfident. If I may speak frankly."

"You may not," Domitian informed him, which effectively ended the conversation. "Julianus, we wish to start in the morning. You will accompany me. Find Lucius Paulinus and tell him that he is coming too. I wish for him to spend the time we are in transit completing his account of the campaign."

–

"Lucius is gnashing his teeth," Flavius told Correus when he woke him at first light. "But he'll have to go. He's only here on the emperor's orders. With luck he'll get back before Julia's baby comes and that will mollify her. Are you planning to send for Ygerna?"

The frontier would settle down now to its usual state of compliant tax paying and occasional small border skirmishes, and rebuilding could get underway, circumstances that would allow the prefect to have his household with him.

"And do you want me to put a letter in the emperor's post?" Flavius went on. "He's sending a stack of triumphal missives ahead of our return. One more won't be noticed."

"Yes, and yes." Correus sat up and Eumenes appeared from the next tent with watered wine and porridge. "I hate porridge. Isn't there anything else?" His leg was throbbing.

"General Fuscus's cook has eggs," Eumenes said.

"I don't suppose he's offering to give you any?" Correus asked.

"Well, no."

"Then don't get caught. And bring me ink and a tablet first."

He scrawled a few lines to Ygerna, promising her a house in Singidunum, although he suspected that any place that didn't have his mother in it would be favored.

Do not let my father try to send Mother with you.

He didn't imagine that she would, but it was always useful to have backup.

Bring Eilenn and the baby and as many nursemaids as you think you will need to keep a grip on them both. I miss you desperately.

He folded the tablet closed and sealed the thin cord with his ring and hot wax. Flavius tucked it in his belt as Eumenes reappeared with four eggs in his hat.

"I shall leave you to your breakfast," Flavius said. "Should I find it distressing that all your slaves have criminal tendencies?"

"You would appreciate that if you weren't eating like a Saturnalia hog out of the emperor's kitchen," Correus retorted.

Flavius chuckled. "If ever I have a field command again, which the gods forfend, I shall send Bericus to you for tutelage."

Flavius departed, whistling, but wondered at the back of his mind whether that might not be preferable to dancing attendance on Domitian. On the whole, he thought not. He had been a competent commander, but it didn't come naturally to him the way it did to Correus, any more than Correus could have navigated a place on the emperor's staff. Paulinus had pointed this out to him when he had also pointed out that Aemelia was, in theory, the perfect wife for him, and was lucky that she had not succeeded in her mad, long ago desire to marry Correus instead. Aemelia would have been, had been, a liability on the frontier, just as Fiorgyn would have been for a man with a place at court. "Even if you could have brought her back to Rome," Paulinus had said ruthlessly, "can you imagine? And you couldn't have married her and kept your position. You'd be like poor old Titus with his unsuitable Jewish mistress."

"I had a certain sympathy for Titus," Flavius had said. "Now drop it."

All the same, he went to his own tent and wrote his own letter.

–

Aemelia read it in Appius's rose garden while Ygerna read hers, and Julia read one from Paulinus that included folded papyrus sketches of herself reading while holding a swaddled infant upside down and of Paulinus in the emperor's train, writing madly, with a pot on his head for a helmet.

Philippos observed the scene in the garden from the window of his master's study, where Appius was consulting the stud books. "It appears that the ladies will be departing for their own domiciles," he commented. He was aware of General Fuscus's victory from the contents of the *Acta Diurna* which had been fetched home by Appius's secretary that morning.

Appius nodded. "Philippos, is it unseemly that I shall be grateful for that?"

"Without my lady to, er, manage things, and emotions and all running high, if I may be so presumptuous, it seems to me a reasonable reaction," Philippos said.

"Thank you, Philippos. There are so many of them."

Julia's baby, which had not waited for Paulinus, was nursing greedily. Marcus sat at Ygerna's feet, trying to eat a bug and being dissuaded by his attendant nurse. Felix was reciting Greek to his tutor under the statue of Athena, while Eilenn, Appia, Paulilla, and Lucian chased each other around the pool.

Their various nurses had settled for a gossip when a shriek announced that someone, predictably, had fallen in.

"Paulilla pushed me!" Appia howled.

"Did not! You're just clumsy!"

"Am not and I saw you!"

Both mothers made ready to put down baby and letters when Helva trotted across the grass and took Appia's damp hand. And where had she come from? "Poor darling. Now you'll catch a chill!" Helva patted her and glared at Paulilla's mother. It was a warm spring morning, abuzz with bees in the roses and no breath of wind. Julia rose in a fury. Aemelia rose with her and both halted when Felix strode across from Athena's courtyard, took Appia's hand, and said quite clearly to Helva, "Go away, Grandmother. You're making trouble again."

Appius put the stud book down and watched with growing interest.

Helva said, "This poor child—" and Felix said, "No, stop it, Grandmother. She's all right." Appia's nurse by this time had wrapped her in a towel.

"Paulilla did push her," Eilenn volunteered.

"She called Paulilla a pigface," Lucian said.

Ygerna stood up. "Eilenn, thank you for your report, which was not strictly necessary. I am going to go and pack. You come with me, and Nurse too."

Everyone else's nurse hustled them off as well, leaving Julia, Aemelia, Helva, and Felix in the garden.

Appius beckoned Philippos over. "Watch."

Felix put an arm around Helva's waist. "You're being naughty, Grandmother. Father says I'm not to let you do that."

Helva attempted to look hurt, but she couldn't quite manage it. She laughed in spite of herself, to the surprise of everyone but Appius. "You're a great deal too much like him," she said and floated off in a cloud of spring draperies.

Julia handed the baby to his nurse and said, "I'm going to bathe."

Aemelia looked at Felix. "That was kind of you," she told him.

"Appia shouldn't be in the middle of Grandmother's quarrels," Felix said. "And she's by herself too," he added with the wisdom of the eldest. "Paulilla has Lucian and the new baby, and Eilenn has me and Marcus, even if he is still trying to eat bugs. Appia is just by herself and I think she's sad when Uncle Flavius isn't home."

"I think she is too," Aemelia said. *And so am I.* Flavius's letter had been conciliatory, an offer to begin again, although she didn't think he knew how to manage it. Was he still thinking of that German woman? It wouldn't be so bad if Aemelia could have given him an heir. But he didn't want her and she couldn't give him what he did want, she thought miserably. And it was probably her own fault for not wanting to marry him in the first place. The gods had a way of remembering things like that.

She gave Felix's shoulder a squeeze and went toward the house, and Felix settled down with his tutor again.

Appius closed the shutters and sat a while thinking.

He was interrupted in his thoughts, not with the expected announcement of lunch, but by Niarchos with a wax tablet on a tray.

"This just came for you, master, by messenger, but he said he was told not to wait for an answer." Niarchos handed over the tablet, an elegant one with mother-of-pearl covers. Appius opened it curiously.

> *Appius, my friend,*
> *I have some news that you may wish to know about and that is best told in person. I will be walking in the Gardens of Sallust near the Via Salaria this afternoon, if you could contrive to be in the City.*
> *Didia Longina*

Appius raised his eyebrows and told Niarchos to have a horse saddled; and no, he didn't want a carriage, why was everyone determined to make him an invalid before his time?

It was, Niarchos said, a matter of dignity, and he was sure that Philippos would concur, but as the master wished.

Appius unnerved the kitchen maids by foraging there for the half-prepared lunch that was to have been set out for him in the dining room, and swung up into the saddle of the big bay that was duly presented at the portico.

In the City he stopped at the Circus where the racing ponies were stabled and paid Julius's groom to water the bay and rub him down. He had pushed him hard on the ride in, whatever Didia had to say gnawing at his mind. He had spent a good deal of time in her company lately, and she was not a hysterical woman, or a gossip either. He walked briskly under the Claudian aqueduct and past the Forum and the new baths, ignoring the urchins offering litters for hire and hawkers trying to sell him dubious sausages and a parasol.

The Gardens of Sallust, Rome's imperial public gardens, sat at the northeast end of the Quirinal Hill, and he found Didia in the dappled shade of the laurels where the Via Salaria entered the City. She was apparently admiring a large statue of a dying Niobid with an arrow in its back, accompanied by one maid with a string bag of parcels, and another with a parasol. She had clearly been watching for him because she saw him at once and sent the maids off to wait on a bench under the mulberry trees along the hippodrome.

"Appius, my friend. I am sorry to be so mysterious. Thank you for trusting me."

She led him to another bench, this one in the center of a low rosemary maze where Sallust's Stream had been channeled into a reflecting pool, and where distance and the burble of the water would make it unlikely for anyone to eavesdrop unnoticed. The rosemary was blooming, thousands of tiny purple-blue flowers drawing in bees and cerulean butterflies.

Appius waved his hand to shoo off a curious bumblebee. He turned to Didia and asked in a low voice, "What is troubling you?"

Didia pressed her lips together for a moment, clearly angry. "It's Livilla. She's pregnant, or she was. Prosper Rufius beat her within an inch of her life and made her drink pennyroyal. It nearly killed her."

Appius raised his eyebrows. "I take it that it wasn't his?"

"I'm afraid he's positive about that. Prosper has certain problems, according to Livilla, who generally tells me things I don't want to know."

Appius considered that. "I am beginning to worry about why you are telling me."

"It's your race driver, or rather your son's. Julius, the young idiot. Prosper is raving that he's going to find him and kill him, and I rather think he will."

"Is Prosper sure of that?"

"It doesn't really matter because Livilla told him so, but I imagine it's true. There's been gossip."

Appius sighed. "I'm grateful to you for telling me. I ought to let Rufius have the fool, but Julius belongs to my son and if Rufius kills him, it will tangle us all up in the courts."

Didia smiled. "You are a practical man."

Appius grinned at her and stood up. "I am not without sympathy for young Julius. But yes, I am a practical man. It's served me well."

He bade her farewell, thinking to himself what a practical woman she was herself, and how attractive that trait was. He returned to the Circus stables, where he told the groom to go away and settled on a hay bale to lie in wait for Julius, who was due to drive a practice course.

Julius appeared startled to see him, particularly when Appius laid a hand on his arm, turned him away from the racing stalls, and said, "Saddle a riding horse. You're coming with me."

Julius's carefree expression vanished. "Has something happened to the prefect?" Correus might be the only person whose hide Julius had ever worried over.

"No. Something is about to happen to you if I don't get you out of here."

"I have a race tomorrow morning!"

"Not after the recent unpleasantness you don't. Trust me on that."

"I didn't do it!" Julius reverted to the street urchin he had once been, covering all possibilities with a blanket denial of guilt.

Appius laughed, which unnerved Julius further, as it had unnerved decades of wayward legionaries. "Yes, you did. You got Prosper Rufius's wife pregnant and he is looking for you. You belong to my son, so if he kills you, I will have to take him to court on Correus's behalf, and I don't want the aggravation. Therefore, you are coming with me."

"Livilla's pregnant?" Julius looked more annoyed than repentant. "She swore that wouldn't happen."

"Livilla is not as clever as she thinks she is," Appius said, "and she's lucky to be alive because Prosper Rufius poured a decoction of pennyroyal down her throat and almost killed her. I suppose she may die yet."

"Are you sure?" Julius looked rebellious. "The City is always gossiping, and half of it's wrong."

"I am sure, and how is not your business." He shouted for Julius's groom. "Get my horse ready, and one for your master."

"What are you going to do with me?"

"Send you to Moesia. You can escort your master's wife and children there for me."

Julius looked horrified. "I have enough money to buy my freedom," he protested.

"Well, I can't sell it to you, fortunately," Appius said. "The only thing keeping you halfway safe is being someone else's property. If Rufius finds out you're in the provinces, he's unlikely to go after you there and stir up trouble with the commander on a military base."

—

The ride out of the City was conducted in businesslike silence on Appius's part and borderline sulks on Julius's, although he was beginning to feel uneasy about Prosper Rufius. By the time they reached Appius's estate, he was, if not resigned, at least compliant.

Ygerna was equally unenthusiastic, but her main goal was to set out on the road as soon as possible, with Julius if she must. She was taking her maid Cottia, Septima the nursery maid, Nurse, and four of Appius's slaves for escort. Julius could replace one of them. At least Appius hadn't mentioned Helva.

"You can mind the horses on shipboard," she informed Julius. That would at least save Forst having to send a man to do it.

They made their farewells in the morning, and Ygerna wrapped her arms around Felix, feeling a pang at leaving him, but Appius was right.

"It is a very great thing that Julius Frontinus is doing for us." Ygerna put her hands on either side of Felix's head to be sure that he was listening to her. "If you are to learn engineering from him as he has promised, you must also learn Greek and sums from Loukas. You cannot, I am told, do one without the other."

"Yes, Mama." Felix's green eyes held a look of thoughtful resignation. It had already dawned on him that without the proper mathematics, one built things that fell down again. When this had sunk in, Julius Frontinus had then informed him that most of the best treatises on the subject were written in Greek, and Julius Frontinus did not propose to translate for his pupil.

"I expect it won't take too long," Felix said, beginning to be cheered. "It isn't like studying oratory. There's only so much mathematics to learn, and then you know it, and you can get on with things."

"Certainly," Ygerna said briskly. She hadn't the faintest idea. Among her own people, only the Druids knew things like that, and they were holy.

Nurse appeared, looking harassed, with a wooden doll under one arm and Marcus under the other. Ygerna kissed Felix on the forehead and they settled with Eilenn, Septima, and Cottia into the carriage that would take them toward the Adriatic coast. The driver shook out his reins, and the rest of their party fell in behind.

At Aternum they sent the carriage home and booked passage on a merchantman, the *Halcyone*, a trireme sailing for Salona. She was square-rigged, bulkier than the lean war galleys of the navy, and a cheerful sight riding at anchor with her hull painted scarlet and azure, with yellow trim and oars. She was loaded with oil and wine and Gaulish cheese, and on her return would carry the Moesian grain harvest back to Rome. There was only one cabin, the captain's, just below the stern gallery, and the captain was happy enough to give it up to the prefect's lady and her household and sleep in the hold with his crew for an extra handful of silver that needn't go into the official books. He made ready to lower the sails as soon as the harbor clearance came through, while Ygerna settled maids, Nurse, and both children in the cabin and went out to explore.

A brisk, pleasant wind was blowing and Ygerna breathed it in greedily. How lovely to be the one in charge of her little entourage, rather than a daughter of the house, despite Nurse's dire predictions of seasickness. The only fly in the wine cup was Julius, who had looked utterly miserable on the road from Rome, and who had never been easy with her, either before or after her marriage to Correus. Something would have to be done about him.

She found him in the hold with the horses and spread her mantle on a bale of hay. The horses whuffled at her with interest in their makeshift stalls. The other end of the hold was stacked with crocks of cheese and clay wine jars cushioned in freshly cut brush. Ygerna sat down on the hay bale and tucked up her elegant traveling shoes out of the manure. They were City-bought, a small extravagance to take to the frontier. "I'm sorry," she said.

Julius straightened up, a hoof pick in one hand. "What about?"

"All of it," Ygerna said. "That woman, and having to leave the Circus. Being sent off."

Julius shrugged. "I earned it," he said.

Ygerna nodded. "Can't I be sorry anyway?"

"I suppose." The ship rolled under his feet and the horses shuffled nervously. Julius steadied himself and whispered to them and they quieted.

"Race drivers don't live long," Ygerna said. "You've got a reputation now. When this blows over, you can train teams and let someone else get killed on the track."

"No one throws their jewelry at the trainers," Julius said sullenly. "Why have you come down here?"

"You didn't like me," Ygerna said. "Then later – I think it was different for a while." Julius flushed. "Now you don't like me much again. That's all very well in Rome. But there isn't a lot of room in Singidunum, I expect. We will have to come to terms."

Julius didn't protest that she was now his master's wife and he was obliged to like her. He looked thoughtful. "Could you not treat me like I'm twelve?" he asked.

"Do I do that?" She looked startled.

"Mostly. I always thought it came from being the royal woman or whatever it was, with your own people."

"I suppose it did," she said. "I didn't have any other weapon."

He considered that. "All right. I'll try. He won't like it if we don't get along."

"Thank you, Julius." Ygerna stood up, shaking the hay out of her mantle, and picking out the bits stuck in her shoes. "He'll have enough on his mind. We won't give him more to worry about."

"I'd just like to know what I'm supposed to *do* there, that's all," Julius muttered.

Ygerna, climbing the ladder from the hold, admitted the same question to herself.

XI

The Horseman

Flavius could feel the sweat trickling down his collarbone, where it itched beneath the silvered parade cuirass and harness tunic, and down his calves between his silvered greaves and his mount's flank. Flower petals littered the street and the smell of incense almost overcame the smell of the crowd. The emperor's triumphal chariot, driven just ahead behind four matched white horses, kicked up occasional bits of stone into the faces of the emperor's escort. The emperor himself was draped in the adornments of Jupiter Capitolinus, the traditional regalia of a triumph: the ancient ceremonial gold and purple *toga picta*, the red boots, and a laurel crown above his scarlet-painted face. Before the chariot a priest led two snow-white oxen with gilded horns and garlands about their necks, destined for sacrifice to Jupiter by his representative on earth.

The procession had gathered at first light in the Campus Martius, where Flavius and Domitian's household staff had wrestled its unwieldy elements into order, and then retrieved those who'd got bored with waiting and drifted away to the public latrines or a handy wine stall. The only obedient element were the several hundred Dacian prisoners, since they were in chains. The captives led the march, followed by the spoils scavenged from their retreat, and wagons bearing recreations of the battle. Behind these came the members of the Senate, on foot according to tradition. Also according to tradition, the Senate had debated and voted on the awarding of a triumph to the emperor, but it was highly unlikely that anyone had considered voting no. They were the most inclined to wander, and Flavius was forced to retrieve one irritable member who had settled himself in a tavern for a second breakfast, commenting that he would be along when they got on with it.

The sacrificial oxen and the imperial chariot came next, followed by the cohorts of the Praetorian Guard, unarmored now, draped in togas and laurel wreaths, chanting "Io triumphe!" beneath their own gilded eagle. Roman law forbade a triumphant general from bringing his cohorts armed into the City, for excellent reasons, and Domitian was a traditionalist.

Anyone not a part of the triumphal parade had turned out to watch it pass. Food sellers were doing a brisk business in figs, fried fish and cups of salted peas, while pigeons and seagulls squabbled over the scraps. Bright parasols floated above the crowd that lined the two and a half miles from the Campus Martius on the banks of the Tiber to the Temple of Jupiter Capitolinus.

Aemelia was somewhere among them, with Appius's household, Lucius Paulinus, Julia, and the children. Flavius's homecoming had been awkward, although he and Aemelia had slept in the same bed the first night, and he had promised her a day in the City to watch the fun, sweetened by a place in the emperor's box at the newly revived Capitoline Games the next day.

The procession inched its way toward the Via Sacra, passed through the Forum and began the ascent up the Capitoline Hill to the Temple of Jupiter, now in its fourth incarnation. The rebuilding was Domitian's gift and he was said to have spent twelve thousand talents of gold in gilding the roof tiles.

They halted before the temple and the white oxen were brought forward. The Flamen Dialis, Jupiter's priest, emerged from the mysterious inner depths of the temple as Domitian mounted the marble steps. Flavius settled firmly in his saddle and watched Domitian's driver grip his reins in both hands. The chariot ponies were not battle trained and the smell of blood overwhelmed the heated air as the first of the oxen went down.

The ponies danced skittishly and tossed their heads, but no ill omen was allowed to occur.

"There's Uncle Flavius! And the emperor!"

Appius had stationed his charges at the temple stairs for the best view. Felix, who was already nearly as tall as his father, put Appia on his shoulders so she could watch the emperor step from his chariot. Overhead the sun gave a festival glow to the gilded tiles and the statues of Jupiter, Juno, and Minerva in painted marble. The steps were strewn with more flowers.

Appia bounced on Felix's shoulders and waved her small parasol at her father. Aemelia put her hand on her daughter's knee. "Felix is not a horse."

"Can he come with us to the games tomorrow, Mama? Please?"

Felix looked hopeful. A day in the City at the games was not guaranteed. His grandfather might well have had his fill of crowds by then. Or Loukas might find his progress in Greek to be lacking.

Aemelia looked thoughtful. "I think so," she said after a moment. "I will ask your father."

She waited until that night after dinner. When Appia had finally allowed herself to be detached from her father and put to bed, Aemelia looked at Flavius tentatively.

"Will you be at home now?" she asked him.

Flavius stretched on his couch. "Unless the emperor takes it in his head to go off again."

"Appia wants to take Felix with us to the games tomorrow. She's fond of him and he's kind to her."

Flavius tried to decide whether any of this was connected.

"Julius Frontinus has taken him under his wing, you know," Aemelia said.

He decided that it definitely was. A slave came to clear away the dinner things and offer an evening cup of wine. Flavius waited while he poured it and mixed in the water before he spoke. "Are you presenting Felix for my inspection?" he asked her. "And has anyone spoken to Correus?"

Aemelia looked at her hands. "I can't give you an heir. And you won't divorce me," she added miserably.

"Do you want me to? Is there someone else?" That hadn't occurred to Flavius.

"No!" She kept her head down. "I meant so you could have an heir."

He closed his eyes. Divorce Aemelia. Take his daughter away from her mother. Marry some brood mare to get a son. And a son wasn't guaranteed even then. "We've been through this," he said wearily. "If I was going to divorce you, I would have sent you to stay with your own father, not mine. And I'll think about the other thing."

–

The allied lords gathered at Sarmizegetusa argued over their dinner, while Decebalus watched them and considered how best to handle their dissatisfactions. The defeat was not sitting well with any of them and they were in need of persuasion that the setback was temporary.

"Did we not bring back spoils?" Diegis inquired. "And are there not more spoils to be had?"

"And were we not chased across the Ister by the Romans to our shame?" Gudila demanded.

The chieftain of the Roxolani reached for another roll of pork and cabbage and crammed it into his mouth. He swallowed, drained his beer, and pointed a finger at Gudila. "The Getae could have stayed and fought," he said. "If they had wished."

Gudila glared at him. "We held the rear while the rest ran for the river."

The chieftain of the Bastarnae nodded. "But because we came away, we lost few men. And there was indeed much spoil beforehand."

"And now," Diegis said, "the emperor has gone home to Rome to boast of his victory and left his prefect here. My translator listened to the tavern gossip while we were in Naissus and he says this prefect is hotheaded. That will serve us."

"That little ferret of a spy of yours is afraid of the Romans," Gudila said.

"Of course he is. They would like to have him back to take to pieces if they knew he was one of theirs. It makes him very loyal to me."

"My brother is wise," Decebalus said now. "This prefect is looking for the passes to Sarmizegetusa. We know this from our scouts. We have only to tempt him to cross the river."

"And why would I be wanting a Roman army in my lands?" Gudila said.

"For the reason that their commander is, as our brother says, impetuous."

Gudila considered the implications of that. Decebalus's emphasis on their kinship did not escape him, although Ziais had proved to be an unpleasant bedmate. She refused to either respond to him or to fight him off, lying like a stone in the sheets until he was finished. That was strangely unsatisfactory. But to lure the Romans into the mountains and defeat them there would leave the southern lands of the Ister open to conquest without entrenched defenses, and as Decebalus's empire spread, so would his kinsman's. Gudila nodded.

Decebalus looked from one to the other now, daring them to argue. None did. "He is looking for the passes now, and has found the Iron Gates road. We will encourage him to cross before his scouts find another route."

—

The journey to deliver Correus's household to him at Singidunum took twice as long as it had taken Correus himself. Nurse complained loudly at each stop about the ubiquitousness of goat meat, about the manners of the innkeepers, and about the beds, inspecting them all for fleas and insisting on unpacking their own linens. They were also slowed by the wagon that carried their baggage and required careful negotiation of the mountain road. Septima and Marcus rode atop the boxes and trunks with Nurse wedged into the seat beside the driver. Nurse was inclined to shriek at each precipitous bend in the road, and Marcus, just beginning to talk, expanded his vocabulary to murmur "Hecate, be careful!" to himself as they went.

Julius carried Eilenn in the saddle in front of him at her insistence and Ygerna and Cottia put breeches on under their gowns and rode. Nurse remained horrified by that, as Roman ladies emphatically did not ride horses, and expressed her disapproval by lecturing Cottia. Cottia said cheekily that Nurse was too fat to ride anyway, Nurse took sulfurous offense, and Ygerna had to step in to put a stop to the squabbling.

"It's different for the mistress, I suppose," Nurse sniffed to the driver, holding her hat onto her head against the wind. "Being from the barbarian north and all and not knowing better."

"Barbarian," Marcus said thoughtfully.

The driver glanced at Nurse. "Best watch your tongue. That young one's better than a parrot."

Ygerna, who had been on horses all of her life until Governor Frontinus sent her to his Aunt Publia to be made a Roman lady of, chose to ignore this. She reined her mare in beside Julius.

"We just have to get them all to Singidunum," she said. She was beginning to be glad of his company. Julius was not exactly a friend, because circumstances hadn't allowed that, but a companion from the old days when she had been a frightened thirteen-year-old hostage in a Roman camp. They knew things about each other that put them on a more equal level.

The land journey ended at Servitium where Ygerna paid for passage for her household on a trader heading downriver along the meandering course of the Savus. The escorts borrowed from Appius would return to Rome. The Savus traffic was heavy with military craft from the Pannonian fleet patrolling from Taurunum, and the ship's master often had to wait for them to pass by, shouting indignantly when they came too close. There was no cabin to be had other than a makeshift space in the hold with the horses, and they all emerged at the Singidunum dock smelling of horse. Ygerna brushed away bits of straw, sat down on the baggage, and listened to the water lapping against the pilings as the trader backed oars and put out into the river again, bound for Viminacium. The Danuvius was even thicker with traffic: squat merchant craft and supply ships wallowing their way downriver, patrols from the Danuvius fleet, and barges pulled against the current along the towpath. The afternoon sky was clear, just white wisps of cloud riding overhead above the towering timber walls of Singidunum Fortress and a smell of bread baking somewhere mingled with the riverine scent of the docks. A troop of Correus's cavalry clattered by, looking to Ygerna like so many armed and helmeted dragons, beak-nosed and scales glittering in the sun.

Julius was sent to announce them at the gates, where a trooper went scurrying to find the prefect.

Ygerna was bone weary, but when she saw him coming down the road from the fort, her heart stopped as it always did, in sheer gratitude that there he was, still alive, holding out his arms. She flung herself into them in spite of his armor and to the approving cheers and whistles of the troopers with him.

Correus fixed them with a glare. "Take these trunks to my house." He kissed her, daring any further comment, and they shouldered the trunks and boxes, grinning.

Eilenn was already clinging to Correus's legs and Ygerna took Marcus from Nurse. "Go with them please," she told the servants, "and start unpacking. Julius, you too."

Julius looked just as happy to have his presence explained by Ygerna.

"What is he doing here?" Correus asked as the procession set off up the riverbank road to the town gates. "Also, I should tell you that we're sharing the fort with the Fourth Flavia and that means their legate has the Praetorium. I've got us a decent house with reliable heat and plumbing and a fresco of lions devouring a gazelle in the bedroom. We can paint that over if it gives you nightmares. Why is Julius here?"

Ygerna put Marcus on her hip and tucked the other arm through Correus's. "Your father sent him," she said in a low voice. "He got that awful woman pregnant and her husband nearly killed her and is hoping to kill Julius. Your father thought that your ownership would give him some protection. I don't understand the laws very well, but apparently it's harder to kill someone else's slave with impunity than it is your own, even for adultery. But the emperor is very strict on morals these days, it seems, so your father thought it best. Also, it's a longish way to the Danuvius from Rome."

"What awful woman?"

"Livilla, Prosper Rufius's wife. She's completely poisonous. She told Aemelia about Flavius and the German woman just to make trouble. She collects race drivers."

"Typhon take him," Correus said. "Here's the house."

The house was a small, elegant villa with a red door and its blind face to the street, Roman fashion. It sat on a corner of the cobbled Street of the Silversmiths, just below the city aqueduct. A small girl peered through the open door of a house across the street as they arrived, and Correus said, "That's Blaesus's daughter. My second. His wife is here too."

"And the legate's wife?" Ygerna asked.

"The legate resides in lonely splendor. He would probably have given me the Praetorium, but I honestly thought this house was a better idea."

"It is," Ygerna said. "It will be nice to be in the town."

Inside, the house had a small Roman-style atrium with red walls and a skylight letting in the sun above an emerald green pool. A somewhat neglected garden courtyard was enclosed on two sides by the wings of the house, on the third by the slaves' quarters and kitchen, and on the fourth by the stable, latrine, and bath.

"I need to go up to the fort for a bit," Correus said. "I'll hand off to Blaesus and be back as soon as I can. Eumenes is here somewhere. Put that fool Julius in the men's quarters with him and tell him to go buy a bed somewhere."

Ygerna saw the servants settled, and the children installed in the nursery where Septima was unpacking their toys and clothes, and went to bathe. Of all the things that Romans felt necessary that Britons did not, the one that Ygerna found seductive was the bath. This one was a small household affair, with a tiny steam chamber barely big enough for two people, a blue-tiled warm pool, and a cold bath. A bottle of rose-scented oil and a strigil sat with a clean towel on a stool by the warm pool, and she stripped her clothes off without waiting for Cottia.

–

When Correus came back, she was waiting for him in the bedroom, in a clean gown, with a pitcher of wine and two cups, and he had most of his armor off before he was through the door.

"Oh, my blessed dear!"

They rolled about in the bed and didn't say anything for a while. Once, they heard Eilenn's voice and the wheels of her bronze doll wagon, then Septima's cajoling voice, and then the footsteps pattered away again down the corridor.

Correus leaned on his elbows above her and kissed the five-petaled flower tattooed between her breasts. She opened her legs and drew him in again. It didn't matter how many babies and formal marriage rituals and Roman clothes and customs made up their life now, every time he lay with her, he saw her as he had the first time, by firelight and moonlight in a hollow in the tall grass among the Silure hills, with her hair a dark waterfall down her back.

Afterward, she laid her head in the hollow of his shoulder and they talked of the small domestic affairs that needed thinking on.

"We need a cook," Ygerna said firmly. "None of the maids can cook and they'll be insulted if we ask them to."

"We had a hired one in Germany," Correus said. "Would that do?"

"It would if you can find one," she said. She was silent a moment. "It still chafes you, doesn't it?"

"Owning slaves?" He turned his head toward her. "I was lucky, but the slave market always makes me feel that I had some kind of narrow escape."

"When did you ever buy a slave out of the slave market?" Ygerna said.

"Just Julius. And they practically paid me to take him. That's not the point. A private sale just means that I know where they come from and that they haven't been mistreated into insanity. It doesn't make me itch any less. I've given Nurse and Septima and your Cottia enough money to buy their freedom any time they want to marry, and if you die first, which is unlikely, I've manumitted them in my will so they won't be part of an estate. They can append 'Liberta Appii' to their names and be proud of it. I don't know why I can't feel that way."

"I don't either," Ygerna said. It was the way of the world and she had a practical mind. She hadn't had any more freedom than a slave herself while Bendigeid had promised her to whatever chieftain he was forging the next uneasy alliance with.

"I always thought I would never own slaves." Correus watched the cloud shadows chase themselves across the painted ones on the ceiling. "I started out with that intention, but things got complicated. There's Eumenes. I bought him out of the arena by bribing someone. I don't know if I can legally free him. And Julius. I've been waiting for him to grow up, if he ever will. And there's the tutor my father so generously bought us. He's much in demand and could be free if he wanted to but everyone thinks a slave is more reliable and he'd find it hard to get a place if he was free. Now I'm going to need a cook."

"You realize if we do hire a cook, it will probably be someone else's slave," Ygerna said. "On the other hand, it will be one less person to take back over the mountains when we shift household again." Which was inevitable as long as he was in the army. "I nearly left the lot of them in Aternum."

Correus chuckled and turned over in the bed to look down at her. "I was half-afraid Father was going to send Mother with you."

"He could have tried," she commented. Her attention was caught by the shifting bedclothes. She jerked the coverlet back from his legs. The scar on his thigh was still an angry red. "That is new and it looks bad. What happened that you couldn't be bothered to tell me?"

"Cavalryman's badge of honor," he said. "It's all right. I'm to ride every day, though, to be sure it doesn't stiffen up. I thought you might come with me. I didn't tell you because I didn't want to worry you."

Ygerna bit her lip. "When I know that you don't tell me things, then I am left to wonder always what you are not telling me," she said. "Also I am not a child. Sometimes you forget that."

He kissed her. "Not lately," he assured her and stood. "I have to go back to the fort tonight, for evening prayers and to get the watchword. I'll be late so I'll sleep there, but then I've awarded myself three days' leave. Would you like to see the countryside?"

She grinned at him from the bedclothes. "After we find the cook."

When he had gone, she dressed again and went out into the twilit house to light some lamps, unpack the household gods and install them in their niche in the atrium. The altar, a white-painted inset in the red walls, was encircled by a braid of painted leaves and a twining black and white snake that embodied the *genius* of the household. Ygerna unwrapped the bronze figures from their woolen bag: two dancing Lares, one holding a drinking horn and one a libation bowl, and a Penate with a basket of grain and grapes. Ygerna's people did not as a rule invite their small gods into the house, but the Romans regarded the trio as guardians and every household had them. These had been a wedding gift from Appius and so they were important for that reason. She settled them in their niche and gave them an offering of incense and a dried fig scavenged from the bare kitchen.

–

When Correus came down from the fort in the morning he found that Ygerna had sent Eumenes to find a bakery and a greengrocer, and was in the kitchen reheating soup bought from a tavern the night before, an apron tied over her gown. A clucking outside the kitchen door informed him that they now had chickens.

Nurse and Septima sat in the sun in the ragged garden, while Marcus napped on a blanket, and Eilenn played with Blaesus's daughter, a fair-haired child with a look of her father. They appeared to be comparing jewelry: Eilenn's gold lunula with the other's amulet, a tiny figure of the Horseman. It was a domestic scene that gave him infinite pleasure.

"Where is Julius?" he inquired, assailed by sudden suspicion.

"I sent him to hire a cook and bring her to Nurse for approval," Ygerna said.

"Do you trust Nurse to make the decision? I had thought we might have a ride while the weather's fair." Singidunum tended to produce unexpected thunderstorms, but so far, the air was crisp and clear with only the scent of the river in it.

"I do. Nurse likes her dinner."

"And you trust Julius to come back, I suppose."

"I do. He is penitent at the moment."

"Then go put some breeches on and I'll throw the prefect's dignity to the winds and saddle the horses myself."

When she came out into the street, he was sitting cheerfully astride Briseis and leading the dappled mare. He watched with admiration as she hung a leather bag from the saddle horns, tucked up her gown, and swung herself over the mare's back without the aid of a mounting block. "I hope there's food in that."

"I also like my dinner," Ygerna said. "I have boiled eggs and figs and a stoppered jar of beer. We will have to ride sedately until we've drunk it," she added. "Where are we going?"

"Surprise," he said and led the way out of the city gates onto the flat plain that bordered the Danuvius beyond the military road. There was no track that Ygerna could see but Correus seemed to know where he was going, skirting around planted fields to stick to open meadow thick with red poppies and the purple of mallow and loosestrife. She watched a harrier overhead as it swooped down and rose again from the rough grass with a lizard in its beak. After a few miles, a series of low green hills rose along the skyline and Correus made for those, finally dismounting at the base of a stone outcrop beside a thicket of willow and hawthorn. He held out a hand for Ygerna. "Bring the lunch."

They tethered the horses under the willows and Correus parted the tangled thicket beyond to show the mouth of a cave, dark against the stone and wild grasses. "Blaesus showed me this," he said over his shoulder, holding back the branches for her.

"Correus—"

He smiled. "Nobody lives here, alive or dead, I promise. If there is old magic left, it's benign."

Ygerna closed her eyes. The air coming from the cave was cool, with a mineral scent and the smell of water, but nothing else. If this was a place of the Goddess, she had left, Ygerna thought. Or she no longer recognized Ygerna, which was also possible.

She opened her eyes. "All right."

Correus took a lantern from his saddle bags and knelt down with flint and iron and a little pile of tinder. Ygerna watched while he patiently struck sparks and coaxed the tinder to a small flame. He lit the lantern and stood, holding it up to cast its light into the cave. "We won't go far," he said. "Blaesus says it's dangerous and I believe him."

The cave entrance was narrow, with a stone outcropping to narrow it further a few feet in. Correus turned sideways to slide past and Ygerna followed. Beyond that it was nearly pitch black. Correus held up the lantern and Ygerna caught her breath. The ceiling was hung with icicles of stone, and more grew upward from the floor.

"Water from the Danuvius makes these, Blaesus says." Correus turned to throw the lantern light around the walls. They were very beautiful, ethereal as silk in shades from cream to cinnamon, a stone bridal veil for some ancient giantess.

"We'll only go in a little way," Correus said. "Just into the next chamber. I've been in enough times to feel our way back from there if we lose the light."

Ygerna followed, trusting him to be right about that. The air was chilly, with the scent of the river in it. In the Silure hills of her homeland, there were caves forbidden not only because they were holy but because they swallowed explorers and rarely spat them out again.

Correus lit the way along a narrow passage that sloped downward into a second, wider room. "This is as far as we'll go," he said. He set the lantern on what looked like a stone table. Here the walls were also hung with petrified lace, but the formations had been cut away around the table by some ancient hand, and on its surface danced a great brown and white horse and his rider, carved into the rock. The stone veiling was beginning to build up again over it from the steady drip of the cavern roof.

"It takes centuries," Correus said, "for these to form. But they do. In hundreds of years more, they will overlay it all again."

"This is ancient," Ygerna said. "Who made it?"

"Blaesus's ancestors, most likely. You'll still see images of the Horseman here. Did you notice the amulet around little Ducci's neck?"

"I did. Correus, don't put the lantern on it."

He picked it up and set it on the floor. "If it makes you uncomfortable, we can leave."

"No, I don't think he minds. We'll give him a bit of the beer." She knelt on the cavern floor and began to unpack her bag. "Do you remember the White Horse on the chalk downs? No one knows who made him either, but they scrape the chalk clear of grass every year. All these old things. They are older than you Romans."

Correus obediently tipped a few drops of beer onto the altar. "It makes me wonder what we have made that will last as long. Long enough for people to forget who built them."

"Romans make plain who built things," Ygerna said. "'The Most Powerful Deified Emperor Somebody Augustus built this temple to mark his victory over yet another people who didn't want him there.'"

"The written word is a powerful weapon," Correus said, declining to be insulted. He took a drink from the jar and passed it to Ygerna, who left off shelling an egg to drink and pass it back.

"Our buildings will last," Ygerna said. "But this frontier you are working so hard to maintain?"

He noticed that she said "our." "I don't know," he said as she handed him the sack of figs. "That's up to the gods, I suppose. It will last a while yet as long as the emperor gives us the men to hold it. The Dacians are still raiding across the river but they never come very far. I think they're just trying to annoy us."

"So much territory," Ygerna said. "I have looked at it on a map in your father's library. Half the world. Why?"

"Because it could be done?" Correus said. "We aren't the first. Look at Alexander."

"Precisely," Ygerna said. "And where is Alexander's empire now? And why does your emperor move legions around like someone who keeps shifting his furniture? No sooner do you make a peace than troops are pulled out and sent somewhere else and then it is all to do again. Even I can see that."

Correus tossed a fig from hand to hand. "It's a juggling game," he said. "Like this. Germany to Britain to put down rebellion." The fig went from left to right. "Britain to Germany to put out fires there." Right to left. "Germany to Dacia to shore up that frontier." He tossed it to Ygerna. "Too many legions under a popular general might breed revolt. We've had too many sword-made emperors for any of them to rest easy."

Ygerna caught the fig and bit into it. "Is that why the emperor recalled Julius Agricola from Britain last year?"

"Very likely. Although that is not something I would like you to speculate about publicly."

Ygerna looked offended. "I am not a fool."

Correus smiled. "You are not." Ygerna had grown up in a nest of adders that could match anything born of the Roman imperial houses.

Ygerna put the last fig on the Horseman's altar. "I don't think he comes here anymore," she said practically, "but your men are his people."

They made their way home across the meadows in the late afternoon sun, Ygerna leaning from the saddle to gather an armful of wildflowers as they went. At Singidunum they threaded their way through the evening traffic along the Street of the Silversmiths. The air was thick with woodsmoke and the scent of dinner cooking in the small houses and the apartments above the shops. There was more traffic in the street than usual. Two centurions from the Fourth Flavia hurried by and another was making the rounds of the taverns and wine shops, pulling men from inside.

Eumenes met them at the stable doors. He said, "They're looking for you at the fort."

Correus groaned. "I'm on leave."

"Apparently you aren't." Eumenes looked grim and watched Ygerna's bouquet fall into the street unnoticed. "General Fuscus's orders and we're to be on the march for Viminacium tomorrow. He's tired of the raids from across the river and he's going after Decebalus."

—

By morning Correus was in the saddle and the household in upheaval. The prospective cook had been sent back, Julius sat a horse just behind Correus, and Eumenes fidgeted unhappily in the doorway beside Ygerna and the children.

"I want Eumenes with you," Correus had told her, pulling on his harness tunic. "I don't know what's going to happen. Fuscus is talking about taking Sarmizegetusa."

"He's going to cross the river?" Ygerna's eyes widened.

"He thinks we've got them on the off foot now, and it's a chance to drive his point home. He's had scouts out for the last weeks, mapping a route."

"What do you think?" Ygerna demanded.

"That I wish Fuscus in Hades," Correus said, kissing her. "You just got here." He wasn't going to tell her anything else he thought.

XII

The Iron Gates

The centurion says here's a bonus
To sign up for twenty-five years—

Whack!
The song came in snatches between the sharp cracks of a pile driver perched on a barge midriver.

You'll march with the Eagles
For the glory of Rome,
So put on your helmet, young soldier,
And leave your poor Chloe at home.

The ratchets clicked and the pile driver's weight rose to the top of its trough. *Whack!* The row of pilings moved steadily across the river, angled against the current. Cornelius Fuscus's bridge across the Danuvius was underway at Viminacium, built atop anchored ships brought from the fleet's base downstream at Sexaginta Prista.

The singer, a legionary of the Seventh Claudia, hefted his hammer and drove another peg home into its socket in a length of lumber laid across the decks. Behind him, closer to shore, crosswise treads were being secured over the lengthwise ones, between railings designed to keep nervous horses from leaping into the river. An earthen ramp ran from the shoreline up to the first anchored ship.

A pair of baleful voices joined the first.

I've just twenty more years
Of the sword and the spear
And leaving poor Chloe to mourn,
Till I can kiss her tits and all of her bits
And drink to those Eagles that never flew home.

The singers went silent as their centurion loomed over them, vine staff under his arm. "A little more work and less music, please, and that peg's in crooked."

The better part of five legions plus auxiliaries camped restively outside Viminacium, waiting for the bridge, while Cornelius Fuscus strode impatiently on the shore, marching out along the finished part every so often to indicate the need for haste. In the meantime, the wine shops and whorehouses in Viminacium did a brisk business and Correus spent much of his time fishing his men out of both, while work on the bridge went on by torchlight. Viminacium had been mostly rebuilt, but the patches were raw and there were still reminders of the burning in blackened walls and scattered piles of rubble. Everyone was twitchy with waiting and Correus yearned to be in the saddle and moving if they were going to do this.

The second night, Julius, who had not been best pleased to be reassigned to the ignominy of a body slave, returned at dawn from an unauthorized outing so drunk he could hardly stand. Correus poured a jugful of river water over him.

"Get up!"

Julius blinked at him.

"This is why I didn't leave you to take care of my wife," Correus growled.

"I just had a drink," Julius said sullenly. "There's nothing else to do."

"Go polish my armor," Correus told him.

Julius retreated to his tent and went to sleep instead. When he woke, Correus's armor was sitting at the foot of his bed, along with its owner.

"I am not in a good mood," Correus informed him.

"I'm not having the time of my life," Julius said.

"You are, however, still alive. Something you would not be in Rome. What possessed you to get involved with Livilla? You might as well have had dinner with Circe."

"She went after me," Julius said. "Gave me presents and all." He put his head, which clearly ached, in his hands. "It was nice. I was somebody."

Correus sighed. "I expect that was hard to resist."

Julius looked up. "I wasn't ever somebody before."

"I expect your disappearance is the talk of Rome," Correus said. "Prosper Rufius won't be popular if he kills you. But you'll have to give him time to realize that, or for us to pay him off. In the meantime, polish my armor." He rose, but turned as he pushed open the tent flap. "Don't think I don't sympathize. Not about Livilla, but the rest. I do know."

–

Two days later, Fuscus's bridge spanned the Danuvius and they marched across it, five abreast, with the gilded Eagles and the cavalry banners bright in the sunshine. The march of mailed sandals and the drumming of thousands of hooves on the boards would be heard for miles, Correus thought. But the Dacians had undoubtedly watched the bridge being built; they were unlikely to be ignorant of the Roman advance. The legions, with auxiliaries and cavalry interspersed, poured across the bridge, Fuscus in the lead ahead of the Fifth Alaudae. Correus, his ala drawn up to wait their turn, watched the Larks go by, the elephants on each shield nose to tail in a circle around the boss. A pair of border wolves, their usual ragtag aspect polished for presentation to the commander, rode beside Fuscus.

The countryside on the north bank of the Danuvius rose abruptly from a flat plain into mountains that lined the Danuvius gorges on either side, south of Viminacium as far as Aquae. The army's route would take them northwest instead and then east into the mountains of Dacia and through a pass, at the end of which, the border wolves said, lay a village called Tapae and an open road to Sarmizegetusa, capital of the Dacian kingdom and stronghold of Decebalus. Cornelius Fuscus intended to make it plain that invading Roman territory had been an ill-fated idea.

It was, the wolves said, at least a ten day march, more with the wagons and catapults to shift through a narrow pass. There were only scattered villages in the hills, not enough to feed an army on the march, and thus they were laden with extra grain wagons. Correus, positioned with the Ala Dardanorum midway down the column, could see the rear of its winding length disappearing behind the foothills they had just ridden through, while the column's lead was already invisible among the stony outcroppings that rose toward Sarmizegetusa. Couriers rode up and down the line with orders to halt for rest, to march double time, to make ready to camp, to shift backward or forward, all as General Fuscus commanded.

As they pressed upward into the mountains, the way grew steeper and they could see the peaks above the tree line capped with the snow that could fall year-round. Coltsfoot and snowdrop blinked among the rough grass in the high meadows, and beech and oak gave way to spruce and fir. Half the time the air was thick with mist and the forest was oppressive, the dank trees on either side too thick to see past, the undergrowth beneath them a tangle of wild briar. They passed a few scattered villages of wooden huts, uninhabited or temporarily deserted while the Roman army passed by, and scavenged what they could, but there was little to find. This was not farm country and any herds that grazed on the ragged hills had been driven out of reach.

They camped where the scouts had noted open meadow, putting up ditch and wall around the perimeter each night, although there was no sign of the Dacians, now presumed to be at Sarmizegetusa fortifying their walls.

"We've lost two scouts, though," Messala Cominius said to Correus as they exchanged the evening watchword. "I don't like that. I had the temerity to say so to Cornelius Fuscus and he said he sent them to sniff out the defenses at Sarmizegetusa again, and they must not know their business as well as they thought they did."

Correus looked at the dark slopes that ringed the meadow where they had camped. Above them the scrub merged into upland forest through an impenetrable tangle of brush and saplings endlessly marching back into any cleared space. The back of his neck itched.

"The general is confident," Cominius said. It was clear that he was quoting.

In the morning they were on the march again under lowering clouds, the camp fortifications knocked down and the ditch filled in, as always. Rome left nothing behind that an enemy might find useful. The way was growing even steeper now, narrowing into the pass that the scouts said the Dacians called the Iron Gates. The tree-ringed upland meadow where they had camped gave way to a narrower stone-walled gap between the mountains. On the right the ground dropped precipitously to a river that had cut its bed deeper over eons until now its rocky course lay thirty feet below. On the left the mountains rose up again, sheer walled and thick with scrub pine. The sound of their passage echoed along the gorge. Fuscus and the Alaudae were in the lead with the catapults and their crews, followed by Messala Cominius's Seventh and the Fourth from Singidunum. To the rear were the Italica and the remnants of the Macedonica.

Correus eyed the hillside above them with unease, and noted that Blaesus, beside him, was doing the same. The ala was in tight formation on the narrow road. According to his own scouts, the ala should be halfway through the length of the Iron Gates now and the whole army was likely to engage the next day. Correus thought again of the scouts that hadn't come back. Tsiru had sworn when he had heard that.

The mist hadn't burned off yet and might not for hours at this altitude. It gave the pass an ominous feel, as if it were some kind of great animal lying coiled around the mountain. The trees loomed out of it, black shapes disembodied in the fog.

Julius had made plain his opinion that the place was cursed. Correus had told him irritably that Julius's idea of wilderness was the public gardens in Rome and to keep his ideas to himself. He was with the baggage wagons now, leading Correus's spare horse. It did not ease Correus's mind that Tsiru had expressed the same thought.

The mist muffled sound as well, so that when it came, the noise took several moments to register above the drum of hooves on the packed earth. Then Correus's eyes widened and he saw Blaesus beside him snap his head toward the moving column as it wound its way around a stony bend ahead. The faint sound of trumpets cut across what they both now recognized as the low rumble of battle far ahead of them: Advance, and then Hold Formation.

While they listened, a hail of arrows came from the mountain above and from the dark trees on the opposite side of the gorge. They saw the Dacian archers emerge from their hiding places in the stone and knew what had happened to the scouts.

"Shields up! Hold formation!" Correus shouted. There was no way to fight back against the archers above them or those across the gorge. Boulders began to fall amid the arrows and Correus saw a horse and rider pitch over the cliff into the fanged river below. The way before them was blocked by the rapidly panicking column. They weren't far into the gorge and at least as much more lay ahead. He made up his mind.

"Reverse in place!" His trumpeter sounded the order and Correus blessed the training of the cavalry games as each rider spun his horse to face the way they had come. Behind him he could hear Fuscus's trumpeter sounding Hold but there was no holding where they were. In open ground they could fight. They

175

struggled back the way they had come, trying to turn the infantry column below them as well, shields up against the relentless rain of Dacian arrows. More stones fell, boulders that took two men to push down the mountain, taking horses and riders into the gorge. Sounds of battle came from below them as well as above, and the foolhardiness of taking a column through the gorge unprepared was clear.

A stone rumbled down and across the way in front of Correus and he pulled Briseis up sharply as another tumbled behind it. They pushed through as fast as they could, shields over their heads, bumping up against the infantry of the Italica also trying to make their way out of the trap and the hail of Dacian arrows. Correus could see the archers in the heights above them nocking arrow after arrow. A horse went down ahead of him with one in its chest and its rider fell beneath the hooves of the horses behind. More went over the cliff into the river as the stones became a landslide. Correus waited and looked for a courier from the front with orders, but none came.

They pushed their way finally out of the gorge, thin of ranks and ragged of formation, into the meadow where they had camped the night before. The rear of the column was in chaos. Dacian archers filled the woods above the meadow. More boulders and the huge trunks of felled trees rumbled down the slopes into the Roman lines, battering holes in their already unstable formation. The baggage wagons were in flames. A wing of Dacian horsemen swept from the slopes above, scattering the infantry braced to meet them. Correus swung his ala around to shield the damaged cohorts.

The mist had burned off here and the sun came from between the darkening clouds as a Dacian horseman swung his falx, bright as flame in the glare. Correus thrust his shield up and rammed his spear into the Dacian's shield, knocking it askew enough to thrust again and feel the spear go in. He dropped it before it was pulled from his hand and drew his cavalry sword. The ala was holding around him, but the orderly formation of a Roman battle line was gone and with it the Roman advantage. Each commander looked to his own and there was no word from the front of the column. The deadly Dacian blades sliced through plate armor with ease and century after century went down.

They held until they could no longer, waiting for some order from the front. Then, too late, trumpet after trumpet sounded the Retreat in Formation but there was no formation left. They streamed through the meadow, falling as they went under arrows and the wicked shining falxes.

"We have to get out!" Correus shouted to Blaesus. The Dacians were aiming for the horses now, then picking off their riders. Briseis collapsed under him with an arrow through her neck, blood spouting, and Correus rolled out of the saddle. Blaesus held a hand down but Correus stooped long enough to stroke her head and cut her throat with his belt knife, weeping, rather than leave her like that. Then he swung up behind Blaesus. All around them the ala was picking up its unhorsed riders, riding double, still in straggling formation behind their prefect, still shielding the scattered infantry as best they could.

Julius appeared out of the chaos as they passed the burning baggage wagons. He was on foot, but he had Ashes by the lead. Correus slid down from Blaesus's horse. "Keep them going!" he said and Blaesus saluted and the ala moved on, fighting its way down the mountain.

Correus took Ashes' reins. "Where's your horse?"

"Dead, where do you think?" Julius said. "What do I do?" He looked panic-stricken. He had been in an army camp before, but he wasn't a soldier.

A riderless horse careened by and Correus grabbed its reins. It reared away from him, but he held on. "Do what you know – ride!" He handed the struggling horse's reins to Julius. "Ride like a fiend and get to Viminacium and tell them to be ready. This is a rout. They'll need to get us all over the bridge – what will be left of us." He swung up on Ashes bareback and didn't wait for Julius to answer.

Julius leaped on the horse as it bucked under him and Correus saw him kick it into a gallop to run out its objections to the stranger on its back. He thought for a moment of the Horseman and said a swift prayer to that old god before he set Ashes' head toward the ala, battling its way through the carnage in the meadow.

Julius lay flat on the horse's back and sent it galloping toward the outskirts of the battle. He could hear arrows overhead but hoped fervently that one small rider might not attract their attention, particularly since the horse had Dacian trappings. He would need to ditch those, he thought, before he got near the Roman forts. If he got there. They were days from the Danuvius.

He kept the horse at a flat gallop until he could edge it out of the meadow and up into the hills from which the Dacians had earlier poured down onto the column. Below him the opposing armies were tangled in the meadow under a dark sky, a chaos of scarlet and steel and blood. The orderly Roman lines were long since shattered and it was clear that they were trying only to claw their way out and down the mountain. The Dacians pursued them, hunting down stragglers with bloody spears or the long falx blades that cut through anything in their path. Julius stopped to let the horse breathe and thought about what to do. Ride, Correus had said. Well, he could do that. He would do that and think about anything else when he stopped. Julius had never been afraid in the Circus. He was afraid now. He resisted the urge to kick the horse into a gallop again. If he killed the horse, it wouldn't help.

The air was thick with the smell of blood and as the threatened rain began to fall, it churned up mud that flew up under the cavalry horses' hooves and sent them sliding on their haunches as they tried to maneuver downhill. Behind them, always behind them, the Dacian warriors kept coming, with flights of arrows and rolling boulders, moving in on foot or on horseback when there was a gap in the Roman lines, which was everywhere now.

Correus, rain dripping from his helmet and clouding his vision, fought frantically with a Dacian horseman, clinging to Ashes' back with his knees until the old thigh wound screamed at him and a muscle spasm threatened to loosen his grip. The scale armor of the cavalry hauberks proved to be more resilient against the blows of the falx blades than the legions' segmented plate, but his men were taking wounds in their sword arms, and a falx blade that landed on a helmet could cleave clear through it. He caught the Dacian with a blow on the shoulder when his horse slid in the mud, and didn't stop to finish him, just rode on, hoping he would stay down. They weren't going to beat them; all they could do was try to hold together and keep moving until the enemy decided they had pursued them far enough.

It was getting dark. They stumbled down the muddy way they had marched up the day before, in no particular order, each ala or cohort clustered around its own commander. For a moment, he caught sight of an Eagle and the standard of the Seventh Claudia in the rainy dusk ahead of him and thought that Messala Cominius had managed to get them out.

As it got dark, the pursuit slackened but there was no way to tell how many were left stumbling toward the Danuvius in retreat as more wounded fell from their horses into the mud, their last strength gone. They kept on another three miles, by Correus's best guess, until there was no sign of the enemy behind them, just the weary tramp of the retreating column. Correus signaled a halt when they came to what looked like open ground as the last light faded. There was no ditch and wall to put up because there was nothing to dig with. They caught the rain in their helmets to water the horses and themselves, and Correus set pickets to stand watch in turn while the rest slept the sleep of the exhausted. In the dusk he stumbled over a gray stone jutting from the earth. He knelt and put his head against its cold face and whispered a prayer to the god of soldiers. *Let me bring them home.*

Julius skirted through the hills until he saw no one below him. It was dusk by then, the sky still lowering, and the rain came as he halted by a small tributary of the river that flowed through the gorge. He let the horse drink and tied it to a tree to graze while he shivered in the cold rain. His stomach growled but he knew that eating grass himself would only make him sick. More than food, he yearned for a place to hide. The hills loomed over him, and the rain transmuted the night sounds that a forest makes into even more eldritch voices. Julius was City-bred, a child of the close, odorous streets and towering apartment buildings of Rome, of the crowds in the Circus and the Forum. Even the army camps had been densely populated, alive with the busyness of drill and target practice. Here in the forest, he felt that terror of wild spaces by which he knew that the forest gods made trespassers run mad. He rolled himself into a ball under his cloak with his belt knife in his hand.

After a thunderous downpour, the sky cleared in the morning, and he rose, ravenous and feeling a little foolish in the daylight, and mounted the horse again. The horse apparently found nothing amiss with its new master, and they made their way steadily downhill until they came to a barn on the edge of one of the small villages they had passed days before. Julius slid into it carefully, emerging with eggs, and rode on, keeping out of sight of the few other farmsteads that clung to the hillside.

–

At first light Correus saw the scattered remnants of Cornelius Fuscus's army spread across the rocky ground around them. The standard of Aurelius Decius, legate of the Fourth Flavia, had sprouted beside Cominius's. The air was clear now, and visibility cruelly sharp after the rain. The carrion birds, reivers of the sky, circled the pass above them. By the time he joined Decius and Cominius, the legate of the Italica had found them also, and he learned that the legate of the Macedonica was somewhere in the high meadow where the carrion birds hovered. Of Cornelius

Fuscus there was no sign, and no sign of the Alaudae. Other auxiliary and cavalry commanders or seconds made their way to the legates' standards; all had taken heavy losses. By common consent, the command returned to Cominius to get the remnants of the column into some kind of order, to bandage the wounded, to get them home, and to feed them on the way.

The surgeons who had survived the chaos had only the instruments they carried on their persons and they wielded those on the muddy ground, overspread with the scavenged cloaks and saddle cloths of the dead. Correus discovered that Nicomedes had survived, but his veterinary surgeon had not, and found Nicomedes was stitching horses as well as riders with hair pulled from their tails, washing their wounds with rainwater because there was no vinegar. Any horse that couldn't walk easily was put down, by men weeping as Correus had, and then butchered for its meat.

On Cominius's orders, the wounded were to be borne by their fellows on makeshift stretchers cut from brush, the cavalry was to take up its horseless members double, and they were all to go hungry until the next nightfall to put some distance between themselves and the Dacian army.

"Send hunting parties ahead," Cominius said. "Tell them there's no such thing as an animal that's inedible. Forage anything left in those villages we passed. We're lucky there's graze this time of year. Prefect Julianus sent a rider yesterday to Viminacium, but we don't know if he made it. Send another now and when we stop again get a beacon lit. Now let's move."

They made fifteen miles that day, far less than a normal day's march, and were stretched thin to do it. When they halted at dusk, they burned the dead who had succumbed to their wounds since morning and prayed for their shades under the legions' gold Eagles. They lit a beacon, hoping it could be seen from Viminacium, and shared out the hunting parties' yield, brought down by archers' arrows, cavalry spears, and makeshift snares and slings. Ygerna had said to Correus once, at an elaborate banquet in the City that included a flamingo, that Romans ate anything.

Correus, exhaustedly devouring a half-cooked weasel, thought now that it was a fortunate habit.

In the morning, they moved out again. It would take at least ten days to reach the Danuvius and the bridge across it to Viminacium, and their numbers grew fewer every day. They lost more horses, more men. The carrion birds began to follow them.

–

Julius wondered how long he could push the Dacian horse before it died under him. Every stop for rest made him frantic, and while the horse found at least sporadic graze, Julius was growing weaker. Setting snares cost time and he was unhandy at it and rarely caught anything. A bush full of unfamiliar berries made him vomit. He caught a lizard and ate that, gagging. Even so, he was far ahead of the column now, if it was even moving, if anyone had got out. Always when he looked back, he saw the black specks riding the sky in the distance behind him.

–

The air grew progressively hotter and more oppressive the farther down the mountain the straggling column came, and the flies clustered on the horses' faces and any open wound. Correus, in a saddle scavenged from a dead troop horse, whose rider clung behind him, saw the Eagle of the Seventh bobbing ahead of them and fixed his eyes on that. The gilded wings seemed about to lift into the pale air and it wavered in his vision. He tried again to count in his head how many more days it might take them to reach Viminacium, but the numbers slid away from him. They had lost more men again overnight. It would be a miracle of Aesculapius if any of the wounded survived the journey.

–

The sentry on the walls at Viminacium saw the rider coming out of the hills on a staggering horse. They had seen the faint smoke of a beacon the day before, but the thinly garrisoned Danuvius forts had no way of knowing what it meant, except that it was most likely bad. Now a patrol went across the bridge to meet the rider who shouted at them in Latin as he approached.

Julius hadn't thought after all to strip the horse's trappings and they met him with pilums bristling until he swore at them, swaying in the saddle, with a fluency and inventiveness that no Dacian could have managed.

Two days after Julius's arrival, Messala Cominius's man rode into Viminacium, and for the second time the garrison commander, a centurion of the Seventh Claudia, shook his head at the request. "We haven't the manpower to send a relief column and leave the border here undefended. Prefect Fuscus took almost every man stationed on the Danuvius. I've done what I can to be ready for them, but they will have to get here as best they can."

–

A military courier came up the road from Viminacium on a lathered horse, and in minutes the whole of Singidunum knew, the news borne on that wind by which the worst word travels the swiftest.

"They've ordered out the surgeons and apprentices, any medical people that are left here," Eumenes said. "Even the orderlies. To Viminacium."

Ygerna steadied herself, hand on the kitchen table. She had known it. Or known something. Eilenn had been weeping and frightened for over five days and couldn't say why except that people were fighting. The last time Eilenn had been that terrified, it had been a collapsing bridge. Ygerna had reluctantly concluded that the child had the Sight, which was not to say that she saw things clearly or even in their entirety. But she had seen a battle, and it had gone wrong.

For five days Ygerna had kept a dish of wine and another of olive oil in front of the household gods in their niche. She had prayed to the Mother, and to the Horseman in his cave, and to Epona, goddess of cavalrymen. She had even prayed to Mithras, who was the soldiers' god and didn't admit women to his mysteries, in the hope that he might listen to Correus's woman.

"Get my horse. I'm going with them," Ygerna told Eumenes.

Eumenes looked appalled. "They won't let you, Lady. Better you send me."

"Can you clean and dress a spear wound?" Ygerna demanded. "I can. I learned it from the emperor's field surgeon in Germany. They'll let me. They can't stop me anyway."

Eumenes prepared to argue, for what that was worth when speaking with Ygerna. "It's not safe. He left me here to take care of you."

"Well, you'll not be taking care of me if you go to Viminacium either, will you?" Ygerna put the turnips she had been cutting up back into their bowl. "If it gets bad here, take them all to Servitium. Right now, tell Nurse to come and finish this. And saddle my horse."

"You don't even know if he's still alive," Eumenes said brutally.

"*Get my horse!*" If she went to Viminacium, he would be alive. And if he wasn't, she would know sooner and that was better than the agony of waiting. Eilenn didn't really understand what the Sight told her – she said her head saw "bits of things" and it didn't come often; Correus didn't more than half believe in it. But Ygerna had asked the Goddess for Correus when she was thirteen. She clung to the fierce belief that if the Goddess, whose domain was death as well as life, had taken him away again, she would know.

–

The junior surgeon and two orderlies left in charge of the Singidunum hospital regarded their companion uneasily, but they hadn't been able to send her back. The prefect's lady had appeared in an old gown tied up over breeches and boots, her hair in a braid down her back, and announced that she would accompany them to Viminacium. What would happen when she tired out and wanted to turn back, they didn't know.

They made half the journey before nightfall, to sleep at Tricornium, whose medical staff had ridden out the day before. Maybe they could leave her there, the junior surgeon thought. But the next morning before they could saddle their horses, she appeared from the quarters allotted her the night before by the startled garrison commander, and they gave up.

They rode out, pushing the horses hard, and came into Viminacium at nightfall, with a growing respect for the prefect's lady. The camp hospital was brightly lit and Ygerna presented herself to the surgeon in charge, a junior of the First Italica. His name was Hirtius, he was only twenty and he was now the most senior medical officer available.

"I can dress a wound, and even stitch it if necessary," she told him before he could object. "The chief field surgeon on the Rhenus frontier taught me. When my husband was primus pilus of the Fourteenth Gemina there," she added, because pulling rank was always useful. "You'll need all the help you can get."

"We will," Hirtius admitted. He looked at her curiously. "Was that the last war? Not Gaius Labienus?"

"It was, and yes."

"Merciful Aesculapius," Hirtius muttered. "I was an apprentice under him when he was with the Eighth Augusta. He was terrifying." He handed her an apron. "Is your husband...?"

"He is with the column," Ygerna said shortly. "Prefect of the Ala Dardanorum." She closed her eyes for a moment. "We don't know."

–

The wounded began to come in before dawn. They arrived in no particular order as to legion or ala, but it was clear that someone had sent the worst ones first. Ygerna found her place in the chaos, no longer the prefect's lady but just one more orderly to fetch and carry, scrub blood and worse off the table before the next man, hold a lamp or a trooper's hand, cover the dead, and note their unit. It was, as she had thought, easier to be busy.

The Viminacium hospital compound was crowded with every medical corps officer and orderly summoned from surrounding garrisons. A triage line stretched into the hall and out to the portico and street, with orderlies examining each man and pulling the worst of them into the surgery first. The Dacian falxes were murderous weapons. Wounds that had been stitched in the field to stop bleeding were festering now and had to be reopened. There were gangrene cases. The small two-bed wards that occupied three wings of the hospital were full and makeshift cots were filling the tile-roofed colonnades around the hospital garden.

"A little closer," Hirtius said, while Ygerna adjusted the lamp stand to shed its glow onto the half-severed arm of a legionary, a man of the Claudia by his belt buckle. It was a wonder he was still alive, and that only by the tourniquet tied so tightly about his upper arm that the rest was almost bloodless despite the wound. She put her other hand against his face to soothe him while Hirtius dropped poppy tears into a cup.

"We're sparing with this just now, you see," Hirtius explained to her, measuring the dose, "not only because we're running low, but in his condition a bit too much could kill him." He seemed to have adopted her as his own pupil, impressed perhaps that she had withstood Gaius Labienus. Or perhaps it steadied him to recite his reasoning to her. He was very young and he had seen the senior surgeon of his legion in the row of dead who had survived their return only by hours.

The hospital stank of vomit and shit and gangrene more than blood. The fresh wounds had bled on the march, then festered. The screams of men enduring the reopening of those abscessed wounds were a grim overlay to the steady solid murmur of instruction and consultation between the surgeons and their staff.

Hirtius cut the man's arm the rest of the way off as swiftly as possible while an orderly held him down, cauterized it, and sent him to the wards. He was replaced in seconds by another and another. At dawn the orderlies brought in a cavalry trooper with the mountain rose insignia of the Ala Dardanorum on his belt buckle. He had a deep spear wound in his chest, and someone in the field had pulled the barbed point, but the wound was infected now.

"Your prefect?" Ygerna whispered to him, but he didn't speak, only tossed his head and moaned.

–

As the gaunt and shattered column neared the river, Messala Cominius had ordered the wounded to the front to be brought in first. They were heartbreakingly fewer than they had been, but they numbered in the hundreds nonetheless. Behind them rode and stumbled the remains of Cornelius Fuscus's army, less than half the number who had marched out.

By nightfall, the chaos of their return had resolved into some kind of order. The survivors whose home forts were elsewhere were parceled out among the empty barracks at Viminacium and in camps on its outskirts, fed, and ordered to rest. When he had seen to his own men, Correus scratched a message to Ygerna and put it in the military post for Singidunum, then hunted Julius down. He found him in the hospital, recovering from a fever that was most likely due to bad water and starvation.

"You're alive," Julius said with satisfaction, opening his eyes at the sound of Correus's voice. "I'm alive," he added. "We're all fucking alive. Your wife's here." He closed his eyes and went back to sleep.

Correus found her in the surgery, holding a lamp and instruments for a junior surgeon who appeared to be the ranking medical officer not on the Unfit for Duty list, as he amputated a legionary's gangrenous leg. The smell was appalling and she was spattered from neck to waist with blood.

Something altered in her eyes when she saw him, a tension leaving her, and she nodded slowly to him, but didn't shift the lamp. "You'll be all right," she whispered to the legionary on the table now. "You'll live."

Correus wondered if his own arrival had brought that conviction with it.

The surgeon stitched the amputated leg closed around the end of the thigh bone and nodded to an orderly to bring the next, an auxiliaryman with a festering gash deep in his sword arm. Pus and blood ran out onto the table and he screamed as the surgeon pulled out the stitches. Ygerna held the lips of the wound open with forceps while the surgeon cleaned it with a swab dipped in vinegar.

Correus left her where she was clearly needed and went to the fortress baths to scrub his aching body and unshaven face, and then to the Temple of Mithras, outside the fort on the edge of the military road. If there was a god to whom Correus gave more heartfelt worship than the respectful veneration due all deities, it was Mithras, the savior and redeemer who was the god of soldiers. His father had been an initiate and he and Flavius had both come to him in their own ways, each finding something different and necessary in his ritual. Now Correus stood at the entrance to the darkened temple and waited until his eyes focused in the dim light. Then he made his way forward to kneel before the figure at the end of the aisle: Mithras astride the great sacrificial bull, lit by the slanting rays that shone through the skylight above the altar, between the twin torchbearers of light and darkness. The god held a knife in his hand, and the bull's head was thrown back awaiting it.

"Unconquered Sun, Redeemer..." Correus stumbled over the invocation. Ordinarily the prayer was for victory. Now he pleaded for healing, victory over the carrion birds and the gods of death. "Let me lose no more men." With no sacrifice to offer, he pricked his thumb with his knife and rubbed the drop of blood into the stone where the stain of old offerings darkened it. "No more losses, no more fools," he whispered. The torchbearers watched silently, one torch flaming upward, the other down.

"I want you to go home again. Back to Rome." Correus held Ygerna tightly in his arms in the dim lamplight of a dingy tent scavenged from the quartermaster's warehouse at Viminacium. She shook her head.

"No."

He rolled over in the narrow camp bed and propped himself on his elbow. "This was a disaster. A rout. We lost almost half our men due to that fool."

"He'll cost you no more men now," Ygerna said.

"He cost us a legion, and its Eagle," Correus said. "I don't know what Domitian will do."

The Fifth Alaudae were gone, the whole legion massacred, by the accounts of those few who had escaped from the vanguard of the column. The loss of an Eagle was a national disgrace. Generals had been ordered to kill themselves for that, if they weren't already dead. Domitian would want revenge. There would be another war.

"They'll have hauled more of our catapults off to Sarmizegetusa," Correus said disgustedly. "And we have reports that they come across the river just long enough to make nuisances of themselves and then vanish under our noses. Cominius has ordered the bridge dismantled but that's not how they're getting here. The fleet patrols report small bands that swim across or launch a quick craft that we can't catch. They may be just trying to get on our nerves, but it's unstable."

"Correus, I am not leaving," Ygerna said. She sat up and pulled her damp hair from the braid in which she had been keeping it from the ghastly detritus of the surgery. She smelled like lavender-scented bath oil. Probably filched from the hospital, Correus thought, where she had been sleeping on a cot in the dispensary. He sighed and buried his face in her loose hair. He wasn't sure he could make her go home, and he wasn't sure he had the strength to keep trying.

XIII

The Border Wolves

*A HISTORY OF THE FLAVIAN EMPERORS
BY M. LUCIUS PAULINUS
DEDICATED TO EMPEROR TITUS FLAVIUS
CAESAR DOMITIANUS AUGUSTUS
IN GRATITUDE FOR HIS IMPERIAL FAVOR*

…Unfortunately, the emperor's triumph was marred by the commander he had left behind in Moesia, the Praetorian Prefect Cornelius Fuscus, who unwisely attacked the Dacians on their home ground and disgraced himself by losing in battle the Fifth Legion Alaudae and their Eagle. The emperor then sent to Moesia two legions from Britain and Germany and wisely reorganized the Province into two parts: Lower Moesia under Marcus Cornelius Nigrinus, and Upper Moesia under Lucius Funisulanus Vettonianus.

Lucius Paulinus always kept two sets of books, and now he laid aside the official history and took out the journal in which he recorded more private thoughts, publishable – possibly – only in the future.

Those of us who voiced less than confidence in Cornelius Fuscus may feel vindicated, but at what cost. The death of a legion. The Alaudae defeated the war elephants of Numidia for Julius Caesar. But they lost their Eagle once before under Augustus, and were nearly wiped out in the infighting of the civil wars. The Senate won't rebuild them this time. The emperor has ordered the First Adiutrix from Germany, which is probably wise for a number of reasons, and the Second Adiutrix from Britain, which may not be. I don't know what to think of Vettonianus as governor. As a military tribune in Syria some twenty-odd years ago he wound up with command of his legion long enough to let it be defeated by the Parthians. Since then, he has had a series of civilian posts followed by a string of provincial governorships. He may not be the best man for a situation like the current one, but I suspect he may also be a place-holder. The emperor is listening quite attentively to Julius Frontinus these days and I think Frontinus is looking for the right man.

In the meantime, everyone is licking their wounds. The accounts of the battle were horrifying. The Dacian armor and particularly those ghastly curved blades are better than anything Rome has ever been up against, including the Parthians. Flavius went white when he heard the news and, while cheered to have learned that his brother has survived, he is perhaps beginning to chafe at a job he can't get out of. His discomfort may also be attributable to domestic affairs. Julia says that Aemelia will come around, but Flavius needs to court her. Flavius did that once before and all Aemelia would say that time was that she was in love with his brother. So he may feel disinclined.

Interestingly, that wretch Julius, having been snatched from Prosper Rufius's clutches, distinguished himself in Moesia with a harrowing ride down the Dacian mountains to the Danuvius with news of the defeat. Prosper Rufius is still stomping about the City swearing vengeance but he hasn't divorced Livilla, which undercuts his moral high ground. On the other hand, she came to him with a healthy dowry and Prosper is a practical man. He confines himself to nasty gossip about Appius Julianus, which my father-in-law shrugs off, probably rightly so.

More interestingly, Appius is courting. They are very discreet, but I am almost sure of it. Aemelia is convinced she is a fortune hunter, out to take away Flavius's inheritance. Julia says no woman in her right mind would marry her father while Helva is there. My Uncle Gentilius offered to buy Helva and take her off Appius's hands (I don't know if he was joking) and there was a household scene because Julia told Helva about it. I am thinking of becoming a playwright. There is so much material available.

Paulinus's prediction that the new governor of Upper Moesia was a stopgap proved accurate. After a fall and winter of relative calm while Domitian, and presumably Decebalus, thought about what they were going to do next, Domitian sent Tettius Julianus from Germany to Moesia as governor of the upper province and military commander of both. Tettius brought with him the First Legion Adiutrix from Moguntiacum and the Second Adiutrix from its previous posting in Britain.

The new governor had served in Moesia before, as legate of the Seventh Claudia, and after that in Numidia and Germany. He was somewhat older than the confident Fuscus, old enough to be less capriciously confident, tall, with curling gray hair, a long face, and a straight nose that flared into a ball at the tip and gave him the look of an erudite horse. As a commander, he whisked through a room like a stiff wind, blowing everyone into shape, and spoke his mind without preliminaries, leaving his listeners to scramble after him if they hadn't been paying attention. He could still throw a pilum farther than most of his men, and Correus thought that he was also a man who could see farther around a corner than most, a conclusion he came to after an interview with Tettius at his headquarters in Viminacium.

"I understand that you served with Julius Frontinus in Britain, Prefect," Tettius said.

"Yes, sir."

"And that you are something of a... what are those lizard things that change their color? My aunt had one for a pet. She used to wear it like a brooch."

"Chameleons, I believe," Correus said.

"That's it. And that you have a gift for picking up the local dialect."

"I'm reasonably good at it," Correus said cautiously.

"I want to know what's on the other side of that pass," Tettius said. "And what other ways there are to get to the head of it."

"The frontier scouts have tried," Correus told him. "But it's like finding a single loose brick in a wall."

"Exactly. I remember these mountains with less than fondness. But there's a back door somewhere. The Dacians have a thriving trade with the east. It doesn't all go through that pass or we would know it."

"The empire taxes everything that sticks a foot over our border," Correus said. "I would think most trade comes in through Pontus Euxinus ports and the Danuvius delta to avoid that."

"Precisely. And where does it go from there? Up the Danuvius to the Iron Gates pass is a very long way round, and they'd be stopped by our fleet."

"Through the Getae lands maybe," Correus said. "They're allied with Decebalus now. He married his sister to their king."

Tettius reached a long arm for the stack of blank tablets on his desk. "Go and find out. Frontinus tells me you would have made an excellent border wolf if you hadn't joined the Centuriate."

–

The king of the Getae came home to Capidava to see to his holdings, consult with his chamberlain and priests on auspices concerning the campaign against the Romans, and visit his counting house. Afterward, he sent for wine, and for the dinner which the palace cooks had been trying to keep both hot and from drying out until he should want it. When he had eaten, he wiped his mouth and shouted for a slave to fetch his wife.

Ziais came grudgingly, which infuriated him. She stood beside him. Her eyes flicked over the mess left on the table and her lip twisted.

"Your brother sends greetings," Gudila grunted.

"That is kind of him," Ziais murmured.

"Look at me!"

She raised her head. Her hair had grown out somewhat and was pinned up with gold clips.

"I want you tonight."

"Bathe first," Ziais said.

He rose and slapped her. "Go to my chamber and wait for me!"

When he came, he had a skinful of wine and could not do much, for which he blamed her and slapped her again. Ziais lay shivering beside him until he began to snore and then rose quietly. She stood in her undershift, looking from him to the small knife that lay on the table where a slave had forgotten it after paring the king's fingernails for him. She picked up the knife. He would beat the slave if he saw it.

Gudila snorted and rolled over. She could have sweetened his temper since the marriage perhaps, if she had been willing to try, to wheedle and simper at him, and pretend to enjoy his touch. She had not been able to bring herself to do that, enduring him instead with a cold hatred that she willed to creep into his fingers when he touched her.

It would be so easy to cut his throat with the little knife. The slave would die along with her, but she wasn't sure she cared. She watched his sleeping form for a long time, until the oil lamp guttered and went out and only the cold moonlight came through a high window. A nightjar called somewhere in the garden outside and shook her from her thoughts. She balled her hands into fists to keep them still. She would put the knife away and wait. She prayed as she had nightly since her marriage. *Make me ill luck to him.*

The trader from the east settled himself into a chair in a corner of the scrubby tavern that sat beneath the walls of Capidava. He was brown-haired and bearded, with the look of a man who has been on the road. Two attendants, presumably slaves, sat cross-legged under a willow tree by the courtyard well, throwing dice and keeping watchful eyes on the pack ponies and the trader's wagon. The air was hot and muggy and it was fly season.

"Stew," the trader told the proprietor who looked at him inquiringly. "Beer. Send some to my men out there." He gestured at the courtyard.

The tavern keeper, a small bow-legged man in a Dacian peaked cap like the trader's, swatted halfheartedly at a fly on the table as he set the stew down and bent a curious eye on his customer. "I haven't seen you before. Going upriver?"

"Possibly," the trader said. He eyed the tavern keeper. Ex-cavalry, he thought. Not Roman, though. "I am Mucatra of Thrace and new to this route. I usually travel farther south, but I was told in the villages that the king is newly married, and thought he might be in the mood to indulge a new queen."

"He is a man with an eye for beautiful goods, most certainly," the proprietor said noncommittally.

The trader wondered if that included the queen. "I shall show him my wares then," he said cheerfully.

"He's north to Sarmizegetusa," the tavern keeper said.

"Really? I have never been there," the trader said with interest. "I have heard it is a very great city."

The small man smiled. "Traders on that route are jealous. You won't find your way."

"Ah. Does the queen go north with the king?"

The proprietor shrugged to indicate that the affairs of kings were not his business to discuss.

The trader looked resignedly at the greasy bowl of stew and picked up his spoon.

The palace at Capidava was not so grand as accounts of Decebalus's hall at Sarmizegetusa, but it towered importantly above the city behind double walls of gray stone, ashlar laid and three courtyards high, surmounted at each level by wooden palisades flying the banners of King Gudila. Its design was not unlike the terraces of tribal holds in Britain, where Correus had once been Rhys the trader, brother under the skin to Mucatra.

He and his attendant border wolves had spent the last months working their way through the Getae villages, spreading out their goods in the public squares: bolts of silk, amber and pearls, ivory and glass and bronzework, counting on Correus's purported Thracian origins to make up for any defects in his accent. All three were bearded and had achieved fine, luxuriant mustaches since they had left Singidunum. Dressed in Thracian-style trousers and tunics, none would be known for a Roman, not even by their parade-ground bearing, which each had the useful talent of discarding at will. Unfortunately, none of the villagers had been to Sarmizegetusa, nor were likely to. To them it was a strange and distant city, mythical in its splendor. All Correus and his companions had gleaned were shrugs and stories of half-human, half-lupine monsters who lurked among the snow-capped peaks to eat unwary travelers. The only caravan bound west had declined forcefully to take on any competition.

Now the three considered the palace gates.

Tsiru hooked his thumbs in his belt, his pale eyes thoughtful under the shock of wheat-straw hair that straggled from beneath his cap. "The queen's servants will have made the trip from the north with her," he commented.

"I've heard no one ever sees her," Dotos said. "The high lords keep their women out of sight." Like Tsiru and most of the other border wolves of the Danuvius, he was native born. The far side of the river was less a foreign land to him than Rome.

"We'll try it," Correus decided. "Maybe we'll have a better chance, with her lord gone north. If she's here."

The guard of the lower gate looked suspicious at their approach until Correus opened a pack and made a goodwill gift of a small amber brooch. The palace was a village in itself, its lower walls enclosing thatch and timber houses, barns and threshing rooms, and the hundreds of slaves and freeborn who served it. At the second level, above a staircase of red marble, an elaborately armored officer of what appeared to be the palace guard inspected them. At the third, a chamberlain in silk trousers, after some persuasion and another gift, sent a slave to inquire. When the slave returned, the chamberlain informed Correus with apparent surprise, or perhaps disapproval, that Queen Ziais would see the trader. The trader only, he said firmly.

Correus was escorted by the slave into the cavernous Great Hall of the palace and then into an antechamber with a red marble floor and painted walls displaying scenes of a boar hunt, and left to cool his heels. The chamber was furnished with a set of gilded chairs, two larger and more ornate than the rest, a pair of shale tables, and a hanging bronze lamp with dragons' heads. Windows on two sides were paned with Roman glass.

After some time, Queen Ziais appeared, trailed by several waiting women, and sat in the smaller of the ornate chairs, while the women fussed about her until she snapped at them. She was dark-haired, from what showed under the edges of her silk coif and gold fillet. Her eyes were pale and luminous as seawater.

"Who are you?" she demanded of Correus.

"Mucatra, Queen." He bowed, resisting the urge to scratch his face. The beard itched and made him feel as if he had stuck his head in a bramble. "Of Thrace. Trader of silks from the silk road in the east, fine amber from the far north." He knelt and laid out the best of his goods on a mat while he spoke.

"We have many traders," she said, "and are not in want of imported luxuries. But I am bored, so you may show me."

"Pearls from the Persian Gulf and perfumes of India," Correus said, smiling. "Ivory from Africa. Fine Roman glass, silver and bronzework. I have kept back the finest of my stock for you, as befits a great house." He waved his hands to indicate the grandeur of the chamber. "But this is a hearth gift." He held out a silver oil lamp shaped like a dolphin. It was exquisite work, finely detailed, with small curling waves encircling the fish. Pearls made bubbles among the waves and the oil receptacle was in its open mouth. It was nearly the most expensive thing in his stock.

She took the lamp from his hands and inspected it while her women watched him suspiciously. Apparently pleased, she nodded at him and pointed at a bolt of indigo silk and a pair of gold trellis-work armbands set with pearls. "Bring me those."

He brought them to her and studied her, still kneeling while she examined them. She was gowned in expensive splendor, bright layers of silk upon silk, and over all a heavy necklace of gold and carnelian with a small gold figure of the Goddess in the center. It was hard to tell, but he thought she was with child. That would cement the alliance no doubt.

"I am told your lord has gone north to Sarmizegetusa," he ventured. "That was your home, was it not, Queen? That is a very long way to come."

"Yes," she said. "I would not willingly make the journey again." She touched the little gold figure that hung among the carnelian beads. "I did not wish to make it the first time."

Her maids made shocked protesting noises and she shot them an evil look. Correus wondered if they were her own people or King Gudila's.

"I had thought perhaps to take my goods to Sarmizegetusa," he ventured, spreading out another bolt of silk.

She smiled, a little grimly. "It is not an easy road. And you would need my brother's permission."

Correus was silent a moment. Then he smiled back. "I heard that the Romans tried that road lately and came to a bad end. I assure you I am carrying only silk and silver."

"Anyone may go by the Iron Gates," she said, trying on the armbands. "Who is not a Roman anyway. The caravans take the Dragon's Road."

"And that is the way that your brother guards so carefully?"

"My brother guards everything carefully."

"As a king should," Correus murmured.

She looked at him. "Where are you from, Mucatra?"

"Thrace, Queen, as I told you."

She raised dark brows above the seawater eyes. "Indeed? I had a nursemaid from Thrace, when I was young."

Correus wished a curse on the nursemaid from Thrace and her no doubt authentic accent. Ziais put her forefinger to the gold figure at her throat again and considered him. Her gaze made him feel oddly naked, stripped bare of beard and mustache and Thracian costume. "So you wish to find the Dragon's Road, Mucatra?" She put a little emphasis on the name. "And sell my brother silks?"

"Indeed, Queen. I have many fine silks besides these. I could carry letters for you," he offered.

"I gave my love to my brother when we parted," Ziais said. She returned her attention to the indigo silk. "It's unlikely they will let you through, but you can sit in Sucidava and wait if you feel inclined."

"There are brighter silks," one of the women suggested nervously. "The colors that your lord favors." Correus wondered if she was trying to change the subject.

Ziais snapped her head around. "I did not ask to know his thoughts. Or yours." The maids looked at each other uneasily. Whatever she did to annoy her lord would probably come back to bite them as well. But he thought they were afraid of her.

There was something about the queen of the Getae that made Correus think of Ygerna – not as he had left her in Singidunum but as she had been in her uncle's hall, a royal woman and grand-daughter of the Dark People of the hollow hills. Correus had not heard that the women of Dacian royal families possessed the authority that the matriarchal Silures accorded to theirs, but he thought that this one had… some power, and had bought it with some price he couldn't guess at.

When she sent the silk back and asked for the other bolt, a changeable weave the color of sunset with bright scarlet threads interwoven, and had her women bring a silver mirror so that she could see it against her skin, he wondered if he was only being fanciful. Then she bought the indigo silk after all and the armbands and a pair of pearl and lapis lazuli earrings, and sent her women for a household slave to find him a bed for the night, and quarters for his men by the kitchen fire. They looked disapproving but did as they were told. Correus thought that she was deliberately doing things that she knew her husband wouldn't like, but that she had probably not been told specifically not to do. It was one of the small powers that the powerless wield.

He knew better than to wander the palace unescorted, but the slave was a chatty soul and happy to entertain the trader instead of whatever chore he was supposed to be doing. When Correus expressed an urge again to visit Sarmizegetusa and the Dacian king's hold there, he shook his head. "A nasty long way, sir, if I may say so, all upriver and then through that pass."

"Where is the pass?"

The slave shook his head. "I couldn't tell you. It's the way we rode when King Gudila came back from the war, to bring the queen home to him, but I was too frightened to pay much attention. We were told strictly not to leave the camp at night too. In the mountains, they don't like strangers going by. Some of the people there can turn into wolves. They'll kill you and just tear your throat out, not like regular wolves."

Correus felt dubious about the wolfmen. The local populace was probably more menacing. "But you ended at Sucidava?" Wherever that was. "And downriver from there?"

"Oh, yes. There are monsters in the water too, you know. And I was seasick."

This disheartening information was enlarged somewhat in the morning when Dotos informed them that he had used his romantic powers on the junior kitchen maid in the guards' quarters and that she had said she knew there was another route because her uncle was a horse trader and he avoided the Iron Gates because the narrow road along the river upset the beasts, but she didn't know where it was exactly, just west of here.

"Why is this accursed pass so hard to find?" Tsiru said, exasperated. The two of them had been all over that country before now, or their fellow wolves had, and all they had managed was vague, evasive information from anyone who might actually know; and yet caravans went over the route.

"Because this Dragon's Road is Decebalus's back door," Dotos said. "The caravan masters won't risk annoying him by babbling about it."

"And you're sure it exists?" Correus asked. Logically, it had to. And Ziais and her seasick slave had both said it did.

"Sure enough that our wolves told Cornelius Fuscus not to go by the Iron Gates," Tsiru said bitterly. The frontier scouts who had accompanied Fuscus there had died with him. "We told him to wait till we found it."

"Then we'll find it," Correus said. "Where is Sucidava?"

"There are two of them," Dotos said unhelpfully.

"Mithras, I hate this country," Correus said. "Do you know where either of them are?"

"One south of here, and one across the river from Oescus, roughly."

"The one to the south is in our territory, technically speaking," Tsiru said. The farthest reaches of Lower Moesia, where the river turned north toward its delta, were under dubious control. "It's the one near Oescus more likely. Oescus is where they hit first last year so that makes sense. Why do you think she told you Sucidava?" he added.

"I'm not sure," Correus said. "But I think it was the truth."

–

They headed west again along the tracks that bordered the Danuvius, unpacking their goods at each small river settlement, while Correus inquired with casual disinterest about any caravans passing through. The roads were passable, not up to Roman standards, but often graded and smoothed for the Dacian patrols that kept a presence on the north side of the river. Where pale limestone bluffs occasionally rose from the southern bank, on the north the land was marshy and the towns set well back from the river and its floodplain. The path off the main road into these was more often a cow track than a road and the wagon lost a wheel in the ruts at predictable intervals. Tsiru and Dotos kept their ears open in the taverns and won a fair amount of silver teaching the other patrons a complicated board and dice game, but no useful information was forthcoming.

They were mending the wagon wheel yet again, now a few miles from the main road down the rutted track to Sucidava and pulled over on the muddy shoulder, when a troop of Dacian horse clattered by. They halted abruptly just beyond and the captain turned back.

"Bad luck," he commented. "Where's your permit?"

"No one's told me a broken wagon wheel requires one," Correus said, looking up from the mud.

"Travel permit and mind your tongue." He stared at Correus under the rim of a peaked helmet and Correus noted that someone had broken his nose at some point.

"For the pass?" Correus ventured.

"No, for the Olympics in Greece. Permit!"

Correus stood up. "We didn't know we needed one, Captain." He touched his cap in apparent repentance. "We come from Thrace, and we'd a mind to see Sarmizegetusa. Everyone says it's a wonder."

"It's a long way upriver to the Iron Gates if you don't fall off the cliff passing the gorges."

Correus looked perplexed. "We had heard there was another pass, near here."

"No."

"No? Not even with a permit?"

"Not if you didn't know you needed one. Fix that wheel and go back the way you came." He put his heel to his horse's flank and kicked him into a gallop, setting up a spit of wet ground.

"Well, that was useful," Tsiru said, wiping mud off his face. "He came out of Sucidava. How far do you suppose his range is, before he turns around?"

"Long enough for us to get there and get lost if we hurry," Correus said.

Dotos had been at work while they talked and he sat up now, tools in hand. "That'll hold. It had better. That spoke's our last spare."

Sucidava was one of the fortified border villages built by Decebalus's allies to defend the river from the Dacian side. It was largely unseen from the gray stone ramparts of the Roman fort across the river at Oescus, but large enough to disappear in if no one was looking for you. They left the wagon in a clump of willows that screened it from the track and took the ponies out of their traces. There was usually a horse market in these towns and that seemed fair enough cover to get them through the gates.

The village lay within mud and timber walls, its gates opening onto a courtyard and municipal fountain basking in the afternoon sun. A caravan was camped not far from the gates and they eyed it with interest. Correus sent Dotos, whose face the cavalry captain hadn't seen, to approach its master with the proposition that they should join it. The answer was not unexpected.

"No one goes past here without a chit from Decebalus," the caravan master said bluntly. "And don't think about following, because you won't get there in one piece."

Dotos frowned at him. "I suppose you don't want the competition," he said sulkily.

"Suppose what you like," the caravan master said. "I've enough to aggravate me and the damn fool horsemaster's gone again."

"How do you lose a horsemaster?" Dotos inquired, interested.

"Down a wine jar's neck. He'll be all right when he's sober. They all drink. Think they're centaurs. One of these days one of them will go over a cliff. Now go away. I can't take you and your wagons up the pass and that's that."

–

The fortuitous horsemaster was very drunk indeed and he had found friends not long after Dotos brought back this useful information. The boy with him was drunk too. In fact, everyone appeared to be drunk, although their friends were somewhat more functional. When the horsemaster and his boy laid their heads down on the table and began to snore, the friends helpfully carried them to the inn's stables to sleep it off. When it was dark, they helpfully took them somewhere even safer.

Correus and the other two went to ground for the night in a different inn, dirt-floored but respectable and possibly without fleas, stabling their unremarkable, and therefore unmemorable, ponies there. The stable smelled of hay and mice and horse dung, a homey and comforting scent. A family of barn swallows had made their mud nests in the rafters. Correus lingered outside, listening to their chatter, as Tsiru and Dotos made their way back through the stable yard. A brisk wind was coming up, driving the first late summer fall of leaves before it and moving patches of cloud across a sky thick with stars and a half-moon just rising through the grove of alders behind the inn. A quiet step behind him made him freeze.

Whoever it was, like Correus, was carrying no lantern. Correus turned silently, waiting. Cloud moved across the moon and then away and he saw the profile for just a moment, silhouetted against the pale wall of the stable, the broken nose unmistakable. Correus eased his dagger from his belt.

"Hold!" The Dacian peered into the darkness. "You!"

Correus stepped backward silently, but the Dacian leaped at him, a curved blade in one hand. He grabbed Correus by the throat. "You were told to leave, not park your wagon by the spring. If you weren't stupid, you'd know those willows had their feet in water and every soul in this town goes there, worse luck for you."

"We just wanted to get a night's sleep," Correus said plaintively, pulling at the man's grip with his right hand. He shifted his grip on the dagger in his left. The moon glinted evilly on the falx in the captain's hand. Correus could see it out of the corner of his eye, terrifyingly close to his head.

The captain tightened his grip. "Well you're for it now. Come with me and don't argue or I'll just kill you here instead of later. You're up to something and people don't get up to something on my watch."

"No, really, we just wanted a beer and some rest." Correus looked at him pleadingly as he brought his knife hand up, silent in the darkness. The captain opened his mouth to speak and Correus's knife went into the gap between his helmet and his hauberk. The falx swung wildly, wavered in mid-motion, and fell as the captain fell.

Correus knelt, heart pounding, and gasped for breath. He took the captain by the heels and pulled him into the alders. When he had him well out of sight of the inn, he picked up the falx and returned to slide it back into its sheath.

Dotos and Tsiru stared at him as he came stumbling through the door of their chamber.

"Mithras god, we parked the cursed wagon by the public spring," he gasped. "It probably feeds that fountain in the square. I saw an inlet by the gates and didn't think anything of it." He looked at Dotos. "Get it out of here now."

–

In the morning, swearing in three separate languages, the caravan master hired another horsemaster and his assistant, who had been let go and cheated of their wages by the thief Dotos.

"He says it's because he can't go to Sarmizegetusa," the one called Mucatra said. "Wherever in Hecate's name that is, it sounds mythical to me. He's probably found someone who'll work for less, poor ape, or bought a slave. I hope he robs him."

The caravan master looked amused in spite of everything. "All right, I'll take you on. I'm short two men. I've a herd of a dozen good horses to get over that pass without injuring them. If you're not competent, I'll know it the first day and you'll be sorry."

They were very fine horses indeed, and Tsiru eyed them enviously as they rode, mounted on the caravan master's somewhat less splendid beasts, with the string on leads between them. The track led out of the river's lowlands and into the hills by way of a gap that looked as if it led only into a walled valley and then twisted through a patch of scrubland and trees into another narrow valley, increasingly shadowed on both sides by limestone outcroppings. Correus let out his breath only when they were well out of sight of Sucidava. With luck the captain had been the sort of man that no one would be surprised to find murdered.

The caravan was a large one: forty heavy wagons laden with goods, and one more with tents and cookpots and the meager possessions of the drivers. There were only ten guards with them and Correus wondered about that until they came through another gap, chosen from a seemingly identical series of possibilities, and met a troop of Dacian horse at its head. The caravan master spoke with the troop's officer, while Correus sweated. The master handed over a series of tablets, the officer stamped something with a seal ring, and they moved on, escorted by one of the troop's riders.

–

Dotos eyed the sleeping figures with mild concern. They were breathing all right, and the prefect had sworn he knew how much to give them. He had it from Nicomedes the surgeon, he had said, with explicit instructions. They stirred, and Dotos felt relieved. He supposed they would wonder how they had got in the cellar of the town granary, but they had been very drunk already before the dose in their beer. Dotos left them there, with the granary door ajar, said good morning to the granary cat, and returned to the inn to wait for whoever came back down the mountain. The wagon was in the bottom of a ravine and its most valuable contents in Dotos's pack.

–

The caravan encountered Dacian troops nearly every day. Each time, the caravan master showed his tablets again and was given more stamps and they were waved through. At each checkpoint, their escort dropped off and was replaced by another from the Dacian guards. Correus almost left off waiting to hear the hoof-beats of a vengeful rider from Sucidava. The mountain valleys narrowed and the trees began to turn their leaves as they climbed, splashing the mountainside with wine and yellow and amber. Everyone on the caravan was strictly forbidden to wander off the trail, and the wagon drivers believed fervently in the wolfmen. Occasionally a hunting party was sent out, and Correus and Tsiru made their contribution with sling and spear and the little Scythian bow that Tsiru carried over his shoulder. Their primary quarry were the goatlike antelope that browsed the rocky slopes, as well as hares, both of which were also hunted by mountain lynxes and actual wolves. The forest was thick and impenetrable-looking even where small farms clung to the slopes. They passed only one or two villages, whose residents made angry gestures at them from the trackside.

"They don't have the coin to buy what we're carrying," Tsiru said, "and I expect this crew isn't above thieving what they can. No wonder we're told not to wander at night."

They were squatting beside their fire, their charges whuffling on their picket line nearby, and debating softly how far to stick with the caravan.

"It looks to me as if we'll climb as far as the ridge tops tomorrow," Tsiru said. "Roof of the damn world, by the look of it. Far enough to see from there?" He stood and stretched. "I have to piss," he added, and disappeared into the darkness, whistling softly.

Correus looked at the ridge top ahead, black as pitch against a slightly paler sky splashed with stars and the wide, luminous ribbon of the Milky Way. Tomorrow maybe. He thought Tsiru was right. Once they were at the crest of the mountains, they should be able to see where the track went. Correus did not want to actually find himself in Sarmizegetusa trying to sell Decebalus a horse.

Tsiru came back, still whistling, and Correus recognized it after a moment; Tsiru's grasp of melody was tenuous.

"Stop that!" he hissed.

"What?" Tsiru looked confused.

"That damn song."

"The guard we picked up today was whistling that. It's a nice tune. What's wrong with it?"

"The Dacian?" Correus lowered his voice even further to a thin whisper.

"Himself. I don't think he's Dacian, though. I think he's German."

Correus swore under his breath. He wasn't a native speaker, which made it difficult to pinpoint other accents laid over the guard's speech.

Tsiru grinned. "Decebalus hires anybody, just like us."

"Whatever he is, that's a Roman cavalry tune," Correus said very quietly. "As a matter of fact, I learned it in Germany."

Tsiru was silent.

"One more day," Correus said. "That's all we can risk."

–

In the morning Correus eyed the Dacian guard as the man rode along the caravan line. He was tallish and fair, clad in Dacian scale, wisps of blond hair visible under the rim of his peaked helmet. He rode a good horse, a buckskin with a white blaze and four white socks, and a Roman army brand on its left flank. Correus had noted that the day before with some irritation, but stolen horses were not a surprise given the past year. Now he also noted a certain posture in the man on its back, and, with increasing irritation, a smaller brand like a bird on the horse's right haunch. Domitian had recruited Germans for the auxiliaries after the last war and shipped most of them out to Moesia. Correus faded back to the end of the caravan and the horse lines. If he recognized the guard, the chances were excellent that the guard would eventually recognize him.

The sky had shifted from the clear expanse of the night before to a dim gray that got darker as they rode. The track switchbacked constantly like a snake climbing the steep terrain, and up above the tree line in the afternoon it began to snow. It was early in the year and the caravan master seemed unworried, which suggested to Correus that they might not have much farther to go. From where they climbed up the mountain, the trees below were patches like dark fur among the tawny grasses and jagged stone. The wagon drivers huddled under their cloaks and urged their reluctant oxen on up the track.

As Correus had hoped, they came at dusk to the skyline and peered out across what indeed looked like the top of the world. If any gods lived here, though, they were hardier than most. The track ahead, showing through the dusting of snow and worn by the passage of numerous wagon wheels, ran along a series of ridges in looping S-bends, as if someone had thrown a coiled rope onto the mountaintop. It was cold and guards and drivers huddled around their fires as night fell.

Correus walked down the caravan line silently. It was dark of the moon and he was nearly invisible to eyes inside the circles of firelight that marked the caravan's length. He had no business being away from his own fire and he went cautiously.

The German guard squatted over a fire in the lee of a wagon, talking with the driver, a litany of complaint about the cold, the pay, the promises that had been made and not kept.

"I might as well have stayed where I was, for all the good I've got here. Fucking Romans. Fucking Dacians. Fuck all of them."

"Well we'll soon be there and you can get drunk and find a girl. That always helps," the driver said.

"Like as not they'll send me out again as soon as we're through the gates. One of the guards in Sucidava was killed and laid out in the alder grove, and now they're all running around looking for spies in everyone's bedclothes."

—

In the morning, Tsiru was gone.

Correus went shouting for him up and down the caravan line, increasingly frantic.

"Fell down a crevasse most like," the caravan master said unsympathetically. "Told you not to run about at night."

"Wolfmen," a wagon driver said, pulling his hat down over his ears.

"Whatever, we can't wait for him," the caravan master said. "Saddle up."

"I can't just leave him!" Correus looked frenziedly about him as if Tsiru might suddenly appear from under a wagon.

"What's the trouble?" The German guard appeared, glaring at all of them.

"That's my sister's boy!" Correus said. "I have to find him!"

The guard shook his head. "You won't find him. Not if he's out there." He waved a hand at the expanse of rocky mountainside.

"I have to," Correus said stubbornly.

"No, you don't," the caravan master said. "You signed on for the whole journey and you'll earn your pay. Now saddle up!"

Correus shook his head, looking near tears. He fished in the purse at his belt. "He's my sister's boy," he said again. "He's all she's got. I'm going to find him." He pulled out a handful of silver and flung it at the caravan master. "Here's your pay back! And the gods curse you for a flint heart!" He stumbled away from them, back down the trail.

"And curse you for a fool," the caravan master shouted after him, gathering up the silver. "You'll go on foot. You're not taking my horse with you!"

The German guard fixed his eyes on the disappearing form, who looked for a moment at the tethered horses and then picked up his pack from beside the ashes of last night's fire and stumbled on.

"You!" The caravan master pointed at one of the wagon guards. "Look to the horses! Get that string going and keep them together."

Correus scrambled down the rocky scree of the track as quickly as he could, shouting for Tsiru. He wouldn't catch up with him until nightfall likely, but it made a good effect.

-

They had been on the trail eight days with the wagons. It would take at least six to get back, maybe more trying to stay out of sight of the Dacian checkpoints and the mountain villages. They had debated stealing the horses, but horses were harder to slide by a suspicious sentry. And the caravan master would have sent someone after them. Better to slink back to Sucidava on foot.

They were congratulating themselves on their cleverness on the fifth night, beside a fire kindled under the lee of a limestone outcrop just above the lowest checkpoint, when a whisper of sound made Tsiru jerk his head up. The hair on the back of Correus's neck went up. Something was out there. He put a hand on Tsiru's arm to hold him still. Whatever it was didn't move again.

Correus was reasonably sure it wasn't wolfmen and most likely not wolves either, as they rarely attacked people unless they were starving. But whatever it was wasn't going away.

Nobody slept, probably including the watcher in the scrub on the hillside. At first light, Correus stood up and stretched, the nondescript sword he had worn at his belt in one hand and his hunting spear in the other. No movement came from the wooded hillside. Then they heard a soft snort and a quick rustle as if someone had clapped a hand around a horse's muzzle. A possibility occurred to Correus and he stuck two fingers in his mouth and gave a sharp three-note whistle. Something rustled in the brush; he did it again and the buckskin horse broke from the trees.

"Get him!" Correus shouted. "Not the horse!" He ran after the fleeing man on the hillside. The horse's rider wouldn't try to fight two of them, but if he got to the checkpoint the hunt would be on, and they'd be lucky to make it back to Sucidava.

The German guard was scrambling through the tangled under-story of a clump of firs that clung precariously to the slope, making his way downhill toward the trail. Correus flew after him. Behind him Tsiru nocked an arrow into his bow and waited for a clear shot. The guard stumbled and Correus threw himself at him, catching him around the ankles. The two of them flailed in the dry scrub and downed branches, rolling over and over on the slope. Correus's sword and spear had fallen and he scrabbled at his belt for his dagger while the guard did the same. The guard had the advantage of a helmet and a hauberk of heavy scale and he got one hand around Correus's throat as Correus tried to pin him down.

"Deserter!" Correus spat at him in German as he struggled, and the man's eyes widened. "Which legion did you betray when you broke your oath?" Correus kneed him in the belly and the fingers slipped. He managed to get his dagger from his belt. The German's dagger was dangerously close to his face and he caught the hand that held it and twisted until he felt the joint crack. The German didn't drop the dagger. Correus felt its tip slice his face open. He could see Tsiru out of the corner of one eye, drawn bow in hand. He tried to hold the German still and hoped that Tsiru wouldn't shoot him instead.

Tsiru had no such intention and took no chances. He stood directly over the thrashing pair and when there was an instant's opening, he put the arrow's tip against the scale hauberk and released it. The arrow drove into the German's chest, nearly pinning him to the ground, blood pouring from his mouth.

Correus sat back, gasping, blood pouring down his own face.

Tsiru slumped beside him. "What do we do with him?" he asked when he had caught his breath. He eyed the dead man in the Dacian armor with disgust.

"Pull that arrow and let the wolves have him," Correus said. "In some ways we ask for this, conscripting our enemies." He whistled again and the buckskin snorted and trotted over obligingly.

"Exactly how in the Horseman's name are you doing that?" Tsiru inquired as Correus got to his feet.

Correus laughed, a short bark that was not exactly of amusement. "He comes from my father's farm. The old man raises cavalry remounts and his horsemaster teaches all the stock to come to that whistle. It's very useful. You can obliterate a brand but apparently you can't unteach a horse something it has firmly in its head." He went through the saddle and its accoutrements and collected a short, unpleasant-looking falx, and shook a handful of coin from the pouch hung on the horns. He slapped the horse on the rear.

"We'd never get him past the checkpoint," he said regretfully. "He'll go back to his barn or wherever his mates are. By the time he does, we had better be down the mountain." He started to whistle, the old cavalry tune that the German had whistled, and checked himself, but some of the words came back to him:

The mountains are tall and my pay's very small
And Caesar expects a lot...

XIV

A Wind out of the World Tree

Harvestnight came to the lands north of the Rhenus on a wet wind, the morning air heavy, the trees still dropping their bright, sodden leaves. The thatched and timbered houses of the Semnone chieftain's hold looked busy with their air of bustle and woodsmoke. Doors stood open to constant coming and going from the well and the garden plots. The packed dirt streets, damp with the morning's rain, were jammed with wagons, dogs, and men on horseback come for the twice-yearly council where tribal matters were decided. At this hinge point in the year, midway between the fall equinox and winter solstice, the borders between the worlds were thin, other winds blew through them, and other visitors might be expected as well. The doors of the hold were scratched with Wuotan's cross to bar the dead who rode with the Wild Hunt, and most were careful to arrive by nightfall. Before the sun fell in a shimmer behind the western slopes, the harvest was brought in, leaving the last sheaf to stand bound in the field for Frey whose festival Harvestnight was. An older power even than Wuotan, Frey was the golden lord, god of fruitfulness and increase who lay with the earth in winter to quicken the seed that would green the land again in spring.

Households who had not seen each other since the spring renewed acquaintance and often enough old quarrels, adding to the matters for the council to sift out. Household dogs barked at the visitors' hounds and thralls waded through the milling packs, breaking up fights until a truce was negotiated.

Ranvig shifted in his chair in the Council Hall and considered the next case before him. He had decided six quarrels so far and his backside ached. It was a dank day and that did not agree with his bones, but as far as he was concerned, it was old Hauk who was giving him a pain there. Hauk must be eighty by now and age had only made him more stubborn, and just now it was directed at Armin, in whose hold he had found a suspicious pig. The council lords gathered under the war spears that hung above the hearth were drinking the chieftain's beer and waiting impatiently for the joint that was roasting on a spit in the hall kitchen. Any one of them would have given Hauk a pig of their own just to get on with it. And then there was the man that Commius had brought. He could wait, Ranvig thought, watching him fidget. The longer the better.

Ranvig held out a hand with his beer horn in it and the thrall crouched at his feet took it to refill. "How came you to suspect that this pig is yours?" he inquired.

"Because I'm missing a pig," Hauk said, as if that was obvious. "Pig man recognized her."

"And why was your pig man in Armin's pens?"

"To look for my pig, of course." Hauk folded his arms across his wolfskin jacket.

The woman who sat to Ranvig's right tapped his arm. "The pig man is quite certain," she whispered. "He is in the kitchen with my women and hasn't reason to lie." She was younger than Ranvig, with rose gold hair and wide blue eyes that had grown considerably shrewder since her marriage to the chieftain.

"Why would Armin take Hauk's pig?" Ranvig whispered back. "Armin isn't poor."

"To annoy Hauk. They quarreled over a game of draughts and they've been at each other ever since. Hauk's daughter-in-law has been driven mad by it."

Ranvig smiled at her, a swift secret smile. Signy's ability to sort through the small daily crises of a large holding was uncanny, and she was almost always right. "Give Hauk back his pig," he told Armin, "and don't argue with me or I'll take it and eat it myself."

Armin looked furious but none of the council lords seemed inclined to come to his defense. The chieftain's decisions were binding once rendered. Hauk and Armin might continue to hate each other but they would not feud and that was the point.

Ranvig sorted out the next cases, including the sale of a stallion that had proved to have only one testicle, the exact dividing line between two lords' barley fields, and the paternity of Alda Jurgens-daughter's baby, which her father demanded to know and which Alda refused to divulge, claiming magical parentage in the form of Donar Thunderer under an oak tree. Ranvig gave no judgment on that as there was no way to make Alda tell what she didn't want to.

Only one case was of serious import. Murder, even attempted murder, was likely to bring blood feud and thus was dangerous to leave unsettled. Both parties were newly made warriors of the last spear-taking, and still seething with anger.

Fiorgyn, on Ranvig's other side, listened silently. Fiorgyn Arngunns-daughter held a position of respect in the tribe that amounted to council status, but she rarely spoke when she didn't have to, content to let Ingvar, who sat among the council lords, be their mutual voice.

Just now she was watching the man who had come with Commius, and Commius himself, who really had no business in a respectable lord's hold, being a river pirate with the morals of Loki. Commius had escaped by the skin of his teeth and without a great deal more of his skin, from the burning of his band's encampment in the marshes of the Rhenus delta by the vengeful forces of Rome. He had not attempted to renew the scope of his former captain's operation but subsisted on small unwary craft and probably thievery. His scarred face appeared occasionally at Ranvig's gates with things he thought the chieftain might like to buy or know. Just now he had a man with him who made Fiorgyn think, for reasons she couldn't quite pinpoint, of coins. He had reddish-brown hair starting to gray and a beard which grew oddly under his chin, and the bright, acquisitive look of a magpie.

Ranvig set a blood price for the attack and ordered the council lords whose holdings the combatants had come from to see that it was paid. "You set household against household with your stupidity!" he said. His people were stiff-necked and disinclined to drop a quarrel as long as anyone felt injured by the other. A feud had to be cut off before it started. He glared at them and went on scathingly, "Neither of you is blameless. And this over a woman. I am told that now she will have neither of you, and if she will, I will not countenance the marriage. You are both infants, and too young to marry. Let your lords take you back home to your mothers."

He turned to Commius as both boys stepped back, shame-faced. "Who is this that you have brought into my hold, Commius?"

Commius's twisted face adopted a clever look and he touched his cap to the chieftain. "The gods have sent the Emperor Nero back to earth and brought him to me," he said.

Arni snorted. "Tell that to a sailor on a cow," he said. "Nero is long dead. And, I have heard, wasn't such a one as the gods would think worth resurrecting."

"How did you come by him?" Ranvig inquired.

"As I said, the gods brought him to me. Look!" Commius held out a coin, a silver denarius with the late emperor's image on it.

That was why she had coins in mind, Fiorgyn thought. She had seen one like it, still circulating in Moguntiacum where there was less urgency to remove every trace of the disgraced emperor by melting it down.

Ranvig inspected the coin. "It is like," he admitted. "But like any number of other men as well. Is this your proof?"

"I have spoken to him at great length," Commius said.

The man who claimed he was Nero spoke loudly in Latin. "I am my own proof!" He struck a pose, incongruous with his ragged shirt and breeches.

"At length," Commius repeated. "You can't shut him up in fact."

"Does he speak German?" Arni inquired.

"No. He speaks Greek and Latin. There's more proof for you," Commius said. "Now what do you suppose would happen if someone took him to Rome with an army behind him?"

"A great deal of trouble, I imagine," Ranvig said. "For someone."

"There are people there who insist he's still alive." Commius nodded to emphasize this bit of information. "I've heard that rumor for years, and now here he comes and we find out it's true. What would that be worth to you?"

"Nothing," Ranvig said shortly but he eyed the man with increasing interest. "Commius, go outside and take him with you. Hauk and Armin, you go with them. It will give you something to watch besides each other." He turned again to the thrall waiting at his feet. "Take them some beer from the kitchen. We are not inhospitable after all. Commius, don't come back until I send for you."

Commius departed looking hopeful, between Armin and Hauk, with the possible emperor going ahead of them – lord-lywise, as Arni said as soon as they were out the door.

"You can't mean to believe in that man!" he demanded.

"And where did that thief Commius come by him?" Steinvar asked. He looked suspicious. Commius was an ill omen as often as not.

"He's not going to say," Horst, seated next to him, said. "But that one is mischief waiting to happen. Commius will use him if we don't and not to our liking maybe."

The council began to thrash it out, until their crosstalk was a cacophony of misheard argument and counterargument. Ranvig sat listening until Barden the priest thumped his staff on the floor to get their attention and they quieted. Barden had been silent up until now, as the small quarrels of men were not a matter for the gods. But this was different. He put his hands on his white-robed knees, the staff with its golden sun disk propped against them, and looked at Ranvig. "If someone has brought this man up from

Hel or wherever it is that Romans go, then it is a matter for us to worry about who. On the other hand, if he is false, then we may wonder what is his purpose before we try to bend him to ours."

"And if he is not restored from Hel but simply didn't die when it was said he did?" Horst asked.

"He was seen to die," Barden said. "We pay attention to the affairs of Rome. People are fools everywhere and see what they wish to. There are many poor in Rome and this Caesar bribed them to love him with food and entertainments, and so of course they did."

"What is he then?" Horst demanded.

Barden closed his eyes. His fingers clenched around the sheaf of wheat at his belt while his lips moved. He sat a long time and they watched him uneasily, and felt a bit of the wind that blows through the World Tree about their ears.

"Not a wanderer," Barden said at last. "I would know."

"A fool then? Who could hope to carry that off?"

Fiorgyn spoke now. "There have been others pretending to be Nero before this."

"Where did you hear this tale?" Arni asked.

"I forget," she said shortly. "But they made much trouble and the Romans were very angry about it."

"They died in the end, I expect," Ingvar said. People who made that kind of trouble for Rome tended to.

She smiled at him. "I believe so." She cocked her head at Barden. "Is the man simply mad then?"

"There is something laid on him," Barden admitted. "Possibly it is madness."

"Commius won't care," Arni said. "He just thinks he can get something for him without risking his own hide."

"He does resemble a hot coal," Ranvig agreed. "Put him in a box it will take a while to burn through, however, and he might be a useful gift for someone. No one near to us, though. I want him elsewhere before Haddon of the Chatti learns of him."

"Haddon has thought of a better way than an ill-advised war to break his treaty with the Romans," Ingvar said. "If the new governor in Moguntiacum is successful, Haddon will have the Romans in his purse."

"Exactly," Ranvig said. "Where they too will no doubt burn a hole, but that isn't our affair. Haddon would try to use this man to pressure the governor and that would be dangerous. I need to buy him from Commius and forestall that."

"Who else would want him?" Horst demanded. "He'll burn anyone's hand eventually."

"Eventually," Ranvig agreed. "Then they may pass him on. I promised the king of the Dacians that the Quadi and the Marcomanni, our kinsmen, would not ally with Rome, in return for his keeping Rome too busy to look to the Free Lands."

"That we did at spearpoint," Arni said. "Or the threat of it."

"Precisely. Now I am in need of a gift better than cattle to sweeten their temper over that." He stood. "We will feast and I will speak with Commius while we do."

—

As the sun dropped, the air was full of the scent of carcasses roasting on spits for the Harvestnight feast. Animals who looked unlikely to make it through the winter had been butchered, and sausage-making and the salting away of the larger joints had gone on while the council met. Now the women of the hold put up their aprons and went to wash and dress in their best. The council lords were shooed from the hall and trestle tables were set up and laid with the best cloths and the chieftain's most valuable plates and cups.

Whoever Commius's man was, Fiorgyn thought, he was going to make trouble. "Ingvar, what will the Romans do when someone makes a noise about this man?" she asked as they changed their clothes in the guest chamber. Their son, attended by his nurse, pulled at the hem of her gown, rubbing the fur trim against his cheek. "That's muddy, small one," she said, and the nurse diverted him with a wooden horse.

Ingvar smiled and picked the boy up and set him on the bed. Never once had he questioned the fact that the child's birth had come early. He must know, of course, but the husband that a babe was born to was the babe's father. Fiorgyn had chosen Ingvar for his kindness as well as his brown hair, and she was content to be the mistress of his hold. It was a lie she told herself often enough to believe.

Now Ingvar said, "They will kill him. It is as well that Ranvig sends him on somewhere. That one is a gift like a coat full of fleas."

Fiorgyn pulled her gown off and stood while her maid dropped her festival dress over her head and straightened its woolen layers. The girl fastened a broad gold collar around Fiorgyn's neck and little gold balls into the ends of her pale braids. "Hauk will want for us to use him," Fiorgyn said thoughtfully. "And Armin too. That's why Ranvig sent them away with Commius. Those two are like fighting cocks. That's all they know. And Arni."

"Then they will bluster and Ranvig will ignore them," Ingvar said. "A useful weapon is what takes the Romans' eyes off the Free Lands when they get bored. Even Arni knows that."

"So now as well as their own governor, we will fight them with a madman, or a possible ghost, although Barden says not, and I suppose he knows."

–

Ranvig, watching the man across the Harvestnight high table, decided that no ghost could have an appetite like that. He ate silently, steadily, with the gluttony of the starving, his face greasy with joint of beef and roasted boar, his hand clenched around a beer horn that emptied as soon as it was filled. Ranvig had put Commius at the high table beside him so that he could talk to him over the din, and the man across so he could watch him.

Ranvig reached a long arm, heavy with gold bracelets, for an apple from the bowl at the center of the table. "You would do well to shed this man as soon as may be," he suggested to Commius. "You will impoverish yourself just by feeding him."

"We appreciate the chieftain's hospitality," Commius said. He drained his own beer horn. "A thousand Roman gold aureus seems a fair price for so useful a man."

Ranvig leaned back in his chair and laughed. "You couldn't get that much to ransom *me*," he said. "Two gold aurei."

Commius looked aggrieved. "The chieftain is joking."

"The chieftain is not. I will give you these bracelets, which are worth five gold aureus, or the equivalent in coin." He held out his wrists, banded with twisted gold set with carnelian and capped with gold stags' heads. "Five gold aureus or the bracelets and you won't have to worry about my telling the commander at the fortress in Moguntiacum that you have him. Or where your boats dock."

"I am insulted," Commius said.

Ranvig shrugged. "Make up your mind before we finish eating or I'll throw you both out of my hold, Harvestnight or no. There are no doubt many of the dead who would like to visit you." He jerked his head at a thrall who refilled Commius's beer horn.

Commius sulked for most of the dinner while his charge got drunker, as did nearly everyone else as the beer and heady harvest mead went around. The Ranvigshold hounds and the visitors' dogs squabbled over bones and scraps under the table. The din grew louder with boasts and arguments and wild bets on improbable things, and new blood feuds would have begun if Barden had not forestalled them.

Ranvig shook Commius's shoulder. Commius blinked at him. "Decide, Commius. Take my offer or ride out tonight." Ranvig pulled off the bracelets and Commius started to protest. Then he shook his head.

"Coin. If you are to cheat a poor man so, then I will have it in coin." After all, the bracelets might be bronze under the gilding.

Ranvig snapped his fingers at a thrall and sent him for the coin. "Tell Lord Arni to take that man and put him in the stable with a lock on the door. And find a place for this one. I wouldn't send him out on Harvestnight." He grinned at Commius. He would send the man to the Quadi and the Marcomanni, he thought. They could pass him back and forth between them while they tried to think of how to use him safely. And if they couldn't, well they might need a gift to sweeten Decebalus in Sarmizegetusa. Although the Quadi and the Marcomanni had agreed not to ally with the Romans, they had not agreed to fight against them for Decebalus, which was no doubt a thorn under his saddle.

--

The beard and the primitive sanitation facilities available on a goat track in the Dacian mountains had left Correus with a scar down the left side of his face that gave him a faintly piratical look and unfortunately also made him instantly recognizable. This was commented on cheerfully by the camp surgeon at Viminacium as he trimmed the hair away from the lower end of the gash and shook his head.

"It's too late to stitch this. I can give you some salve that may help fade it," he offered.

"I'm not a dancing girl," Correus grumbled. "Just leave it alone. If it doesn't get infected, that's enough."

The barber also felt the need to remark on it as he shaved the remainder of his customer's face. Ordinarily Correus shaved himself, or let Eumenes do it, but the beard, which felt more and more like some hideous overgrowth colonizing his head, was more than he could deal with.

"Now I could trim your hair to put some curls over your forehead, the way the late Emperor Nero wore it. That would distract from the scar a bit, you see." The barber held a mirror hopefully in front of Correus. "You've got nice hair. You'd hardly have to use a curling iron at all."

"Mithras, no," Correus said, revolted. "Just give me a good military cut and get rid of the beard."

The barber made a tutting noise indicative of his disapproval of the prefect's decision, but did as he was told. Correus, shaven, trimmed and bathed, presented himself to Tettius Julianus in company with Tsiru and Dotos. The three of them saluted, fists to chest, and tried not to look overly pleased with themselves.

"This is most useful." Tettius consulted the papyrus bearing Correus's scribbled map. "You are in agreement that this road leads to Sarmizegetusa?"

"We are," Correus said. "It would be best if one of us rode with the column if you take that route, however. It's not exactly a road, and it's tricky country."

"I will remember that." Tettius nodded at Tsiru and Dotos. "You are dismissed. I will tell the optio that I've given you a week's leave, but don't get so drunk you don't come back, please."

When they had departed, he looked at Correus. "Now then, Prefect."

Correus waited, puzzled and mildly impatient. He had sent a message to Singidunum to let Ygerna know where he was, but he was more than eager to go home, make love to his wife, kiss his children, and see that his ala hadn't fallen apart in his absence.

"I'm transferring you," Tettius said abruptly.

Correus felt unnerved and tried to think what part of his report had been unsatisfactory. Or politically improvident. Or had the ala actually come apart in his absence and disgraced itself? All seemed unlikely.

"I'm giving you command of the Fifth," Tettius said.

Correus blinked. "The Macedonica?" A legionary command? He wondered if how much he wanted that showed on his face.

"You may want to wait to thank me," Tettius said. "They're a demoralized disaster just now. They were nearly cut in half, between the first attack on Oescus and the defeat at that accursed pass. We've sent them replacements, again, but they'll have to be knocked into line. I'm told that you took over the Fourteenth in Germany when its legate... er, died, and that you pulled it off. The Macedonica's primus pilus was killed too, and the Second

Cohort commander isn't up to this. I am aware that your family does not have senatorial rank – your father's choice, I believe, and in your case... at any rate, I have the emperor's dispensation for this."

"I'll do my best to earn that, sir." Correus tried to keep from grinning. It wouldn't make a good impression. "Is the transfer immediate? I have a household at Singidunum to move."

"You have two weeks," Tettius said. "We've mostly driven the Dacians back across the river again but keeping them there until we can deal with them properly is going to be another matter."

"Thank you. If I may suggest it, sir, my second at Singidunum, Decurion Blaesus, is well suited for command and the men are used to him."

Tettius made a note on a tablet. "I'll consider that. Now go pack up your household. Two weeks is really more than you can spare just now."

–

Three days later, in a semi-miraculous turnaround organized by Ygerna, the household was on the road. She had widened her eyes a bit at the gash on his face, kissed him, and begun packing up the household gods. Now they and the house's mortal inhabitants, including the chickens, were loaded onto a wagon or astride a horse. They went by the military road as far as Aquae, taking a detour south to avoid the suspended road above the gorges, which was not made for wagons, would have engendered hysterics in Nurse, and made even Correus uneasy with his family in tow. From there, they took a patrol craft of the Danuvius fleet for the rest of the journey.

Eumenes and Julius were cheered by their master's promotion, the importance of which they both understood. Nurse and Septima were silently disapproving of the upheaval and consequent disturbance of the children's routine, and Cottia was excited, as she was by anything new. Julius seemed to have become older and oddly thoughtful in his absence, possibly the result of his adventure, a near-death experience with more behind it than a handful of coin and dubious fame. He was pleased with himself, Correus thought, in a different way than previously. He was also restless and it was evident.

At least they didn't have to find a house. The Praetorium at the Oescus fortress was Correus's as legionary legate. Cornelius Nigrinus, the governor of the newly split-off Province of Lower Moesia, occupied his own house in the city on the bluffs above the River Oescus, where its waters flowed out of the southern mountains into the Danuvius.

Correus delivered his belongings, chickens and all, to the Praetorium, an establishment palatial by army standards, containing its own baths, stables, and an extensive garden in a walled courtyard of marble and rose brick. The previous legate had come from Surrentum on the Bay of Neapolis and had apparently missed it. The floors featured mosaics of fish and lobsters as well as Triton surrounded by Nereids on dolphins. The kitchen was decorated with octopi and squid, the dining room walls with a school of hippocamps, and a giant flounder looked up at them from the bedroom floor. Their own furnishings were too sparse for such a house and Correus sent Eumenes to find more, particularly beds and anything else that didn't have fish on it. Ygerna set off to hire a cook, having done without as long as she intended to, and Correus went to make his respects to the governor and then to take up his command in the Principia.

There he found himself welcomed by the command optio and a military tribune, also newly arrived and relieved to find a legate in charge. The tribune saluted and introduced himself as Favonius Marcellinus. Military tribunes were of the senatorial class and probably destined for their own command someday, the short road to it for the promising among them. "I can't tell you how glad we are to see you, sir," this one said, showing a deference that Correus found promising in its own way. He hoped no one had told him what had happened to the Macedonica's last tribune.

"I'm delighted to be here," Correus said. "I want to see the Second Cohort commander; I understand you've lost your primus pilus. I'd like you to be here for that, Favonius." The tribune nodded. "Also the quartermaster, the senior surgeon, and the armorer." He set his horse-tailed cavalry helmet on the desk, a beautifully made expanse of polished oak with a map shelf set in just below the writing surface.

"You'll find the armorer and the quartermaster with their heads together, I should think," the optio said. "You'll be wanting a new helmet and cuirass, but you might just keep that cavalry scale to wear under it. It's funny, we're replacing all the lorica plate with old-fashioned mail or fishscale. It turns those nasty blades better."

"It does, I was grateful to find. How far along is the replacement process?" Tettius had examined the armor of the survivors of the Iron Gates massacre and given orders for the wholesale abandonment of segmented plate, and the addition of greaves, and of manica for the arms, as well as cross-braced reinforcement of helmets, all requested to be done yesterday.

"About halfway, I'd say," the optio said. "With most of it shipped from Rome. We haven't the capacity to do it all here, or the stock. No one except for officers has worn greaves in years. And then the governor ordered all the manica taken apart and reversed when he saw them. They'd made them like they do for the gladiators, but what he wants is the other way round; says he tested them and they do better against a Dacian sword that way." They both eyed the scar on Correus's face with some curiosity.

"If you won't mind my asking, sir," Favonius said hesitantly, "was that a cut through your helmet cheekpiece that did that?"

Correus grinned at them and decided that it wouldn't hurt to augment the legate's reputation. "I went out with the border wolves. It's an experience everyone should have. I recommend it, Tribune. Just don't gamble with them."

–

The Fifth Legion Macedonica turned out in parade dress under the watchful gaze of its centurions to welcome its new legate.

Correus had promoted the centurion of the Second Cohort to primus pilus after meeting him and this had bumped a number of officers up a notch in hierarchy, there being no time to do anything other than promote from within the legion. They wore the readopted mail hauberks, lengthened in hem and sleeve according to the governor's orders, over leather harness and scarlet military tunics that echoed the horsehair helmet crests. Their shields were army red, painted with thunderbolts crossed behind the legion's rose-and-thorns insignia. They looked splendid and Correus felt proprietary about them.

Correus himself was resplendent in an embossed silvered cuirass adorned with the bull of the Macedonica and all his medals, and tied with the white legate's sash that had given him infinite pleasure to put on. The Macedonica's banner fluttered over his head, and the great gold Eagle of the legion rose above him on its staff, perched on crossed thunderbolts with silver wings swept back as if about to take flight. His helmet, adorned with a legate's eagle-feather crest, was under his arm, leaving his scarred face visible.

"I am aware of what this legion has suffered," he said, "and that many in your ranks are new to the Eagles and the rest are weary." That was a euphemism and they knew it. With the legate dead, a lack of discipline had spread like mold through the thin, leaderless ranks, and transferred itself unfortunately to the newcomers.

"The Fifth must be a legion worthy of the name again, and quickly, and how painlessly that is done will be up to you. We have less than two months before the river freezes and we are vulnerable." A little wind whipped up and a spattering of fall leaves danced around his head and whisked across the reviewing stand. When the Danuvius froze the entire river became a bridge. The assembled cohorts eyed him warily.

"I watched you at drill yesterday, and the man who tripped playing the fool and sent the man in front of him to the surgeon with a pilum point an inch into his back should be glad that the governor wasn't there. He will be," he added ominously. "Next week." The centurion in charge of yesterday's culprit blanched, as intended. A general shift among the Centuriate was another destabilizing factor and the newly promoted also included a number pulled from the ranks to replace the dead.

Correus dismissed them, doomed to a morning of drill in full marching kit, and went back to the Praetorium to change his own kit. They would no doubt be surprised when he appeared beside them, but he had discovered long ago the salutary effects of watching your commander do what he has requested you to do, and do it better.

—

"You are not twenty," Ygerna remarked as Correus lay face down on a bench beside the little blue-tiled hot pool of the Praetorium baths and let Eumenes massage his aching muscles. The water in the pool gave off a pleasant steam in the fall air.

"I'm not dead yet either," Correus said grumpily.

Ygerna considered the scarred body under Eumenes's hands. It was infinitely familiar to her after all these years and never undesirable. Just now she hoped it was going to stay in residence for a while. It seemed likely. Tettius Julianus wouldn't launch a campaign until spring. Ygerna took comfort from the fact that Correus put more faith in him than he had in the confident Cornelius Fuscus.

Correus groaned and sat up. "That will do. I'm going to soak in the pool."

Eumenes arranged the legate's comb and a clean towel on the bench, collected the rubbing oil, strigil, and pile of damp towels from the floor, and departed. Correus slid into the pool and Ygerna took off her sandals and sat on the edge with her feet in it. A little statue of Fortuna just above the infill spout held a cornucopia overflowing with marble coins and what might be eels, and Ygerna regarded it with amusement.

"Correus, this house is luxurious in spite of all the fish. We've never had a place this fine. It's like living in your father's house without—"

"Without my mother," Correus said.

"Or your sister or your father or your stepmother, may her shade be at peace, or Aemelia, or Flavius, or any of your hundreds of relatives."

Correus floated blissfully on his back in the hot pool. "You need to be your own mistress, I know that. We'll have a house in Rome when I retire, I promise. I would have done it before now, but I don't want my father to put my mother in it."

"He will," Ygerna predicted. "He's courting someone. I have it on the best authority."

Correus righted himself in the pool and put his elbows on the edge. "Indeed?" That was startling. "Who is this reliable source?"

"Julia," Ygerna said. "Now that things are settled between us over Felix, we are friends." Julia had raised Felix for his first five years and not been pleased to part with him. "We need to talk about Felix, too."

"The adoption idea?" Correus ran his wet hand up her leg under the soft woolen folds of her gown. "I'm not against it. Why don't you get in the water with me and we'll talk about it?"

"Because we won't talk," Ygerna said, but she pulled the gown and her shift off over her head and shed her underthings. She rearranged a pair of silver combs to pull her hair higher on her head, posing for a moment on the edge of the pool because she knew he liked to look at her. She slid into the water.

Correus kissed her and ran his hands over her breasts. "You're right. This is luxury. Have the servants settled in? I haven't heard any squabbles."

Ygerna leaned against him and wrapped her legs around his. "Eilenn, who feels the need to tell me these things, informed me that Julius and the new cook were kissing in the kitchen while the buns burned. I'll have to do something about that."

"Blast Julius. Tell him if he interferes with my dinner, I'll beat him." Correus boosted himself onto the edge of the pool in a shower of water and picked her up to set her on his lap astride him. The light from the high windows slanted through the glass, reflecting the water on the painted ceiling like silver ripples in the air.

"Correus, what if someone comes in?"

"They won't if they know what's good for them." He shifted her again so that he could enter her gently, and she buried her face in his shoulder, moving with him. Years of marriage had taught them things about each other, different from the old wild first days, but just as strong, just as necessary. *I asked the Goddess for you when I was thirteen*, he remembered her saying once, and it flashed through his mind to wonder what the queen of the Getae had asked the Goddess for, and then the thought was gone, lost in the moment.

Afterward they slunk into the bedroom for Correus to dress, were sidetracked by the bed which had acquired a new quilted silk and woolen coverlet, and then went to sleep by mistake in its tangled folds.

They awoke when the setting sun made a bright splotch high among the school of silver fish on the green wall, like something seen from the bottom of a mysterious well. Correus felt on the floor for his sandals. "I feel like I've found lost Atlantis. Didn't that man ever think of anything but fish? I have to be at evening prayers in an hour. You wanted to talk about Felix, but I'm not against the idea. It would benefit Felix and Marcus both. Assuming Flavius is in favor." He hesitated. "But there's an… issue. Or may be. I don't know."

"That's less than clear," Ygerna observed.

"Tettius Julianus told me something before I went haring off impersonating a frontier scout and I haven't known what to do with it."

Ygerna sat up and found her undershift. "What on earth could alarm Tettius Julianus? I thought he was such a distant relative that nobody even knows what kind."

Correus was silent as he slid his tunic over his head. "Tettius came out here from the Rhenus with the Second Adiutrix. They were at Moguntiacum, and there is considerable trade there with the free Germans from across the river, including Ranvig's Semnones."

Ygerna was quiet, listening, an uneasy idea beginning to creep into her head.

"It seems that he has some acquaintance with Ranvig, which is an excellent idea, to the extent that he invited him to dinner while Ranvig's household was in Moguntiacum. Nyall Sigmundson's widow was among the lords and their women accompanying the chieftain."

"I felt sorry for that woman," Ygerna commented.

"She has remarried, according to Tettius, and has a young son who looks rather unlike her husband except for his coloring, and greatly like Flavius. Tettius had heard the gossip, of course, since my idiot brother was recklessly public about it, and he drew a logical conclusion."

"Oh Mother of us all," Ygerna said. "Does Flavius know?"

"No. And I don't know whether to tell him. He couldn't do anything about it. At least nothing sane."

"And you're worried he might do something not sane?" Ygerna stood and pulled her gown on.

"The not sane part was taking up with her in the first place," Correus observed. Ygerna didn't answer, and it occurred to him that taking up with Ygerna, at the time he had first done so, had not been sane either.

"We were lucky," Ygerna said, following this obvious thought, unconsciously echoing Lucius Paulinus. "Will Tettius tell anyone else? It was bad enough that Aemelia heard gossip about the woman, and it's made dreadful trouble. If she hears this…"

"No. He said he told me because he thought someone in the family should decide whether to tell Flavius. I think he just wanted it out of his own hands. Flavius is on the emperor's staff and anything the emperor might feel the need to get involved in is always marshy ground." Domitian was capricious. There was no telling what he might decide was his business.

"Does this affect the idea of Flavius adopting Felix?" Ygerna asked.

Correus studied the flounder in the mosaic floor. "Not really, except emotionally. This child belongs to someone else whatever his actual bloodline, is German, and completely unavailable, legally and in every other respect."

"But you have the idea that allowing Flavius to adopt your son, without knowing about his own, is dishonorable?" It was only half a question.

Correus was silent while he finished dressing. He fastened his sandals and combed his hair in the mirror on Ygerna's dressing table. It unnerved him that the face that looked back at him, also greatly like Flavius's, was walking around on a three-year-old in Germany. "I don't know," he said.

-

The Macedonica's Eagle, dressed in its battle honors, threw its long winged shadow across the parade ground with the cohort standards ranged behind it. The sun was just going down in a flaming pool behind the western bluffs. The rituals of prayer before the standards never failed to move Correus. Whatever other gods the soldiers prayed to, these were the prayers that bound them together: to Jupiter Best and Greatest, to Juno and Minerva, to Mars, the ancient god of war and mythological father of the Roman people, and even to the imperial *genius* of the Emperor Domitian, current father of his country. Correus's prayers to Mithras were something personal, and his wary regard for the Mother in all her guises was genuine, but the ceremony of the standards caught at his throat every time.

All the same, his confession to Ygerna stayed in the back of his mind, and when he and the newly minted primus pilus had escorted the standards back into the chapel, he went to the hearth in the atrium of the Praetorium and knelt before it. Vesta, goddess of home and family, had shrines that no one but her priestesses could enter, but she inhabited the hearth of every Roman house. The child would be Marcus's age, and only a little younger than the son that Aemelia had lost, Correus told her in a whisper. And what was he going to do about it? The hearth was silent.

XV

Baiae

Flavius thought, encouraged, that tonight Aemelia looked almost as she used to, excitedly selecting the best pieces from her jewelry box while her maid arranged her hair in front of the mirror. Her new gown was of pale rose silk bordered with a wave pattern in deep red, the sleeves fastened with a matching set of gold pins set with pearls. It was the first night of the Ludi Saeculares, not held since Claudius's time, and as the wife of an important member of the emperor's staff, Aemelia was chosen to lead the matrons who would make their sacrifice to Terra Mater on the third night.

Theoretically, the Ludi Saeculares were held every one hundred and ten years, thought to be the maximum lifespan of a man, but there were several ways of calculating the correct date, and despite the Emperor Claudius's observance only forty-one years ago, Domitian had declared this spring to be the proper year. During the three-day festival, the Fates, the Ilithyian goddesses of childbirth, and Terra Mater would receive their offerings by torchlight above the subterranean altars of Dis and Proserpina on the Campus Martius, and Jupiter, Juno, Apollo, and Minerva by day on the Capitoline Hill, each followed by a theatrical perform-ance. Another week of classical works by Greek and Roman playwrights would come next, and a final day of chariot racing for those exhausted by so much education.

Aemelia cocked her head at the mirror. "That will do, Rusonia. Thank you. Bring me my slippers." She stretched her feet out to let her maid lace the delicate rose-colored shoes. They tied with red ribbons threaded through the flower-shaped eyelets and were the latest fashion.

"Those are very nice," Flavius said. "They make you look like you're wearing a rose garden."

Aemelia turned around on her cushioned bench and stretched her feet out to show off the ribbons.

"Who are we dining with tonight?" Flavius asked her.

"Your father. And tomorrow night we're dining with my father. And the third night, they're all coming here and Cook is baking a peacock. Do you think she'll be there tonight?"

"Who?"

"That woman your father is seeing, and don't pretend you don't know. It's all over the City."

"He'll love that," Flavius remarked. "I don't think she'll be at the dinner but he's bringing her to Baiae. That's why we're invited."

"What?"

"For respectability," Flavius said, grinning.

A trip to the seashore was a treat and Flavius had wangled a month's leave for them to spend at Baiae. Aemelia looked horrified at the prospect of her father-in-law spending it with Didia Longina in his lap. "Aren't you worried? What if he marries her?"

"He might, I suppose." Flavius shook his head, bemused. The idea of the old man courting was a new one.

Aemelia bit her lip. "What about... well, particularly since you haven't an heir... Livilla told me about her cousin. His father married an awful woman and her son got his hands on everything."

Flavius pulled up a chair, a flimsy wicker thing that seemed doubtful about supporting his weight, and sat down in it gingerly. "First of all, why are you listening to that woman, and second, this woman of Father's hasn't got any children and she's a distant cousin of Prosper Rufius so Livilla should mind her tongue, and third, not every family is a nest of vipers, unlike Livilla's."

Aemelia brought her chin up. "You may not like her, but she hasn't told me anything that was untrue, has she?"

"No," Flavius admitted. "And are you actually happier for knowing it?"

"Well, I can't unknow it, can I?" Aemelia slid a pair of gold bracelets over her wrists and concentrated on threading a pair of pearl earrings through her ears. "I think Felix is old enough to be invited to dine here when your father comes, don't you?" When Flavius was silent, she said, "Julia thinks that Correus would favor the idea. It wouldn't take him out of the immediate family. I know you didn't care for his mother," she added, "but the poor woman's dead."

Flavius chuckled. Aemelia most definitely hadn't cared for Freita. "I didn't dislike her," he said, "I just thought she was bad for Correus. But you're right about Felix. He's thirteen and old enough to join us."

–

Didia Longina was not present at the dinner at Appius's estate that night, but by the time Flavius's household hosted its own banquet at the end of the three-day games, Flavius had heard all of the gossip, some spoken outright, some whispered because "a friend" thought he "ought to know." Appius Julianus had always had an odd kick in his gallop, he was losing his faculties since his wife died, why would anyone refuse senatorial rank, he was disgracefully old and the woman was plainly a fortune hunter.

Flavius ground his teeth and said blandly that he was certain his father knew his own mind, and thus it was no business of his son's. He rightly put the source down to Prosper Rufius, who was Didia's cousin, knew perfectly well that she had money of her own, and quite possibly had his eye on it for himself. Gossip about Livilla's pregnancy, Julius, and Appius's hand in Julius's disappearance had also made the rounds, being far too entertaining not to, and had done nothing to improve Prosper Rufius's temper. Flavius understood why his father wanted to go hide out in Baiae, where scandal was practically a local industry and nobody cared because they too were doing something that wouldn't travel well.

The third night dinner party gathered at his house on the Esquiline Hill following the torchlit sacrifices at the Campus Martius and that evening's play. The statue of Terra Mater had been carried in a litter from her nearby temple and Aemelia had led a quintet of well-born matrons in procession to oversee the bloody gift of a pregnant sow. Flavius knew that blood always made her feel faint and he admired her grit and determined ignoring of the droplets that splattered the hem of her white gown, simply tucking it under her seat where she couldn't see it during the performance that followed. The new Flavian Amphitheater was draped with lanterns and flowers and the emperor's banners fluttered overhead. The play was Aeschylus's *The Eumenides*, the final chapter in his tale of the doomed House of Atreus. It involved enough stage blood to float a ship, but Flavius could see that his wife's mind was mainly on the dinner to follow. She had spent the day either supervising the slaves polishing the new floor in the dining room, or in the kitchen with the cooks, approving and disapproving every sauce, until they were all probably ready to fall on their own knives, and she was happier than he had seen her in a long time.

The dinner guests included Julia and Lucius Paulinus, Aemelia's father and mother, a senator and a City magistrate and their wives, Paulinus's uncle Gentilius, Appius, and Felix, in a new toga which threatened to desert him at every move.

"Keep your arm pressed against your ribs," Flavius whispered. "Once we settle to dinner you won't have to worry about it."

Felix looked relieved. "I thought it was going to fall off every time I moved when we climbed the steps at the theater. I liked the play, though. Did you?"

"Very satisfactory," Flavius said. "Revenge, blood, justice, mercy, in that order. As it should be."

"Do you suppose the Furies really became nice ladies just because Athena gave them a new name?" Felix asked.

"No," Flavius said and they both laughed.

The dinner party was a success. The food was good, and sufficiently elaborate, and the new floor was much admired. It was the latest fashion, a fool-the-eye depiction of the aftermath of a lavish dinner: lobster claws, oyster shells, the spiny shell of a murex, mulberries from the East, ginger, and figs, each with its own shadow to increase the illusion, and a mouse gnawing a mulberry at the corner. Flavius called it "the midden" but Aemelia was immensely proud of it and the senator's wife was jealous.

The peacock was duly baked and then encased in pastry, its tail feathers reattached in a luminescent fan. There were oysters, roasted snails, a roast suckling pig with a white sauce of damsons, whole lobsters, boiled lamb with honey and dill sauce, grilled bream with an onion and raisin compote, an egg sponge, cheeses, poppyseed cake, and milk tarts, all accompanied by a fire-colored Setinian wine and an amber Falernian, presented in silver pitchers with matching water vessels.

Appius kept an interested eye on Felix. Aemelia reclined beside him, an honor not normally bestowed by the hostess on a child. Roman adoptions were legal matters of money and inheritance, rather than sentiment, and growing up in Flavius's household wouldn't distance him from his father, but Appius thought they seemed a good match. The boy wouldn't even have to change his name. He would write to Correus, he decided. There was the other matter weighing on him as well; he might as well heave both bricks at the same time, once he was certain.

–

"My dear." Didia looked at Appius with a good deal of affection but a steely glint in her eye. She put a hand on his arm. "I am growing surprisingly fond of you, but you have an encumbrance I am not willing to live with."

They were reclining, head-to-head, in the open breakfast room of the villa he had rented on the coast at Baiae. The table displayed the remains of the morning meal: a jumble of eggshells, fruit peelings, and a wine pitcher. Appius smiled ruefully. "This is not a situation I anticipated when…"

"No," Didia said thoughtfully. "You anticipated bringing a mistress home to a dutiful wife who couldn't object. Or was too proud to."

"I won't make excuses for that," Appius said. "Not now."

The morning air smelled freshly laundered in the breezes off the Bay of Neapolis, like washing hung out in the sun. The villa hugged the low rocky cliffs above the shore, and marble steps ran from the roofed terrace where they were dining down to the beach and the blue water. Below them a dozen fishermen were hauling in a net amid the nearly naked bathers in the waves, and a pantomime theater was setting up its tents on the sand. Flavius and Aemelia had left early with Appia and Felix and a parade of servants carrying hampers and parasols to take in the seaside entertainments along the piers and ogle the villas of the wealthiest, with their private canals and artificial islands.

Didia shredded the remainder of her bun and flung the bits into the air. A gaggle of seagulls swarmed down on them, squabbling on the rocks. Appius held out his hand and she took it.

"It is my intention," he said gravely, "to remedy the situation."

"Will that make trouble?" she asked him. "I can't think that it wouldn't."

Appius rose and tugged her up from her couch. "Navigable trouble, I think. And in any case, things can't go on as they are, whether you consent to marry me or not."

"Then let us shelve that question," Didia said. "I don't think one is supposed to come to Baiae and not misbehave."

He eyed her appraisingly. "Do you want to misbehave?"

"I should like to try it out." She smiled at him and he felt his heart turn over in his chest. This was new to him – lust overlaid with something else entirely, something old and deep.

By mutual consent they went hand in hand back to the bedroom where she had slept. Outside on the beach, a water organ accompanied the pantomime, the music drifting through the open windows over the bed. A gull flew in at the window and snatched a grape from a bowl on her dressing table and Appius, laughing, cursed it and threw a sandal at it.

Appius put his hands on Didia's shoulders and kissed her slowly and more thoroughly than he had ever done before. She wrapped her arms around his back. He felt her quiver in his arms, something possibly years dormant waking in her, he thought. She hadn't cared for being married, he knew, and he remembered saying drunkenly the night he met her that that meant she'd had the wrong husband. It would matter now not to be greedy, to be the right husband, with benefit of priests or no. He picked her up and set her on the bed and she watched him pull his tunic over his head while she unpinned the sleeves of her gown. He had a soldier's body, still lean and muscled, and marked with old white scars. He knelt beside the bed naked and pulled the folds of her gown away. Her olive skin was paler on her breasts and belly, her hair a dark cloud around her head and between her legs. She followed the fashion for shaving under her arms, he noted, but wasn't vain enough – or pain-tolerant enough – to have them plucked instead. For some reason he found knowing this small detail endearing and wondered if he was completely besotted. Probably. Her skin was soft, but there was muscle under it. She wasn't sedentary. He saw her watching him and wondered how she found him. He cupped both breasts with his hands and she lay back on the bed. He rose and lay down beside her. He put one hand between her legs and felt her respond, and wondered how long it had been since she had lain with a man. He was afraid to hurt her, but she pulled him closer and parted her knees and made a small contented noise, and then a gasp.

He tried to slow his response and give her time, but she didn't need it. Whatever her husband hadn't roused in her had been there and waiting for Appius. She shuddered and moaned and lay still beneath him, until he too stilled and rolled over, one hand on her breast as if in fear that she might fly out the window with the gull.

Afterward they made the bed again, on the slim chance that her maid didn't already know what there was to know, and went like proper tourists to admire the great lighthouse of Baiae and buy cups of fried squid from the vendors along the seaside arcade.

–

Flavius had taken his party farther afield, in the hope of evading any summons from the emperor, which was bound to come simply because he had managed a month's leave and that generally convinced Domitian of his immediate need for him. Respectable enough to visit only in the daytime, Puteoli harbor was famous for the gigantic marble sea horses that adorned each pier, and the maritime traffic of one of the world's busiest ports. Here visitors could watch the huge grain ships from Egypt come in to dock, the maneuvers of the triremes from the naval base at Misenum, and the occasional ponderous imperial bulk of a quinquireme. Felix was captivated by all of them.

The sulfuric smell of the volcanic vents that heated the baths hung in the air, mixed with the smell of fried calamari and fish stew hawked by pierside restaurants and washed down with local wine served in conch shells. After a lunch at one of these, Flavius took Felix to see the baths while Aemelia and Appia rested on a bench and admired the private yachts anchored in the bay.

The shoreside baths were all enormous, luxurious edifices built to lure the weary and hungover tourist. Puteoli's was famous for its size and grandeur. Enormous columns of red marble supported its vaulted ceiling and the inner courtyard was dotted with oversize bronze statues of Neptune, Amphitrite, and other ocean divinities. The complex included sweat rooms, exercise yards, fountains, and swimming pools of all temperatures, elaborately decorated with statuary, oceanic frescoes, patterned tile, and mosaics made of shell. Felix was uninterested in the decor, agreeing with his uncle who had remarked unsuitably that it made it look like a high-class brothel. But anything mechanical enthralled him and he asked endless questions of the bath attendants about the plumbing and heating systems, getting no satisfactory answers, until they encountered Julius Frontinus, of all people, sitting half-submerged on the steps of the tepid pool with a conch shell of wine in one hand and a fan in the other.

"Escaping the emperor's call," he said when Flavius inquired as to what he was doing in a tourist trap like Puteoli. "Not unlike yourself, I expect."

"I'm on leave," Flavius said firmly. "But yes. He's sent off a message to the Quadi and the Marcomanni politely requesting their help against Decebalus's army. That will take a while to go there and back, and there is nothing to be done until it has, whatever the emperor wishes otherwise."

"Indeed," Frontinus said. "And will they?"

"I think that's a roll of the dice. They're related to the Semnones and the Semnones have been very chummy with Decebalus, although it doesn't look as if he has got them to send actual fighting men."

"No," Frontinus said. "That would not be like Ranvig of the Semnones at all. To stir the pot in other ways, yes."

"In the meantime," Flavius said, "my nephew burns to know how the water supply in this place is managed."

Frontinus heaved himself up out of the water and handed his conch shell to a slave. He draped a towel about his middle and grinned at Felix. "Come along. We'll find my clothes and I'll show you the mysteries of hydraulic engineering."

Flavius watched them disappear, trailing wet footprints on the onyx floor, and smiled. Everyone seemed to think it was a good idea, so it probably was. He'd make a sacrifice for the shade of the child's mother, in gratitude – or expiation maybe.

—

He said as much to Appius when the family reunited to watch the sunset from the terrace of their villa. As the sun went down behind the western promontory, the jugglers and storytellers and the pantomime theater packed up their kits. The shadows of the hills fell across the sea and the waves steamed gently from the volcanic heat that was everywhere along the bay. The steam was jokingly called Cupid's libido, for the goings-on that were typical of Baiae after dark, but it also served as an unsettling reminder of the eruption and earthquake that had buried Pompeii and Herculaneum, midway across the great bay, less than ten years ago. Only the scavengers tunneling down to the houses whose rooftops showed above the hardened ash lived there now. Perhaps that was why the nightlife of Baiae and Puteoli was so frenzied, moving endlessly from the yachts moored in the bay to the beachside tents to the water palaces on the cliffs, clinging to the entertainments of the living.

Appius watched Felix playing rota with Appia at the foot of the steps on a wheel scratched in the sand, and letting her win; Flavius and Aemelia talking softly; and Didia sitting quietly, her head cocked, watching him back. Once, he knew, he might have slipped down the steps to the beach, drawn by the lanterns bobbing on the dark bay or weaving down the sand to increasingly drunken shrieks of laughter, to take his pleasure where he found it. Tonight he felt no such urge.

–

"Appius!"

Appius turned his head slowly and raised his eyebrows. He had returned from Baiae with business on his mind. He was on foot now, as was his habit in the City, formally toga-clad, and had come from a consultation with his lawyer. Now in a narrow street outside the Baths of Titus, he found Prosper Rufius glaring at him from the curtains of a litter, while the litter bearers shifted from foot to foot under his weight, and an annoyed crowd bound for the baths surged around the bottleneck. The confrontation with Rufius was chance made but not unexpected, since Appius had had three infuriated letters from him already, all of which he had ignored.

Rufius leaned over the side of the litter, threatening to over-balance it. "Stay away from my cousin, Appius, or I will take you to court!"

Appius's eyebrows went higher. "You aren't her guardian, Prosper. And let those poor men set that litter down before you break their backs."

Prosper Rufius ignored the suggestion. He was red with anger. "Her old uncle isn't fit to be guardian to a cat. I'll take him to court. I forbid it. You'll be lucky if I don't bring charges against you for transferring that slave out of Italy."

Appius smiled, a not entirely pleasant expression. "You should be grateful to me. I saved you from killing him and being hounded by his fans every time you left your house. They're very loyal. I knew a man who beat his driver and they pelted him with rotten apples in the street."

"Do you understand me?" Rufius looked dangerous. "I can still arrange for something to happen to that slave."

"You haven't divorced Livilla," Appius pointed out. "You can't legally kill her lover if you don't divorce her. Financial reasons, I suppose. That's a shame."

"I forbid any association with my cousin from here on! My house will not be dishonored by scandal."

"Your wife's behavior does make that awkward," Appius said. "Has she found another race driver yet? She can't be very fond of you after the pennyroyal. One of these days you'll find yourself dead in your bed, Prosper. And in any case, my intentions are entirely honorable. I trust you'll find your way home safely." He nodded, made his way around the litter, which had created a substantial clog in the narrow street, and disappeared into the baths.

-

Appius eased himself into one of the delicate gilt chairs in Helva's chamber. She rose and turned her back on him.

"Helva, stop that."

She turned around, her face tragic in the slant of late afternoon sun through the window glass. "You are going to abandon me."

Appius sighed. "I am going to free you. I am going to settle a generous amount of money on you. And I am going to buy our son a house for you to live in. You may feel free to define that as abandonment if you wish."

"You are driving me from this house." Helva waved sad, expressive hands at the blue chamber with its silver fittings and poppies on the walls. It was her own design.

"You can have your chamber in the new house painted any way you want it," Appius said, exasperated.

"It won't be the same," she said sadly. "And my lovely elephants." The floor was an African scene, or at any rate the artist's vision of Africa. Monkeys rode on the elephants' backs on the edge of a green river.

"Helva, there is no way to turn back time and events." Appius felt like one of the monkeys, riding a conversational elephant in endless circles around her sitting room. "Are you happy the way you are now?"

"No!" she snapped at him. "No, I am not happy. Why would you expect me to be happy? You never pay attention to me anymore, your daughter counters *all* of my efforts to make your house run smoothly, and everyone is laughing at you because you've fallen in love. At your age! It's disgraceful."

"Very likely. I've never been disgraceful before." He grinned at her. "That's been your department." He took a peach out of the glass bowl on her table and began to peel it with the silver fruit knife she kept there.

"I've been faithful to you," she observed. "I've kept my end of the bargain."

"Very true. Now you won't need to."

Reluctantly she drew up one of the little gilt chairs and settled herself in it where the light was most flattering. She was practical and she really knew there was no going back, he thought, not with Antonia dead. Even if he had not met Didia he would have had to do something.

"I will need an allowance to keep up this house I do not want. And servants."

"Correus will have an allowance to keep the house up. You will have an allowance for spending money. A generous one. And I will provide any servants that you feel you need, within reason. Naturally, you may take Decima with you." Decima was her personal maid.

"So, this will not be my house, then. It will be Correus's wife's house. I shall be a neglected afterthought."

He bit into the peach. "Bring me a napkin. I'm making a mess on your silk cushion."

She fetched a linen cloth from a carved chest in the corner and gave it to him. "Here. For Juno's sake." She wiped the peach juice from his fingers and chin.

She didn't love him, but he thought that she needed a man to belong to, to cajole and please, and wind around her finger. And if so, that was his fault over the years. And why freedom frightened her so.

"You might even marry," he offered. "You'll have a substantial dowry if you do. And then you would have your own house." She was still heart-stoppingly beautiful. Freedwoman's status was not an impediment to anyone but a senator.

She eyed her reflection in the silver tray that held the bowl of peaches and rearranged a strand of silken hair. "You have broken my heart," she informed him. "My head hurts and I feel faint. Send Decima to me with a cloth for my head, and then leave me alone."

–

My dear Correus,

I have freed your mother.

She has had a good deal to say about being cast off like worn-out clothing, but I have settled a substantial amount of money on her, and on you to maintain the house which I have purchased for you. She will have a personal allowance and beyond that the principal will be in your hands and those of Lucius Paulinus. You, of course, will have final say in all matters, but Paulinus may serve as a responsible party when you are not in Rome. The house is not far outside the City, off the Via Salaris, but secluded enough to have a bit of land attached for gardens, stables, and such. If you don't care for it, or Ygerna doesn't, you can always sell it and buy elsewhere.

I realize that you may not be best pleased with these events. I hope that your brother's agreement with the notion of his adopting Felix will come as more welcome news. They have become fond of each other, I believe, and between Flavius and Julius Frontinus, they can launch young Felix on the engineering career for which he is so obviously destined. Julius Frontinus took him down into the bowels of the plumbing under the baths at Puteoli and they spent all afternoon there.

Correus read his father's letter through again and it still said the same thing. He stared at it harder. The letters refused to change. The headquarters optio stuck his head in to remind the legate that he had wished to observe the Fifth Cohort at pilum practice this afternoon, due to certain errors on their part yesterday. But if the legate was busy, the optio suggested, he could arrange for him to terrify them later.

"No, I'll come." Correus put his helmet on and left the letter on his desk, held down with an onyx paperweight in case it should decide to go off and acquire more dismaying content.

The Fifth Cohort was much improved in performance and attitude, orderly ranks bristling with pilums like a porcupine with six-and-a-half-foot quills, and managing mostly to hit their targets. Correus congratulated their progress while making it clear that their shortcomings would not be forgotten, all while he mulled over his father's letter in his head. He had promised Ygerna a house. He had not meant one with his mother in it. And without Felix as a buffer. It was all very well to buy him a house in Rome, but the thought of leaving Helva to her own devices in it, even with Lucius Paulinus keeping an eye on her, was hair-raising. Equally hair-raising was the thought of bringing her to the frontier with him. What in Mithras's name did Appius think he was doing? At least there was one thing he could hand off, Correus thought savagely.

–

Dear Father,

Since we are discussing family developments, I have information which I have not known what to do with, and thus I am sending it to you. I feel that you will know better than anyone what, if anything, to do. Tettius Julianus was in Moguntiacum, as you probably know, before coming out here as governor, and had some dealings with the chieftain of the Semnones, in the course of which he saw Nyall Sigmundson's widow. I am sure you have heard the gossip on the subject of my brother and this woman, as nothing much escapes you. Tettius has informed me, rather hesitantly but thinking that someone should know, that she is now remarried and with a young son who looks nothing like his father and rather a lot like Flavius. Given the situation with Felix, I feel most uncomfortable deciding what to do, so I leave it to you as paterfamilias whether to say anything to Flavius about this or not.

He folded the tablet closed, sealed it, and put it personally in the military post destined for Rome.

–

Flavius watched Felix with some amusement, and a growing affection, as he stared enthralled at the great Map of Agrippa on the Campus Martius. He had seen it before, of course – it occupied a colonnade fifteen hundred feet long and was hard to miss – but as he said accusingly to Loukas, no one had ever told him what it *was*.

"The whole world?" he asked Loukas. "Where are we?"

Loukas pointed to the city of Rome, a green malachite oval set into the thin layers of surrounding stone. The map itself was almost thirty feet high and twice that long, encircled by a blue marble ocean. The continents were ranged around the Mediterranean and the Pontus Euxinus, each territory carved from a different stone, and all marked with the arrow-straight lines of the empire's roads, converging on Rome, the heart of the world.

"Beyond the empire, it gets a little fanciful, no doubt," Loukas said. "And there are a few inaccuracies corrected since Agrippa's day, but all the same, it's a marvel, isn't it?" The stone landscape was marked with every city, port, mountain range, and river known to Roman geographers. The major shipping lanes were chiseled across the chrysoprase seas.

Appius had deposited Loukas and Felix with Flavius at the Forum, remarking that he had personally been to most of that map and could stand to miss the remainder. He had departed for the baths with a scroll under one arm and the promise to meet them and Julius Frontinus for lunch, an informal celebration of Felix's pending adoption. Felix seemed perfectly happy with the idea. It wouldn't really change his life. He would go on living with his grandfather, he was told, because Flavius wasn't at home any more than his father was, and Aemelia had a tendency to spoil him. Felix had accepted that assessment since he was a philosophical child, and a practical one, despite an almost fiendish imagination. If there was a complicated idea that could end in either triumph or disaster, Felix would think of it. It was considered better that whatever it was should happen at his grandfather's house.

"Where is Father?" he asked now, squinting to see the lettering of provincial names.

"That buff-colored bit, just below the river up there." Loukas pointed. "That's the Danuvius, that blue line."

"General Agrippa made this?" They had been studying Agrippa, war hero and architect to the Deified Augustus, the man who had built modern Rome.

"Julius Caesar ordered it to begin with," Loukas said, "but Agrippa took over under Augustus. The army and the fleet supplied most of the information. You need maps, you know. Otherwise you set out to conquer Britain and find you've invaded Campania instead. They sent surveyors to chart the unknown bits."

"Here," Flavius said. "This is where your mother was born." He pointed to Upper Germany. "And your stepmother, here in Britain, where you were born too. And that is Gallia Belgica, where your grandmother comes from."

"That makes me just a quarter Roman, doesn't it?" Felix said thoughtfully.

"It makes you all Roman," Flavius said. "And very classically so." He had once thought, when he was young and possessed of the rigidity of youth, that foreign blood somehow diluted the family, made it lesser. He was a little ashamed of that now, particularly after a chat with his father over various distant grandmothers and great-grandfathers, including the Gaulish grandsire three times removed who had had a niche full of human skulls in his hall, most of them personally acquired. "We're all a mixture," he said. "Like dogs, a varied pedigree is the strongest."

That seemed to satisfy Felix. The crowd surrounding the colonnade made his uncle's point: City-dwellers, tourists from the country come to see the wonders of the map, beggars, food vendors, and students with their tutors, an array of skin and hair color, height, and facial structure.

He was still full of the excitement of it all, and wavering between a career as a hydraulics engineer and one as a surveyor, when they met Appius and Julius Frontinus at one of the more respectable of Rome's not very respectable taverns. The odors of stew and fish drifted from the pots set into the tavern counter and a woman behind it was filling red clay bowls with a ladle. Appius and Frontinus had found a table at the far corner, and Flavius noted that Julius Frontinus looked aggravated and Appius wary.

Flavius cast a glance at Felix and Loukas. "Go and order us wine and some fish," he told them. He made his way through the crowded room to the table in the corner.

"I'm to take you back to the Palace," Frontinus said by way of greeting. "The emperor has had his answer from the chieftains of the Quadi and the Marcomanni. It wasn't polite."

XVI

The Shades in the Pass

Tettius Julianus addressed a council of his generals, summoned from Singidunum and the lower Danuvius forts to his headquarters at Viminacium. A breakfast of boiled eggs, olives, fruit and cheese, along with bread and local beer, was laid out on a map table in acknowledgment of the fact that it was barely dawn. Tettius Julianus was not a man who slept late. He ran a scarred hand though his gray curls and tilted his long face consideringly as he read aloud to them from the emperor's infuriated message.

"I will be frank," he said when he had laid the papyrus down. "I shall be delighted to do without any assistance from the tribes in question. The Marcomanni and the Quadi are unstable and too closely connected to the Semnones, with whom some of you have acquaintance. Their loyalties are suspect at the best of times."

The Marcomanni and the Quadi maintained a relationship with Rome that generally amounted to outward observance of a treaty no one was actually abiding by and occasional sheep-stealing. The prospect of having their fighting men under his command gave Correus the shudders and he said so.

"Precisely." Tettius cracked an egg on the edge of the table and peeled it with quick, careful motions. "The emperor is in a temper about it, of course, as no emperor likes to be told to go and put his head in the Tiber, which was about the tenor of their response. The question is whether they will fight for Decebalus instead."

Correus looked thoughtful. "Ranvig of the Semnones, or someone very like him, was reputed to be at Decebalus's court two years ago," he offered, "before they attacked Oescus. But we haven't seen any Germans among the Dacian fighting men, then or since."

"It's possible that all he's done for Decebalus is to keep them from fighting on our side," Tettius said. "He'll abet what trouble he can to keep us occupied here and on our side of the Rhenus in Germany, but I suspect he won't destabilize the border otherwise. He just wants us to stay out of the German Free Lands."

"And is making sure we don't have leisure to do otherwise?" Aurelius Decius of the Fourth inquired.

"Oh, I think so," Messala Cominius said and Tettius nodded.

The legate of the Second Adiutrix listened attentively, quartering an apple. The Second had come from Britain and the complexities of the Danuvius and Rhenus frontiers were new ground.

"Ranvig is wily, and a diplomat in the most dangerous sense of the word," Tettius said. "He was a lord of the Nicretes fifteen years ago when Nyall Sigmundson of the Semnones decided to drive Rome off the Rhenus and brought the Nicretes in with him. That effort ended with Nyall Sigmundson in chains. Anyone we left alive pulled back to Semnone lands, and the next we heard of Ranvig, he was somehow the new chieftain. He's held them ever since, through another war and a realignment of the border in our favor to take in the Agri Decumates, but he's made it clear that it will cost us to go further."

"I agree with Appius Julianus," Marcus Licinius, the legate of the Italica, said. He was a stocky, sandy man with a look of his Gaulish ancestors. "The last thing I want under my command is a detachment of the Marcomanni."

Correus felt the same gentle shock he had been experiencing ever since Tettius Julianus had arrived and his fellow commanders had needed to distinguish between the two of them. Correus was a family name, an intimate name, not the address used by his fellow soldiers. To them he was Julianus, and now Appius Julianus, the clan name every man in his family bore. Appius Julianus was his father, but, unsettlingly, now also himself.

Tettius Julianus set the emperor's orders on his desk and pulled a papyrus scroll from the map cabinet beside it. He signaled to an attendant slave to clear the breakfast away and unrolled the map's length on the table. It was a larger and more elaborate copy of the sketch that Correus had given to him, extended now by the addition of the Danuvius forts, the Iron Gates pass, estimated distances, and their best guess as to the location of Decebalus's stronghold in relation to the eastern pass.

He looked at Correus. "I sent your wolves back out again over the winter to track the route the whole way now that we know where it runs, and this is what we have." He pointed to the broken line that went northward on the map from Oescus into the little inverted V's that indicated the Dacian mountain ranges. Well into the mountains the line forked, north to where a small square marked the site of Sarmizegetusa, and west, through a smaller square marked TAPAE to connect with a second pass that Correus recognized must be the Iron Gates, with its approach running back down through the mountains and then east again to Viminacium.

"The emperor's orders are to take Sarmizegetusa and remove Decebalus from our hair on a permanent basis." Tettius Julianus tapped the larger of the two squares on the map. He tapped again where the Iron Gates were marked, his expression darkening. "Here is where we lost the Alaudae and that must not be allowed to happen again. When we take Sarmizegetusa, we will bring back their Eagle for Rome."

The other commanders nodded, faces grim. A lost Eagle was lost honor, and more. It was not just a legion's soul; in some ways each one was a piece of the soul of Rome.

"First, we will employ sufficient scouts to ensure that there is not another ambush. Second, we will turn Decebalus's attention elsewhere, with an attack through the eastern pass instead. When the four legions of that column are near enough to engage with the enemy, only then will the other two legions move up into the western pass."

"And catch them before and behind," Marcus Licinius said. "With the mouth of the Iron Gates and two legions to halt a retreat, unless they fall back to Sarmizegetusa."

Aurelius Decius looked thoughtful. "Which legions will you send each way?"

"There I wish to know your thoughts," Tettius said. "Those of you who fought through that pass with Fuscus. Are they more likely to have the horrors, and feel the unburied shades of their dead battering at their ears, or to burn with a desire for revenge?" He paused, letting them consider. "Either would be understandable, but it is crucial that we know which. I could send the Adiutrix legions, which are new to the province. Or the Italica, which took the lightest losses." He nodded at Marcus Licinius. "Or I could send two of the others. Through the bones of their dead."

The legates were silent, even the Second Adiutrix commander, who knew it was a decision for the others. The retreating army had burned those who had died on the road home but no burial party other than the carrion birds had ventured back into that hostile pass for the rest.

Correus was the first to speak, uncomfortably aware that he was the most junior of them. "The Macedonica is two-thirds replacement recruits. Their cohort commanders as well, although those generally were posted from other legions and aren't dangerously green. A lot of the others were promoted from the ranks. But I've had them for nine months now and I would vouch for them against anything alive or dead." He smiled a little. "Also, my primus pilus has informed me that those who survived the Iron Gates came to him to answer just this question, most emphatically."

Tettius raised his eyebrows. "Before it was asked?"

Messala Cominius ran his finger up the map toward the haunted pass. "Mine as well. They know it's coming and they want their chance."

"The new Roman governor is building an army." Gudila crossed his arms on his chest and stared at Decebalus to remind him that he had told him so.

"Not unusual, since we destroyed his last one," Decebalus said. "My scouts know this without your advice. They will be bones in the pass again. The Romans learn little, it seems."

"What does the king learn?" Gudila snapped. "Why are we not crossing the Ister to put a stop to it?"

"For the reason that it is better ground here in our mountains," Decebalus said. "Also the king of Parthia has been most interested in our gift."

"That fool? If Pacorus believes in him, he is a greater fool."

"The Parthians have fought a border war with Rome for a century. They will use any blade that comes to hand."

"Why did you not keep him then? If he is so sharp a blade?"

"He's an ill-fitted blade likely to turn in the hand," Decebalus said. "The Quadi thought he was sharp enough to cut them and thus they sent him to me. To inform the Roman emperor that a returned Nero resides in their hall would risk finding Romans in their hall as well."

"He would appear to be a gift that no one wants to keep," Diegis observed. He had been listening to them quarrel for an hour and would have preferred to be at his dinner.

"The Parthians have supported a claimant to be Nero's ghost before now. What good will this new one do them?" Gudila looked suspicious. He had a dislike of complicated schemes.

"They believe this one to be genuine."

Diegis had seen the man and he looked like the coins with Nero's face, but he was mad as the full moon. Neither he nor Decebalus would say that to Gudila, any more than they had to the Parthian minister who had been so impressed with the claimant's imperious bearing and knowledge of Rome.

"In the meantime," Decebalus said, "they will pull at the Roman emperor's attention from the east while the Germans do so from the west. Thus in the middle of their frontier, this new army will lose the emperor's attention, and that means their supply lines, their reinforcements, their levies of fresh horses, everything will slow. Then we will cross the Ister if they have not come to us."

"We should do it now," Gudila said stubbornly.

"The Romans may make a mistake twice," Decebalus said. "I will not."

After a great deal more thought than the confident Cornelius Fuscus had given to anything, Tettius Julianus divided his avenging army: four legions under his own command to take the eastern pass, and two, the Second Adiutrix and the First Italica, to go up through the Iron Gates again.

The outraged legates of the other legions, who had assured him that their men were ready to pass through any number of shades to pay retribution to Decebalus, bit their lips, but Tettius was uncharacteristically inclined to elaborate. "I am confident of that and less so of their inclination to halt or fall back when told to. Our success rests on precise discipline. It is reckless enthusiasm I fear, not the lack of it."

"And I couldn't argue with the bastard," Messala Cominius said afterward to Correus, "because he's right. I've seen a battle nearly lost because disciplined legionaries started acting like German berserkers. This one's going to depend on timing."

An elaborate system of communication by the smoke of signal fires was rehearsed, as the only courier who could take a crow's flight path between the two armies would be an actual crow or a mountain goat. Bridges were constructed again across the river, laid on anchored ships at both Oescus and Viminacium. Every garrison along the Danuvius settled into a state of organized upheaval as the legionary and cohort standards were fitted out for the march, armorers counting spare pilum points, medical officers counting bandages, and optios counting everything. The entrepreneurs who followed any campaign packed their tents and their wares, demonstrating a gratifying confidence in Tettius Julianus that they had not shown in Cornelius Fuscus's headlong advance. Lavinia, shuttering her wine shop in Naissus and loading her brightly painted traveling wagon, remarked to her girls that a campaign was always an opportunity.

Ygerna packed a trunk to follow the column, deciding to leave Julius with the female servants and the children in the Oescus Praetorium, under the wing of the remaining garrison. If he seduced the cook while they were gone, she couldn't help it. Correus debated only halfheartedly with her, knowing that she would come whether he gave her permission or no. This campaign might take over a year if they were to lay siege to Sarmizegetusa. Ygerna had followed the army before. She would attach herself to the medical staff and make herself useful. The children, with what was left of a bored garrison to spoil them, seemed content with the arrangement and Correus gave up arguing.

It was early fall by the time they were ready to march. The column clattered across the bridge from Oescus in battle dress, past the dun-colored walls of Sucidava into a morning still thick with September heat. The civilian population of Oescus turned out to cheer them along, with children lifted onto their fathers' shoulders and the ubiquitous sellers of dubious things to eat circulating among them. Julius brought Eilenn and Marcus out to see their father off.

The auxiliary infantry formed the vanguard, with the pioneers, axes on their backs, to clear the way for the army to pass in battle order. The governor rode just behind them, accompanied by Correus and the other legates. There was no sign of movement from Sucidava, which was clearly disinclined to defend anything from four Roman legions.

Correus, in a new scarlet cloak and the eagle-feather crest of a legionary legate, was accompanied by his optio and by Favonius Marcellinus, the young military tribune of the Fifth. Favonius was, Correus had decided, going to have a successful career, judging by the tribune's careful observation of the preparations and his lack of suggestions offering a better way to do things. The generals were followed by auxiliary cavalry and the four legions in their new scale armor, greaves, and manica, marching six abreast, a sea of gold and steel and scarlet under their gilded Eagles. Sosius Alpinus, primus pilus of the Fifth Macedonica, rode at their head beneath the legionary banner, with the aquilifer beside him, face shadowed by his lion's-head hood, claws pinned over his breastplate, and the gold Eagle raised to the sun. Correus noted the precision of their column, perfectly aligned behind their shields with the sun glinting off the gilded lightning bolts and the bull's gold horns, with considerable pride and the same proprietary glow he had felt when he first addressed them. They were his. They were showing well. They were, in fact, his heart's desire, other than Ygerna.

At mid-column were the legionary cavalry, the artillery mules pulling disassembled catapults including the huge stone-throwing siege engines, and the officers' personal tents, furnishings, and slaves. In the rear, the legionary baggage carts and the hospital wagons rumbled along ahead of a final auxiliary force of both infantry and mounted troops that included Correus's old ala, now, as Correus had suggested, under the command of Blaesus. Clinging to the cloak hem of these last was the rolling entertainment district of wine shops and whorehouses that was technically forbidden but tolerated as long as they kept their heads down and their customers well behaved.

Lavinia, regarding the grinning legionaries who swarmed her wagon on the first night in camp, told them, "The first one who pulls a knife or starts a fight, I'll send you to your centurion in a sack and I'll know by your belt buckle where you come from." She was a muscular woman of nearly six feet, with a startling blond wig and a mustache. No one in their right mind argued with her, any more than with the two elephantine slaves who sat throwing dice in the wagon's shadow, or the dog, apparently constructed from the spare parts of a wolf and a boar, which was asleep under the wagon.

The camp lay in the narrow valley shadowed by limestone outcroppings where Correus and Tsiru had passed with the merchant caravan. It was ideally situated to defend against attack from the hills above, and had been surveyed and dug in behind multiple rings of ditch and wall even before the tail end of the column had reached it. There had been no sign, unsurprisingly, of the Dacian sentries who had been posted along the caravan route the year before, but Decebalus plainly knew they were on the way and, by their presence, that they had found the pass into Sarmizegetusa. What he was going to do about that was still uncertain. His scouts would tell him that a second army was coming up the track to the Iron Gates. He could fight both now and split his forces. He could hope to meet the eastern legions and defeat them before the western ones could get through the pass. He could also note the signals floating in black clouds of smoke above the red and gold hills, that both armies seemed to be approaching at precisely the same distance from their goal, and that the geometry was not promising.

Ygerna made her way on her mare through the camp to Correus's tent in the Fifth Macedonica's quadrant. It was red leather with a wooden floor and three separate rooms, and modest by most generals' standards, but its ingenious folding furniture and practicality of design delighted her.

"This army of the governor's is bigger even than the one in Germany," she said, while Eumenes served them dinner from an elaborate camp stove. "It's like an entire city that moves. And two more legions to the west. How long will that last?" she murmured.

"Only long enough to take Sarmizegetusa," Correus said. Six legions in one province, even if it was technically split into two, was dangerous, and gave governors ideas. "He'll transfer a couple out of this command as soon as the border's secure. Or into Dacia for a garrison under a new governor there."

"Is Dacia to be the empire's next province?" Ygerna inquired. "Another conquest to proclaim?"

"And collect taxes from," Correus said. "And yes. Decebalus asked for it, so I'm not feeling sympathetic. You weren't at the Iron Gates. You didn't see Viminacium burning."

"No." Ygerna put her hand over his and brushed his scarred face with her other one. "And the Legions were your love before I was, and I am not the kind of fool who asks for choices. It's only that I am always afraid when you march."

"Not this time. This time we are going to march down Decebalus's throat."

–

From Ygerna's vantage point at the end of the column, the army that wound up the mountain ahead of her flowed like a broad river, inexplicably upward as water did sometimes at high tide. The empire was the tide and it would push the river up and over Decebalus's banks. Sarmizegetusa was said to be the center of a kingdom with great wealth in gold and iron mines, a multi-terraced marvel of architectural engineering hidden within a forbidding wall of mountain ranges. No wonder Rome wanted it.

The trees were already turning as they moved through the lower reaches of the pass, and in two days the evergreens bore the only clothed branches, and then they were above even that tree line, and below them the conifers were dark-furred patches among the gray rock. They saw no other living thing, but what living thing would cross the path of their march?

–

With no good options left, Decebalus waited, arguing with his generals, and then led his army out to meet Tettius's eastern legions, with a furious Gudila, who told him every hour how right he had been, in command of the cavalry. A smaller unit under Diegis was sent to hold the pass against the ones approaching through the Iron Gates. There had been no opportunity to post an ambush unnoticed this time; his spies never saw

Tettius's spies, but they both knew the others were there, and approximately where.

They met a day's march south of Sarmizegetusa, on ground chosen by Tettius Julianus, who simply halted and let the Dacian army come to him if it would, rather than push the column on down an uneven slope, a 'stepmother' terrain that no general liked, and through a narrow valley into the land around the village of Tapae. Decebalus didn't have a choice. If he didn't meet the Roman army, it would encircle him and pick off his smaller fortified cities one by one.

The sky was gray with the promise of snow and at this elevation the wind was a freezing curtain sweeping across the bare mountain. Correus could see Ashes' hot breath blowing in little puffs when he snorted at the trumpet call that came clearly in the high cold air. He put his heels to the horse's flanks and rode along the Macedonica's place in the column, spreading them out according to Tettius's orders behind the auxiliary infantry, ready to move up when the auxiliaries had blunted the first charge. Up and down the line his centurions were dismounting and sending their horses to the rear. The legions were infantry and an officer fought with his men. The days when he had locked his own shield into the familiar spot at the left-hand end of his cohort's front line came back to him, but a legate had a different place.

He chose a spot where his primus pilus could see him and so could Tettius's couriers, and halted there with the Fifth Macedonica's banner over his head and Favonius and an optio beside him. Ahead of the auxiliaries, slightly down the ragged slope that fell away into the valley, he could see the dark massed ranks of the Dacian army, dragon banners shrieking in the wind and the light catching the wicked curved sword blades. They hurled themselves at the Roman front lines, not in the wild exuberant style of the Germans or the Britons but in orderly ranks, swinging long two-handed falx blades to cut through the massed wall of pilum points that greeted them and to hook the Romans' shields. The auxiliaries held, the first rank closing shields into a solid wall and the second rank laying theirs over the heads of the first in tortoise formation. When a Dacian blade broke through and a man fell, the line opened to take him in and another moved up, closing the shield wall with a snap. The cavalry circled around to either side, engaging the Dacian horsemen, driving them off the Roman flanks.

Correus could see Tettius Julianus on a hillock overlooking the battle, and the riders who came and went at his command, fanning out with new orders through the column. The other legions were ranged beside and behind the Macedonica, their own legates identifiable by their banners.

"The governor's compliments and you're to move up at the signal," a courier said, drawing rein beside Correus. "Oh, and the Iron Gates legions have engaged." He spurred his horse away down the line.

Correus nodded to Favonius as they heard the trumpet call. The auxiliaries began to pull back and the front lines of the Fifth Macedonica and the Seventh Claudia moved up into their place. The Eagle of the Macedonica rose above the massed cohorts and went before them like a bird of prey, the cold gray air dimming its silver wings to stone.

The Dacian front ranks were thinning too, and the heavier troops behind them moved up under the howl of their dragon standards. They were close enough for Correus to look a Dacian commander in the eye now, a grim snouted face under a peaked helmet and a red brush of mustache and beard. The helmet was gilded, his hauberk of brightly polished scale, and his horse's harness decorated with gold fittings. A man of some rank then and, like Correus, not one to give orders from a distance. He took note of Correus and rode straight at him.

Correus raised his shield and the Dacian blade bit into the edge. Correus thanked Mars Avenger that Tettius Julianus had also ordered shield edges reinforced as he swung at the Dacian with the cavalry sword that every mounted officer wore. He caught another blow on his arm guard that nearly cut it off, but his own blow landed, biting into the Dacian's hauberk at the shoulder below the ring of a heavy gold torque. Out of the corner of his eye he saw his own men moving up around him. He swung Ashes about beside the Dacian commander's horse, hooked the edge of his ragged shield behind the Dacian's shield and yanked. The man slid sideways in the saddle for an instant and Correus got his sword up under the shield and drove it in. The Dacian troop horse reared and Correus pulled Ashes back barely in time, but he saw the Dacian go down. The man tried to rise, but his own horse put a hoof on his chest. Correus caught a glimpse of a black-feathered something that flicked past the body, but there was no time to puzzle over that. Another horseman swung at his head. He felt the blow land at an angle and slide off, but it knocked the helmet halfway across his face. By the time he could see again, a handful of men from the Sixth Cohort had surged around him, and Favonius had knocked the man off his horse and was pulling his short sword out of the body. Correus gave him a grin. Favonius would do.

–

Ygerna held a lamp up for the Macedonica's surgeon to see his work better. She had gone to make herself useful in the hospital, knowing that no good came of having nothing to do but fret until she had envisioned all the various ways in which Correus could have been killed. She was mildly startled to find Lavinia and her girls, all of whom she had seen in the baggage train, and about whose profession she had no doubts.

"There now," one of them was crooning softly to an auxiliaryman with a nearly severed arm. "The surgeon is going to have to take that off, you know, but you drink this and hold still for him and I'll give you something to make you feel better later on, sweet boy." She bent her brilliantly hennaed head over his. "You just come to Naissus and ask for Merope."

On the other hand, Ygerna decided, if any other officers' wives had chosen to follow the column, they had not chosen to get their hands bloody in the hospital. She smiled at Merope, who smiled back at her.

After that, the day was an endless parade of blood, and savagely wounded men in spite of the armor modifications, and unreliable news. The western column was retreating. No, it had pushed through the pass and was on the tail of the Dacian army. The two columns had the Dacians encircled. The Dacians had barricaded the pass and torn through the Roman lines. Dis Pater himself had appeared over the haunted pass.

"Enough!" The chief surgeon, a tall cadaverous soul with a long face and equally long, delicate fingers, glowered at the wounded waiting their turn. "If you're well enough to gossip like housemaids, then go back to the line."

"Hold this," the Macedonica's surgeon said to Ygerna, and gave her the end of a suture, and she turned her attention to the boy on the table, who looked to her maternal eye no older than Felix, and who was pale with blood loss from the gash in his ribs. His breath came in shallower and shallower gasps. He wasn't going to live.

–

The First Italica was into the Iron Gates pass, with the Second Adiutrix hard on its heels, and those that caught sight of the scattered bones that were all that was left of the dead of two years before murmured a prayer under their breath and marched on. The auxiliaries in the vanguard emerged from the mouth of the pass in disciplined order, with the vengeful shades at their backs, and pushed the Dacians back and back again. Their archers scaled the slopes on either side and rained death from above, thinning the Dacian ranks so that those in the bottleneck of the pass could push through, splitting the defenders' line. As soon as there was another gap, they pushed again, and the bulk of two legions came after them, shields locked, across the outer fields and hedges of Tapae and through the village beyond them.

The knowledge that there was another army at their backs served the Dacian troops as the notion that a wolf is just behind a man's shoulder in the brush will do. Or perhaps they felt the shades' presence. They faltered beyond the ruins of Tapae, waiting for word that the legions that had poured through the eastern pass had been halted. None came.

Slowly Decebalus's army collapsed on itself, driven from east and west by Tettius Julianus's legions. The Dacians never lost their discipline, but they fell to the Roman numbers by the thousands, and took an almost equal number with them. Only when the battle tipped, when their war trumpet's Fall Back changed to Retreat, did the Dacian lines crumble and victory become pursuit and then a hunt.

–

A courier stopped beside Correus. "Governor says we're to let them go now. They're making for Sarmizegetusa and the governor says we won't get in there without siege engines and it's going to be wolf winter up here in a day or two. We'll let them bottle themselves up and we'll see how long they last." As he spoke, the Roman trumpets called the order to Halt Pursuit.

Correus let his breath out. It had been a bloody victory and his legion had lost more men than he wished, but they had done it. In the spring they would knock the walls of Sarmizegetusa into rubble and avenge the dead of the Iron Gates pass, as well as every other needless death caused by Decebalus's wandering eye.

–

They prayed for the shades of their dead, including the bones in the pass below Tapae, as the first white flakes came drifting on the wind like little wandering ghosts. Tettius Julianus built his camp on a high flat plain outside Sarmizegetusa and settled in for the winter. Neither army could fight in the blinding snow that began to fall or over the ice that clothed the ground, and the catapults were unworkable when their torsion springs froze. Decebalus might have warmer quarters within the walls of Sarmizegetusa, but he had too many people to feed and no supply chain to supplement whatever was in the granaries. What was in store was likely to be a good deal, but they would be hungry by the thaw.

The Romans, on the other hand, had the advantage of regular supply trains that pushed through the snow-packed passes from the Danuvius forts. The mules that pulled them wore studded iron shoes and plowed through the great frozen drifts that blanketed the mountainsides. The Romans' camp, being built to last the winter, was more elaborate than the usual marching camp, its walls reinforced with stone and timber, and double ditched outside the perimeter. As the steady snowfalls filled the ditches, they were scraped and shoveled clear again by cursing legionaries bundled in fur leggings and sheepskin cloaks. The army and all its entourage were gathered in, including such followers as Lavinia and her girls, various wine sellers, and a few enterprising brewers of beer from grain pilfered from the army's store. Tettius Julianus was a believer in allowing a certain amount of well-regulated entertainment to flourish lest his charges decide to look elsewhere, and the Dacian mountains were not a hospitable place for a legionary who slipped through the camp gates at night even in fair weather. He made sure the wolfmen rumors circulated and levied a reasonable tax on Lavinia's income, and a balance was struck.

"You started that wolfmen story," Ygerna said accusingly to Correus and he grinned at her.

"They're usually more afraid of something otherworldly than they are of actual sheep herders with a temper and a pitchfork."

"All the same," Ygerna said, "wolfmen wouldn't surprise me in these mountains. It's nearly Samhain. Whatever crosses the veil up here isn't something I want to meet." At the dying of the year, the doors between the worlds stood open.

Correus braced his helmet upside down between his knees, gave the cheek piece a twist with a pair of pliers and shook his head. He handed it off to Eumenes, who sat polishing his master's breastplate by the brazier that warmed the tent. "This needs to go to the armorer. I can't straighten it out."

"Extra bracing saved your head, I expect," Eumenes said. He set it on the tent floor. "I'll take it in the morning. The armorers are piecing everybody's kit back together. I never saw anything like the damage those Dacian blades can do."

"I saw it in the hospital," Ygerna said softly. "Too many amputations." And now too many new graves outside the camp walls, jars of ashes dug into the iron-hard frozen ground with picks and marked with uniform rows of stones: DIS MANIBUS, the soldier's name and his unit. Despite what the surgeons could do, infection killed more amputees than blood loss. The bones from the pass had been collected too and burned together in a common grave.

She pulled her chair closer to the brazier and watched Correus, who had moved to his camp desk and was signing supply lists and Fit for Duty rosters and whatever else had come his way today in the endless paperwork that went with a command. Twelve years ago in another tent, its leather walls closed not against the cold snow but the soaking rain of West Britain, she had asked the Goddess to give him to her, while she was still a royal woman and a priestess of the Mother, offering to trade that, which had never brought her anything but ill, for this man. The Goddess had done so, and Ygerna had made an offering this afternoon to thank her, in her guise as the Morrigan of Battles, that she still had him. Outside the snow fell, sealing them all in until spring.

–

King Gudila of the Getae came home to Capidava on a bier, along a circuitous route that brought most of his remaining men and horses in single file around the Roman lines. The icy weather kept the body from decay and so the flesh of the face was barely shrunken away from the bones when it was presented to his queen.

Ziais inspected the bier. The baby in her arms reached out a fat hand, intrigued by the gold torque and the bright silk hangings. Her women hovered about her, and one offered to take the baby, who by rights should have been with his nurse, but Ziais waved her away with an angry gesture.

269

"He is king now," she said. "He should look." She swept a triumphant glance around the room as Gudila's chamberlain and high priest watched her uneasily. "So should you all. You know the law." The dark mourning veil gave her face a predatory cast, like the painted huntsmen who chased the painted boar around the chamber walls.

There was an uncomfortable stirring. Ziais had been a necessity in order to provide the king with an heir, but Gudila had not required that she be given any more than the minimal respect that his own rank demanded for her and gave her none himself. Now the landscape had shifted dangerously. By ancient law, the mother of an infant king became his regent until his majority at twelve.

The chamberlain and the priest both knelt hastily. So did the lords who had ridden beside the bier.

"Your brother King Decebalus sends you greetings and consolation," one of them ventured. "There is a letter here for you." He reached into the leather pouch at his waist.

Ziais took it in her free hand, a fat sheaf of papyrus sealed with Decebalus's ring. She walked to the bronze fire bowl that warmed the chamber and dropped it in.

XVII

Nero Redivivus

Domitian's face was scarlet with fury. Flavius thought for a moment that he was going to order the man's execution and steeled himself to try to talk him out of it. Then the color flowed away slowly from the broad brow and squared-off jaw, giving him the uncanny look of his father. The emperor took a deep breath and Flavius let his out.

"I do not know from what marsh you dredged up this new upstart," Domitian said quietly and with some menace. "You are aware, I believe, that this is the third? Your king's late brother dispatched the last one when he proved to be false. Let me assure King Pacorus that this one is also a fraud. You have Rome's word on it."

The Parthian envoy fidgeted in his bright yellow boots and started to reply. Domitian glared him into silence.

"The Emperor Nero is dead and caused enormous trouble in his leaving. Rome will not stand for his name causing any further uproar. I suggest you go home to your king and tell him that."

The envoy looked as if that was the last thing he wanted to do.

The emperor tapped the ivory-inlaid arm of his chair. "You may also tell them that I shall send an envoy of my own to meet with your council who have sent me this dangerously threatening letter by your hand. It will take Ambassadorial Legate Julianus approximately a week to arrange transport, and then I shall expect them to hand over this imposter to him. Now take your leave before I decide to send a legion instead."

The envoy was escorted out by two of Domitian's Praetorians and the emperor turned to Flavius. "Don't argue with me, Julianus."

"I assure you that I was not going to, sir." He had been, but there was really no point.

Domitian looked grim, thoughtful now rather than angry once the first rush of temper had passed. "I was eighteen when Nero died. My father was fighting Vitellius and my brother was in Judaea. I was in Rome and I ended up under house arrest and barely escaped being killed by Vitellius's faction. They caught my uncle and murdered him in the street before my father's army got here. You are a bit younger, I think, but I expect you remember."

"I do," Flavius admitted. Appius had been with Vespasian's army. And anyone who had been alive during the Year of Four Emperors shuddered at the idea of reliving that chaos.

"I have no idea whether you like me or not, Julianus," Domitian said unexpectedly. "But I do have an idea that you are loyal, which is what I require. Your family has that reputation. Your father could have contended with mine for the purple when the civil wars began, but he didn't. I think you inherit that."

"I think the last thing my father would want is to be emperor," Flavius said truthfully.

"And for that reason, I trust you both," Domitian said. "I would find it hard to count up the men I trust in that way on the fingers of one hand. Therefore, you are going to Parthia to remove this imposter."

—

Lucius Paulinus and Flavius had been trying to outwit each other at latrunculi for an hour in the little courtyard beside the fish pond at Paulinus's country house. Paulinus's hand hesitated over the latrunculi board while its owner considered. Flavius sat back in his chair, studiously blank-faced.

Paulinus came to a decision and moved a stone on the board. "How many does this make now?" he asked, taking up the underlying conversation, and the reason for Flavius's visit.

"Three." Flavius studied the board. He and Correus had grown up trying to beat each other at latrunculi but Paulinus was a wilier player than Correus. Also, Flavius and his brother, when playing each other, had generally tried to cheat. "I am to leave tomorrow, a week behind the Parthians' envoy," he said. "The delay being designed to give the Parthian King of Kings, assuming it's still the same one by the time I get there, a suitable sense of my importance." Flavius moved a stone but shook his head. "I'll concede this, I think."

Paulinus looked pleased, which made his brother-in-law suspect that there was some way that he could still have won, which Paulinus could see and he could not.

"And when you get there?"

"Convince the Parthians that this new imposter is not Nero either. And convince them to kill him, preferably. That or to give him to me."

Paulinus pushed the board away and called for Tullius. "Wine, please. The Falernian. And some figs. I should send him with you," he added.

"The Parthians aren't going to do anything to the emperor's ambassadorial legate," Flavius said. "If you're going to lend Tullius, have him follow my father around. I'm half-serious. It's why I'm here. I don't trust Prosper Rufius. He's up to something."

Paulinus looked thoughtful. "To do with your father?"

"I don't know. But my father is besotted with Rufius's cousin and Rufius has threatened him over it, probably because of money. Rufius has been spending a lot to keep up his popularity and the well may be going dry."

Paulinus nodded. "I will observe. And anything else necessary."

Flavius thought it as well not to ask what else might be necessary but he drank the wine that Tullius brought them with a freer mind. There were too many flies round his head just now and he was relieved to leave Paulinus to swat this one. There was absolutely no dissuading the emperor from sending him to Parthia. And he probably shouldn't even if he could. An ambassadorial legate with an eye to his own advantage somewhat more than the emperor's well-being would be a dangerous thing, and that pretty much described everyone else at court. He had told Aemelia that while he was preparing to drag her and everyone else to his father's estate once again.

—

Paulinus sat quietly in the garden for a while after Flavius had ridden away, and then wandered into the house for his journal, his usual way of thinking things through. He would record the demise of the new false Nero in the official history once it had actually occurred.

> *Nero Redivivus. Again. It is dismayingly easy to convince a group of people not adept at critical thought that a man who was seen to die and be buried by several people has not actually died at all and has been hiding in disguise all this time. This is the third manifestation of a claim, tenuously based on a resemblance to the late emperor and an ability to play the lyre, to surface in the twenty years since Nero's suicide forestalled outright assassination. The plebeians loved him since he was so openhanded with them, and they still strew flowers all over his tomb. It's probably reasonable for them to hope for his return. During the Year of Four Emperors a series of forged imperial edicts circulated in his name, which didn't help the general upheaval. The last thing that Domitian, heir to the last of those four, wants is another outbreak of that. Neither should anyone else in their right mind. Domitian is already in a temper over the refusal of the Marcomanni and Quadi tribes to come to our aid (although Correus says that the Danuvius commanders emphatically do not want them) and he is most dangerous, not to say capricious, when he is angry.*

274

Paulinus thought a moment and then scratched that last bit out.

The first imposter, who popped up in Achaea immediately after Nero's death, was a freedman who gathered a bunch of army deserters, took up piracy, and apparently thereby convinced the Greeks of his legitimacy. Galba had a short-lived grip on the principate by then and his new governor in Achaea promptly squashed the imposter and sent his head on a tour of the empire by way of warning. The second one nearly started a war with the Parthian Empire in Titus's reign. That one appeared in the province of Asia and headed for Parthia when things got hot. He tried to convince the Parthians to support him in exchange for the actual Nero's having ceded Armenia to them, got himself embroiled in a fight between three princes for the throne of their late father, and was finally executed for making a fool of the victor when his real identity was discovered.

Now a new one has appeared and the Parthian king has sent the Roman Senate a message demanding that Domitian abdicate immediately and restore this Nero to his throne. Domitian understandably did not receive this well (I am glad I was not there) and the Parthian king is lucky, in my estimation, that Domitian is otherwise occupied at the moment, or the king would get several legions instead of an ambassadorial legate to explain the error of his assumptions.

The current King of Kings is Pacorus II, the ultimate survivor of the succession squabble with his brothers, who took turns overthrowing each other for three years until Pacorus was the only one standing. His brother Artabanus, in a short reign in the middle of it, was the one who executed the last false Nero.

The Parthians have achieved what Decebalus aspires to: a highly developed empire with all the luxuries of modern civilization. They are a power in world trade, speak both Greek and Parthian, with Aramaic as a common tongue, and are reputed to be excellent cooks as well as warriors. I must remember to ask Flavius about that.

Rome and Parthia are, at the moment, ostensibly at peace after centuries of periodic war. With Decebalus trying to destabilize the northern border by setting up his own empire across the Danuvius, Domitian must feel strongly that this is not a good time to jeopardize the eastern provinces. It would not in fact surprise me if Decebalus hasn't had some kind of sideways hand in this. Or for that matter Ranvig of the Semnones, who I would not want to play latrunculi with. There are whispers in the wind that there is something going on in Germany too.

And then there is the matter of Prosper Rufius. I don't know what he's doing, but it's something that he shouldn't be, and Flavius thinks so too. If it's unsavory (it's bound to be), it will be a necessity to separate Didia Longina absolutely, either from him or from Appius.

-

Flavius, bearing the official letters of an ambassadorial legate and accompanied by Bericus and two centuries of the Praetorian Guard, sailed from Misenum aboard a trireme of the fleet that made its way through the Mediterranean in a rough sea to Laodicea on the coast of Palestine. From Laodicea they rode overland to Palmyra, and from Palmyra to the fertile rolling hills along the Euphrates River where a representative of the King of Kings waited at a Parthian border fort to escort them to Pacorus's winter capital at Ctesiphon. The river was heavy with traffic moving beneath the bridge as they crossed, traders and merchantmen under sail, round boats like coracles poled along in the shallows, and gracefully curving reed boats like giant chrysalids.

Flavius was amused to notice that they slowly ascended the hierarchy of Parthian aristocracy as they rode southeast from the Euphrates toward the Tigris River and Ctesiphon. Their first escort was captained by a clan chief of the land that lay along the border. He wore a suit of scale over leather riding breeches and was respectful of the Roman ambassador's status, but also fluent in Greek and chatty, and Flavius knew most of his family's history and the names and accomplishments of his children by the time they clattered across the much larger and more impressive bridge that spanned the Tigris, with the capital on its far bank. There they were met by a captain of the king's guards named Vaerka, son of a collateral branch of the family of a sub-king who held his lands from the King of Kings. These relationships were announced upon introduction and Flavius realized that they constituted the same sort of division of the upper classes that senators, equites, and the old patrician class did in Rome. Vaerka, who spoke more educated Greek than Flavius's first escort, wore loose trousers of scarlet wool, pleated horizontally down each leg, a scale hauberk over an emerald green tunic, a wide red leather belt with a gold buckle, and a conical helmet studded with gilded rivets. His close-cut beard and substantial mustache seemed to be the Parthian fashion.

The city of Ctesiphon, on the verdant banks of the Tigris, was a stop on the silk route from the east, a sprawling, energetic place of domed buildings, bustling shops, and public squares and gardens centered on elaborate waterworks. The winter palace at the heart of it was surrounded by a series of walled courtyards, each with its own outbuildings. Vaerka politely suggested that Flavius's Praetorian escort should halt in the outer plaza and Flavius assented. A hundred and twenty armed men would not be of any use if Pacorus decided to kill him, and Flavius could think of no reason why he should want to anyway.

"While you are in conference with the minister, they will be quartered in the palace barracks," Vaerka assured him. "Most comfortable. I will send your slave to the chamber we have prepared for you."

Flavius thanked him and was handed off again, first to a slave of the minister and then to the minister himself.

Clearly this was another step up in the hierarchy. The minister's saffron and emerald tunic and trousers were even more voluminous and elaborately pleated than Vaerka's, and Flavius found himself impressed by the luxury and ambition of the minister's mustache. His hair was puffed into a crown, back-combed at the sides, and secured with a broad gold headband.

"Pacorus, the King of Kings, welcomes the Roman Senate's envoy," he said, bowing formally, a gesture which Flavius returned. "I am Artapan of the House of Suren. It is our inherited privilege to crown the kings of the House of Arsaces."

"I am Flavius Appius Julianus, of the House of Appius," Flavius said. "I serve both the Senate of Rome and its emperor Caesar Domitianus Augustus. The situation just now is awkward in that respect, as you understand."

"Of course." Artapan smiled. "My slave will show you to your chamber where you may refresh yourself. Then let us dine and after that we will think about it like civilized men."

Flavius, washing in the basin provided in his sumptuous quarters, wondered not for the first time exactly how much King Pacorus actually believed the new Nero's dubious claims. It probably didn't matter, he decided as Bericus dropped a clean tunic over his head and arranged the formal folds of his toga. If Parthia could install him as emperor in Rome, whoever he was, it would be greatly to their advantage. It would be to Rome's advantage to put a stop to that without a war.

The diplomatic dinner was elaborate and lengthy, and attended by several lower functionaries, two secretaries, and a poet who recited in Greek, and no doubt by design they spoke of everything except the man who claimed to be Nero. The king did not make an appearance, nor did Nero. The Parthians had a reputation as lovers of good food and that at least was borne out with a baked peppered whole lamb. Their wine was excellent and Flavius was careful not to drink much of it.

Artapan took note of Flavius's hands and raised his eyebrows solicitously. "A battle injury, Ambassador?" he asked. "Quite unusual, if I may mention it."

"In a way," Flavius said. "It is long healed, and as you see, I have learned to adapt."

"Our astrologers consider your appearance an omen," Artapan confided. "Of old grievances shed, and new friendship between Parthia and Rome."

"Indeed," Flavius said. How convenient of them. "That is greatly to be wished," he added.

When the slaves had cleared the meal away and the poet had departed, Flavius pushed Artapan toward the matter at hand. "I must speak to your king and to this man who claims to be Nero returned," he insisted. "I cannot give the Senate any advice until I have done that."

"Of course," Artapan agreed. "In the morning."

In the morning, a slave brought Flavius and Bericus both a breakfast of honey and fruit in their chamber, and clean water in a basin. The slave bowed, gave Flavius's hands a sidelong, curious look, and departed. Flavius supposed he was now a wonder in the insular circle of the palace, source of the gods knew what speculation and rumor. Artapan appeared as they were about to venture out to the palace latrine and accompanied them chattily on this errand.

"It is a lovely day. One of those beautiful, unexpected gifts that winter sometimes brings us," Artapan said. "We should take advantage of it. I have arranged for a guide to show us about the city."

"I am to meet with King Pacorus this morning." Flavius cut him short. "And with this supposed Emperor Nero."

"The emperor is indisposed at the moment, I am most sorry to say," Artapan confessed. "But our physician assures me it is temporary. In the meantime, you would like to see our city. It is most wonderful."

"And the king?"

"He is in council. That will take all day," Artapan said. It was beginning to be clear that Flavius's business in the Parthian court was to be conducted with Artapan. The Parthian kings were notoriously afraid of poison, which might make them disinclined to associate with foreign envoys. "But the king is pleased that the Senate in Rome gives the situation its attention," Artapan said.

"The Senate is considering the matter," Flavius said. In the sense that the Senate was greatly annoyed by it.

Artapan looked pleased and Flavius resigned himself to a tour of the city. They were no doubt sizing him up before allowing him to meet with the imposter. Or consulting their astrologers. The Parthian king was said to rely heavily on their advice.

"I will escort you myself," Artapan said happily.

The guide brought by Artapan to accompany them was a small scholarly soul with a squint and the pleated garb of the Parthian upper class, although far less grand than Artapan's. He was introduced as Artapan's secretary.

"Note the frescoes in the inner court," he instructed them, "the fineness of the color. Also the stucco reliefs as we pass through the outer court, and the stone carving depicting horsemen in battle dress."

Flavius duly noted them all, and they proceeded down the palace steps and into the bustle of Ctesiphon on a fine day. The air was cold but the sky was that bright astounding blue that clear winter days sometimes achieve. He admired the vaulted arches of the counting house and a columned temple in the Greek style.

In the city market along the riverbank, stalls offered winter fruit, dried meat, fish, and bins of grain and dates and olives. Warehouses of sun-dried brick housed shops beneath their arched fronts offering jewelry, silks from the east, cotton from Egypt, saddles and bridle fittings, pottery, silver, and bronze pots. Flavius inspected the bolts of silk while Bericus halted in front of a shop selling statues of gods from the recognizable to the utterly mysterious.

The day concluded with another state dinner. Flavius brought Bericus, who spoke adequate Greek, to serve him and glean any information that he could from the palace slaves. There were more poets and a trio of dancing girls, but no appearance of the supposed Nero.

In the morning, the "emperor" was still indisposed. Bericus reported that all he had heard in the palace kitchen was that the Roman ambassador might be a demon, who were known to have four fingers, and Flavius was losing his temper. Artapan appeared to note that and assured him he would consult with the physician again.

"Oddly," Flavius said, "I begin to lose faith in his recovery. If this Nero dies, then there is no need for our continued discussion."

"I assure you he is greatly improved."

"I will wait one more day," Flavius said. There was no telling what was wrong with the man, but some forms of madness tended to come and go. This one might be in his chamber sticking feathers from the bedding into his hair.

By morning the man had apparently improved, or the astrologers had told Pacorus that the stars were favorable, or the great god Ahura Mazda had come down from the sky and said to get on with it. There was no telling. Artapan was pleased to inform the ambassador that a meeting could now take place.

"My secretary will take notes for you," Artapan added. It was obvious that Flavius wasn't going to be allowed to talk to him unattended.

Conversation so far had been conducted in Greek and that continued as the claimant was presented to Flavius in the palace's sunny conservatory, a circular chamber with arched windows throwing gold light across the tessellated floor, and the sort of potted plants that a listener could conveniently sit behind. Artapan's secretary was perched on a wide window ledge, and a pair of guards stood on either side of the doorway. The minister himself occupied one of the three chairs ranged in the center of the room.

Flavius had to admit that the purported Nero bore a remarkable resemblance to the late emperor, if he had lived to age another twenty years: chubby and bull-necked with the emperor's blue eyes and red-brown hair, now going a bit gray, brushed forward over his brow, and the distinctive beard grown below his chin to hide the second one.

Flavius regarded him thoughtfully when introductions had been made. "If you are indeed the Emperor Nero, where have you been?" he inquired.

"Hiding from the traitorous Senate," the man said. He had been lounging in his chair and now he sat up straight. "Where is my lyre?" he demanded of the slave who had escorted him. "I will prove myself to you."

From what Flavius knew of the unstable emperor who had died when Flavius was fourteen, that offer did not seem out of character. He waited while the slave brought the lyre and the man played it and sang determinedly, and not badly.

Artapan nodded in approval as if that clinched it. "You see," he said.

Flavius raised his eyebrows to indicate that he did not – not just yet.

A period of questions regarding Nero's actual history and certain aspects of Rome's layout followed, which the man answered accurately enough in an imperious tone, lounging in his chair again. He gave an account of twenty years in hiding outside the Roman Empire's borders, which was possible if not entirely plausible and included pirates, sea caves, oracles, and at least one visit from the goddess Minerva.

Flavius switched to Latin.

"I have been assured by my secretary that he is fluent in Latin," Artapan said.

"He does seem to be," Flavius agreed, and went on nonetheless. Certainly the man answered his questions with the ease and colloquial vocabulary of a native speaker, and the arrogant tone of a possible emperor. However. "And does your secretary come from Rome?" he asked Artapan when he had finished.

The secretary shook his head. "No, lord. I am from Alexandria."

Flavius smiled. It was not a heartening expression. He looked at Artapan. "This man is not Nero."

282

Artapan appeared startled at the sudden pronouncement. His faith in the imposter's credentials, or probably in his potential usefulness, was not going to be shaken. "How can you prove that? He has answered all your questions. And you have only to look at him!"

The false Nero sat up in his chair. "How dare you? When I am emperor again, I will have you crucified. The gods have decreed my return." He took up his lyre again and began to play, sulky and imperious.

"If you go back to Rome that statement will come back to bite you," Flavius said. "Be quiet and hope the king keeps you here." Flavius wondered about him. He still thought the man was delusional. Merely an eye to whatever his claim might bring him wouldn't justify such a risk. The real game was being played by whoever had sent him to Pacorus.

The supposed Nero shouted a furious order for the Roman envoy's immediate execution that would have done credit to the original. Flavius ignored him and turned to Artapan again. "His speech has the accent of the City, but it is the accent of the streets and not the palace."

Artapan frowned, suspicious. "What does that mean?"

"His speech lacks breeding. It is not the speech of the educated class, much less of the imperial family of Augustus."

"And how does the educated class speak?" Artapan demanded.

"Like me," Flavius informed him.

The hopeful emperor grew abruptly silent.

"He will be laughed off his horse if he goes to Rome and speaks like a street-corner fishmonger," Flavius said while Artapan digested this. "He won't last two hours. Since you don't believe me, find someone who was born in Rome and ask him, which you should have done to begin with." He eyed the imposter and then Artapan, gauging how far to push the situation while he had the upper hand. "He has cost me an unpleasant journey, and the emperor and the Senate a great deal of annoyance, and made a fool of you. I will take him with me if you wish or leave him here. It's all one to me. But don't tell me that you yourself couldn't distinguish between the voice of a bricklayer and the voice of your king."

Artapan looked pale. Flavius wondered how much he had had to do with convincing the king that the man was legitimate. The Parthians wouldn't be willing to raise an army to back the man now, which had been the main worry, not after they found a native speaker to confirm Flavius's assertion. It wouldn't be hard to find one in a city as cosmopolitan as Ctesiphon, and the imposter's usefulness had rested on Rome and at least some of the legions rising to welcome him. That no one had thought of the importance of his accent was a gift from the god Mercury himself, patron and guardian of travelers and thieves.

Flavius accorded Artapan a diplomatic bow for politics' sake. "I shall leave for Rome this afternoon," he informed him. "My escort and I are grateful for your king's hospitality."

Artapan bowed back, silently thoughtful. The man who had claimed to be Nero began to rise from his chair. Artapan nodded at the guards in the doorway and he sat down again.

"The king is grateful for your advice," Artapan said finally.

Flavius bowed again and took his leave. He'd had the sensation the entire time that someone had been sitting behind the forest of potted palms and he strongly suspected that it might have been Pacorus himself. It was likely that the king would make the same disposition of this claimant that his brother had made of the last one, and Flavius hoped so. He would much prefer that to his hauling the wretched man back to Rome for Domitian to kill as horribly as possible. At worst, Pacorus would not be pleased with whoever had sent him this unreliable bargaining chip, and if he had contemplated an alliance with whoever that was – and Flavius could think of some names – that was likely off the table as well.

–

"It appears that the Emperor Nero has not been resurrected, yet again," Correus said. A long aggravated letter from Flavius had arrived in the military post. "The Parthian king has expressed his displeasure with that in a fatal way, according to my brother."

"Well, I expect the Boatman will know who he is when he~gets there," Tettius Julianus said. He stretched his legs out to the warmth of the brazier and Eumenes refilled his cup with the precise mixture of water and wine which he had learned the governor favored.

For some reason, Tettius had taken to stopping by the Macedonica legate's tent when he had finished his evening prowl about the camp. Perhaps it was because he was an old friend of Appius, despite their age difference, and they were relatives of a sort. Or perhaps he enjoyed Ygerna's graceful presence; she was the only legate's wife who had unfashionably considered her husband's company worth being ice-bound in the Dacian mountains. Or perhaps Correus was favored because, due to his birth, he had risen as high as he was likely to go and thus was no competition for a man with higher ambitions. He would never be named consul, for instance, a fact that troubled him not at all and Tettius knew it. The army and command of a legion were what Correus had wanted, and all he had wanted.

At any rate, Tettius was here tonight, with the gift of a piece of excellent cheese, a jar of apples preserved in honey and ginger, and a glass flask of bath oil for Ygerna that only a military governor could have ordered into the army supply train.

It was Saturnalia and Tettius Julianus had approved a camp-wide holiday. The Macedonica legionary who had drawn the Fifth's lucky bean as Saturnalia Princeps had ordered his legate to sing a song in praise of beetles while dressed in his wife's tunic, and Correus had complied. Afterward Correus had retreated to his tent, leaving his primus pilus and the optio on duty to see that things didn't get dangerously out of hand. Outside in the snow, Sosius Alpinus and the senior centurions were doing a dance with cook pots on their heads at the direction of the Princeps while their cohorts howled with laughter.

Ygerna stuck her head out the tent door. "They're terrible at it," she announced. "One of them just fell down. I can't tell who. He had a pot over his eyes."

Tettius chuckled. "That's the point. Io Saturnalia!"

At Saturnalia, the lowest ranks drew lots to annoy their superiors without danger of retaliation. Master and slave reversed roles, small presents were given, most often silly things or the little figures called sigillaria, and everyone worked a lot of midwinter boredom out of their skins.

"I notice the governor is hiding in here, however," Ygerna commented with a grin.

"I don't know how many spare clothes you have," Tettius said, "and if I show my face, I'm likely to find out." He took a thoughtful drink and eyed Correus. "Does your brother have any ideas about who put this new Nero up to it? Usually they don't just decide on their own to be fools."

"None besides the obvious, which would be Decebalus," Correus said. "And possibly Ranvig of the Semnones, although I am aware that certain quarters think I have a bug in my helmet about him."

"I'm not sure I think that's an imaginary bug," Tettius said. "A centurion of the First Adiutrix had leave to go back to Upper Germany and see his wife. He just came back with the last supply wagons and says there was tavern talk there, about what he wasn't sure, because it died down immediately every time he showed his face, but he thought the Chatti were much too comfortable in Moguntiacum. Coming and going 'a bit too assuming' was the way he put it, and no one asking for their pass."

"Did he think there was war brewing with the Chatti?" The last time the Chatti had attacked Rome, they had been allied with Ranvig.

"He thought it might be possible but the governor there didn't seem concerned."

Correus's eyebrows went up. He glanced at Eumenes, who had been served his dinner by Correus and given a bag of silver, and was now throwing dice with himself, left hand against right. "Eumenes. It's Saturnalia. You have my leave to go and do whatever strikes you until morning, as long as you don't get in a fight." A slave could only give evidence under torture. He was beginning to think it was best that Eumenes not be there. "Isn't that Antonius Saturninus?" he asked Tettius when they were alone.

"It is. And he's no fool. The Chatti aren't running tame on our side of the river because he doesn't know about it. There are four legions in Upper Germany," he added. "Two of them in Moguntiacum."

Correus was silent for a long moment. Ygerna looked from one man to the other and waited for one of them to say whatever it was that they were both thinking.

"It's always awkward, not to mention dangerous," Tettius said finally, "to accuse a fellow commander, particularly one's successor. But – I understand your brother is on the emperor's staff and your brother-in-law is his tame historian."

Correus nodded. It was clear that Tettius realized that neither was an honor that could have been declined.

Tettius stood up. "If you want to answer your brother's letter, I'll see that it gets in the first courier bag going down." He drained his cup and bowed to Ygerna. "Thank you for letting a lonely bachelor invade your household. I shall go and make sure that none of our revelers have fallen off the ramparts."

Ygerna cocked her head at Correus when the tent door had closed behind him. "What does he think this governor in Germany is up to?" she asked bluntly.

"Treason," Correus said. "That's not to go any farther. And I shan't say it to Flavius or Lucius either, just pass along the facts. That's enough, if not too much."

"Too many legions gives governors ideas. You said that was dangerous." Ygerna looked thoughtful. "And Germany…"

"Precisely," Correus said. He didn't know how much, if anything, Tettius knew of the old failed plot against Domitian that had caught fire in the plotters' hands and nearly ensnared his family, thanks to that fool Lucius. More likely he simply regarded him as a discreet conduit for giving the emperor information that he preferred not to send personally.

–

It was raining, a miserable January drizzle that made Flavius think of staying in the house until spring and made Lucius Paulinus's fur boots look like wet muskrats. Paulinus stamped the water off them on the portico floor and was hustled inside with much tutting and dabbing with towels by Flavius's steward.

"What are you doing out in this mess? Courting a water nymph?" Flavius asked him. Paulinus's dislike of being rained on was notorious. "Bring us hot wine," he told the steward.

Paulinus sneezed. "I came in a litter, but the canopy leaked and the litter bearers slipped in the wet and nearly upended me. I would have done better to walk. I'm spending the night with you if it doesn't clear up."

"By all means." Flavius looked at Paulinus speculatively, and led him into his study, a comfortable, masculine room with brown walls decorated with painted urns and draperies. Shelves of scrolls and a few bound codices flanked the window that looked onto the inner court. The floor and walls were warm with hot air from the hypocaust beneath the house. "I don't suppose you had a letter from my brother?" he suggested.

"I thought he was bound to have written to you too," Paulinus said. "Mine was a masterpiece of evasion and understatement. I could have written it myself." The steward brought the hot wine and Paulinus warmed his hands on the cup. "I had heard hints of some such," he added.

"I've heard rumors of things I don't like," Flavius said. "But nothing that touched on Saturninus. Why have you kept that to yourself?"

"I've been cautious. Not wanting to make mistakes, so to speak."

Flavius snorted. "Well, yes. I've done my best to mend that. If there are any other attempts at, shall we say destabilization, they won't be done by me."

"You relieve my mind." Flavius was the emperor's man, whoever the emperor was, and would remain so. His loyalty was to Rome, and the emperor was Rome. He had remembered the Year of Four Emperors with a bone-deep horror without Domitian's prompting.

"Where is Prosper Rufius in this?" Paulinus asked.

"I don't know. We may be dealing with two issues or one. I'm very reluctant to pass along rumors about Rufius yet. There are enough informers gibbering in his ear and these things can turn around unpleasantly. But this gives substance to the worries about Germany, and that much we need to take to the emperor as soon as tonight. I've just been waiting to see if you would stop by. I think it should come from both of us, for bona fides, so to speak."

Paulinus sighed. "In the rain."

"In the rain. And most tactfully. Tettius Julianus has six legions up there, and he needs them. That's why he doesn't want to call attention to himself, I expect, and invite any comparisons."

"Is that what Correus says?"

"Elliptically, yes."

–

Decebalus stared angrily through the dark window at the sleet falling in icy curtains on the mountainside, at the distant glow of the Roman camp in the valley far below, and then at the courier from Capidava who stood trembling in his sodden boots. The king's brother stood beside the throne, reading over his shoulder the message on the papyrus clenched in the king's fist. A splotch of wax with the seal of the Getae royal house lay on the floor at Decebalus's feet where he had thrown it.

"Whore," Decebalus said. "Lying, ungrateful whore. I made her a queen."

"She doesn't seem to have appreciated it," Diegis said.

"What right gave her leave to send this?" He glared at the courier. "Go back to the lords of the Getae and tell them to be ready to ride at spring thaw against the Romans' backs as soon as we have word from the Germans. I, Decebalus, uncle of your king, say this."

The courier looked miserable. "I cannot go against her orders, lord. We swore to her by the Great God and also by the Mother and the Horseman."

Decebalus closed his fist around the papyrus and crumpled it into a ball. "Do you mean to tell me that your clan has made a *woman* king?"

The courier stood his ground, but he looked torn between two terrors. "It is ancient law, older than any of us. The mother of an heir rules until his twelfth year. It is to prevent male regents from attempting to keep power and disputes over the title. I cannot break it, lord, and even if I could, none of the lords would do so."

"They will break it if I send you back to them dead and tied across your horse."

The courier flinched. "No, King, not even then."

"Get out!" Decebalus rose abruptly, shouting. "Go and tell your queen that I will drag her dead by her hair through Capidava! I leave you alive to tell her that!"

The courier fled before he could change his mind.

Diegis grinned. "I am not without sympathy, but perhaps you shouldn't have paraded her naked, or should have asked about their inheritance laws. One of those anyway."

Decebalus turned on him. "Don't push me, Diegis. I don't need you."

Diegis picked up the crumpled papyrus from where his brother had thrown that too. It amused him to see Decebalus come up against something he couldn't budge. "You will when you want an envoy to the Romans again."

"There are other lords."

Diegis bowed. "As the king says."

XVIII

Saturninus

"Livilla called on me," Aemelia said to Flavius. "You were right about that woman." She was brushing out her hair, a curtain of curling black silk, before her mirror. It had become their evening habit, now that things were mending between them, that she should do it herself and Flavius should watch while they talked of things that weren't meant for the servants. "I thought it was her aunt or I wouldn't have let her in."

"You mean Livilla Drusa Major?" Flavius asked. "That old gorgon terrifies me. The last time I saw her she made me bring her hot milk and told me all about her digestion."

"She knows all the gossip," Aemelia said, "but she's not vicious. I'm fond of her. I didn't realize it wasn't her until she was in."

"And what did Livilla Minor want?" Flavius inquired uneasily.

"I don't know. I think she was afraid of something. She kept asking me what you were doing and how you were liking the emperor's service."

"I don't want her here."

"Well, neither did I. I really don't want to see her anymore. I've given orders she's not to be let in again."

"Particularly when I'm gone."

Aemelia put the brush down. "Are you likely to be gone? Again?"

"I don't know. There's something brewing that I can't talk about yet," he admitted. "It's probably what Livilla was fishing for, so it's best you don't know. If I do leave, I want you to go to my father again. Or yours if you like. I'm sorry."

"I'll go to yours. We seem to practically live there, but Appia will like it better. She's very pleased about having a brother, you know, and informed me that an older one is much better than a nasty baby." Aemelia laughed so he would know she could talk about babies without flinching.

Flavius smiled back at her. "With my father's, um, encumbrance settled elsewhere, it may be calmer there now."

"It is," Aemelia said. "Livilla wanted to talk about that too, just trying to stir up more scandal, I think. She wouldn't be seen talking to Helva herself, of course. Of the two, I think I'd take Helva."

"Livilla is a siren, in the least flattering interpretation of the tale," Flavius said. "And, my previous sentiments notwith-standing, I wish you'd call on Helva if you're willing. My reputation can stand it. The emperor simply thinks it's funny. I expect she's lonesome and if she has some company, she's less likely to be foolish and get herself in some fix. Correus flatly refuses to have her on the frontier. He sent me a scorching letter to that effect. I suppose Father got the same, or worse. Father can go see her of course, since she's his freedwoman, but I don't suppose he wants to make a habit of it. He's really in love. It's terrifying to watch, like seeing your parent regress to a schoolboy."

"Can you imagine Helva on an army post?" Aemelia murmured.

A discreet cough at the door interrupted that thought. A centurion of the Praetorian Guard loomed behind the steward's shoulder. His dripping helmet crest proclaimed that it was raining again.

The centurion held out a tablet sealed with the imperial stamp. "I'm to give you this immediately, sir."

It was what he had been expecting, Aemelia thought, watching Flavius as he read it. He'd be gone tonight no doubt, but she was feeling affectionate toward him. When he came home, she thought she would try the silver cap again.

Flavius was on the Via Cassia north out of Rome in the rainy dark in less than an hour, leaving Aemelia to close up the house. Bericus rode beside him, but no one else other than Domitian's courier. They had orders to change horses at every post and get to Titus Flavius Norbanus, the procurator of Raetia, in Augusta Vindelicorum yesterday. Tettius had been right about Antonius Saturninus and only his suspicions had prevented Domitian from being completely unprepared. For reasons which could be hashed out later, if they amounted to anything but ambition and too many legions under his command, Saturninus had confiscated the savings banks of both legions in Moguntiacum, thereby rendering those legions practically incapable of anything other than following his orders. Those orders had apparently been to declare him emperor and to march on Rome with the other two legions of Upper Germany, and with help from the German Chatti.

Norbanus was to bring his Raetian troops, consisting of four cavalry alae and eight auxiliary cohorts, and meet the four legions of Lower Germany, and a legion from Hispania for good measure, and take care of Saturninus before his efforts encouraged anyone else to his side.

Flavius's position was that of Domitian's personal represent- ative, with orders to get to the site of the rebellion and await the emperor's arrival. Lucius Paulinus had been kept in Rome, since no one knew yet who else was involved, and Domitian had no wish for Lucius Paulinus to know either. If Domitian lost his grip on the Rhenus, Flavius thought dismally, they would be at civil war again, legion against legion.

"They were warned, weren't they?" Bericus asked. "The Lower German commanders? They won't stand for backing a rebellion, will they?" It was too dark to see Flavius's face but Bericus had been Flavius's personal slave since he first joined the army and he knew certain things without needing to see.

"We'll hope not," Flavius said. "Otherwise, we've warned the wrong people."

—

The most direct route from Augusta Vindelicorum to Moguntiacum was through the Agri Decumates and the Black Forest, on a road that Flavius had some acquaintance with, having helped to build it on his first posting. The Agri Decumates, the triangle of land between the Rhenus and the Danuvius, was sparsely inhabited, more a buffer than anything else, and the road was still a log road, laid along a causeway between ditches to prevent flooding. The forest was kept cleared on both sides of the road for a quarter mile, but beyond that the mountains were inky black on either side.

It was a week's march to Moguntiacum at speed, with no knowing what was transpiring there. A courier sent ahead wouldn't be back for four days, even changing horses at each small fort along the road, and there was no telling if there would even be a garrison at those forts, which were manned by the other two Upper German legions, or if they would have ridden out for Moguntiacum. And the Agri Decumates forest felt unwelcoming, a place of unseen presences.

—

"The Rhenus has thawed," Arni said disgustedly, pulling off his sodden cloak. At this time of the year, it should have been as solid as the stone in Haddon of the Chatti's head, but melting snow was dripping from the dragon's head that capped the rooftree of Ranvig's hall. As he passed beneath it, it had looked as if it were slavering, and Arni mirrored its mood.

"They have not crossed the river?" Steinvar asked.

"No, Haddon is sitting in his hold because the weather warmed and the river is wet!" Arni stalked across the hall to the fire, his dogs at his heels.

"He can hardly cross by bridge under the Romans' noses," Ranvig observed.

"The commander of the Eagles in Moguntiacum was to have opened the gates for him," Arni said. "He could have crossed by bridge then, when the ice first started to go soft. But he waited for it to freeze again and now there are other Romans fighting the commander's Romans, and Haddon, who was so fierce to wave a spear in our faces, has gone to his hold and gone back to bed."

Ranvig considered. The new commander of the Eagles at Moguntiacum was unreliable in a number of ways, beginning with being as hungry for war fame as any warrior of Ranvig's people. He had tried to overthrow his own emperor and it now appeared that the emperor was fighting back sooner than expected. Haddon might actually have been wise.

Arni stamped the slush from his boots and eyed the chieftain, sitting on the piled deer hides of the council chair with Signy and Fiorgyn Arngunns-daughter on either side of him like Wuotan's ravens. The council lords, summoned to hear his news, crowded on a bench before the hearth, fur cloaks dripping from pegs by the door and boots stuck to the fire's heat.

"If we went with enough spears of our own, we could prod them across the river," Arni said. He sat on the end of the bench and the dogs lay down in the straw at his feet, fussing with Steinvar's dogs for the warmest spot.

"That was never the plan, was it?" Ingvar cast a dubious eye at the spear he had left by the hall door. "And a worse one now."

"And why should we go? Merely to throw the Chatti, who are kin to us, to the Romans?" Steinvar asked.

"The Chatti are the ones who ran tame in Moguntiacum and saw the chance to raise an emperor who would make pets of them," Arni said contemptuously.

"And how likely was that to succeed?" Horst asked.

"It has happened," Thrain said. "Although not lately." He was paring his fingernails with his belt knife and kept his eyes on his work. "We knew that. But any disturbance to their rule keeps them from looking at us, and that *was* the plan. I have had Romans in my lands before now and I do not have those lands anymore." He stuck the knife in the bench beside him for emphasis.

Ranvig leaned forward, hands on the carved arms of his chair. "And which of the Roman forces is winning?" he asked Arni.

"I don't know. For one thing, I can't tell them apart. They are fighting each other like stoats in the same den."

"Then we will wait until we see which side wins," Ranvig said. "If this new commander of the Eagles at Moguntiacum wins, he will march on Rome with all his men, as well as the ones who have lost to him if they will switch sides. And it will be a very long time before any Roman army thinks of crossing north into our hunting runs. And if he doesn't win, it will also be a long while before the emperor risks leaving enough legions stationed on our border to be a threat to us. I am not unhappy."

"Is this all we want?" Arni demanded. "To sit back and let the Romans fight over their own bones like dogs under the table?"

"What else do you want?" Fiorgyn asked him. "We have fought Rome, Arni. You have fought Rome. You and I know what it cost us."

"We all know," Thrain said quietly.

"I thought Rome could be beaten, once," Ranvig said. "We failed and there is no reclaiming the lost land. They would have taken that whether we fought them or no, to settle old scores and also because it gives them an easier frontier to defend. The commander before this one made that clear. He was a man I found worth trusting. I ate in his house. This new governor is hungry. He had four legions in his province and no war to fight, and he wanted one. If he didn't fight his own people, he would have looked to us."

"That was the reason we sent aid to the Chatti," Steinvar said. "Because they thought to use the governor's ambition to their advantage."

"What does it matter whether the Chatti made good on their pledge or not?" Fiorgyn demanded. "The Romans are occupied fighting each other nonetheless, as Arni saw."

"So we buy our safety with trickery," Arni said, sullen. "When we come to Valhalla shall we brag of our cleverness and not of our honor?" He scratched his scarred ear.

Horst nodded his head. "I countenanced the plan, but it sat ill with me. It may be we have bought our peace too dear."

Ranvig smacked both fists on his chair. "Horst and Arni, if you want to fight someone, go and raid each other's cattle. If you fight Rome again, then you may brag in Valhalla of how you fought a war that left your wives and children homeless."

Arni subsided, barely, and Horst shook his head stubbornly but didn't say anything more. They knew Ranvig was right, but they needn't like it.

"So by our cleverness we have made trouble for Rome and laid the blame on the Chatti," Steinvar said thoughtfully.

"The Chatti nearly cost us the last battle," Ingvar retorted. "Marbod got the fate he looked for and took nearly the whole of his fighting men to Wuotan – at least the ones that didn't go to a Roman slave market. If his successor has decided to be less headlong, it may not be surprising."

"If by less headlong you mean making alliance with a Roman commander to fight Rome, which is like making alliance with an adder to fight the rest of its nest, then yes," Steinvar admitted.

"The Chatti don't care who they fight," old Hauk said.

Ranvig stood, signaling the end of the discussion, as Arni was opening his mouth again. Signy rose also, wading through the dogs, and sent for beer and meat. It was not possible to entertain the council lords without a meal, and more often several. Old Hauk had been known to stay for days, drinking the chieftain's beer instead of his own.

The council settled to the table, the dogs rearranged themselves hopefully beneath it, and thralls went round with bowls of hot stew.

"And what when the adders have finished their quarrel?" said Arni, who could rarely let a thing go.

Ranvig kicked his chair back and stood to point a finger at Arni, the last of his patience gone into his beer horn. "Ask me anything else, Arni, and I will send you to eat in the cow byre, council lord or no. When they have settled the matter, we will send an envoy with our good wishes to whoever has won." He glared at Arni again. "Plainly not you."

–

At the highest point of the Agri Decumates, on a stretch of open moor sodden with melting snow and lumpy with outcroppings of stone and a few windblown trees, Flavius crossed the crest of the world, or at least that part of it where the waters ran either westward down to the Rhenus Valley and then north to the great delta on the edge of the German Ocean, or eastward to the Danuvius to empty into the Pontus Euxinus.

At the first way station fort they came to, the garrison commander claimed to have no knowledge of anything irregular in Moguntiacum, said he had given their courier a fresh horse, and was clearly disinclined to ask any questions. Which, as Norbanus said, indicated that he already had the answers and wanted none of it. The commanders at the next forts proved to be as disinterested in the column's purpose as the first. As snowmelt turned the ditches beside the road into bog, the courier came back to say that he hadn't crossed the Rhenus but that there were men of the Sixth Victrix from Lower Germany on patrol along the Rhenus road and a camp outside Moguntiacum Fortress that looked like it meant to stay.

Norbanus found that ambiguous and sent out a handful of frontier scouts. As the Raetian column approached, no one seemed inclined to march out and fight them, and the scouts returned with further information: the Lower German legions had arrived the day before, stood fast for Domitian, and Saturninus had fallen on his sword.

The Raetian troops marched down to Moguntiacum Bridge through a narrow band of bare winter fields. The river was flowing swiftly, ice-free, and across it the terraced vineyard slopes around Moguntiacum were pruned back for the winter, black against the snow that lingered on the brown shale terraces. Below, a pair of patrol galleys of the Rhenus fleet moved downriver under sail, flying the insignia of their home port at Castra Vetera in Lower Germany.

Whatever the Chatti had intended, they hadn't been able to cross a free-flowing river without fighting off the four Lower German legions who had besieged Moguntiacum and were guarding the nearby bridge as well as the one upriver where the Moenus met the Rhenus. The Raetian auxiliaries and the Seventh Gemina from Hispania came squelching through the melting snow and sealed the end of Saturninus's short-lived rebellion. The two other legions of Upper Germany, the Eighth Augusta at Argentoratum and the Eleventh Claudia at Vindonissa, had ignored his call and stayed in their camps.

Lappius Maximus, governor of Lower Germany, had taken half his troops across the bridge into Chatti lands and burned the nearest holds in retaliation for the watchtowers that Haddon of the Chatti had destroyed – for reasons no one could discern other than that Haddon was ready to fight someone over something, an urge that had always been a Chatti trait. Haddon's warriors had melted into the forest of his home hills and Maximus had declined to pursue them, having made his point.

The upheaval in the empire was another matter. Lappius Maximus found his own strength of four Lower German legions now suspect, despite his loyalty and position as one of Domitian's confidants. The governor of Britain, Sallustius Lucullus, successor to Agricola, was suspected of involvement, and that rapidly became common knowledge. And there was the question of what to do about the officers of the two Upper German legions who had been blackmailed into rebelling against their emperor.

Domitian's arrival was imminent and Flavius and Lappius Maximus contemplated the possible aftermath of that in Saturninus's quarters in the Praetorium at Moguntiacum. They had already been through the papers in his office in the Principia and the contents had made both of them ill.

"There's no saving Sallustius Lucullus, and I don't want to anyway," Lappius Maximus said. "Damn fool." He was an angular, scholarly soldier with a thick shock of dark hair and crooked incisors that gave a crocodilian aspect to his smile. Just now he wasn't smiling. "Both the First Cohort commanders here might as well be dead already. I don't think we can fish them out. And everyone else is already turning on each other. Those two legions fought each other in the civil wars. I can't imagine how they've done now as campmates. I don't know what Domitian thought he was doing posting the Rapax here. He should have sent it to the Danuvius and left the Adiutrix."

So many careers ruined, Flavius thought, for the ambitions of Saturninus. Both legions would be given new officers down the line to the lowest ranking centurion. The current officers who survived would be posted elsewhere and never in all their lives get another promotion. Correus had briefly commanded the Fourteenth Gemina in the last German campaign. Flavius thanked Mithras under his breath that he had not stayed with it.

Now they considered the locked chest that sat beside Saturninus's bed in his private quarters. They hadn't opened that yet. If Saturninus had unknown backers, they would be found in there.

Flavius ran his hands through his hair. He was dog tired and had forgotten when he last slept. On the road, on his horse maybe. "The whole Rhenus–Danuvius frontier feels like a marsh," Maximus said. "Like twitchy bog with spots of soft. There are more connections than we've seen yet. The Semnones are somewhere in this, my scouts are sure of it. And there has been traffic between them and the Marcomanni and the Quadi."

"My brother thinks the Semnones have been having dealings with the Dacians," Flavius said. "Is there anywhere the Semnones are actually minding their own business?"

"They sent an envoy to me this morning," Maximus said. "Ranvig wants to assure Rome that they had no hand in this matter. Which of course means they did."

"Ranvig makes my head ache," Flavius said. He looked at the chest. How useful were wholesale executions of people who changed their minds when they saw how the wind blew? He was extremely glad Lucius Paulinus hadn't come. For everyone's sake, Paulinus needed to be miles from this particular bog. "Keep a grip on that," he said. "I don't want to know what's in it yet. I want some sleep before I make any stupid decisions."

"Do you want to meet with the envoy? Or will the emperor? I don't think you'll get much that's useful out of her. She knows her business."

"She?"

"The old Semnone chieftain's widow. She's a force in the tribe because her husband gave himself to Rome to save the rest when we beat them in Vespasian's reign. The Germans value acts like that."

Flavius felt his stomach turn over. The nausea that had risen at the contents of Saturninus's papers came again. "That was my first post, that campaign," he murmured.

"Do you know her?"

"I am acquainted with her, yes."

Maximus looked abruptly tactful, old gossip no doubt occurring to him. They hadn't been discreet. They had both known another war was coming and that after that it wouldn't matter.

Maximus eyed him thoughtfully. "You're dead on your feet. Go get some rest. We've got two days at least before we'll have to report to the emperor. I'll put a guard on this box. I don't want to open it without the emperor's representative on hand."

—

Moguntiacum was ominously quiet. The Principia was now occupied by the staff of Governor Maximus, who were investigating its contents with the thoroughness of tax men. The men of the Fourteenth Gemina and the Rapax were confined to quarters and the wet streets patrolled by the invading cohorts of the Seventh Gemina from Hispania. The legates of the other two Upper German legions had sent their assurances of loyalty and remained in their quarters along the borders of the Agri Decumates.

Flavius retreated to the inn where Bericus had bought them rooms. He gave Bericus, who had slept, his boots and cuirass to clean, collapsed on a bed, and slept, too tired even for the dreams he had feared might come. He slept through the day and woke in the morning wondering where he was. It came back to him alarmingly quickly.

The inn was among the market stalls under Jupiter's Column, and the face of someone who nearly always knew things that no one else did came into his mind. If she was in Moguntiacum and not in Colonia, where the clientele was more fashionable and the trouble less, she might well be in her old house near the column.

The house was still there and as he remembered it, an L-shaped building with a portico and an upper story, melting snow dripping from the tile roof. The door was painted in scalloped bands of yellow and scarlet and a bronze figure of Faunus adorned with an enormous phallus leered at him from the wall beside it. He pulled on the phallus and heard a bell ring inside. The girl who opened the door was unfamiliar, a slight blond with wide blue eyes and a suspicious glance. It was early in the day.

"Is this still Rhodope's place?" Flavius asked her. The door-bell's modest advertisement suggested that it was. "Don't look at me like that. I'm not here to collect taxes or protection money."

"Then you can come in," she said.

Inside, the house was furnished to Rhodope's taste, which leaned toward eastern splendor, with brilliant silk draperies, piles of rugs, and tastefully salacious scenes on the walls. Through the reception room Flavius could see a dining chamber where another girl with a long black braid was doing the flowers and setting fresh incense into the bronze burners on the walls. He didn't recognize her either. The room was furnished with silk-cushioned couches on a mosaic floor where a collection of satyrs were prancing among naked nymphs, members erect. This seemed to be a motif, but the house felt remarkably homey all the same. Rhodope herself sat in the dining room doorway where she could oversee things from a wicker chair with an enormous peacock tail back and red silk cushions. She widened her eyes delightedly when she saw him.

"Correus!" She paused and then shook her head. "No, it is the other brother."

"I hope you aren't disappointed," Flavius said.

She looked exactly as she always had, her bulk still topped by a head of brilliantly red-hennaed hair. She wore a red and gold gown, a purple mantle pinned with an enormous emerald, and bright blue shoes. Her dark eyes were friendly. "Not in the least. I was taken by surprise to see either of you. Although you are on the emperor's staff, are you not? So I can guess your business here."

"I'm afraid you can," Flavius said.

"Difficult times. Sit down. It is fine to see an old acquaintance. Amalthea, bring some wine, and some pastries for the centurion. Is that your rank still?"

"It is. I'm still attached to the army as well as to the emperor." Centurion covered a lot of ground, from the lowliest commander of the Sixth Century of the Tenth Cohort to a primus pilus, second in command to a legate. "I wondered if I would find you here," he ventured.

Rhodope gave a whoop of laughter. "With five legions with time on their hands and in need of something to take their minds off the situation? I'm not counting the ones you have locked in the fort. But we've been here since the last campaign. The army gave me my start and I'm loyal."

Flavius grinned. "The army appreciates it." He was edging toward what he wanted to know when the blonde girl, Amalthea, brought a silver pitcher of wine and small water pitcher to match, and a redware plate of cakes. The plate was embossed with a couple doing acrobatic things that he suspected would put him in the hospital.

"I hear the Germans have sent Nyall Sigmundson's widow as an envoy," Rhodope said and Flavius jerked his head up. He had forgotten that the things she knew probably included things about him.

"Oh dear." She looked contrite. "Did you not know? I thought perhaps you were looking for distraction yourself."

"With one of your girls?" Flavius asked ruefully. There was a time when that would have sounded like a fine idea.

Rhodope shrugged. "Leza is still with me. She always liked you."

"I had other things in mind," Flavius said. "And I did know."

"No man is always wise," Rhodope pronounced. "You're too much like your brother."

Flavius stiffened. "Really? I had always thought us rather different."

"As in the flesh, so under it, in my opinion." Rhodope poured a little more wine into his redware cup. It displayed the same couple in a different position. "Too much heart, both of you."

"I always thought that of Correus, but that I was rather more like the old man," Flavius said. "Although that notion has gone down the river. He's fallen in love with a middle-aged widow."

"I had heard that he was widowed himself," Rhodope said. "News travels. Your father is a famous man. My condolences about your mother."

"Thank you."

Rhodope settled herself in her peacock tail chair. She looked over her shoulder at Amalthea and the black-haired girl, who were staring at the newcomer with interest. "You're too ugly for him," she told them. "Go make the beds. Scoot!"

They departed and he heard their footsteps pattering on the stairs. Rhodope regarded Flavius with a shrewd eye. "So. If you won't console yourself with one of my girls, why are you here?"

Flavius sighed. "I have to…" He trailed off, then started again. "Decisions must be made. The emperor will be here in a few days. It's not going to be pretty."

"And you're wondering who else may have been involved," Rhodope said. "And thinking that my girls hear things. And you're also wondering who's going to be crucified and who you can get off, and whether they're worth the risk."

"You terrify me," Flavius said. "But yes, all of those. A bloodbath won't be good for stability or morale." And that was always Domitian's first instinct. "Also, I can't risk letting anyone really dangerous slip away."

"I have become successful," Rhodope remarked, "by not attending to anything that a customer is drunk or foolish enough to whisper in a girl's ear, to impress her or to soothe his conscience. But…"

Flavius waited.

"But I listen, of course. I am not stupid. Governor Saturninus kept a list and used it to frighten others into compliance. A little mistake here, some debt there, a drunken joke here. You see."

"I do." It was a technique too familiar in the contorted politics of the empire.

"And there are people on it who do not deserve to die, not for that. The others… they no doubt knew the Boatman would be by sooner or later."

"I expect right now they can hear his oars," Flavius said. "Are they dangerous now that Saturninus is dead?"

"In my opinion, no," Rhodope said. "But that is only my opinion."

Flavius thought he would bet a good deal on Rhodope's opinion.

–

The chest still sat on the late commander's desk. Flavius and Lappius Maximus regarded it with the wary eyes of people about to open a box of wasps. A double-faced head of Janus on the lid's edge rested above an iron lock. A courier had brought word that the emperor, accompanied by Julius Frontinus, had passed through Augusta Raurica some days ago and was expected to reach Moguntiacum in two more.

"All right, let's get on with it." Maximus produced an iron bar and a mallet from his satchel. "I borrowed these from the work yards," he commented, wedging the bar into the lock. "I didn't fancy asking anyone else to do this."

It was a gray day and a lamp on a bronze stand was lit, as were the coals in the commander's brazier. According to Lappius Maximus, the fortress hypocaust was inadequate for his oncoming ague and an optio had been sent for those. Flavius wondered if he was catching the governor's imaginary ague. The back of his neck felt as if the melting snow was dripping down it.

Maximus smacked the end of the bar with the mallet, and it went part way in, but the latch didn't open. He hit it again, and the wood cracked around the lock. A third blow nearly took the lid off. Maximus stood back and set the mallet down.

"I don't..." Flavius said and stopped.

"Want to know what's in it?" Maximus suggested.

"Want to be responsible for what the emperor will do with it."

Maximus nodded. Domitian would already be suspicious of wider-ranging involvement. Anyone implicated even by a whisper was likely to be executed, or exiled at the very least. "Let's look at it first," he said hopefully.

Flavius lifted the lid. The box was full. Papyrus sheets and scraps, small wooden tablet leaves, one small scroll that unwound with a horrifying, unending list of names. None were the names on the records that had already destroyed Sallustius Lucullus of Britain and several others. This was the list Rhodope had told him about of favors owed and done, money lent and due, conversations recorded or overheard, adultery, quoting the wrong philosopher, consulting astrologers on the health of the emperor, any small dangerous thing that could be used to bring a reluctant participant in treason to heel.

To Flavius's vast relief, he saw no one directly connected to his family, but enough senators and magistrates, high ranking equites, and army officers to fill an arena with the blood that Domitian would extract for their participation, voluntary or no.

Maximus looked over his shoulder and grew pale. "I'm remembering seven years ago," he said. "I wasn't here, I was in Bithynia at the time, grateful to say, but I've always thought it fortunate that Marius Vettius's house burned down before anyone could go through it."

Flavius didn't say anything to that. A great many people had thought it fortunate, except for Domitian. A similar accident would be highly suspicious, but in this case, they knew where the documents were: in their hands like a fistful of snakes.

"You're an *amicus* of the emperor," Flavius said finally. "He respects your advice."

"He respects yours," Maximus retorted. "Do you think either of us could defend anyone implicated here without being suspect ourselves? I don't."

Flavius was silent again. How did you weigh loyalty on this kind of scale? What was worse? He had faced something like this once before and pulled both his wife's father and Lucius Paulinus out of the flames. Why was he reluctant now? Because Domitian had said that he trusted him? Could he stretch that trust to include keeping Domitian from the wholesale death sentences that his blind fury would demand, because the backlash could easily lead to the assassination Domitian constantly feared? Was that specious thinking?

Finally, Flavius looked pointedly at the brazier and Maximus nodded. The governor arranged the coals to suit him, carefully, methodically, as if they were about to toast bread. They fed the contents of the box into the fire piece by piece, breaking up the ashes with the mallet and scooping them into the ash bucket. The wooden tablet leaves were reluctant to burn and Flavius pounded them into splinters first.

When they were finished, they broke the box into pieces as well, took them to the cellar, and shoved them into the furnace that fed the hypocaust. Maximus dropped the iron lock over the bridge into the Rhenus during a casual stroll through the vicus for refreshment, and if he noticed that Flavius had shoved a single sheet of papyrus down the front of his tunic, he didn't mention it.

XIX

Fiorgyn

The Emperor Titus Flavius Caesar Domitianus Augustus received the envoy from the Semnones in the Hall of Justice of the Moguntiacum basilica from a gilded chair set on a two-foot-high dais. A pageboy with a flask of wine and a fan knelt beside the emperor's chair and a dozen of the Praetorian Guard troops who had accompanied him from Rome stood behind it, splendid in parade dress cuirasses and scarlet plumes. A chair for the envoy had been set below the dais. Outside, a crowd of the curious had assembled in the wet streets to see her arrival.

"Germans!" A guardsman whispered to his centurion. "They let their women gallop around on horseback like sluts. I saw her ride in, with her skirts up around her waist and breeches on like a man. Whoever heard of sending a woman to treaty talks."

"If they want to send a woman, or a cow or a mermaid, they've a right to," the centurion said repressively. "Anyway, they're barbarians. Eyes front and mind your business."

A flurry of action on the basilica's steps announced the envoy's arrival. She was tall, clad in a gown of deep blue and an over-tunic of a lighter sky shade, fur-lined boots and cloak, and a broad gold collar. Her pale braids hung over her shoulders, tipped with enameled bands. Ten Semnone warriors walked behind her, weaponless and dressed in woolen breeches and wolf and fox skin cloaks, their hair knotted in the fashion of the northern tribes, and their standing showing in gold torques and armbands and the fineness of embroidered woolen shirts. Two of them carried a wooden box between them.

The envoy made a deep bow to the Roman emperor and spoke in awkward Latin. "I am Fiorgyn Arngunns-daughter, and sister's daughter's daughter to the mother of Ranvig, chieftain of the Semnones. The Lord Ranvig sends me."

Domitian waved the pageboy's fan away and gestured to the man standing expressionless on his other side. "This is Centurion Flavius Appius Julianus. He will translate for us. You may speak in German if that is more comfortable." He sounded benevolent, almost fatherly.

Flavius repeated the greeting, in the language he had learned from Fiorgyn. Fiorgyn met his eyes as she took her seat. He thought she had seen him as soon as she walked in. "Thank you, Emperor of Rome. I am indeed more comfortable in my own language."

"Why have you requested audience with the Emperor Domitian?" Flavius asked her, repeating the emperor's question, which everyone knew the answer to. He remembered her eyes. Sky color.

"I have come with the Lord Ranvig's assurances that our people had no hand in the recent rebellion among your legions. We wish the emperor nothing but good fortune, and according to our treaty, we have since maintained the border between us in peace."

"I see. Can your chieftain say the same of the men of the Chatti?" Domitian rested his elbow on his chair, chin in hand.

"The Chatti, Emperor, have never been wise. It would seem that they have grown no wiser. To ally ourselves with them would be foolish and we are not fools." She kept her eyes on Domitian to Flavius's relief. If he did not look at her, he could probably get through the meeting. Her hair was still blonde.

Domitian laughed. "The Chatti did not fare as well in the war between us as did your people. It is a shame that all are not as wise as the Semnones."

"Indeed, Emperor. We wish nothing in the future but good relations with Rome. I have brought a gift to honor that friendship." Flavius translated. She was still slim.

"That is gracious of you." Domitian looked pleased. He liked presents. Two of the Semnone warriors set the box before him and opened its clasp. They lifted out a pair of bronze lamps, finely modeled in the figures of a stag and doe, the oil cups set into their backs.

Domitian admired them. "Very fine workmanship. I shall have them in my private study."

"I am glad that they please you." She curled one hand over the other in her lap, thumb to thumb, an infinitely familiar gesture.

Domitian rose. "We accept the Semnones' assurance of their neutrality. You and your escort are welcome to stay in Moguntiacum as long as you wish."

Fiorgyn rose as well. "The emperor is most gracious." There was a ring on her finger.

The Semnone delegation waited while the emperor's retinue swept from the hall, pausing in the dripping portico for the page to raise a parasol above the emperor's head. Flavius followed, the tension that he had fought off throughout the meeting suddenly clenching his stomach into a knot. He knew that the actual diplomatic dance had already been conducted between Fiorgyn and Lappius Maximus. This meeting was for show, but because of that, perhaps even more important. The emperor had been publicly shown to have a firm and steady hand on the border. With luck he wouldn't have to see her again. A little hawk cocked an eye at him from its perch on the Drusus cenotaph, memorial to an Augustan general. Flavius felt like the unwary sparrows eating crumbs on the wet stones as danger lurked above him – something too swift to dodge.

"Julianus, you're in a fine state." Domitian clapped him jovially on the back.

Flavius jumped. "I beg your pardon, sir?"

"No wonder Ranvig sent that woman for his ambassador. Probably hoping she'd have the same effect on me she did on you. Don't think I never heard the gossip."

Flavius went cold. "I assure you—"

"Oh, I don't think you told her any military secrets. Probably the other way around. Very useful." Domitian looked pleased with this deduction. "Go and see her. I'll send you with a little present. Ought to reciprocate."

"Emperor, that would not be wise." Flavius's distress was so obvious that Domitian paused uncharacteristically to consider.

"No? Well, perhaps not. There will be enough to attend to just now, cleaning house."

Flavius fled to his chamber at the inn, where Bericus was occupied with brushing his clothes and polishing his spare boots.

"If anyone is looking for me, I have gone out and you don't know where. Even the emperor... particularly the emperor."

"This came for you," Bericus said dubiously. "The man who brought it said it was from General Frontinus."

"He came from Rome with the emperor," Flavius said, "but I haven't seen him." He took the folded, sealed sheet. The seal wasn't Frontinus's. It was his father's.

> *My dear son,*
>
> *I am sending this with Julius Frontinus who is going out to the Rhenus with the emperor tonight, hard on your heels.*
>
> *I have debated for some time whether to tell you this or not, but now that the upheaval on the Rhenus has begun again and now that you will be there possibly for some time, I feel that I must. I have heard the gossip about the woman in Germany, of course, although I have not mentioned it since it is none of my business and I have very little standing to complain about your taking a mistress. Leaving her behind in Germany was the wisest part of that. But you do need to know that she has a son and he is almost undoubtedly yours.*

Flavius sat down on the bed and closed his eyes. Bericus looked at him uncertainly. It was some kind of dreadful news, he was sure.

Please, not the old general or the master's wife. He saw Flavius take a deep breath and go on reading.

> *This information came to me indirectly, and I am not going to go into how I heard it, but its source is probably sound. Gossip generally comes to me to die, but in this case, I thought it best to pass it on to you alone. It is not general knowledge, so do not worry about it distressing your wife or making the rounds of Rome's dinner parties. I fear that I have that distinction at the moment.*
>
> *I have no idea whether you will even see the woman, but I understand that her people come into Moguntiacum and other Rhenus towns to trade, so it is a distinct possibility. If you do see her, it is possible that she may exert some pressure on you, so you should know that it is probably true. Please do not be insulted at my practical assessment of her possible course of action. I know that you felt deeply about her or you would not, quite frankly, have made the scandal that you did. And she may also, quite reasonably, wish for you not to know. If need be, however, you may make her a decent settlement with my permission. I am sure I do not need to caution you NOT to try to bring this child back to Rome, but I shall do so anyway.*
>
> *Your loving father,*
> *Appius Julianus*

Flavius put his head in his hands and Bericus couldn't bear it. "Please, master, who is dead?"

Flavius looked up. "No one. No one is dead." He folded the letter, two sheets of papyrus in his father's familiar hand.

Bericus looked worried but he went back to his task. He had served Flavius Julianus for over seventeen years and recognized his moods. If it was not a death, it was deeply private and best left alone.

It took Flavius the better part of the afternoon to steel himself. Then he went to find Domitian, hoping he was still feeling avuncular.

Domitian was having lunch in the villa that had been taken over for the emperor's use in Moguntiacum. Orders had gone out already for the execution of Sallustius Lucullus in Britain and a number of others. The higher ranking officers of both guilty legions who had failed to kill themselves in time had been summarily and publicly executed while Domitian was meeting with the Semnone envoy. She would have seen their heads in the agora on her way back to her lodgings, a fine bloody welcome to Rome's side of the river.

"Julianus!" Domitian waved him into the room.

Flavius gave an inaudible sigh of relief at the emperor's mood. It was clear that the speedy dissolution of the rebellion had pleased him. Political executions left Domitian either suspicious of everyone else around him or cheerfully confident and magnanimous, depending on circumstance. Today he was the latter, taking dishes from the hands of his taster and eating greedily. Flavius thought that he and Lappius Maximus had done the right thing. He could take comfort in that at least.

"Here, have something to drink." The emperor snapped his fingers at the slave serving him and pointed to Flavius. "And an oyster."

Flavius admired a kitchen staff that could procure oysters this far up the Rhenus on a day's notice when all merchant traffic on the river had been held up by the fleet patrols.

"You have my permission to sit."

He sat down and ate the oyster that the slave presented on a silver plate bearing the emperor's image.

"I've sent for Julius Frontinus to discuss redistribution of the army out here," Domitian said, rinsing his fingers in a bowl of scented water. "It was unwise to leave so many legions in one province, that much is clear."

Flavius nodded, sipping his wine, waiting for an opening for what he had to ask. Domitian gave it to him without asking.

"I'm going to send you back to that Semnone woman, Julianus. I appreciate your personal scruples but I have no time for them. I want to know what she knows about the Chatti. Julius Frontinus agrees with me that we need to make a decision as to whether to send another army across the Rhenus and teach them more manners or offer a treaty while they are still rebuilding the holds that Lappius Maximus burned for them."

Flavius suspected he knew the answer that Frontinus wanted. Battles with the German tribes in the Free Lands tended to be unwieldy and inconclusive. There were too many places for retreating warriors to go to ground and reappear later in ambushed patrols, burned farms, and dead sheep in the water. An all-out war with the Chatti now might be an entanglement best left untried. Domitian, on the other hand, might be in a mood for reprisal regardless. His current frame of mind could signal that as well.

Flavius saluted. "Of course, sir."

"Excellent. I have prepared a little present for her, to take with you. A diplomatic gift for form's sake and a reason to call on her."

"Thank you, sir."

Domitian's page presented Flavius with a small carved box.

"Ear drops," Domitian said. "Women like jewelry."

"Yes, sir."

"And don't worry, I shan't tell your wife that I sent you. That's all water under the bridge now. This is just diplomacy, a mission for your emperor." He was still jovial, a kindly uncle chaffing a favorite nephew.

"Yes, sir." Flavius saluted again and made his escape. On his way out he encountered Julius Frontinus.

"How is his mood?"

"Cheerful," Flavius said grimly.

Frontinus's lips moved but the words were inaudible. Flavius thought he said "Oh dear."

–

The Inn of the Oak Trees sat under the bare branches of a small grove somehow left standing during the constant expansion of the

Moguntiacum civilian quarter. The oaks were hung with lanterns that would be lit with the dusk, above a path of flat stones set among evergreen hedges. A Semnone guard stood in the doorway of the inn's thatched portico and regarded Flavius with suspicion. "I will ask," he said grudgingly when Flavius inquired for Fiorgyn.

There was the possibility that she wouldn't see him, Flavius thought, while he waited under the roof of the portico. That would make it easier. Or not.

After a long while, a girl came to fetch him. "My lady says you are to come with me."

"Thank you." Flavius followed her down a corridor to a set of rooms at the rear of the inn. The door opened onto a reception room where Fiorgyn sat in a cushioned chair by a brazier that sent a ripple of warm air across the cold room.

"You can go, child." She sent the maid away and waited, hands in her lap, for him to speak first.

"Fiorgyn…"

"I didn't know if you would come," she said then.

"I almost didn't," he admitted. *Oh gods, Fiorgyn…*

"You have gray in your hair," she said.

He smiled. "You don't." *Fiorgyn…*

She shook her head. "Blonde hair hides it better. I asked the gods once just not to let me forget your face when you were gone. I'm glad I didn't."

Flavius was still standing in the doorway, the old wild longing surging up in him.

"Come and sit," Fiorgyn said. There was a chair on the opposite side of the brazier and he took it. "Did the emperor send you?"

"The emperor sent me to pry information about the Chatti from you," he said ruefully, resorting to truth. "I tell you that honestly because I know you won't give me any. He sent you a gift as well." He held out the box.

Fiorgyn took it and lifted the lid. She put one of the ear drops in the palm of her hand. It was fashioned from a gold bar set with an emerald boss; three small emeralds dangled from its pendant chains. "You must thank your emperor for me," she remarked.

"I believe they are very fashionable," Flavius said. "I don't know whether he sent a slave to buy them in Moguntiacum or simply travels with a supply of suitable gifts for all eventualities." His words were flippant and stiff.

"Is that the only reason you are here?" she asked quietly.

"I don't know!" His voice was desperate. "I want everything I can't have and I make a disaster of everything else." He took a deep breath. "I understand that you are married."

"Yes."

"And have a son."

"Yes."

"I am glad of that." *Is he mine?*

"My husband dotes on him."

"I am glad of that too." He looked wildly around the chamber as if some disembodied hand might write the words to speak to her on the walls. The Jews had a story about that, Ygerna had told him once. She had been friends with the old emperor's Jewish mistress, a dangerous indiscretion that Flavius had not, thank the gods, known about until later. Nothing appeared now, and in any case the king in the story had not been able to read it, and when translated, it had prophesied his death. The thoughts in his head collapsed in a jumble and he stared at her. Her eyes were still sky color, not the bright blue of a bird's egg, but the pale hue of a fresh day.

"If the emperor hadn't sent me, I would have come anyway," he murmured.

"Will it make trouble if we are seen together?" she asked.

"No. You are the envoy of the Semnones and I am the emperor's aide. And translator. That is thanks to you. I was never good at German before you."

Fiorgyn rose. "Then let us take a walk." She took the fur-lined cloak from a hook on the wall and settled it around her shoulders.

Flavius followed her out into the sunlit afternoon. It was still thawing and the paving stones were glossy with trickling water that carried the oily detritus from the food stalls, iridescent as a pigeon's coat. By unspoken consent, they walked toward the river, away from the town and the bloody remains of the morning's executions.

"Why did Ranvig send you as envoy?" Flavius asked her. He could take that back to the emperor at least. "Is it common to use women in this fashion?" Previous negotiators had been men, including the chieftain himself.

"In circumstances like this, yes," Fiorgyn said. "A woman is less likely to provoke a man's instinct to... to..." She waved her hands, searching for the words.

"Prove his virility with a sword?" Flavius suggested.

Fiorgyn laughed. She cocked her head up at him and smiled. "Yes, precisely. Your governor here, the one who thought to make himself Caesar, was troubled by that. He wanted glory, and if he could not manage it this way, he would have looked to the Free Lands."

"Thus a rebellion here might be usefully helped along?" Flavius asked.

"Certainly not. Not by us. That is why I am here, to assure the emperor of that. Also because, as a woman, I am a less tempting hostage than a council lord might be."

He was reasonably sure she was lying about the Semnones' involvement, but he suspected that it amounted to little, if anything, more than egging the Chatti on.

As they neared the river, the street faded into a dirt track leading down toward the towpath and they followed it, walking in the shade of the trees that fringed the bank. Snowdrops were coming up among last year's fallen leaves, white as pearls. Fiorgyn lifted her skirts above the mud as they made their way down. Her fur boots were hobnailed on the soles like military boots. The sun came through the bare branches in cross-hatched light, casting their shadows across the towpath into the water where they rippled with the current. A patrol craft of the fleet slid by, its oars moving like a single waterborne insect with a scarlet shell. There was no one else about and even here, in the shadow of Rome's bridge, Flavius thought that this was the country of Pan Silvanus, the horned god of the forests and wild lands, whose name changed with the province but whose presence never diminished.

"He's your child," Fiorgyn said abruptly. "You have a right to know that."

They were alone on the sandy track of the towpath. Flavius halted and put his mutilated hand against her cheek. "Is he with you here?" he whispered.

She shook her head and put her own hand over his. "He is at home with his father and his nurse. That is better, Flavius."

"Most likely." He turned away to look at the river. "Do you need... need anything? I could send..."

"No." She shook her head. "Anything you gave me for him would bind you to him. We've been given this time together again for some reason, but we can't keep it."

He thought about that, and how often the gods' gifts sent madness along with them, and whether that mattered.

They began to walk along the towpath again under a brightening sky. The air was odd, luminous, Flavius thought, like a storm that hadn't been there lifting, and full of birds, wheeling above them. As the towpath reached the bridge, she took his hand. She smelled of woodsmoke and rosemary.

A small hut sat below the bankside pier of the bridge, home to a toll collector who levied tax on barges coming upriver. The toll collector was asleep outside the hut on a bench in the thin sun, feet on the concrete base of the pier, and Flavius shook him awake.

The man snorted and looked up. "Who are you?" He had a squint in one eye and a crooked nose and made Flavius think of trolls.

"Go and get yourself a cup of hot wine," Flavius told him and held out a coin. "Two in fact."

"What about my barges?" The toll collector looked suspicious. "Who's going to collect the fees?"

"There aren't any just now," Flavius said. "Order of the fleet. All traffic going upriver past Bonna is stopped."

The toll collector bit the edge of the coin. "I've got a bit of stew on the fire in there. I want to find it when I come back."

"You will," Flavius said. "Don't come back until dark and you might find another coin fallen in it. Now go."

The troll put the coin in his pouch and shambled up the towpath. He didn't ask what the Roman wanted with his hut. Romans never made sense anyway.

Fiorgyn looked ready to burst into laughter, or tears, Flavius wasn't sure which. Her face was fine-drawn and there was a translucent quality to her, like someone whose heart is too close to the skin. "It's a place to be alone," he said helplessly. She nodded and he took her by the hand and they went in.

It was dim inside and cold. A bench, a rough table, a cot, and one shelf were the only furnishings. The pot of stew sat odoriferously on a small raised hearth that smoked badly; the smoke hole above it was clogged with what looked like an old jackdaw's nest. Flavius found a stick of kindling and stood on the table to poke at it. The nest came down in a shower of decaying twigs and feathers, and the smoke abated somewhat.

Flavius spread his cloak over the cot while Fiorgyn watched him solemnly. "If this has fleas, I will apologize later," he told her.

"Whatever is in that pot is probably enough to drive fleas off," Fiorgyn said. "You got bits of nest in it, though."

Flavius inspected the pot. "I'm not sure he'll notice."

Fiorgyn smiled and shed her own cloak, and he held out his hands to her. She came to him and he put his arms around her and kissed the base of her neck and then her hair. Outside the light changed, the trees shook themselves into new leaf, and the air grew green and watery.

"We can't keep this," Fiorgyn whispered. "Only for an afternoon."

He sat on the cot and drew her down to him. He slipped the enameled bands from the ends of her braids and pulled them loose to run his fingers through her hair. It shimmered in waves in the dim light and a quick, bright image of fields of barley came into his mind. She kissed his mouth and his face and his hands.

Flavius unlaced her gown, conscious that they were both in the toll collector's hut on his possibly fleasome cot, and at the same time somewhere else where the trees bent over them in the grass and there was the sound of pipes, soft and silvery and very faint. Whatever gods gave their favors to lovers had given them this. He would take it gratefully, knowing that it could not be kept.

He pulled her gown from her shoulders and she wriggled out of it and under her fur cloak for warmth while he shed his woolen tunic and the breeches and winter leggings that the Rhenus frontier required. He slid under the cloak with her, kissing her again hungrily, hands on her breasts while she wrapped her arms around his back, shaking with the urgency and magic that infused the air.

Her bare breasts were milky pale, and dark rose at the tips, and his hands must have been cold but she didn't flinch. She leaned into his touch and the smell of the toll collector's stew was overlaid with the scent of spring water from deep in the earth, and new grass, and the call of the birds overhead became a tune, a little running song, light and shining as silver.

—

They left at dusk. Flavius half expected to step out into an unfamiliar land but the green leaves had dissolved and it was still the same world, full of mud and melting snow and bloody executions in the public square. They were people who had slept where the *alfar* danced and by rights the world should have been different when they woke, but it wasn't.

They walked silently, no longer hand in hand, by mutual consent peeling away the strands that had linked them, layer by layer like unwinding a skein of wool knotted in the middle, until the two ends were separate countries. When they reached the track that climbed from the towpath to the street, they turned in opposite directions.

–

"You can take this chit to the aquilifer." Flavius handed the farmer a wooden tablet with the due amount on it and signaled the optio beside him for the next claimant in the line that clogged the main hall in the Principia. The aquilifers, the Eagle-bearers when on the march, were also legionary treasurers. The savings banks of the ill-fated Rapax and Gemina had been re-confiscated and were being used to pay the claims of farmers whose fields and livestock had suffered from the encampment of four legions. The remains of the Rapax and Gemina troops had been sent in disgrace to postings in Pannonia, and the Twenty-Second Primigenia from Lower Germany installed in Moguntiacum.

The farmer didn't budge. "That's not enough."

"It's what we pay for a cow."

"That was a fine cow."

"I'm sure it was." They had all been fine cows, and prize-winning pigs, and chickens who laid three eggs a day. Flavius consulted the accounts spread on the table before him until the farmer gave up. "Next."

Fiorgyn's entourage had ridden out of Moguntiacum in the dawn light, but he felt as if the previous afternoon sat next to him, invisible but embodied, a glass flask with the day captured in it. It had taken on a mythic quality, intangible but always with him. That would be enough, he thought. He had been given something he didn't deserve but the gods were capricious and did things for their own reasons. He had given the *genii* of the place an offering of wine and olive oil at the well in the agora.

"A whole section of vine trampled by their great hobnailed feet," the woman in front of him was saying. She crossed muscular arms across her woolen front. "What are you going to do about that? That's what I want to know!"

"How many vines?"

"Twenty."

Flavius suspected that probably meant ten, but he wrote the chit anyway.

"And bothering the farm maids. By rights you ought to pay for that too."

"Was someone hurt?"

She snorted. "No, she had a knife and Cook had a cleaver."

Flavius grinned. "I expect he's a reformed man, then." He scribbled on the chit again. "But I've added a bit for you to give to the girl."

The woman looked startled. She hadn't expected him to care about that. Men never did, just thought it their due, and not just the Romans.

"Down the steps to your left. Just follow everyone else." He couldn't pay off every girl accosted by soldiers in a war, but this hadn't been the civilians' war. Extra goodwill among the city populace just now would be useful. He eyed the line that circled around the standards of the Twenty-Second in the center of the hall and saw three who had been through once before. He pointed them out to the optio.

"Tell them that if they try that on I'll rescind what we've paid them, forcefully if necessary. I'm losing patience. So far, I've had nine or ten claiming entirely imaginary pigs, and one old harridan who smelled like a sheep and cursed me."

"Yes, sir." The optio set out purposefully for the repeaters.

Flavius returned to the claims before him. It was full dark by the time the last of them left. He sent for Bericus and bathed in the fortress baths, only to be summoned still dripping to report to the emperor at his villa in the city.

Domitian's quarters were an anthill of activity: pages, Praetorian officers, and secretaries hustling in and out at the emperor's command, and Lappius Maximus and Julius Frontinus already attending him.

"I trust that all have been made happy?" Domitian inquired as Flavius saluted. "Yes? Very good. Now that you are no longer besieged by importunate farmers, Julianus, we'll have your report. Did the Semnones' envoy succumb to your charms?" The emperor reclined on his couch and smiled benignly at Flavius. He was enjoying this, in the way that he sometimes did with a favorite, teasing him for the fun of seeing him blush.

Flavius declined to blush. "No, sir. And such as they are."

Julius Frontinus and Lappius Maximus sat to either side of the emperor's couch, helmets on knees, attentive.

"Sit down, Julianus," Domitian said. "What did you find out?"

Flavius sat. "That the Chatti were afraid of Antonius Saturninus's ambition, to the best of her belief. He had more legions here than was good for him and no one to fight. She thinks that he was looking to the nearest German Free Lands for a military victory and they encouraged him in the other direction, so to speak."

"That seems likely," Frontinus said.

"I agree." Lappius Maximus considered this information. "That being the case, they are unlikely to be further trouble if the new governor is not so dangerously ambitious."

"If I thought that Javolenus Priscus was ambitious, I would not have chosen him," Domitian said shortly. He studied the three men, sifting out their information and possible prejudices. "I think," he said at length, "that we will leave the Chatti be, as you suggested, Frontinus, unless they give us further reason not to. They have been paid for the burned watchtowers. Their chieftain Haddon appears to be even more foolish than the old one, and Marbod was a fool who provided me with a triumph for his pains."

"And Lower Germany?" Frontinus inquired. Lappius Maximus had that morning been assigned to the consular legateship of Syria in the general rearrangement. He could not object, of course, and it was politely considered a promotion of sorts, but also a way of removing from the Rhenus anyone who had commanded more than one legion there. The assignment of the Twenty-Second to Moguntiacum had additionally reduced both the Upper and Lower German legions to three in each province.

"I am considering that assignment," Domitian said. "The legate of the Seventh Gemina may stay on for a while."

"I like Traianus," Frontinus commented. "He won't put up with any nonsense from Germans running tame on this side of the river, and he's a professional soldier, not a rabble-rouser."

"Precisely," Domitian said. "Now then. Frontinus and Julianus, we leave for Rome in the morning. Maximus, I expect you'll want to ride with us and spend some time in Rome before you set out."

It was clear that Domitian did not intend to linger in Germany or to leave behind him anyone who had been connected with the revolt or its aftermath.

–

As ordered, they were on the road at first light, the whole column of Praetorians, generals, aides, slaves, baggage, and silver oyster dishes.

Flavius was afflicted with a sudden longing for home that startled him. There was business to take care of there, and Aemelia. The afternoon with Fiorgyn was still with him, invisible, a talisman no one else could see, that somehow, counterintuitively, made his wife more dear to him. He had found since yesterday that he could go back to that other country in his mind whenever he wanted to, where Fiorgyn lived with the son he would never see. He hadn't asked the boy's name. In his head he would just be "the boy" and that was better.

The papyrus filched from Saturninus's dreadful files was in his saddle bag.

XX

A Chat with Prosper Rufus

As far as Ygerna could tell, the signs of spring in the Dacian mountains were mud, followed by a refreezing of the snow, followed by more mud. A few determined crocuses pushed their heads up in the fields that had become parade ground and exercise yard, and she picked her way around them, although someone would trample them soon enough. Five months in winter camp made even the jaunty unfurling of a crocus valuable. She bent and picked one and tucked it into her cloak pin, proof that the earth would eventually awaken again.

She was carrying an empty basket, having delivered a rib bone to Lavinia's dog and a jar of salve to Merope, who had twisted her ankle. Correus had halfheartedly objected to her acquaintance with Lavinia's girls, but when she had said that she was not so fine that she could not play Wisdom with the whores when he was off drilling his men to march around in squares, he had shrugged and let it alone. Ygerna was not a woman who could be idle. She had spent the winter learning to read Greek from the Macedonica surgeon's copy of Dioscorides's herbal, took her mare bareback over the jumps in the cavalry exercise yard to the horror of everyone but Correus, and magicked up two chickens from somewhere that Eumenes kept in a coop in his tent.

There seemed to her to be an unusual amount of coming and going across the camp as she neared the Macedonica's quarter, and a great many people in and out of its Principia tent. Maybe they were getting ready to begin the siege of Sarmizegetusa that was the reason they had all frozen in these mountains since fall. That would make Correus happy.

When she got to the legate's tent, it was clear that Correus was not happy.

"Typhon swallow them all up! We were ready to march on his city! Now we're to go *home*?"

"What is it?" Ygerna set her basket down and pulled off her cloak. Eumenes was silently putting things in trunks.

Correus slammed his helmet into the corner of the tent and Eumenes retrieved it. "We're ordered back to the Danuvius!"

"Why?"

"Because there has been a rebellion among the Upper German legions." He was practically shaking with fury.

"A rebellion?"

"The governor of Upper Germany tried to make himself emperor, got nowhere with it and ruined two good legions for at least a generation, including the one I used to command, and now we're to pull back to the border and Domitian is sending the First Adiutrix *and* the Second to Pannonia when we get there."

"No doubt the emperor thinks there are too many legions here," Eumenes said. "That's always in their heads, the chance that some governor will get ideas."

"Tettius Julianus's idea was to take Sarmizegetusa!" Correus snapped. "We could have done it! And now this again! We get close and he pulls us back. Agricola got close in Britain and he was pulled back. I was part of that campaign. And he was going to do it. He could have taken the highlands and brought the whole island into the empire, and Domitian called him back and put Sallustius Lucullus in his place, and from what I hear now Sallustius Lucullus has been executed for being involved with Germany."

"I doubt your Agricola could have held the highlands," Ygerna said. "The Picts are not easily held. And the ones in the far north are half seal anyway, so it's said."

"Half seal?" Correus was momentarily distracted.

327

"They shed their skins and come up on land," Ygerna said. "So my grandmother said."

"I don't care if they're bats," Correus said. "We could have taken it."

Ygerna sighed. "Correus, you weren't even there. You were posted to Misenum by then."

"That was thanks to Flavius trying to help my career along, blast him. I wanted a promotion in Britain and to stay with Agricola."

"Who got recalled," Ygerna said.

"Which isn't my point." He glared at her. "I didn't join the army to march around in circles and retreat when we've won."

"I'll see to the horses," Eumenes said and made his escape.

"Now we've driven poor Eumenes off to the horse barns." Ygerna warmed her hands at the brazier and tried to make amends. "I do know how you feel. It seems foolish to me too, but I am not an emperor with fear riding on his back like a Samhain wind. He must be afraid of everything: rebellion, assassination, mysterious illnesses that were probably poison, all the things that have befallen other emperors. How many have died a natural death, before Vespasian and Titus?"

"Not many," Correus admitted. "Augustus."

"Wouldn't you be afraid?"

"Petrified," Correus said. "And the more he runs from it, the more likely he makes it. This will destabilize the whole Danuvius frontier again. He could have got another triumph out of it when we took Sarmizegetusa. Instead, he's leaving the border open to Decebalus to do it all again. I am disgusted and I want to retire and keep goats."

"That would be very nice," Ygerna said. "I like goats."

–

Correus had retrieved his temper by the time they began their journey down the mountains. What opportunity Decebalus might make of their withdrawal the scouts left behind were unable to say. Tettius Julianus was tight-lipped about the orders, merely relaying them to his legates and announcing that of course they would obey. An emperor unnerved by the events in Germany would be wary of a field general with even the four legions left to Tettius. Now that "peace was restored," Domitian had ordered Tettius to confine himself to the defense of Upper Moesia while Cornelius Nigrinus took charge of Oescus and the legions of the lower Danuvius. One of the reassigned legions had been the First Adiutrix, Tettius's own troops.

There was, Correus told himself determinedly, something to be said for a life in the legionary fortress at Oescus, the luxuries that provided, and the presence of his children. Marcus and Eilenn were both visibly bigger and Marcus more talkative. He also found a letter from Flavius awaiting him.

> *My dear Correus,*
>
> *I expect you will have received the emperor's orders well before this arrives, therefore I am directing it to you at Oescus. There is a possibility that we will be out to the Danuvius again and I look forward to seeing you there, if so. It is possible that we may not be far behind this letter, but one never knows. This is mainly to assure you that your mother is well, and if you wish to write to her Aemelia will read the letter to her. I asked Aemelia to call on her, and she has done so and reports that she is in good spirits. It is fairly obvious now to everyone that Father is going to remarry. I quite like the woman, Didia Longina, a distant relative of Prosper Rufius, with all the excellent qualities that Rufius does not possess. With the frontier quiet, I hope you will be able to travel to Rome for the wedding this fall. You needn't worry if you wish to bring that young fiend Julius with you. That matter is settled and he should be in no danger. Felix had a long conversation with Julius Frontinus about the cliff road along the Danuvius and now hopes to add aerial engineering to his studies. Julia and*

> *Lucius send their love and regards respectively, and please convey mine to Ygerna.*
>   *Flavius*

Correus sat blinking at this missive. He read it again to be sure that it actually said that Aemelia had called on Helva. That was fascinating, if terrifying in its possibilities. The offhand line about Julius caught his eye on this reading. He read it a third time. If Flavius gave no explanation, it was because he didn't want to.

And what was the emperor planning to do on the Danuvius frontier if he had recalled his army from Dacia?

—

Prosper Rufius was half dozing in one of the hot chambers of the baths, letting a slave rub his back in the hope of distracting him from his sour stomach, and trying to sweat out the results of drinking too much the night before. His stomach heaved and he was beginning to think that the heat had been a mistake. Someone stood next to him, and Rufius's eyes opened and then narrowed.

"What do you want, Julianus?"

"A chat," Flavius said. He settled on a bench beside Rufius, damp hair hanging in curls over his eyes, and adjusted his towel. Steam rose from the hot pool in the center of the chamber. "Your slave told me where to find you. You really ought to train them better."

Rufius grunted irritably. "Did your father send you?"

"Certainly not. You really should stay out of his affairs, however. He's going to marry your cousin, you know, and we wouldn't like any scandal beyond what you've already created. It's not auspicious."

"Then he had better leave Didia Longina alone. She will shortly be under my charge instead of that senile old uncle. I have lawyers."

"That's excellent," Flavius said. "You may need them." He glanced at the slave who was massaging Rufius's hips. "Are you sure you want an audience for this?"

Rufius sat up furiously, swinging around on the bench to stare belligerently at Flavius. Flavius gave him a bland stare back. Rufius tightened his lips but he sent the slave away. "What are you implying?"

"I went out to Germany with the emperor," Flavius remarked.

"We heard the news," Rufius said. "Did you come merely to tell me that? The Senate has been informed. A very distressing affair."

"Very. Saturninus kept lists, you know."

Rufius didn't respond. He stared at the steam rising from the water.

"It wasn't a good idea to owe him money."

"Are you threatening me, Julianus?" Rufius's face darkened.

"Certainly not," Flavius said. "Why should I? Senatorial rank demands a certain income, I understand that, and sometimes it's difficult to maintain, particularly when one is a friend of the emperor with an image to keep up. And an expensive wife. I completely understand." He shook his head sympathetically.

"What are you getting at?"

"Only that these things often become difficult when one borrows from the wrong person. There is pressure afterward, you know, for support in dangerous enterprises. Then one borrows again, elsewhere maybe, to pay the interest, and it just goes on."

"My accounts are none of your business. I have sufficient resources," Rufius said.

Flavius smiled. Lucius Paulinus made a study of the rivers and tributaries along which the money supply of the City flowed and had said otherwise.

"What do you want?"

"The Moguntiacum Principia looked like a badger's den when the dogs have got in," Flavius said. "We sifted out what we could but it's possible Saturninus destroyed some of his records before we could get to them." He paused thoughtfully. "Still, you never know what might turn up later. I imagine there are a number of people, even senators – maybe particularly senators – who are a bit uncomfortable right now, wondering and all."

"Nothing else has 'turned up' or the emperor would have it by now," Rufius said.

"You never know. Sometimes he likes to make people wait and worry about it." Flavius smiled at him again, and it made Rufius twitch. "Do you know, if I were you, Prosper, I should buy a house in the country and go live in it."

"What exactly are you saying?"

"I am saying that you had best leave your cousin alone, leave my father alone, and while we're at it, leave my brother's slave alone."

"If you have anything you didn't hand over to Domitian, he would execute you too, for withholding it," Rufius said bluntly.

"Maybe I don't have anything. Maybe I just hear rumors, and an amount — shall I tell you the exact amount? — and it turns out that it can be verified. Money leaves a trail, Rufius."

"Get out." Prosper Rufius sat stolidly, his face gray, until Flavius stood up.

Flavius rewrapped his towel with infinite care. "Just remember what I told you. Incidentally, I've provided for you in my will, in case you're thinking I might have an accident or be set on by robbers and tragically killed. We're dining with my father tonight. I'll tell him you send your best wishes."

–

"My father asked us for dinner tonight." Flavius kissed the top of Aemelia's head as she sat among the pots on her dressing table. He was freshly shaved and his hair was still damp from the baths. "Would you still like to go? I accepted but we'll stay home if you'd rather."

"No, let's go." Aemelia patted a touch of rouge onto her cheeks. Flavius was different again. Different from the way he had been when she married him *and* different from the way he had been after the German woman. There was something easier about him. She wasn't sure what to make of it. "Is it a family party?"

"Yes, just us. I do want to see him before I leave."

"When you will drop us under his portico like a parcel and ride off again." She smiled at him to be sure he knew she was joking. He had only been home a week and they had barely got the house open. They had used the ointment and the silver cap last night and it hadn't been so bad. She had thought about asking to go with him when he left again, but everyone was being very careful with Domitian right now, and asking for the wrong favor could have consequences. And if she was honest with herself, she liked her comforts. Her rooms at Appius's house were almost another home with Flavius gone so much, and Appia liked it there. Appius's estate bordered her parents' and it made it easy to visit without having to stay there and let her mother tell her all the things that she was no doubt doing the wrong way.

When they arrived, Niarchos directed them to the dining room, with the murmured note that Cook's egg sponge was ready and it would be well to eat it fresh before Cook had the opportunity for a temperament. Cook appeared unnerved at the idea of a new mistress and had been on edge lately.

The meal was arranged with couches for three around a four-sided table where the servants could place the dinner dishes and then leave the family in private. Appius had spent the afternoon in his study with the farm books by the look of it and now attempted to hide a long smear of ink in the folds of his tunic. He was cheerful but he eyed Flavius with mild annoyance. "Your message was most informative, but I had that situation well in hand and I do not require looking after."

"Is that why you invited us to dinner, to tell me that?"

"Partly. I am always glad to see you, however. And you, my dear." He bowed to Aemelia.

Flavius allowed himself to be herded to a couch. "I did have a certain interest in the matter," he informed his father. "As did Correus. And, with as much respect as I can muster in the circumstances, you are not in a position to question who requires looking after."

"That was a very long time ago," Appius said with dignity, "and I have long since noted it in my Great Book of Mistakes, which I keep in my head."

Aemelia listened silently. She knew the story. Flavius had told it to her, not long ago and unexpectedly. Appius had thought Correus the stronger of them when they both entered the Centuriate and had extracted a promise from Correus to look after his brother. It had come close to ruining both of them.

"Well, then," Flavius said cheerfully, "we are even." He folded a piece of egg sponge over between his fingers and took a bite. "Very good. You have a better cook than the emperor."

"Don't tell Domitian that," Appius said, "or he'll want him."

"Domitian will be too much occupied to steal other people's cooks," Flavius said. "We're leaving again. For Pannonia this time. My backside is acquiring the shape of a saddle. Let me know if it grows knobs front and rear."

Appius set his wine cup down. "Pannonia?"

"He's been brooding since the Quadi and the Marcomanni refused to send him men."

"What does he intend to do about that?" Appius inquired.

Flavius wiped his fingers on a napkin. "Send a detachment to punish them for their impudence, essentially. I have tried to talk him out of it, but I can only go so far before he decides I'm the enemy too."

Appius took a long thoughtful drink from his wine cup and stared into its depths, reading something inscrutable there. "That is the drawback of a post at court."

Aemelia was silent, biting the flesh from an olive, slowly. None of this was news to her. Flavius told her things now, unexpectedly, as if she had suddenly become a person and not a wife. That was the only way she could think of to describe it. As for what Flavius had done about Prosper Rufius, he had told her that too. Then she had watched him burn the scrap of papyrus, which was too dangerous to keep any longer. It had curled in the brazier, twisting as if it were alive.

"I feel as if I'm floundering," Flavius said. "Trying to save him from his own worst instincts. He won't simply send an army, the way his father and brother did. He insists on going himself, where he drives the generals mad and offers tips on strategy that they can't ignore. And the one time he did ride back to Rome and leave his general to get on with it, it was Fuscus. Who both Julius Frontinus and Cornelius Nigrinus told him not trust."

Appius nodded. They were so alike, Aemelia thought. Neither of his sons seemed to have any stamp of their mothers, but looked like coins struck from the same mold, thirty years apart. There was nothing lesser about Flavius, despite his having grown up terrified that there was.

"That is the difficulty with being close to power," Appius said now. "His father and brother were dangerous, in the sense that a strung catapult is dangerous, but you knew where it was going to shoot its bolt."

"Your suggestion is that this one has the torsion springs in the wrong way round?" Flavius asked. "I have wondered. But how do you distinguish madness from the conviction of divinity?"

"You don't," Appius said.

"Does anyone really think that emperors become gods just because they say so, or the next emperor does?" Aemelia asked. "My father would be horrified by that question, but honestly I can't help but wonder."

"That's what comes of marrying into this family," Flavius told her. "Blasphemy and dangerous philosophical thought." He leaned across his couch to hers and kissed her cheek, so that she thought he was actually pleased.

"Only the emperors in question," Appius said, "but it is not politic to say so." He refilled his wine cup from the pitchers on the table.

The conversation turned to lighter topics, and Felix and Loukas made an appearance after the meal to pay their respects. It was late when they left, and Appius laid a hand on Aemelia's shoulder at the door.

"Thank you for calling on Helva, my dear. That was generous of you." He smiled at her.

"Flavius said I should," she murmured. She wanted to be sure Appius knew that. "But I didn't mind. I always did like her." She smiled back at him. "She told me she is reduced to utter poverty."

"I put Lucius Paulinus in charge of her accounts with Correus to spare Flavius that," Appius said. "But I assure you she is not."

"Oh, I know. She's just lonely. I'll try to persuade some of my friends to come with me next time. It will seem a little daring to them, so they'll like it."

They climbed into the carriage where Bericus was waiting with the driver. Flavius tucked a rug around her fashionably sandal-shod feet and settled himself next to her. She smiled at him too. Usually he rode beside the carriage, but tonight he had climbed in with her. She tucked herself into his arm and dozed as the carriage rattled along the road.

-

The City was dark, with only a few lights still showing in the doorways of places whose customers came mainly by night. Other than the yellow pools cast by occasional streetlamps, the Esquiline Hill was black, as was the house, save for the torches in their stands in the portico. Flavius was lifting Aemelia down when he saw that his steward had not come out to meet them. He shouted irritably but no one came.

"I'll go." Bericus hopped down from the driver's seat. The door opened at his first touch with no key and the torchlight showed a dark shape on the atrium floor.

Flavius told Aemelia to stay in the carriage and ran for the door. The dark shape was the steward, face down in a pool of blood. A sound from the study caught his ear, followed by hammering and screams from the slaves' wing. Bericus sprinted for the study and Flavius ran to Appia's room. It was empty. He flung himself at the door that shut off the slaves' wing and found the steward's key in the lock. When he opened it, Rusonia shrieked in terror before she recognized him.

"Where's my daughter?"

"She's here with Nurse," Rusonia's words ran together, "she gets lonely, we take her in with us sometimes when everyone is gone, then he came and he had a knife and it was all bloody and he told us not to come out."

Flavius turned back to the corridor. In the study, Bericus was struggling with a thrashing figure and the floor was strewn with the scrolls and tablets from the shelves. Two records chests had been hacked open and their contents dumped on the pile. The tile floor was slick and Flavius's feet skidded on it, sending him sprawling. Lamp oil. It had been poured over everything and the small lamp still burning on the desk told what the intruder's intentions had been.

Flavius picked himself up in a rage and grabbed at the invader, but he lost his grip as the man pulled from Bericus's hold. The knife gleamed red in the flickering light and Bericus put a hand to his arm. Blood seeped between his fingers.

The man fled down the corridor, sprinting for the atrium. Flavius was two paces behind him as he burst through the portico into the street. Flavius slipped again as the lamp oil that had coated his sandals sent him skidding, and the man's lead widened. He fled down the sloping street. Flavius pulled his own knife from his belt and cut the traces from one of the carriage horses. He flung himself onto it bareback and kicked it into a gallop, winding the trailing reins into his hand.

The intruder dodged between two houses and Flavius urged the horse after him in the narrow passage. As the alley opened onto another street, the carriage horse shied at the line of washing hung from an apartment window, but it obeyed the man on its back. The fleeing man had better footing on the stones that paved the streets and Flavius almost lost sight of him, dodging through the rabbit warren of shops and apartments and back alleys, hoping he wouldn't break the horse's leg. Streetlamps cast only dim light.

The man was avoiding the main streets not only out of fear of Flavius but probably of the Watch, who had a tendency to capture anyone running from something and ask what afterward. The pursuit swerved through shuttered market stalls and a trio of drunken partygoers stumbling down a back street, who shouted curses after them.

Flavius still had his quarry in sight as they plunged onto the wide Via Tiburtina and out into open countryside under a half-moon that hung behind scudding clouds. He steered the horse onto the sanded bridle path where it gathered speed. The fleeing man looked over his shoulder and dove across the far side of the road, scrambling across the drainage ditch into a field. Flavius turned the horse after him, kicking it hard to make it leap the ditch, one half of his mind aware of the dangers of riding a carriage nag bareback through unknown countryside, the other half consumed completely by a rising fury that did not abate as he closed on his quarry. The man scrambled over a stone wall and Flavius set the carriage horse at it. The horse balked and he kicked it savagely and reined it around again to take the wall. This time it jumped. He kicked it into a gallop and came up behind the man, who turned a terrified glance over his shoulder as he ran.

"Stop now or I'll ride over you!"

The man stumbled on across the field. Flavius brought the horse up on his heels, close enough to hear his gasping breath, reached down with a loop of the long carriage rein and dropped it around the man's neck. He yanked hard and the man went over. Flavius halted the horse before he dragged his captive to death and slid down from its back. The man fought him furiously, his knife out again. It raked across Flavius's collarbone. Flavius brought his fist up into the man's stomach and when he doubled over, he caught the knife hand and twisted it until the dagger fell. Flavius hit him again, he stumbled, and Flavius pinned him to the ground amid someone's onion field, the sharp scent mingling with the acrid odor of sweat and fear. The man had a silver armband of the kind that household slaves wore, and Flavius jerked that arm

338

up, none too gently, to peer at it in the moonlight. He felt beside him for the man's dagger, closed his hand around it and threw it into the onions. He put his own to the man's throat.

"I should kill you," he said between his teeth. "The only reason I won't is that I want you to take a message: tell your master that if he so much as looks at me or anyone in my household again, he will regret it bitterly." Flavius pressed the knife point to the man's skin for emphasis. "And you will pay the price that murderers pay."

The man whimpered and tried to pull away from the knife. "I didn't mean to kill him. That was an accident. He came after me. He should have been in bed!"

"He was waiting up for me. You were going to burn my house down. With my *daughter* in it!" The knife point broke the skin.

The man was silent now, sweating and pallid in the faint moonlight.

"You will go home to Prosper Rufius and tell him that you looked everywhere and found nothing," Flavius said. "You had best convince him because if anyone comes after me or mine again, I will take him to court for robbery and murder. You do know that slaves can only give evidence under torture, do you not?" The fingers of his other hand bit into the man's shoulder. "No matter the outcome?"

"Yes." His voice was hoarse, a whisper. A thin trickle of blood, black in the moonlight, ran down his neck.

"Whose idea was it to burn the house afterward? Yours or your master's?"

"Master's," he whispered. He twisted his head, trying to get away from the knife. "I would have let them out, once it was alight, I would have."

"Did he tell you to do that?"

"No."

"And you wouldn't have, would you? You're just trying to save your filthy skin."

The slave twisted in his grip again. Flavius could find no sympathy for him despite the fact that he had probably had no choice in the matter. Prosper Rufius was known to be a vicious master. He had been a fool, Flavius thought, for telling Rufius he would be away from home that night. The knife dug a little deeper into the throat. "Do you understand what I've told you?"

"Yes."

Flavius got off him. The man didn't move. "Go home. Make sacrifice for the shade of the man you killed. And don't try running away, because I know where to start the dogs on your trail and I will. I would hate for Prosper Rufius to lose such a valuable slave. *Get up!*"

He drew his foot back to kick him and the man scrambled to his feet. Flavius took a step toward him and he ran. The carriage horse was eating grass between the onion rows and Flavius swung up on its back again. His whole body itched with the urge to ride the man down again and kill him, and then whisper Prosper Rufius's death warrant into Domitian's ear. Rufius's connection to Didia Longina made that dangerous. The emperor was in a vengeful mood and when that was the case, he was not selective about it.

XXI

Two Deaths in Sirmium

Correus stood staring at Tettius Julianus across his desk in the governor's villa at Viminacium. Messala Cominius, who had been in conference with the governor, had taken one look at Correus's expression and beat a retreat.

"Sit down, Julianus," Tettius said. "I appreciate your stopping by."

Correus saluted, the thin wooden leaves of the tablet with his orders still in his fist. He handed the tablet to Tettius and sat silently, waiting for an explanation.

Tettius handed it back. "I know what's in it. I signed it. I want the transfer accomplished as quickly as possible," he added. "Yesterday, for instance."

"Transfer from the Macedonica to the Flavia. And Aurelius Decius from the Flavia to the Macedonica. Why? Is someone just bored?"

"Are you questioning orders?"

"No, sir. Yes, actually." Correus was determined to get some clarification. "I had just gotten the Fifth in shape. My wife liked it in Oescus. I'd just gotten used to all the fish."

"Fish?"

"Never mind. Just please give me a reasonable explanation, if there is one. Sir."

"All right, Julianus. Domitian is coming out to Pannonia, he'll most likely have his headquarters in Sirmium, and I want Aurelius Decius out from under his nose."

"Decius is a good officer," Correus protested. "I shared Singidunum with him."

"Precisely. And Singidunum is on the border with Pannonia, and less than fifty miles from Sirmium. Decius's mother is a connection of Antonius Saturninus."

Correus was silent at that.

"I think it likely that the emperor is still looking around for people who may have been involved, or who he suspects may have been involved, or are merely connected in some way. I don't want Decius to occur to him, or some disgruntled tale-bearer to bring it up."

"No." Correus didn't either and he also thought it likely. And why in Mithras's name did Domitian feel the need to come to Pannonia in the first place?

"Generally, a legate's appointment needs to be confirmed by the emperor," Tettius said, "but you both already hold that rank. Cornelius Nigrinus agrees with me that this offers the simplest solution."

Correus sifted that out in his head and nodded. The Moesian governors had seen a straightforward way to protect one of their generals and taken it. "Very well, sir. I didn't suppose I could talk you out of it, I just wanted to know why. I appreciate your telling me; you didn't have to. My household is on the road behind me already."

"Excellent. Thank you."

Correus saluted and departed. He supposed he might as well sit about in Singidunum as in Oescus to watch his command make roof tiles and drainpipe instead of besieging Sarmizegetusa. Civil construction projects were almost always the chore of the peacetime army.

In the meantime, he superintended the moving of his household to Singidunum once again, this time into the Praetorium, and met with the primus pilus and tribune of the Fourth Flavia. They also looked perplexed at the transfer but were disciplined enough not to say so. Correus implied that he had no idea, and the question passed. The primus pilus, Silvius Vindex, was also newly appointed and turned out to be an old comrade, as was the way with the upper ranks of the Centuriate, and Correus invited him to dinner because he had known Ygerna in Britain.

Ygerna was philosophical about the move. As long as she was where Correus was, she was reasonably content, and the Singidunum Praetorium was as comfortable as the one at Oescus. She set out the household gods in their niche in the atrium, Eilenn renewed her friendship with Blaesus's daughter Ducci, and Correus sat Julius down and informed him that he could go home.

Julius was mending a saddle girth in the stable. His scarred face looked suspicious. "He's not looking for me?"

"Flavius says no, and I trust him."

"What's your brother got on him?" That seemed to both of them the only possible explanation.

"I have no idea." Correus wanted to know that too.

"Well, I'll think on it. I'd want to take Tiati."

Correus blinked. Tiati was the cook. Ygerna, who had a more practical turn of mind than Correus where slaves were concerned, had picked her out when they had first settled in Oescus, after bringing her home for the evening to see if her efforts were edible. Tiati had belonged to a wine merchant and he had put her on the market when she bit him, which Ygerna had considered a recommendation. Apparently she hadn't bitten Julius.

"I told her I wouldn't leave her if I went back," Julius said stubbornly.

Oho. "Not a passing fancy?" Correus inquired. Julius's romances had been many and fleeting, although generally not as deadly as the one with Livilla.

"Give me some credit for growing up a bit," Julius said. "Going down that mountain made the Circus look like a stick horse race. I'm not so sure I want to get killed behind a chariot anymore, or as sure that I won't, for that matter." The mare whuffled in his ear and he pulled an apple from his tunic. "Who's going to spoil you then, if I leave?" he asked her and she slobbered apple on his shoulder.

"Diulius would take you on," Correus said. "You'll live longer training than driving."

"Can I have Tiati?"

"You've got enough to buy both of you with what you have banked," Correus said. "I'm not made of money."

–

As he had suggested he might, Flavius arrived on the frontier with the emperor. In Singidunum he found Correus occupied with a hapless legionary caught writing scurrilous verses about his centurion on the barracks' stucco wall. Vindex was beside him, vine staff ominously under one arm. Ordinarily this was not a matter for the legate's exalted attention, but the verses had made Vindex laugh so hard that he had brought Correus to see, and then they both had to be involved in the discipline to soothe the centurion's ruffled feathers. Vindex had not changed much. His sleek cap of dark hair had a bit of gray in it but that was all. He eyed Flavius with amused recognition and salaamed eastern fashion before the gilded splendor of his parade cuirass and the spotless white leather skirt of his harness tunic.

"Hail, representative of Caesar!"

"Shut up," Flavius said from his saddle. "I brought my brother a present of some decent wine and I'll tell him not to let you have any if you aren't respectful. What are you doing here anyway?" He widened his eyes at Correus's scarred face. "And what happened to you? No one's going to mix us up again."

"Intentionally arranged," Correus said. "Defrauded innkeepers and jilted women were stopping me in the street thinking I was you. Get down off your horse and read this before we make him scrub it out."

Flavius dismounted and inspected the wall. "A promising poet."

"All right then," Vindex said to the culprit. "Scrub that off and whitewash it and then you belong to Centurion Mucius here." He nodded at the affronted officer. "Latrines, I should think, and

344

then perhaps you could lend him to Prefect Blaesus to clean his stables."

"Vindex has risen to the exalted post of primus pilus," Correus said. "He rules with an iron hand."

"I shall go and apply it to other matters." He saluted Correus. "Until tonight, sir."

"He's coming to dine with us," Correus said to Flavius. "You'll stay and join us, I hope. And thank you for the wine. The local supply is not impressive."

"I imagine not," Flavius said. "It's in the crates on that wagon. I told them to take it to the Praetorium. How did Ygerna take to winter camp? The poor woman never gets a chance to settle, following you about. Tettius Julianus sent me a quiet note to let me know where you were."

"Ygerna is adaptable," Correus said. "She spent the winter teaching Lavinia's whores to play Wisdom. What have you done to Prosper Rufius?"

"Not nearly enough and I can't tell you."

"Well, I'm glad we have that settled then." Correus was beginning to have a reasonably good idea anyway. "How are the family?"

"My wife and daughter are with Father and there are two hired guards living in my house," Flavius said. "I want to borrow young Julius, and I can't tell him either, so make that clear."

"Borrow him?"

"I'm looking at a team of ponies that's on the market in Sirmium. I've driven them but I want to watch someone else drive them and I assume you aren't available."

"No, alas. I must attend to the important job of overseeing drainpipe production."

"A noble calling."

"Flavius, I am about to lose my wits. We could have taken Sarmizegetusa."

"Probably."

"Not probably. Now I'm filling orders for drainpipe. Decebalus has a free hand. The army is still trying to stabilize a

345

border that the emperor is apparently determined to destabilize by starting and abandoning campaigns, and now he's out here again. He wanders about the empire poking his fingers in things. Why can't he stay in Italy worrying about tax reform the way his father did?"

"Got it out of your system?" Flavius inquired. "Because I would suggest not repeating any of that to anyone but me."

"Of course not," Correus said irritably. "That's why I said it to you. I've been saving it up. Come see Ygerna. She'll be glad to see you. And I'll find Julius and tell him he's on loan. He'll like a chance to drive something besides wagon nags."

–

Ygerna had put considerable effort into the dinner, partly because Centurion Vindex remembered her as a sullen hostage and she thought it would be interesting, and satisfactory, to see his reaction. She had had the dining room arranged with four couches, two each head-to-head, and the mosaic floor polished. Whoever had designed the interior of this praetorium had mercifully not been obsessed with sea life, and the floors all depicted scenes from the lives of the gods. In the dining room Bacchus rode a flower-garlanded donkey, attended by nymphs bearing platters of fruit.

Tiati produced a feast that made Ygerna regret the prospect of parting with her, and the wine that Flavius had brought was indeed excellent. Vindex's greeting was thoroughly satisfactory. His eyes widened and it was clear that he was about to be tactless in his surprise, but he caught himself, and said, "*Salve*, lady. I rejoice to meet you again."

"Good evening, Centurion. I am delighted to meet you again too. It appears that we have all risen in the world."

"I'll lose him soon," Correus said. "He's due for a command of his own. It should have happened by now," he added.

"As soon as we have someone to fight," Vindex said placidly. "Stop worrying about me, I am not overripe fruit."

They settled to dinner, served by Eumenes. A first course of salmon from the Danuvius was accompanied by caviar from the huge sturgeon that swam upstream in its waters as far as Vindobona.

"So the emperor has sent old Velius Rufus to make the Quadi and Marcomanni regret their decision to withhold aid," Vindex said, dipping a spoon in the caviar and dabbing it on a piece of bread.

"He has vexillations from nine legions," Flavius said. "That will be enough to cause serious regret, I expect."

"All from Britain and Upper Germany," Correus noted. "And none with their senior officers attached."

"I doubt that Velius Rufus feels he needs them," Flavius said. "He's what you call a commanding personality." Velius Rufus had commanded Domitian's troops during the last campaign on the Rhenus, a frog-faced little man with a thick shock of hair brushed down over his forehead and a reputation for eating a pilum shaft every morning before breakfast, just to keep his spirits up.

"The Iazyges are raiding across the river now too, and they're supposed to be a client state. Perhaps we'll be allowed to fend them off," Correus said irritably.

"They've just spotted a chance to be a nuisance," Flavius said. The Iazyges formed a buffer between the western reaches of Dacian territory and the Roman province of Pannonia. "It won't last. Rufus has enough troops to settle them simultaneously."

"Let us know if they need drainpipe," Correus muttered. The emperor's intention was obvious – to exact revenge on the Quadi and Marcomanni with vexillations designed to weaken the legions available to the governors of their home provinces, and at the same time to prevent the Danuvius governors from earning any dangerous victories.

"Flavius," Ygerna said, "tell us the news from Rome. How is Felix? He writes occasionally, when Loukas makes him, I think."

"Studying assiduously," Flavius said gratefully. "Julius Frontinus has gone back to Ephesus, but he promised him a job and a commission recommendation in another four years."

The conversation turned to family matters, the growth and accomplishments of children, the new crop of foals at the home farm, and to Flavius's possible purchase of a team in Sirmium. The capital of Pannonia was a thriving Roman colonia with a hippodrome with regular races.

They parted near midnight and in the morning, Flavius rode out with Julius behind him, having extracted a promise from Correus to stop grousing before it was noticed. Noticed by whom he did not need to say.

News came sketchily into Sirmium, via couriers from Velius Rufus, who always said that the campaign was well in hand and neglected in his next report to reply to Domitian's insistent questions as to exactly what that meant. Rufus disliked being managed.

Flavius occupied himself with vetting the prospective team. They were a matched quartet of pale sorrels with white manes. "Showy," Julius commented disparagingly, but he changed his tune when he drove them.

"These are as good as anything your father breeds. Why are they on the market?"

Flavius grinned. "The previous owner thought he could drive them himself. Broke his collarbone and cracked his head."

"I could drive them for you," Julius said wistfully. "I know I'm not supposed to ask questions, but thank you for whatever it was I'm not supposed to know about."

"I intend to drive them myself, and you're welcome."

A rider from the city's landward gate clattered past as they walked the ponies out of the hippodrome. His passage sent up a flock of the pigeons that roosted in the track's eaves and Flavius watched him uneasily. He handed the ponies' leads to Julius. "Take them back and say I'll buy them if he sends them round to me. Here. Half of this is earnest money and the other half's for you. Tell my brother I'm grateful to have borrowed you."

He put a pile of coins in Julius's hand and headed at a trot for the palace of the Pannonian consular legate, whose household had recently been dislodged to provide the emperor with suitable accommodation. Domitian had just received the standard report from Rufus yesterday morning. This was something new.

–

Flavius heard the emperor's furious voice well before he found him glaring at a tablet bearing Rufus's seal, his face an angry scarlet. The message had interrupted his leisurely breakfast and he had expected news of a victory. "Peace?" He was nearly shouting. "They are asking for peace? Rome will accept nothing but unconditional surrender. This is a deliberate insult!"

The courier, not the usual rider but an officer of Rufus's command, stood stolidly while the emperor voiced his opinion. He looked grateful when Flavius strode in and Domitian handed him the tablet. Centurion Julianus had the reputation of being able to persuade the emperor to sort through complicated possibilities.

"Peace, sir?" Flavius asked. "That's promising."

"Not in the least." Domitian waved at the slave hovering with a tray of eggs and olives. "Take that away. Disappointment has cost me my appetite."

Flavius flicked an eye at the courier, a junior tribune who stood at attention, helmet under one arm. Domitian didn't like the offer and Velius Rufus probably wouldn't like Domitian's answer, and the tribune was going to bear the brunt of both tempers.

Domitian sat up. "The Quadi and Marcomanni are suggesting that we make peace by withdrawing from their territory and in return they will guarantee not to send their raiding parties across the river into our provinces," he said acidly.

"I see." In other words, exactly what Domitian should have expected, but that was beside the point. The Quadi and Marcomanni were numerous and well armed. That they had not come into the war with Decebalus on the Dacian side should probably have been enough, particularly now that Decebalus was loose from Sarmizegetusa. And what he was doing, no one knew. Despite Correus's grumbling about drain tiles, his cohorts made regular patrols along the Danuvius and neither they nor the scouts reported any sign of the Dacians.

"What will you tell them, sir?" Flavius inquired cautiously.

"I will tell them to prepare to see their fields burned, their army slaughtered, and their women in the slave market!" Domitian said. "And tell Velius Rufus not to send me any more such insulting offers. He should know better!" He glared at the tribune, who saluted and fled.

Domitian lay back down on his couch. "Where is my breakfast? Why was it taken away?"

The slave had plainly been waiting in the corridor, since he reappeared immediately with Domitian's taster on his heels, the food having been out of the emperor's sight.

"Go away and leave me alone. I shall finish breakfast and take my morning walk." Domitian glowered at them all until they departed.

The air was heavy under gray scudding clouds and the trees were turning up their leaves to a fitful wind. Flavius hoped it held off. Domitian was in the habit of taking a solitary walk after breakfast, trailed at a discreet distance only by two Praetorians. If it rained on him in this mood, he would take it as a personal affront.

Flavius avoided the emperor's usual route, which went around the Temple of Jupiter and along the riverbank where the Savus flowed past twin islands. He found the ponies and their seller's slave waiting for him in the palace stables and paid the rest of their price. One of the mares snuffled at his chest, inspecting his tunic front for possible apples.

"Busted up the last fellow, did you?" he asked her. "Not your fault, I shouldn't think. You're a good girl."

A stable boy hovered admiringly nearby and Flavius handed him the reins. "Walk them cool, rub them down, and give them a feed of grain. Then put them in the loose boxes. Who do you belong to?"

"The legate, sir. He's left his horses here because the villa he's taken hasn't a stable."

"We've put everyone out, haven't we?" Flavius gave the boy a coin. "If I'm not here to exercise them in the mornings, take them out for me. Just on leads. Don't try to run them." He would race them under Domitian's colors, he thought, and the emperor could bet on him and win. That would please him.

Most of his concern lately seemed to be with pleasing the emperor and thus preventing him from doing things simply because he was in a temper. Why Domitian had fixed on the Quadi and the Marcomanni instead of the Chatti was anyone's guess, but he wanted another triumph, another showing of the military victories that he hadn't been allowed to achieve under his father and brother. It was becoming more and more evident why they had kept him out of the field.

–

Velius Rufus sent a terse report advising the emperor that the Quadi and Marcomanni had the strength to hold out for years simply by retreating north into their mountain holds. From there they could launch intermittent raids south to keep the emperor from establishing any settlements on their land, which Velius Rufus did not advise anyway. What he did advise was to accept their offer, having made his point. They did not want a war, they had merely wanted to stay out of Rome's war with Decebalus, and Rufus felt that Roman displeasure at that had been adequately expressed in burned villages.

Domitian refused in terms that Velius Rufus had no choice but to act on. The Quadi and Marcomanni surprised him by sending envoys to negotiate further. It was clear that they did not want all-out war, an unusual attitude from a particularly bellicose people. Velius Rufus made one more plea to Domitian to hear them out.

This time there were no such formalities as had been accorded to Decebalus's brother. The envoys, one each from the Quadi and their kin the Marcomanni, and the twenty warriors that Velius Rufus had allowed through the Roman lines to accompany them were escorted immediately to the Sirmium basilica to present their terms. They were tall men, their hair pinned in the knot that the Suevian Germans all affected, clad in fine woolen shirts and breeches, gold at their throats and wrists, high-born in their tribes and high-handed in their manners.

Domitian received them with a century of the Second Adiutrix behind him, as well as his personal century of Praetorians. Flavius stood beside him to translate, facing the envoys' own interpreter, a thin man with a thrall collar that seemed more a message than a necessity. Flavius suspected that he was a provincial Roman, captured in some raid.

"We have offered the emperor of the Eagles peace and been sent insults instead," the Marcomanni envoy said flatly, and Flavius translated. "Therefore, we have come to state our terms in person that the emperor of the Eagles may know that we are serious."

"The Emperor Domitian finds that your terms have insulted him," Flavius said, softening the statement as much as he dared. "He requested your aid and you denied him. One does not deny the emperor of Rome. Therefore, he will now accept nothing less than this: hostages to the number of half your fighting men, an equal number of women, two-thirds of your grain harvest, five thousand talents in gold, and the destruction of any holding within a day's ride of the border." The terms were unreasonable and Flavius knew it. Domitian was deliberately pushing war because he wanted a victory, not a treaty. Flavius braced himself for their answer.

The German envoys stiffened. One of them spoke quietly to the interpreter with the thrall collar and the man nodded.

"There will be no more talk of peace," the Quadi envoy said. "To accept such terms is to disgrace ourselves before the gods. Better we fight and go to Valhalla, even if our bodies lie unburied. The emperor has made a mistake."

The Marcomanni envoy took a furious step forward. "The Roman emperor sits in his palace, drinking wine like a woman while his warlords do his fighting for him," he spat. "When we have driven them into the river, we will come for him!"

Domitian's face reddened at their tone and he raised a hand to his Praetorian Guard. Flavius softened the envoys' words as much as he could, but Domitian wasn't listening. He had understood enough and had held his hand enough. The Praetorians moved as one and surrounded the German warriors, and the centurion of the Adiutrix stepped forward with his men behind him. Domitian snapped an order and they pinned the envoys to the floor and cut their throats.

Flavius stood helplessly as the men of the Adiutrix dragged the envoys' bodies to their horses and lashed them across their saddles. The Praetorians herded the German escort behind them.

"Mount!" the centurion of the Praetorians said. "Ride out of here before you meet the same end and tell your chieftains the emperor's answer."

Blood pooled on the black and white floor of the basilica's Hall of Justice. There would be no undoing this.

–

The Quadi and the Marcomanni came across the border in a red rage at Aquincum where the Danuvius could be forded. They came in force at dawn, fought their way past half-awake garrisons and took their blood gold in burned and looted houses, driving horses, sheep, and pigs before them back through the ford, sacks full of gold jewelry and silver dishes tied to their saddles. They rode out as swiftly as they had come, leaving behind as many dead civilians in the doorways of their houses as dead legionaries in the streets.

Velius Rufus sent his army across the river after them but they vanished into the mountains. He rode into Sirmium to report in no good mood. Rufus had sent a report ahead of him, to give the emperor time to think on it, in the hope that he would think something useful, or that Flavius Julianus could talk him into a useful thought.

"Unless you want a year's campaign to get them fully under control and turn them into a province and not just a client state, we can't go further than we have," Rufus said bluntly. "And the Iazyges will rebel because they'll think they're next."

Flavius eyed Domitian uneasily, but he appeared to be listening.

"It would mean another province to hold," Rufus said pointedly, "with at least four legions on a permanent basis. I can't recommend it, sir."

That was his selling point, and the suggestion that Flavius had quietly made that morning. Rumors of other plots were already bubbling in the froth of tale-telling that always stewed at court. That they seemed to be without substance was perpetually open to argument in Domitian's mind. Giving another provincial governor four legions at his disposal should make the emperor uneasy, and it did.

"What do you suggest?" he asked Rufus reluctantly.

Flavius could see the grim set to Rufus's froglike face relax just a shade. "Leave them be, Imperator. They've taken their revenge and they didn't want war to begin with. Reaffirm our treaties with their neighbors and box them in."

"The Iazyges?" Domitian demanded. "The Iazyges have been raiding across our border!"

"We've put a stop to that, mostly. A diplomatic mission will reinstate our treaty and they'll look unkindly on any efforts by the Quadi to overset it. To the other side, the Hermanduri who inhabit the land west of the Marcomanni have been sworn to Rome for fifteen years."

"That was my first campaign," Flavius said. "The Hermanduri will swear to whoever offers promise of the most gold. Or frightens them the most. They were sorry they followed Nyall Sigmundson into that war. I suspect they would be unlikely to listen to anything the Marcomanni have to say."

354

"We will make sure of it," Velius Rufus said.

Domitian was silent, thinking. They both watched the possibilities chase each other across his face. To expand the empire with another province was attractive but dangerous. The Dacians were still a looming threat despite some recent intelligence from the frontier scouts. And even here on the frontier, messages reached him from the various informers that swarmed around his court, all with their own agendas. The emperor reluctantly made his mind up.

"Very well."

Domitian had acquiesced grudgingly but Velius Rufus and Flavius left the audience with considerable relief.

"He trusts you," Rufus said with a certain amount of wonder when they stepped out into the palace courtyard, returning the salutes of the Praetorians stationed outside.

"I have made a point of never giving him reason not to," Flavius said. "He trusts you as well, I suspect for the same reasons."

Rufus stopped to scratch the ears of a ginger cat that was sunning itself on the edge of a blue-tiled pond and looking with interest at the small silver fish that swam among the lotus. "A limit to one's ambition is an excellent recipe for longevity," he commented.

–

"And why should I be trusting a man who has killed an envoy?" Zosines, chieftain of the Iazyges, inquired, inspecting the emperor's proxy gift of a silver-mounted bridle. He sat with the Roman ambassador in a chair outside his wagon, while three of his fighting men and three of Flavius's escort stood by. "There is a curse on the man who does that and your emperor will be wearing it about his neck now."

Flavius thought so too. "For the reason that he has sent me," he offered. The Iazyges' language was beyond Flavius and an interpreter translated.

Their chairs were arranged on a fine rug spread on the rough grass. The wagon was high, with a living chamber behind the driver's seat. The oxen that drew it were unhitched and grazed among the other wagons, while the dark shapes of the chieftain's cattle herd spread out across the plain. The carefully constructed earthen firepit told Flavius that the camp had been there for several days. They would move on when the graze was depleted. To the east, a dark tree line marked the course of the Tissus, the flat river valley of the Iazyges. To the west, the sun was starting to sink and the clump of oak and hawthorn in whose shade the chieftain's wagon rested was alive with small birds chittering in the leaves.

"The emperor is aware that you could do the same to me," Flavius said. "But I am here nonetheless."

"Thus he trusts my people to have more honor than yours," Zosines said brusquely. "Rome grows soft, and softness breeds dishonor. That is what I think."

The Iazyges were semi-nomadic cattle herders who lived in their ox-drawn wagons or in scattered settlements on the edge of the cattle graze and their notion of honor was a harsh one – Iazyge sons were reputed to kill their elderly fathers when they were too old to fight – but they were not above accepting a grain and salt dole from Rome in exchange for their loyalty. Flavius mentioned that.

Zosines snorted. "Rome receives more than she gives. And drives stone roads through other peoples' graze."

"That has not been done here," Flavius said mildly. "The emperor wishes the treaty which ensures that to continue," he added.

"The emperor has poked a thumb into a hornet's nest," Zosines said. "Let him fight the Dacians instead of courting the hornets to do it for him."

"We do not ask for fighting men," Flavius said. "Despite the fact that yours have been raiding our villages' cattle from across the river."

Zosines shrugged. "Who can tell one ox from another?" He turned and spoke to someone within the wagon. "My wife will bring us food and drink so that you may tell your emperor that you have been treated with hospitality."

They sat in silence until a woman pushed aside the wagon's red-painted shutters and came carefully down the wooden steps, carrying a basket of seeded bread, dried meat, a flagon, and two wooden cups. She filled both and handed them to her husband and to Flavius. Zosines drank, watching for Flavius's reaction over the rim of his cup. It was beer, strong and dark and very good.

Flavius smiled.

Zosines smiled back. "We are not a wealthy people, but we brew good beer," he said. "I will send a barrel to your emperor to improve his temper that he may not curse himself further, and we will give you leave to camp among us for the night."

Flavius knew that was the best he was going to get. The only bright spot, which he did not mention to Zosines, was that Domitian was not the only ruler with disappointing allies. The scouts reported that for unknown reasons, the Getae had withdrawn their support from Decebalus.

XXII

The Goddess Never Goes Away Entirely

"Kneel!" Ziais pointed a finger at her brother and he stared back at her in a fury.

"I will ride a cow backward through the public streets before I kneel to you!" Decebalus spat at her.

"Very well. Then leave."

Ziais sat on the dais of the reception room in the palace at Capidava, on the larger chair now. She wore a gold fillet in her dark hair, which was twisted up in the fashion of the Getae women, and a gown of brilliant indigo silk heavily sewn with gold thread and bronze beads. The gold and carnelian necklace that had been her wedding gift hung around her throat, the small gold figure of the Goddess at the center, and the ceremonial sword of the king of the Getae lay across her lap. She regarded her brother with loathing and a certain amount of triumph.

"For what reason have you withdrawn the support your husband swore to me?" Decebalus demanded. His face was white with anger and his boots and breeches were mud-spattered after the journey from Sarmizegetusa; the rage he had set out in had not abated on the way.

Ziais looked to the guards stationed by the red marble pillars that flanked the doorway. "Kneel or I will have them take you away."

"Whore! I made you queen. I can undo that."

Her eyes narrowed into a poisonous stare. "Call me a whore again and I will have you killed."

They were both aware that Decebalus could bring the army of Sarmizegetusa and its remaining allies and crush the Getae if he wished. Also that it would seriously deplete his ability to fight Rome, which was already depleted by the loss of the Getae. They stared at each other for a long moment and then Decebalus flung himself to his knees and up again in one motion. He spat some curse at her and she spat one back while the Getae guards, with Decebalus's men behind them, watched uneasily. A guard made the Sign of Horns. The atmosphere in the room was thick with anger, charged as before a thunderstorm, lifting the hair on his forearms. The queen and her brother the king might have been Old Ones, Zalmoxis with his thunderbolt facing down the Mother of War, old magic snapping in the air.

"Now we will speak," Ziais said with a smile that bared her teeth. "I told you that you would pay for what you did to me, Decebalus. You didn't listen because I was only a woman, something for you to barter for the right price. He was a pig and you didn't care. If he hadn't died in battle, I was near to killing him myself, no matter what would happen to me after."

Decebalus glared at her. "I should have given him your sister."

"That is another matter," Ziais said. "You will send Rescuturme to live with me."

"And why should I do that? She is worth more than your ill-trained men who are willing to follow a woman, if that is the exchange you are offering."

"I am not. I am telling you that you will send her to me or I will make a treaty with the Romans."

"You disgrace your family and our father!" Now he was shouting, which pleased her.

"My father did nothing to keep you from marrying me to the pig."

"And you play with fire," Decebalus said. "The Romans won't abide by any treaty. They'll devour you and your little kingdom for their breakfast."

Ziais smiled again. "They have reason to be grateful to me, and one of them knows it, if I was right about him." She fingered the indigo folds of her gown, pleating the silk between her fingers. "How do you think they found your pass, Decebalus, that you guard so carefully? Go ahead, try me. Send my sister to me or see what else I can do to put rocks in your path."

"I can arrange your death, Ziais. And thus I will be regent."

The guards in the doorway stiffened and moved to block Decebalus's men.

Ziais laid a hand on the sword across her lap. It was not a fighting weapon, but a ceremonial one, ancient and with old power attached to it. "Do not make useless threats. If I die, my closest female relative becomes regent in my place. It is always a woman so that she cannot continue to rule once the heir is of age. If you kill me, my men will come for Rescuturme and they will fight you to a standstill for her."

"When we have beaten the Romans," Decebalus said between his teeth, "I will come for you. The Roman emperor has withdrawn his siege because events have pulled his attention from the Danuvius, as I arranged. My time to make an empire is now."

"I have no interest in your empire. Send me Rescuturme and I won't ally with the Romans against you."

"You would fight your own kin? Your father's household? You shame our lineage!"

"You should have thought of that earlier."

Decebalus glared at her, fury in every line of his body. Until now, she had been a small obstacle, easily overcome, and bringing her to heel with a marriage that suited him had been a gratifying experience. Now she had a power that he had not intended to give her.

"You won't beat the Romans," Ziais said now. "I will give you practical advice: make peace while the emperor of Rome is distracted by other matters. He is not the strategist that his father and brother were. You will get better terms now than you will with the next one."

"The next one?"

"There is always a next one, even for you, brother." Ziais touched a finger to the gold figure at her throat and the other hand to the sword, a gesture that Decebalus found unsettling. "Take the pig's death as an omen and take what you can get from the Romans."

The Fourth Legion Flavia Felix at pilum practice was at any rate a sight to warm a new commander's heart. Correus watched the front ranks of the shield wall hit their targets, pull back into the gaps opened for them by the second rank, and the second rank do the same, with fluid precision. It was a shame, Correus thought, not to have given them Dacians to throw at.

"The thing to be said for making drainpipe," Vindex said, "is that when you take them off it, they appreciate pilum practice."

"I had a lecture from Tettius Julianus on the necessity of drainpipe to the empire," Correus said. "Fresh water arrives via drainpipe, noxious substances leave the same way, and civilization is achieved."

"Generally," Vindex said. "The Third Cohort latrine caught fire yesterday." The noxious miasma that built up in uncleaned latrines occasionally exploded in flames from the seats. "I lectured their centurion on the necessity for regular mucking out and suggested that he supervise. I imagine it will stay well cleaned after that."

"And thus we serve the empire," Correus said. "Soldiers of the spade and bucket."

The Eighth Cohort finished its drill and its commander gave a salute to the legate and the primus pilus. The drillmaster held up a hand while the battered straw men were taken down and fresh ones put up, and then the Seventh stepped up to the targets.

"I heard," Vindex said, "that the Dacians made a peace offer. Any truth to that?"

"I think so, according to my brother, who stops by occasionally with wine when he thinks I ought to know something – because he thinks the governor ought to know it. Nothing he's been specifically told to keep quiet, you understand, just… developments."

The spring weather was turning toward summer's heat and Vindex swatted at an insect that seemed determined to crawl into his helmet. "What was the answer?"

"So far, no. It was sent by courier through Iazyge territory and the courier handed it off to the Praetorian commander in Sirmium to be passed along. What happened to the Quadi and Marcomanni envoys didn't make a good impression. Flavius says that a brisk message consisting mainly of 'No, never, go jump in the Styx' was sent back, but he thinks it's just the opening gambit. They'll send an envoy when they get serious, and Flavius says the emperor is restless and wants to go home with some kind of victory."

"You don't think he'll change his mind about going after Sarmizegetusa then?" Vindex asked. "Now that Decebalus seems to be short his Getae allies?"

"No, not now." Correus watched the Seventh Cohort step back and the Sixth come up. He returned the Seventh commander's salute. "We've lost two of the legions we would have needed."

"I did think we were going to do it," Vindex said wistfully.

"We'll have to eventually," Correus said. "Or somebody will. This frontier bubbles like leaven every time we take our eye off it. A stronger hand will come along and that will be the end of Decebalus."

"In the far future, the gods protect the emperor," Vindex said carefully.

"Of course. But in the meantime, we will patrol the riverbank because anyone who thinks the Dacians aren't going to raid us once we've made a treaty will believe anything."

"Sarsinus in the Third Century says the Dacian soldiers all turn into wolves once a month," Vindex said. "He saw one do it in the middle of the last battle. It's why we can't kill them properly, he says."

"Well, there you are," Correus said. "Frankly, he's not far off."

"He saw an auxiliary standard bearer in a wolfskin," Vindex said.

"Borderlands are strange places," Correus said. "I'd got to half believing that story myself by the time we pulled back."

He was mulling that over when the courier from Sirmium came, requesting the immediate presence of General Correus Appius Julianus at the emperor's side in Sirmium, to serve as translator for the ambassador from Sarmizegetusa. Flavius, in a separate message, suggested that the legate should bring his wife, emphasizing the social and diplomatic nature of the meeting, and in the hope, Correus read between the lines, that her presence would remind the emperor of that.

Correus lost his temper. "My wife is not set dressing for a stage farce about barbarians and the emperor!"

"The emperor seemed to like me the time I met him in Rome," Ygerna said. "He thinks I'm an example of a civilized barbarian, I expect. What the Dacians might be if you make a treaty, although I doubt that. If Flavius thinks it will be useful, I'll go."

Correus muttered a number of things about high-handedness and wishful thinking, but finally said that he supposed if her presence reminded the emperor not to murder the envoy, that would be useful.

The envoy from Decebalus proved to be his brother Diegis again, and the prince was accorded the same ceremony as he had been given in Naissus. The blood had been scrubbed from the basilica floor and the tile polished as if it had never been there. In one place where it had seeped between the black and white squares, the tiles were prised up, their edges cleaned, and reset.

Diegis arrived with an escort of warriors as before, dragon banners snapping over their heads, and his household behind them: grooms, slaves, secretaries, and the black-haired interpreter Natoporus. Ygerna watched them ride in from a vantage point along the landward road that ran below the city aqueduct to the courtyard of the basilica. They struck her as not unlike the Romans in their demeanor. The escort rode as Correus's cavalry ala had, in tight formation, with the look of riders who had been drilled. They lacked the wild air of the Germans or the Britons of her home country, although horses and riders were heavy with the gold adornments of a people used to carrying much of their wealth on their bodies. There were gold mines as well as iron in their mountains, Lucius Paulinus had said, another reason for Rome to look greedily in their direction.

Cottia, standing beside her mistress, gaped at their splendor. "Eumenes says the walls in their palaces are made out of gold," she whispered.

Julius snorted. "Eumenes doesn't know as much as he thinks he does." He was feeling superior over the fact that Eumenes had been left behind in Singidunum and Correus had brought Julius to wait on him.

"Neither one of you has any idea," Ygerna said. She watched the cavalcade sweep by, halting where Correus and Flavius waited to welcome the envoy. Certainly they were very fine. The envoy dismounted and walked toward them lordlike, the sun glinting off his gold fishscale and the peaked ridge of his helmet. Preliminaries apparently conducted, they dispersed to their lodgings, accompanied by escorts from the emperor's staff. The gawking civilians in the street and the souvenir and sausage sellers departed to reopen their shops and lay out their best wares, plates depicting the Temple of Jupiter in Rome and fanciful scenes of Dacia on vases. The countryside around Sirmium had not suffered from the war to the east and its residents were prepared to welcome the foreigners and encourage them to spend their money, as well as collect the compensation the emperor was offering for the use of the city's best residences.

Official negotiations would take place the next morning. Domitian had ordered a banquet for the evening to which his senior staff and such family as attended them were invited to entertain the Dacian prince and his senior officers.

"He's making this look like his idea," Correus said to Ygerna while they dressed in the guest wing of the house where Flavius was quartered.

"If he feeds them, he can't kill them, can he?" Ygerna asked. "I suppose that's good."

Correus snorted, his dress uniform tunic half over his head. "That may be the point of tonight's dinner, to demonstrate that." Domitian had been known to ignore that tradition, but it still served as a statement of benign intent – until it didn't.

The emperor, at dinner, appeared to be in a convivial mood, his couch at right angles with the envoy's, with a table in between, Flavius on one opposite side, Correus and his wife on the other. The interpreter Natoporus stood behind the envoy's shoulder, not invited to dine himself, but to serve in a professional capacity. The Dacian officers were scattered among the Roman guests in groups of six or seven and appeared to be trying to decide how best to eat while lying down, which was not a Dacian custom. There were few women besides Ygerna: three magistrates' wives from Sirmium, and the Pannonian consular legate's wife, all placed beside their husbands, like vases of flowers, Ygerna thought, and set herself to be decorative since that was apparently what was required. There were actual flowers strewn on the floor, rose petals several inches thick so that the scent when they were trodden on was overwhelming. Slaves circulated with trays of elaborate delicacies and flagons of wine and water.

Diegis, the Dacian prince, was affable, not to say chatty. He asked Ygerna about her homeland and told both Correus and Flavius that he was delighted to see them again. He eyed Correus's scar with interest and remarked that he was distressed to see that some misfortune had befallen him. His Latin was excellent and really required no interpreter, although he asked Natoporus to repeat occasional phrases in Dacian, nodding and smiling at the translation. The man looked uncomfortable and Ygerna remembered something that Correus had said about him looking like a man who had been drilled. She thought that Correus and Flavius were both rather determinedly not looking his way.

"Tell me," Diegis said to Ygerna, "do your people follow the gods of the Romans? I was told that you were a priestess in your own land."

"Not a priestess as the Romans count it," Ygerna said carefully, "but a woman of the royal line, who represents the Goddess in an earthly body. Some among the Silures have taken to Roman gods, I expect, now that my uncle is dead. While he lived, no." She saw Natoporus's eyes widen and thought he looked frightened. "That went from me when I became Roman," she added. "It was not a thing I could take with me, or would want to."

"Ah," Diegis said. "Very wise. We hope to make peace also, between our people and Rome."

Ygerna smiled. "I was not the one who made the peace. I was only a very small difficulty to those who did."

"Whereas I am a large difficulty," Diegis said. "But we will make peace all the same."

Domitian had been silent through this exchange. Now he said, with avuncular jollity, "The legate's lady is only one of the fine things Rome acquired from our conquest of Britain, but a most decorative one." He beamed at her.

"What is he up to?" Correus demanded of Flavius when the dinner had finally ended, after twelve courses, music, two very beautiful blond dancing boys, and a tame leopard that caught chunks of meat, thrown by Domitian from his own plate, in a snap of its jaws.

"Which one?" Flavius said.

"Either. I meant Domitian."

"Obviously he would prefer that negotiations appear to have been the result of superior statesmanship on Rome's part."

Ygerna yawned. "That sounds perfectly reasonable."

"It will be the only thing that does," Correus said. "He thinks he's outfoxed Decebalus in some way, and Decebalus's brother thinks the same of him. They will exchange unwieldy, message-laden gifts, argue minutiae, and come to some kind of terms that will let them both declare victory. What are we giving him this time?"

"A marble statue of Alexander the Great, very old, Greek workmanship. It weighs over twelve hundred librae."

Ygerna began to laugh. "That is so appropriate and insulting at the same time, and how is he to get it home?"

"That may be the point," Flavius said.

—

The statue, in a martial pose with one arm uplifted, was mounted on a wheeled cart and delivered to the basilica in the morning, draped in gold and purple cloth so that it looked, Correus refrained from saying, like someone caught in the imperial bedsheets. Diegis duly presented the emperor with an onyx and ivory board and pieces for playing latrunculi, enclosed in a golden box.

Then they proceeded to lie to each other about the strength of their armies, the will of their people to sacrifice for the benefit of their rulers, and the loyalty of their various allies. Both had come reluctantly to the treaty table and both were determined to prove that they had not needed to, but only wished to be merciful to an enemy at a disadvantage. Correus developed a headache and the interpreter Natoporus was beginning to look terrified and he couldn't figure out why. When the talk turned to the return of prisoners, Correus thought perhaps he was afraid of that, as well he might be if he was a deserter from the auxiliaries, but he was an unlikely candidate to be handed over.

It was obvious that the negotiations were going to go on for several days, until each side felt that it had made all the requisite points, and extracted as much as possible from the other. Flavius took his turn to entertain the envoy the second night at a small all-male party with two officers of the Sirmium cavalry garrison who had not fought in the recent war. Diegis dispensed with the need for an interpreter and conversed in formal Latin and more colloquial Greek, describing the marvels of the palace at Sarmizegetusa and the impenetrability of its defenses.

Correus and Ygerna, thankfully released from diplomatic duty, kept to the guest wing. Before they went to bed, Ygerna put her cloak over her nightshift and went out into the garden to the wing that housed the latrine and the baths. There was only a waning moon, barely enough to see by, so she took a lamp from their chamber, a small lidded saucer with a flickering flame like a will-o-the-wisp in the dark. The garden hummed with insect noise, the homely chirp of crickets punctuating the eldritch wail of summer cicadas. Lights from the main house indicated that the party was still going on, and she halted in the doorway, hoping that no one else was there. Romans were remarkably communal in their use of latrines, and while she appreciated the convenience and functionality of Roman plumbing, she was not fond of company. The anteroom and the latrine and baths beyond were dark and still. Ygerna took her cloak off and a hand grabbed her from behind, while another came down over her mouth. The lamp fell to the stone floor and a foot stamped out the flame.

Ygerna writhed in his grip and sank her teeth into the hand over her mouth. The grip tightened. She kicked at him, trying to turn and bring a knee up. In the faint spill of moonlight coming through the open door, she saw the glint of a knife. She bit deeper and the hand came away from her mouth and slapped her as she screamed, then closed over it again. She flailed in his grip, trying to make herself an unwieldy target, and then someone else was there, pulling the attacker away. The newcomer threw him against the wall and Ygerna, gasping, bent to pick up the knife that had fallen. Julius kicked the man in the ribs and then in the head and knelt on him.

"Get a light!" he said, breathing hard.

Ygerna picked up the spilled lamp and looked for a flame. A small mound of dying coals in a brazier warmed the chilly anteroom and she picked one out with the tongs and touched it gingerly to the lamp's wick. The little flame flickered fitfully in the oil that was left and she carried it to the man on the floor.

It was the Dacian interpreter, Natoporus.

"Now the knife," Julius said.

"Julius, wait! Don't kill him."

"He was trying to kill you. Why shouldn't I? Mistook you for the legate, I expect, or his brother. You're lucky I had to piss and I'm too civilized to do it in the garden."

"No, that's ridiculous. If you grabbed me in the dark, would you think I was Correus?" She bent over the figure on the floor. "Who are you? Tell me or I'll let him use the knife."

The man stared up at her in despair. "You know me. Or I would not have done this."

Ygerna stared back at him. "I do not." She paused. "Julius, pull his shirt up."

Julius grabbed a handful of cloth and yanked it past the man's ribs. Ygerna bent over him and drew in her breath.

The pattern of the Spear Mark, different for every tribe, and given to every boy of her people in the year of his manhood, showed on his chest, old now and faded to a bluish gray. She had seen the Demetae's pattern often enough: she had been sent by her uncle to marry their chief's son to cement an alliance. "You were Gruffyd's man."

"I was Fillin. Before I was a prisoner of the Romans and given the choice between their cavalry and the slave market. You knew me in Carn Goch and would have told."

"Pah! Your bad conscience makes you stupid," Ygerna said, in her home hills' dialect. "I did not remember your face, but I know it now. You were one of those who tortured the Roman that you caught, who is my husband's brother, ill luck for you. But why kill me and not him?"

"No! I was not the one who questioned him. But you would say my name to him."

"To kill a royal woman is to bring the Black Goddess's curse down on you, did you stop to think of that?"

"You said, at the Roman emperor's table, that the Goddess is gone from you now," he whispered. "And I was afraid."

"You had better be," Julius said, picking up enough of the talk to follow it. "Deserters are executed. You don't need worse than that. I saw one once."

"Julius, be quiet." Ygerna turned back to the man on the floor. "The Goddess never goes away entirely. If you had killed me, she would have turned your gut to molten iron and your skin to flame, and I will ask her to do it now if you are not careful."

Her pale face and black hair flickered in the oil lamp's dim light and the five-petaled mark of the Goddess between her breasts showed at the top of her nightshift. Fillin shuddered. He was Fillin now, Natoporus gone into the daylight hours of another life.

A second light filled the doorway, this one from a lantern in Correus's hand. "What in the name of Mithras's bull is going on here? Ygerna!" He saw the torn nightshift and the marks on her face and pulled her to him.

"Tried to knife her," Julius said. "Thought she knew him from Britain, the poor fool." The man tried to rise and Julius put a knee on his neck.

Correus went white and the hand with the lantern shook. *No. Not again.* "Give him to me," he said grimly and set the lantern down. "I'm not even going to leave him for the army."

"No!" Ygerna pulled away and faced him. "You took him from his people and put him in your army! You gave him a commander who did something to make him run. It wasn't cowardice. My people do not shame themselves in battle."

"I never saw him before," Correus protested, still shaking with fury and fear.

"Well, your brother did. He's one of the ones who took his fingers off," Julius said.

"No, lord! I was only there, I did not…"

"Rome has done this and you are the soldier and servant of Rome," Ygerna said to Correus. She looked from Correus to Fillin.

"That is ridiculous," Correus said, distracted now from the man at his feet, but his heart still pounded. *Ygerna.*

"I am the one he wanted to kill. Do you allow me any say in my own life or am I just another conscript?" Her eyes were fierce and he thought of the half-wild child he had met at thirteen.

Ygerna had not changed so greatly. No wonder Fillin was afraid of her.

"Ygerna—"

Ygerna stamped her foot on the stone floor. "Listen to me! Rome is responsible for what has happened here. Rome took this man and shook all of his soul out of him and filled it with marching in squares and fighting strangers in a foreign country for no reason of his own, and now blames him for escaping to yet another foreign life because he can never go home. And he is so broken that he would risk the curse of the Dark Mother for killing her priestess rather than go back."

In some ways we ask for this, conscripting our enemies. Correus remembered saying that. *Shouldn't you ask what I want?* Ygerna had said that to him in Aquae Sulis when he had left her there because he was afraid of taking another wife to follow the army with him and die. Both memories had the capacity to be the stuff of nightmares, frightening visions out of Erebus of what he could not control. Ygerna was still glaring at him, demanding to be neither a conscript nor the vessel of the Goddess but his wife, a woman he must let take her own chances. That was not an easy thing.

"What do you want me to do with him?" he said helplessly. "Let him go? To come back and try again?"

"I will not," Fillin whispered hoarsely. "I will swear it if you wish."

"And what is your oath worth?" Correus demanded. "Since you also swore to Rome?"

"I swore to Rome by Rome's gods," Fillin said dismissively. "I will swear now to you by the Goddess and by Lugh Sunlord. *She* knows what that means."

"He won't break that," Ygerna said, softening her voice now. "Also, I have told him I will curse him and he believes me."

"*I* believe you," Julius said, unnerved. If the Goddess had left her, then he was the Deified Augustus.

"All right," Correus said, giving in. "Get off him."

Fillin stood, somewhat shakily. His face was black with spilled lamp oil and dirt from the floor.

"How did you get in?" Correus demanded.

"Over the back gate from the alley."

"Then leave that way. If my brother's dinner party sees you, I won't be able to stop anything. And even if I can, your prince won't be pleased to have his spy caught."

Fillin bowed to Ygerna, touching his forehead. "I am sorry, lady," he whispered and fled into the dark garden. In a moment they heard him scramble over the gate.

Correus put his arm around Ygerna's shoulders again, too tightly for comfort but she didn't protest. Outside, the cicadas' otherworldly call rose and fell in the warm night.

"You are still fearful," she said softly. "But there are three of us. He can't kill you and Julius as well."

"Heart, I can't help but be fearful. You must leave me that if I leave you your freedom."

-

Negotiations continued for two more days, thrashing out the minutiae of an agreement. Correus continued to translate, as did Natoporus, who was mercifully unmarked by the night's encounter. As fiercely as Correus had wished to kill him, and still did, the reflection that it would have made unwanted trouble for the negotiations dampened this urge enough that in the daylight he managed to look disinterested in anything but the careful translation of suggested terms.

Everyone was being extremely polite. Correus thought that Diegis was enjoying himself. Domitian had made his point sufficiently with the Quadi and Marcomanni envoys that he could adopt a benevolent interest in the support of Dacia as a client state, and pretend that the eight million sesterces a year that Diegis was demanding was a reasonable sum to pay for access by Roman troops to Dacian territory should they require it.

"That's blackmail!" Correus said disgustedly, unbuckling his parade cuirass and handing it off to Julius. "Flavius, you know it is!"

"Diegis agreed to come to Rome to receive the crown and patronage," Flavius said. "That will play well at home."

Correus snorted. "You note that Decebalus isn't the one coming. Decebalus won't put himself in Rome's hands."

"Wise of him," Flavius said.

In the end, all the more that Rome could pry from Diegis was the return of a handful of prisoners taken in raids across the Danuvius and at Cornelius Fuscus's debacle at Tapae. In exchange, Rome would return an equal number of Dacian prisoners. When the question of Roman deserters was raised, Diegis shrugged his shoulders.

"We have none, I assure the emperor," he said.

"The emperor wishes to know who taught you to make catapults in that case?" Correus retorted.

Diegis leaned back in his chair, marginally smaller and less grand than the emperor's but not by much. Careful measurements had been taken by the emperor's diplomatic staff before negotiations had begun. "We are not without our own engineers," he said and waited, tapping his fingers against the spiral of red gold bracelets that reached halfway up his forearm. His brother's seal ring sat heavily on his right forefinger.

There was a long silence. Correus did not so much as flick his eyes at Natoporus, who had been a cavalryman while he was still Fillin. The catapult crews were a specialized unit. He wouldn't have been responsible for that. *I am making excuses for him*, he thought. *Is it because he is of Ygerna's people? Who tried to kill her when she had been too long among Romans? Who cut my brother's fingers off?* He waited to see what Domitian would say in response.

The emperor chose not to argue and Correus suppressed a furious rage and gritted his teeth. Where was the price for Oppius Sabinus and Cornelius Fuscus and the Fifth Alaudae? It could be argued that Sabinus and Fuscus had bought their own fates, but the Alaudae were another matter. Correus had watched the Larks march out behind their elephant shields and their Eagle and none of them had returned. Diegis also claimed to have no knowledge of the Eagle, which was unlikely but unprovable. Correus thought of telling the emperor that the envoy's interpreter was a deserter who had tortured the emperor's aide, and letting things fall as they might. He bit his tongue. Domitian's reaction was too unpredictable. He had told Flavius and Flavius had looked at his hands for a long time and then said to keep that to himself.

Domitian waved a hand for his secretary, and the scribe squeezed through the half-circle of Praetorian Guards and past Flavius to kneel at the emperor's feet. "Rome agrees to accept Dacia as a client state," Domitian announced. "To be accorded all the benefits that come with such status. Take this down," he said to the secretary. He held up a finger as he made each point. "Prisoners will be exchanged and the King Decebalus agrees to withdraw all troops from Roman provincial soil. In addition, Rome will have free access across Dacian borders in the event of conflict with any of Dacia's unfriendly neighbors. In return, Rome will send the support that the client king Decebalus has asked for, through his envoy and brother Diegis, together with the engineers and advisers he requests."

"To teach them any other of our tactics that they may have missed!" Correus said furiously.

They were in a chariot in the Sirmium hippodrome behind Flavius's new team and well out of anyone's earshot, a circumstance that Flavius had thought prudent, given his brother's mood.

"I'll do what I can about that," Flavius said. "But they already have most of it. They are a particularly adaptive culture, when they aren't fighting each other. If Decebalus can hold them all together, he'll have his own empire whether we like it or not. As long as he doesn't push Rome too far."

"How much farther than this can he go? And what can you do about it?"

Flavius shook out the reins, sending the ponies into a trot. "They need to be run more. Would you like to take them out while you're here? And I was getting to that. He's sending me with the advisers, as ambassadorial legate to the new client kingdom. I am to take my family and spend a year there as a goodwill gesture. We will leave with Diegis after he makes his state visit to Rome."

"Do you have any choice?" Correus demanded.

"Not really," Flavius said. "Not without awkwardness. But I rather like the idea. It's not the wilderness, you know. And I think Aemelia will like it. It's exotic and interesting but she'll have luxurious quarters. She'll have stories to dine out on for months afterward. The advisers will all be military, you understand. There's a post open for their commander."

Correus was silent for a moment before the implication hit him. "No!"

"You might think about it," Flavius said.

"Flavius, if you have so much as whispered in the emperor's ear about this—"

"Well, no, but—"

"The last posting you helped me to had me shipping hippos up the Tiber for a year. No!"

Flavius handed him the reins. "Give them a run."

Correus shook the ponies into a canter and then a full-out gallop, their pale tails flying like banners. They were, as Julius had said, a fine team. He missed driving. He supposed if he settled somewhere for any length of time, he could have a stable. They flew down the straightaway and took the far turn around the obelisk at speed while Flavius braced himself against the chariot's rim and watched him drive. The chariot was heavy and unwieldy on the turns. When they had made a circuit of the track and slowed, all Correus said was, "You need a better rig than this. It handles like a grain wagon."

"I bought it from the man who sold the ponies," Flavius said. "He didn't know better. I have something else on order. Well?"

"I told you. No. I'd sooner command a troop of camel cavalry. If you think there is a chance of my getting those orders, you had better get me out of it."

"It could be a step to senatorial rank. Despite, er, everything."

"I don't *want* senatorial rank," Correus said flatly. "You do." He wouldn't get it anyway. There was a limit to how far a freedman could go, even Appius Julianus's son. He let the ponies amble, reins lightly in one hand, and regarded his brother. "Why do you feel bound to arrange to give me what you have, whether I want it or not?"

Flavius fixed his eyes on the ponies' red backsides. "Is that what I'm doing?"

"Yes. And I don't want it. I have what I want."

"A frontier command. On the border of Nowhere and Not Much."

"Command of a legion," Correus said. "I have wanted that since I was five."

Flavius slewed his glance around at him, turning his head to see past his helmet's face guard. "Because that's what Father had?"

"To begin with. But I went on wanting it. You just thought you were supposed to."

Flavius took the ponies' reins back, but he kept them to a walk. "Father was a hard man to measure up to."

"You've more than done that," Correus said. "He couldn't have handled a diplomatic post and nor could I. He's proud of you, you fool."

"Perhaps he is." Flavius smiled. "I was beginning to think so, you know, the last time I saw him."

"Good. Now make it clear to Domitian or whoever needs to hear it that your brother would be a most unsuitable candidate for that command."

"Given that he cannot mind his temper and has no discretion," Flavius murmured.

"Precisely."

In the morning, Domitian made ready to return to Rome, leaving any further border troubles in Velius Rufus's hands, to everyone's relief. Diegis and his retinue would ride out the following day, taking Domitian's signed agreement to Decebalus while arrangements were made for his state visit to Rome.

Correus, lazing in bed simply because he could, was prodded awake by Julius who came to inform him that "Old Velius Rufus is here looking for you, dressed like a Tiber bargeman."

Correus got up and put a cloak over his night tunic. "I'll go see him. And watch your manners." *Now what?*

Rufus was waiting for him in the guest quarters atrium. He wore an ancient pair of cavalry breeches, a frayed German–style shirt, and a straw hat that would have embarrassed a donkey. "Julianus! Go get some clothes on. We're going fishing."

"Fishing?" Correus blinked at him.

"Good for the soul. Nothing better than fishing. Get some old clothes on. Fishing is a muddy occupation."

Correus had seen little of Rufus other than at the emperor's banquet for the Dacian diplomatic mission, but he had fought under him in Germany, and had a healthy respect for the general. He sketched a salute and padded back into the bedroom.

"I'm going fishing," he informed Ygerna as he rummaged in his trunk for something he didn't mind ruining. "For what, I'm not sure." He pulled an old tunic over his head and fastened his sandals without waiting for Julius to reappear.

"With Velius Rufus?"

"Indeed. I have no idea what the old toad wants, but unless he's lost his mind, he wants something."

Rufus inspected Correus's attire and nodded. "Excellent, you don't look like yourself at all. Come along."

Outside the villa's main door, a pair of fishing poles and a basket awaited them. Rufus picked up the basket and a pole. "You're a country boy, Julianus. Grew up on your father's farm. I trust you fish?"

"Occasionally," Correus said.

"These are excellent waters for trout this time of year." Rufus set out briskly past the basilica and through the crowded market quarter, dodging between a cart selling pottery busts of the emperor and a carriage disgorging a farm family come to have a last look at the foreigners. The ubiquitous gulls and pigeons squabbled for the detritus in the streets, hurtling upward in an annoyed huff of feathers when anyone got too close.

Beyond the market the road led through the city's river gates, forking at the banks of the Savus. Correus followed Rufus's bow-legged figure along the downstream path and across the stone and timber bridge that led to one of the river's twin islands. A little shrine to the eponymous river god, Savus Flumen, stood on the far side: a stone niche enclosing a statue and an altar where someone had left a silver coin. Rufus paused to add another from the pouch at his belt. The ground was soft, and the banks overgrown with willow and alder. It was deserted except for the rustle of some small creature in the undergrowth. Upstream from the bridgehead, a limestone ledge jutted into the water above a pool where the willows reached their feet and fronds into the river. Velius Rufus settled himself on the stone in the shade of the willow, sandaled feet dangling over the edge. He opened the basket and produced a sack of buns and a small clay jar of worms. He unstoppered the jar and offered it to Correus, followed by the buns.

"How often do you fish here?" Correus asked, amused. It was clear that he knew the place.

"I always find a fishing spot when I want to think," Rufus said, putting a worm on his hook. "Or talk quietly."

Correus baited his own hook and cast it into the pool while he waited to see what else Rufus had to say.

Velius Rufus watched the ripples spreading where his line had gone into the water. A dragonfly skimmed the surface just above them. "Tettius Julianus is going to be recalled."

"I am sorry to hear that." Correus was, but not surprised. Tettius Julianus had recently commanded far too many legions to make Domitian comfortable with leaving him on the frontier.

Rufus tested his line, which had tugged a bit. The line came up easily, the hook bare. "Extraordinary how crafty fish can be," he commented. He baited the hook again. "Nigrinus as well. I assume both will be replaced, but in the meantime, I have been given the task of keeping an army ready along the length of the Danuvius, including the Moesian sections, against whatever may come next, because of course something will."

"I see," Correus said carefully. Velius Rufus had risen to equestrian rank and made it plain that he wished to go no further. It made him an excellent choice, from Domitian's point of view, to command a large army.

"I want sound commanders on that border and I've convinced the emperor to leave their choice to me. And thus I have saved your ass, so you can thank me now." Rufus turned to grin at him from under the disreputable hat. "Your brother tells me that you are distressed at the thought of a certain posting."

"I am," Correus said frankly.

"Furthermore, playing posting rota with legates and legions is all very well when necessity demands it," Rufus said, "but I have told Tettius and Nigrinus that they need to move you and Aurelius Decius back again now that the court is leaving for Rome. You just got the Fifth into shape and led them in a successful campaign, and this is no time to be handing them off to another commander. That's a tricky job and it merits consistency. I watched you pull the Fourteenth Gemina back together in Germany, and in my opinion if you still had them, they would have told Antonius Saturninus to swim in the Styx, no matter what he had over their heads."

"Thank you," Correus said. "Does this mean I'm posted back to Oescus?"

"It means you will be."

"For how long?"

"Several years at least. Probably no more. We are soldiers. We go where we're sent. You have a fish on your line, I think."

Correus pulled up a small, irritated-looking turtle. He detached it and dropped it back and it sculled away into the river. He looked at Rufus gratefully. He would stay on the frontier and he had the Fifth Macedonica back again. They were a legion that he had made into something to be proud of and to part with them had grieved him more than he had admitted. A cloud of midges materialized, swarming around their heads, and Rufus batted them away with his hat. He returned to his line and pulled in a middle-sized trout, stunned it and tucked it into the basket, mottled scales luminous in the sun, and announced them finished.

XXIII

A More Auspicious Gathering

The Emperor Domitian celebrated his third triumph in Rome that fall. Aemelia took Helva to see it. The nearer the calendar got to Appius's wedding, the more morose and quarrelsome Helva was becoming, and it seemed a favor to all concerned to keep her entertained.

Helva shaded her eyes under the bright green parasol that Decima held above her head. Behind them, Aemelia's maid and two pages were laden with everything that might be required for them to view the emperor's procession in comfort, and Felix had helped cajole his grandmother into a sunnier mood with the promise of an escort to the games afterward. At fourteen, Felix's height almost made unnecessary the two muscular slaves who had accompanied the party for protection from thieves and unwanted male attention. The day was fair for November and the promised rain had blown away, leaving the sky an almost summer blue.

"Is that the Dacian prince?" Felix stared admiringly at Diegis as he rode behind Domitian's chariot, lordly on a black horse, arms and throat heavy with a red gold collar and spiraling gold armbands. The prince's head was topped with a gilded helmet that peaked like the cloth caps that lesser men wore, and his beard and mustache were oiled and curled.

Helva left her folding chair and stood on tiptoes, interested now. "He's very handsome." She shuddered slightly. "But I think it's too bad to make you travel all that way. Flavius must be insane. Who knows what goes on in a place like that?"

"That's what my mother says," Aemelia agreed. "But the emperor wishes it, so that is that." All in all, it did not sound so very bad to her. It would be an adventure, undertaken in the most comfortable fashion.

The procession had halted in front of the Basilica Julia, where the ceremonial conferring of a crown on Decebalus's representative would take place. Aemelia's party had an excellent view from the steps of the Temple of Saturn, staked out by slaves in the early hours and stoutly defended since then. The crowd milled about, waiting, getting under the feet of the emperor's horses who snorted and danced in protest. It would be a dismal omen if they trampled someone, and guards hurried the bystanders away.

The emperor and Diegis reappeared from the shadows of the basilica's portico with more guards clearing their way through the crowd. Diegis was helmetless now, his curling hair crowned with a circlet of twisted gold in token of the fact that he gave fealty to Rome in his brother's stead. Domitian stepped up into his scarlet chariot, Diegis remounted, and the procession reformed and moved up the Capitoline heights.

"Are you ready to go, dear?" Aemelia asked Helva. The wind had picked up and was whirling scraps of trash about them, and it looked a daunting prospect to follow the procession up the hill. Felix, thank Juno, had volunteered to escort his grandmother to the games. Aemelia could hardly bring her back to lunch with her father-in-law, Julia and Lucius, and Didia Longina.

"Be careful, and take at least one man with you," Aemelia told Felix. "And bring her away before any bloodshed."

"I will. I don't like those things either. Grandmother just wants to see the trained animals and the races. She's planning to catch one of the prizes." Domitian's representatives would throw little wooden balls to the crowd throughout the show, each with a ticket inside for some present: wine or gold or new clothes. Felix was aware that his grandmother had everything that she could possibly want, but that wasn't the point. It was the thrill of the catch. She was still pretty enough that they would likely throw one her way, and that would make her happy.

Felix decided that he would avoid women until he found one that he was both permitted to and actually wanted to marry. His grandfather and uncle already had their eyes on several girls they considered suitable for him, but he would put his foot down. An army career building bridges in inaccessible places would make that easier. He tucked his grandmother's arm through his and smiled at her affectionately. *You're a mistake I won't make,* he thought.

–

Aemelia inspected preparations in the kitchen and wondered if there was a way to convince Cook to come to Sarmizegetusa with them without his immediately demanding to buy his freedom. Her father-in-law's wedding was in a week and their departure would take place when it was over, as soon as the Dacian prince had concluded his state visit to Rome.

It was as if someone had put the family in a dice cup and shaken them, she thought, tumbling them over each other until they fell with new sides topmost. Appius and Lucius Paulinus were in Flavius's study with him, and Julia and Didia Longina were making small talk in the atrium where Didia was admiring Julia's new way of dressing her hair and wondering if she might try it herself for the wedding. Correus and Ygerna and their household were expected the next day, to settle as well as possible into the house that Appius had bought them, and which had Helva in it.

In his study, Flavius perched in the sunny windowsill, parade cuirass discarded, his white dress tunic a snowy splotch against the warm brown of the wall. The gold garlanding painted on the plaster behind him gave him an imperial aspect. He eyed Lucius Paulinus. "No."

"I didn't ask," Paulinus protested. "I only asked when you were leaving."

"You may record the emperor's triumph," Flavius said. "And the visit of the representative of the king of Dacia. That should take several chapters. Lucius, don't put your fingers in this, and don't involve Julia. It's bad enough as it is."

"That's sound advice," Appius said. "I understand that the Senate is not best pleased by the treaty."

"Or by the emperor?"

"Short of a return to the Republic, there is only one solution to a problematic emperor," Appius said, "and the Senate is not so minded, particularly now and particularly not since the lower ranks of the army are solidly behind him."

"They should be," Flavius said. "He raised their pay by a third. An astute, if expensive, move. Lucius, this treaty is tricky, so keep out of it. You have a fine line to walk as long as you are in the emperor's employ."

"However long that is," Paulinus said. "There are some holes in the flooring."

"Then it's up to us to shore it up," Flavius said. "For everyone's sake."

Appius sighed. "The more unstable and capricious a ruler becomes, the likelier it grows that someone will react, often an unexpected someone. Given your positions, the two of you will know when it's coming, I believe. If you cannot prevent it, or in an extreme case if you do not wish to, you must be well away."

–

Correus would no doubt have agreed, but just now the failings of the emperor were less on his mind than the question of whether his wife could manage not to kill his mother. Helva had greeted them on their arrival, the adults travel weary and the children contentious, and insisted on showing them the entire house, with an unfortunately proprietary air, before they had unpacked. In addition, she had had the guest wing made up for them. You couldn't really fault that, since they would not be staying but a month, but the message was pointed.

"And what on earth is a nymphaeum?" Ygerna asked Correus as they soaked in the bath. There appeared to be one in the house, still half-built, with the beginnings of elaborate, and expensive, mosaics to cover the walls and ceiling as well as the floor.

"It's a kind of grotto, with a decorative fountain and a niche for statues to the local water deities," Correus said. "Very fashionable. You can have parties there."

"Not if your mother is still in it," Ygerna said. "And who is paying for it?"

Correus sighed. "I suppose I am." He sank into the pool until only his eyes and nose showed. He wondered if he could just stay there.

"Didia Longina, whom I have not yet met, is a most prescient woman," Ygerna remarked.

Correus surfaced enough to talk without a mouthful of water. "For refusing to share a house with my mother? Ygerna, we only have to stand it for my month's leave, to wish my father well and see the sights. Then we'll be back to the Danuvius again."

"I'm almost sorry you wouldn't go to Sarmizegetusa. It's farther away."

"Flavius says that Aemelia has been calling on her," Correus said, "and persuading her friends to come too. I don't think my mother has ever had friends before. Talk to Aemelia."

"Your mother wanted Aemelia to marry you," Ygerna said. "She told me so."

"She's not tactful." Correus sank into the water again.

Ygerna pulled herself out of the pool and held out her arms for Cottia to wrap her in a towel. "I shall consult Aemelia. If she's been calling on your mother, something new has come over that woman."

–

In the morning, Ygerna sent a message to Aemelia, making it quite clear that the invitation came from her, which made Helva click her tongue and flounce out of the breakfast room. Correus told Eumenes to saddle Ashes and rode to his father's estate on the ostensible errand of selecting another troop horse to replace Briseis.

Helva was sulking in the garden since Aemelia was "your guest," as she had told Ygerna pointedly. Ygerna eyed her through the atrium window. "I feel as if I've moved into a house with an unfriendly *anima* in it, except that she's so solid."

"What you want to do," Aemelia said, selecting one of the small pastries from the silver dish presented by Helva's kitchen maid, "is find her a husband."

"I wouldn't even know where to start," Ygerna said despairingly. "She's the only thing about marrying Correus that I haven't been able to cope with."

"Put a notice in the *Acta Diurna*," Aemelia said solemnly. "Eligible mother-in-law, expensive tastes but stunningly beautiful."

Ygerna couldn't help laughing. Aemelia had more sense of humor than she had expected. "I wish we could. How do I even begin?"

"Well, not with senators, since she's a freedwoman. They aren't allowed. But a nice old equestrian gentleman with no children to get upset. I'll help you. We know most of the equestrian families. It's a shame we can't take her to the wedding and show her around. They'll all be there."

Ygerna envisioned that scenario. "Appius would make Correus divorce me. But what a thought."

"Well, most of them saw her at the funeral," Aemelia said practically. "And she's memorable."

–

The wedding of Flavius Appius Julianus the Elder and Didia Longina took place in the garden of the bride's country house on a day carefully chosen for its propitious aspect. The bride was attended by the groom's daughter and daughters-in-law and given in marriage, at least theoretically, by her uncle. The uncle, who Correus decided must be nearly a hundred, seemed unclear on exactly what they were doing, but was game, signing the contract and offering prayers as instructed by Didia, and then settling in a chair to watch the proceedings as if he were at a play.

Since the bridal couple had been the subject of endless gossip and speculation, everyone who could wangle an invitation came to see them wed. The poet Martial arrived with a scroll under one arm, prepared to read a celebratory ode in honor of the day, of which a number of people took due note and sought out places to hide before he began. Martial could exhibit a biting wit, but his commemorative works ran to platitudes designed to extract largesse from their subject. Domitian himself attended, an announcement that had sent Didia's household into even more fevered preparations and Julia into a complete rearrangement of the couches for dinner.

The bride was dressed in white, with a flame-colored veil and shoes, the groom in a spotless toga, and both were crowned with garlands of roses that gave Appius the look of a military statue that someone had hung his wreath on.

The emperor had offered the services of the Flamen Dialis himself, a high honor which Appius had politely declined by reason of practicality since the Flamen Dialis was so hedged about with ritual restrictions that his presence at any function was a constant problem. His prohibitions included touching horses, iron, dogs, she-goats, ivy, beans, raw flesh, flour, or bread, or walking under trellises.

"Can't say I blame you," Domitian had confided. "Perfect nuisance, but I thought I'd make the offer."

"Caesar is most gracious."

Domitian was given a chair beside the altar and seemed to be enjoying himself, while giving everyone else heart palpitations for fear of someone accidentally offending him.

The couple said their vows in the garden before a lesser priest and offered a plate of cakes to Jupiter and to Juno. The guests showered them with shelled nuts from small linen bags distributed beforehand, and they ran hand in hand, laughing, through the rainfall of almonds and walnuts.

"Very handsome performance," Livilla Drusa Major said to Aemelia. She was an imposing figure with her hair dressed in the stiff globe of curls made fashionable by the imperial family. "I sent them a nice pair of candlesticks. I suppose you've heard about Prosper. He's drowning in debt and has no prospects now that Didia has married. My niece is divorcing him," she added.

"That's unfortunate," Aemelia said carefully.

"I don't suppose you invited either of them," Livilla Major said. "I wouldn't either. I hear he shouted at Appius in the street. And she's a grasping little ferret and always has been. Her father's trying to get the settlement back – what's left of it anyway. Prosper's had to sell the racing ponies."

Aemelia found that entirely satisfactory, but it wouldn't be prudent to say so. She cast about for some appropriate platitude.

"Her father's behind the divorce," Livilla Major went on. "A sex scandal is one thing. That side of the family doesn't set high standards for their morals, I regret to say. But Prosper did something politically unfortunate, I suspect, and he's not having that in the family."

Slaves began circulating with trays of food and cups of wine while everyone settled to the pre-dinner entertainment. Aemelia seized the opportunity. "I need to find Uncle Longinus and see that he's fed."

Martial had begun his laudatory recitation in front of the fountain, enticing his audience to stay for the verses in praise of marital harmony and the House of Appius with the promise to next recite a few of the epigrams from his newest book, a prospect that even Appius seemed to find preferable.

"Get on with it then," he suggested. "Any further paean to my family tree can wait. As long as possible."

Didia's uncle Longinus, provided with wine and a plate of figs and pastries, rested his hands and then his chin on his cane and beamed approvingly. Martial's epigrams were notorious for insulting everyone. It was a game to see who could be identified behind their aliases.

Felix had attached himself to Julius Frontinus as soon as he saw him. Flavius watched them with some amusement. He had attempted to introduce Felix to the daughter of one of the wedding guests, a pretty child a year younger than he, and Felix had reacted like a fish evading a suspicious bait. He supposed the boy had good reason, given the example his male relatives had set. Even now the memory of Fiorgyn floated beside him as it always did, and he had the odd, mad thought that Felix could see it.

Aemelia found Ygerna and drew her into the shadow of the colonnade. "Old Opilius is here. He's the perfect prospect. I'll introduce you and you can ask him to dinner."

"Won't he think that odd?"

"Not in the least. He's a retired military man so he'll be interested in what Correus has to say about the frontier. And he has a weakness for pretty women."

Ygerna let Aemelia lead her across the garden to a man with a thinning fringe of curly brown hair and a cheerful face. As predicted, he was charmed to meet the wife of General Julianus the Younger and happily accepted a dinner invitation. Aemelia made certain that he got a fresh cup of wine and one of the prawns in pastry that were being carried around, then drew Ygerna toward another man, this one a bit older and plumply prosperous-looking. "Servius Gallienus is in grain imports in the City," Aemelia whispered. "We'll ask him too. It's as well for them to think they have competition."

Martial's recitation in praise of the happy couple wound to its conclusion and he rewarded his listeners with a few of his more scandalous verses, including a new and not very veiled reference to Prosper Rufius and his wife's unfortunate pregnancy. Since no one much liked Rufius, it was received with enthusiasm. The poet looked pleased. That one would be all over the City by the end of the day.

Correus listened with some amusement, trying to decide whether Julius would like to hear that verse or not. Julius appeared to be an entirely new person and had gone off to see Diulius on their arrival. Everyone seemed to be remaking themselves. Even Ygerna flickered in his vision now when he looked at her, her Roman self dissolving into the Silure princess through some old dark magic that wasn't gone after all. She had blandly informed him that morning that she had a plan for his mother, and he was reasonably sure that it had to do with a suitable match and not some ancient unbinding spell.

Domitian beamed at the happy couple, accepted their gratitude for a wedding gift of eight embossed gold dishes, and everyone but Julia breathed a sigh of relief as he departed, trailing his bodyguard, secretary, two pages, and a food taster in his wake.

"He's not staying for the dinner?" Julia demanded.

"Apparently not," Lucius Paulinus said, "for which small mercies we thank all gods known and unknown."

"I redid the entire dinner arrangements when he said he was coming," Julia said.

"Then put your father in his place. He won't have anybody executed over the dessert course."

She departed for the dining room and he turned to find Correus beside him.

Paulinus greeted him happily. "A more auspicious gathering than the last time you were home." His eyes widened at the scar that ran from Correus's left eye to his jaw. "Who spoiled your beauty?"

"A ghost of our own making," Correus said. "A German mercenary of the Dacian army and one of our own conscripts from the last war."

"I take it that he is in worse condition?"

"If by that you mean dead, yes," Correus said. "Conscripting our enemies has its drawbacks."

"Whatever happened to that interpreter that Diegis had with him?" Paulinus asked.

Correus paused a moment. "What brings him to mind?"

"Just a thought. Do you know, I thought he looked British."

"He was. You're uncomfortably observant. Honestly, why do we think we can enforce loyalty with an oath to a god they don't

390

believe in and an emperor they hate? The auxiliaries or the slave market? Who wouldn't take the auxiliaries, and then run?"

"Well, with an oath and a vine staff, but I take your point." A slave came around with more cups of wine and Paulinus put his empty one on it and took two more. "Here. Drink to the old general's happiness and tell me, when you left for the Centuriate, did you think the empire was perfect?"

"No, of course not." Correus paused. "Yes." He lifted the cup and drank, laughing.

"Disillusionment comes to us all," Paulinus commented.

"It seems to have come to you at birth," Correus said.

"And thus I have survived, albeit with some dreadful mistakes and the help of friends."

"Father expressed particular pleasure at my posting to Oescus," Correus said. "I wasn't sure whether he was proud of me for the command or relieved to have me miles from Rome."

"I rather think both," Paulinus said. "He told your brother and me that we would know when it was coming and that if we couldn't stop it, to be well away. I assume I needn't elaborate?"

"No, for Mithras's sake, don't!" Correus looked horrified. So even his father thought it would eventually come to murder.

"I don't sense anything imminent, if that's a comfort. The trouble with you, Correus, is that you can't ever rest easy and inhabit the moment."

"Am I really that jumpy?"

"When you're making a dead set at something you want, no. Once you have it, yes."

"I suppose I'm afraid that the gods will come along and take it back," Correus said. He had to admit that. It had always been his underlying fear. Whatever he gained was so fragile in his grasp.

"Isn't it time you left that off?" Paulinus asked him.

"Recent developments on the frontier don't encourage it," Correus said. That was an easier example to speak of than Freita's death or a knife in the dark. "We could have taken Sarmize-getusa."

"Decebalus is the one who ought to be looking over his shoulder for the Fates," Paulinus said. "Being king is an even jumpier proposition than being a legionary legate with a frontier command and enough medals to decorate a horse."

Correus looked away and caught sight of his father across the garden with his arm around Didia. Under its rose wreath, Appius's dark face was alight with pleasure at this late life gift. Appius had known how much his slave-born son had wanted a career with the legions and he had adopted him over his wife's objections to give it to him. Something slid into place now for no particular reason other than his father's face: that he owed it to Appius to take that as his right, finally.

If Paulinus was correct, Decebalus would overreach eventually. And maybe this time the border commanders would be able to finish it and the Danuvius would be stable. If Domitian over-reached too, that wasn't the army's affair, other than to hold the border while kings and emperors rose and fell. *We go where we're posted*, Velius Rufus had said. The army *was* the border, Correus thought. Wolves of the rivers and hills, the small dusty forts and the great legionary bases. Wolves in fishscale and segmented plate. And he, Correus Appius Julianus, had a whole legion under his command, and two comfortable houses, of which his mother could only inhabit one. He had Ygerna. He had Felix, who also had Flavius, and he had Eilenn and Marcus. He would free Julius, he decided, and give him Tiati. It was more than enough to believe in. He didn't know why he had thought it wasn't. He tipped a little wine out of his cup onto the grass for whatever god was watching.

Glossary

Aesculapius: god of healing.

Agri Decumates: the lands between the Rhine and the Danube.

ala: a unit of cavalry, consisting of 500 or 1000 men.

alfar: elves.

amicus: a member of the emperor's inner circle.

anima: soul, ghost or spirit.

aquilifer: the standard bearer who carries the legion's Eagle.

Aquincum: Budapest.

atrium: the central room of a Roman house, frequently built around a pool.

aureus: a gold coin worth twenty-five silver denarii.

auxiliaries: cavalry, light troops, bowmen, etc., recruited from the provinces; term applied to all units other than the legions. The officers were Roman, and the men received Roman citizenship upon their discharge.

Baiae: Roman resort town on the northwest shore of the Gulf of Naples.

basilica: public building housing law courts and exchange.

Bellona: Roman goddess of war.

the Boatman: Charon, who ferried the dead across the River Styx.

Centuriate: collective term for the centurions of the Roman Army.

century: a unit of eighty men; six centuries made a cohort.

cohort: six centuries; ten cohorts made up a legion.

colonia: a provincial settlement given Roman city status.

consuls: formerly the two highest Republican magistrates in Rome; under the empire a much less powerful office, but still a great honor. The emperor was generally a consul.

cuirass: close-fitting body armor covering the torso.

Danuvius: the Danube River.

decurion: officer of cavalry or auxiliaries.

Eagle: the standard of a Roman legion; it personified the legion's honor, and its loss was a disgrace.

Eagles: the Roman legions.

Epona: Celtic goddess of horses.

equites: Roman social class ranking below senators.

Erebus: the darkness through which the souls of the dead travel to Hades.

Fates: three goddesses who spin, fix the length, and finally cut the thread of life.

Furies: avenging goddesses.

games: gladiatorial combats, wild beast shows, and other spectacles put on for public amusement.

genius: the spirit of a place, person, or thing.

German Free Lands: Germany east of the Rhine and north of the Danube.

Germany, Lower: the west bank of the Lower Rhine and modern Netherlands.

Germany, Upper: the west bank of the Upper Rhine and parts of modern France and Switzerland.

the Goddess: Earth Mother in her many forms.

Gorgons: three frightful sisters whose look turns the beholder to stone.

greaves: lower leg armor.

Hades: lord of the underworld; also the name of the underworld itself.

Hel: German goddess of the underworld; also the name of her domain.

Hephaestus: lame god of the forge.

hypocaust: Roman hot air heating system.

Iazyges: free tribe inhabiting the land between Dacia and the Roman province of Pannonia.

Ister: Dacian name for the Danube.

Janus: two-faced god of beginnings and endings of all undertakings.

Juno: wife of Jupiter, goddess of marriage and childbirth.

Jupiter: Roman name of Zeus, all-powerful father of the gods, protector of Rome.

latrunculi: literally "bandits," Roman board game.

legate: commander of a legion; a title also given to holders of other positions, such as ambassadorial legate.

legionary: the enlisted man of the legions; he was a Roman citizen.

libra: Roman unit of weight; about .725 of a modern pound.

lictor: an officer attending a consul or other official.

lorica: body armor of several types; at this time, scale or segmented plates.

Marcomanni: German tribe living north of the Upper Danube.

Mithras: Persian god of light and truth, mediator between man and the supreme god; his worship was popular in the Roman army.

Moenus: the Main River.

Moesia: Serbia and Bulgaria.

Moguntiacum: Mainz.

the Mother: Earth Mother in any of her many forms.

naiad: freshwater nymph.

Naissus: Niš, Serbia.

optio: second-in-command and general aide assigned to all officers.

Pan: god of woodlands and horned beasts.

Pannonia: parts of Austria, Hungary, and Yugoslavia south and west of the Danube.

Parthia: empire stretching from eastern Turkey to Iraq, Iran and Afghanistan.

Picts: barbarian tribe of northern Britain, called Picti or Painted Ones from their custom of all-over tattooing.

pilum: Roman military javelin.

Praetorian Guards: the home guard of Rome, the elite of the army, and the personal bodyguard of the emperor.

praetorium: the commander's quarters in a Roman fort.

prefect: Roman cavalry commander; title of various other Roman military commands.

primus pilus: commander of the First Cohort; in the field, second-in-command of the legion.

Principia: headquarters building in a Roman fort.

Quadi: German tribe living north of the Upper Danube.

Rhenus: the Rhine River.

Roman gods: In addition to their own gods, the Romans imported cults from almost all the peoples with whom they came in contact. The Greek pantheon was almost entirely reflected in the Roman one, and Romans tended to use their names interchangeably. Gods mentioned in this book are listed individually.

rota: a simple game played on a round board.

Samhain: Celtic Feast of the Dead beginning the night of October 31.

Saturnalia: Roman winter festival when slaves impersonated their masters and vice versa.

sesterce: bronze coin worth one-fourth of a denarius.

Sign of Horns: invoking the Horned God (similar to Pan) to ward off evil.

Singidunum: Belgrade.

Sirens: sea nymphs whose songs charm sailors to their death.

suffect consul: consul for a shorter term than a full year, succeeding the ordinary consul.

tribune: officer in a legion, generally a young man serving a short term before beginning a political career.

trireme: galley with three banks of oars.

Typhon: fire-breathing monster and creator of hurricanes, said to have a hundred heads and terrible voices.

Vestal Virgins: priestesses of Vesta, supposed to be incorruptible.

vexillations: detachments from regular legions.

vicus: the civil settlement outside a Roman fort.

vine staff: a centurion's staff of office; literally a cane cut from vine wood.

Wisdom: a Celtic board game resembling chess.

Wuotan: German chief of all the gods; sky god; god of light, war, and knowledge, giver of life breath to men.

Author's Note

It would be another seven years, in 96 CE by our reckoning, before Domitian was finally assassinated by his own household. He was succeeded by the elderly Nerva, followed at Nerva's death less than two years later by Trajan, who expanded the empire to its greatest extent, and after two Dacian wars, sent Decebalus's head back to Rome. After that, Dacia became a Roman province and remained so for more than 150 years.

Any accounting of events of ancient Rome is always subject to information available from historians of the time, with due attention given to the habit of what we have come to call *damnatio memoriae*, the erasing of all statues and inscriptions to disgraced persons, and *vituperatio*, the accounting of the sins of the past regime by the historians of the current one, as well as to the sometimes conflicting opinions of modern historians about it all. We form our conclusions from best guesses and hope to be not too far off. There are numerous good histories available about the empire itself and Domitian's reign. For those more intrigued by the minutiae of daily life, I found two books to be invaluable: *Pagan Holiday: On the Trail of Roman Tourists* by Tony Perrottet and *A Cabinet of Roman Curiosities* by classics professor J. C. McKeown. The classic on Roman food is the first century *Art of Cookery* of Apicius, preserved in a ninth-century version of a fifth-century copy, and available in translation by Barbara Flower and Elisabeth Rosenbaum. *Doctors and Diseases in the Roman Empire* by Ralph Jackson is an excellent account of the peculiarities of Roman medicine.

I want to thank my editor Kit Nevile and the rest of the team at Canelo for the chance to wind up this series begun so many years ago.